About the Author

Levi Samuel was born in 1986 in Elk City Oklahoma, though he was raised in Springfield Missouri. While in high school, he discovered the game, Dungeons and Dragons, as well as a Live Action Role Playing group, where he truly discovered who he was. Graduating high school, he joined the Army, but quickly realized that wasn't the life for him. He returned home and went to work in manual labor jobs. Being a quick study, he became a skilled tradesman in a number of fields, but the quest for happiness and purpose evaded him. In 2008 he became a father and has raised his daughter by himself ever since. In 2009, he decided to write a book, which was the start to a lifelong and rewarding career. His first book was published in 2013 under a penname. He's since established a laundry list of qualifications and achievements. Levi lives with his daughter and their cat, Alona.

Please subscribe to my newsletter for first access to all new content. http://eepurl.com/dxRUvL

What you hold here is the product of several years of growth. This was his first completed book, though it's since been revised many times and is far from the original concept. Whether you enjoy this book or not, leave us a review at any online retailer. Reviews help open the door for other readers, as well as teach the author new ways to entertain.

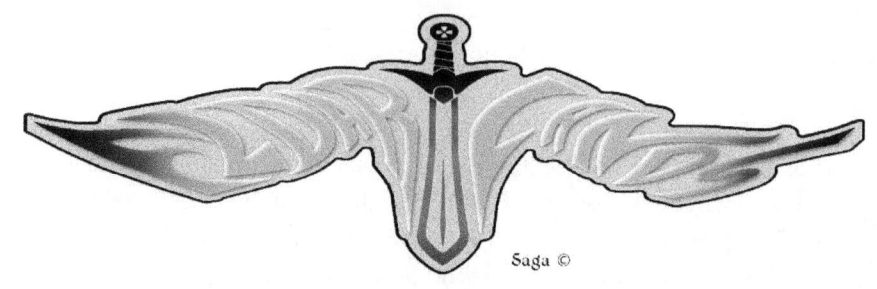

Heroes of Order Trilogy

by Levi Samuel

Izaryle's Will

Izaryle's Prison

Izaryle's Key

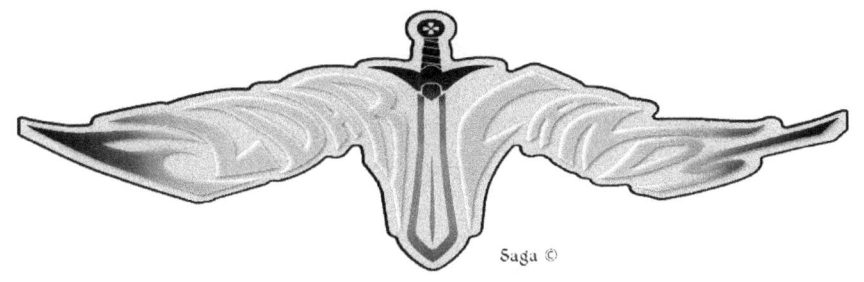

Saga ©

Heroes of Order Trilogy
Volume One

IZARYLE'S WILL

Levi Samuel

PUBLISHING

ELDARLANDS©
Heroes of Order Trilogy – Volume One

IZARYLE'S WILL
Eldarlands Publishing
Copyright © 2015-2018

The story, cover art, and illustrations by Levi Samuel.
Edited by Edward Gehlert
Foreword by Ben S. Reeder

Genre: Fantasy / Series

ISBN: 1-7321471-2-4
ISBN-13: 978-1-7321471-2-6

Find all the author's projects at http://www.LeviSamuel.com

Foreword

Do you feel like a hero? Like a trailblazer in a new realm of storytelling? Spare me just a moment of your attention, dear reader, and you might.

Once upon a time, there were a select few who adventured in the literary realms. Like knights of old, they often underwent years of training and went on legendary quests, enduring unending trials until they succeeded, where so many had failed before them, in getting published. And though I make it seem like a difficult process…it was really much harder than it sounds. Less than 2% of aspiring authors used to even get agents, and less than half of those authors actually got manuscripts published.

In the past decade, though, things have begun to change. The advent of e-readers and the subsequent rise of print-on-demand companies have made e-books more accessible, so that in 2009, more e-books were sold than actual print copies. And with that has come the rise of the self-published author. Unlike the mythical traditional author in days of old, the self-published author faced far fewer challenges to getting their work out in front of readers. In other words, the bar was set low and it showed. Self-published authors had a reputation for…well, it wasn't a good one. The word "stigma" got revived to describe them.

That reputation has slowly, painfully changed. Make no mistake, the bar is still low, but enough good writers have self-published that people no longer dismiss them out of hand. Then along comes a guy like Levi. The first time I met Levi was during a Live-Action Role-Playing game, or LARP. He was one of those rare players who stayed in character the whole time they were "in game." He was serious about what he was doing, because he was one of the players who wasn't there just to pretend he was a bad ass with a sword. He was there to play through his character's story. A story that he worked at diligently, and never took the easy way out with. He knew that story so far, and he always knew *how* he wanted that story to go. I remember hearing him tell his character's story to one of the other folks who helped run the game, and seeing a few other players come over and listen as he wove the details.

We went in separate directions after that, until a convention a few years ago, when I learned that he'd taken his penchant for telling stories and earned a couple of contracts for a small press whose owner I knew and would eventually work for myself. They have exacting standards and reject most submissions. Levi had already worked with them on three books, and was working on another novel, a story that would end up being the very one you hold in your hands right now. Once again, he had refused to take shortcuts, and had taken the time and effort to learn the ropes in publishing before undertaking the process of self-publishing.

The actual process of self-publishing can be incredibly easy. Doing it well? That's hard. Anyone can tell a story. Telling it well is the harder part. Writers like Levi, who work to tell a compelling story, who work to get the process *right,* are the reason self-published authors have gone from being considered the pariah of the industry to being heralded as its new pioneers. He takes no shortcuts, pulls no punches and tells the story to the best of his ability. More importantly, he's constantly honing his skills as a writer.

Because being a writer isn't easy. Being a good writer takes a lot of hard work, and it means you're going to take a lot of hits to your ego. You're going to get bloodied and bruised, after a fashion, when you enter the arena of public scrutiny. Levi has been there and back more than once. He's earned his chops in the arena and then some, and this book is the product of that experience. What you hold is his best work…until the next one.

You, dear reader, are part of the democratization of publishing. You are the new gatekeepers, and in supporting new voices like Levi Samuel, you are blazing new trails in publishing and making it possible for hard-working authors like him to make a difference in the industry. So, read on, and enjoy. And then, please, leave a review. Feedback from readers is how authors like Levi go from being damn fine writers to being great ones.

Welcome to the new frontier!

Ben Reeder
September 2016

To my daughter, Breanna. Thank you for your patience while I spent entirely too many hours trying to finish this book. Were it not for you, I've no doubt it would have been done in half the time. I love you and hopefully one day, very soon, I'll be writing throughout the day, so that I can spend my evenings with you.

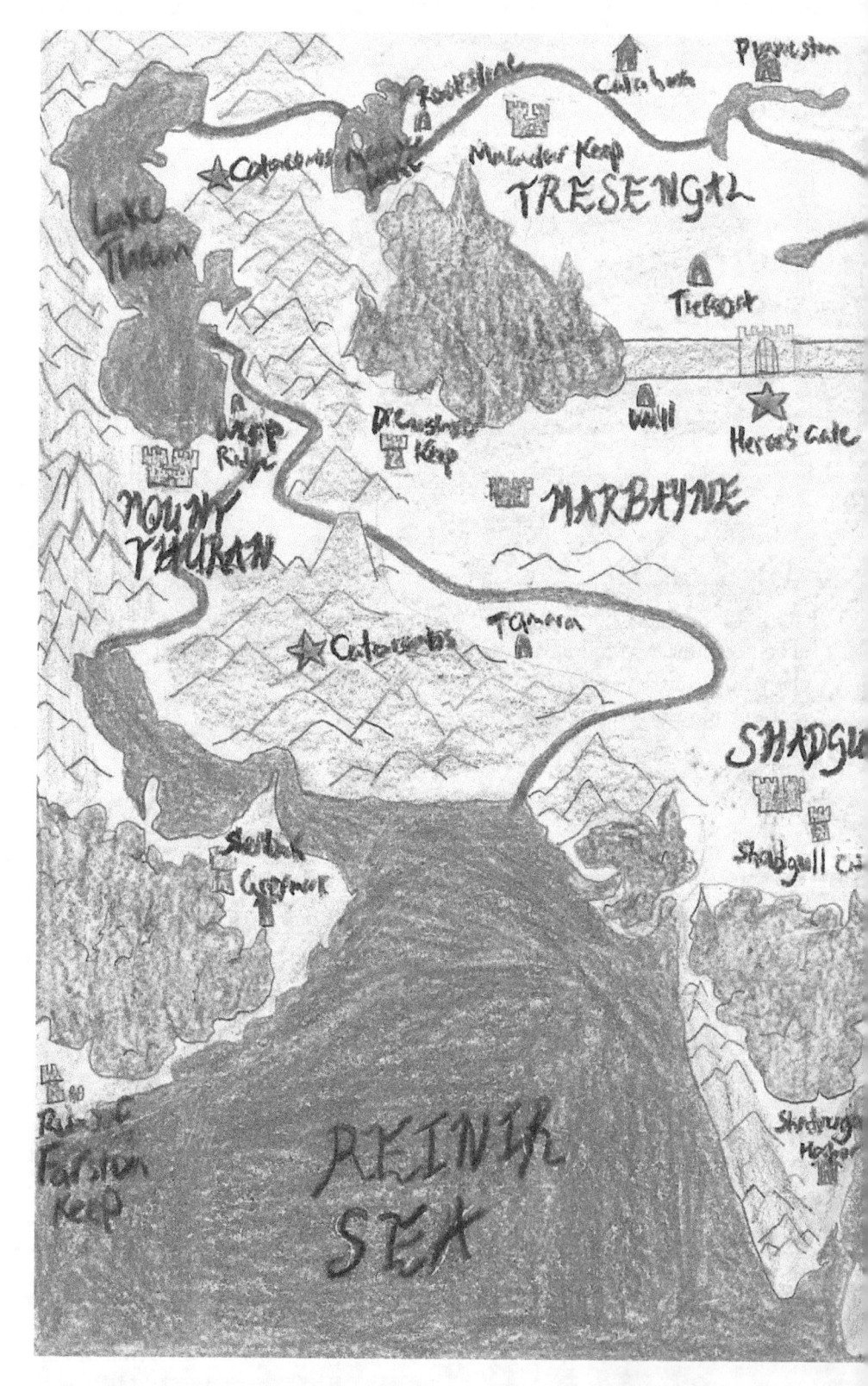

Elven Ruins

EVENWOOD

Tilia Fith
Citadel

Timberland

Gate

Greymotte

Halgarde

The Hot
Plains

KRONDAR

DSULL

ll City

Fender's Spear

Marshield

CullHaven

AERIN

Contents

Chapter 1
Eldarian

The ancient city filled the valley. Once buried beneath a shroud of dust and debris accumulated over millennia, the streets now teemed with invaders. The ring of pickaxes chipping away at stone echoed off walls and monuments as the seething mass of dalari excavated the ruins. Jostling for space, they ignored the few stone spires that soared above them, spared no glances for the delicate carvings that adorned the facades. Faces were turned downward, focused on one thing.

The site overflowed with arcane power, stronger than any they'd felt before. None of them knew what had opened the wellspring and none of them cared. Drawn by a sudden awareness of the energies that lay beneath the mystical city, they had grabbed whatever tools were at hand and trekked to the valley. Once there they followed each trickling flow of energy, digging eagerly, hoping to possess even the slightest amount of the ancient power known only to them.

Desire turned to obsession, leaving them unwitting slaves to their devotion. They dug tirelessly toward the source, their actions changing them with each scoop of dirt. Their skin blackened with exposure to the corrupted energies. Their ears elongated much like those of the alfar, their first creation. Their hair leached its color, leaving stringy white locks where various shades once rested. They continued to dig without rest or sustenance, dying by the thousands. Their greed for power fueled them, removing any ability to stop. All the while a silent promise poured into their ears, leaving the passage of time and their change unnoticed.

A young dreualfar working in an alcove felt the head of his pick penetrate the stone and disappear into the void beyond. After working so long in silent concentration, he had to clear his throat before he could speak. "Fazeen, we've broken through!" His voice rasped from dust and disuse.

The elder beside him stopped and stared at the crack in the casket. "Well, what are you waiting for, boy? Gain entry so that we may study it."

Rezerik heaved the pickaxe overhead and struck the surface beside the crack. Another piece chipped off.

"Hurry up, boy. We haven't got all day!"

"I've been at it for days without—" He swung, putting every ounce of his strength into it, "food or break. If you're—" With another swing, the fracture split open into a small hole. "in such a hurry, get me some help!"

Fazeen glared his disappointment at his apprentice. "You're a good lad with potential and you might realize it if you weren't so damn lazy." Shaking his head, he waved a team forward.

The corrupted dalari climbed in and went to work, chiseling the stone casing away. Musty air rose from the hole and Fazeen took a step back. Within minutes, the team had enlarged the hole to expose the mold-covered black walls of a buried room. A large statue of a man clad in thick armor stood in the center, facing them. Its material comprised of the same stone as the walls.

The purple cloak draped down its back glimmered in reflected daylight, seeming to ripple as if alive with energy. A pendant hung around its neck, set with a small, drab stone. No mold marred the jewelry. Motion behind the statue caught attention. The far wall reflected the room with a dark haze, the movement of the excavators little more than brief shadow on the polished surface.

Rezerik shoved the workers aside and climbed into the tomb for a closer look. He stared into the statue's face. Feeling the cold eyes stare back, as if reaching into his soul.

"Rezerik, what have you found? Is there treasure?"

His master's voice echoed in the room. Irritation shivered across his skin. "There's a statue and a dark mirror, nothing more."

"Don't be absurd, there has to be more. I no longer feel the power! There's no way it just disappeared into nothingness, without being detected."

"Check for yourself if you don't believe me!" Rezerik retorted, snatching the pendant from the statue. He felt it break free of its blackened chain. Glancing at the broken sigil he stuffed it in the pocket of his brown woolen breeches, hoping no one would notice the alteration of mold and dust clinging to the stone.

The elder dreualfar set his foot into one of the carved holes and carefully climbed into the entrance, keeping his frail body from missing the steps and tumbling into darkness. He pressed past the excavators standing just inside the fracture, trapped in the gaze of the towering figure. Wiping the stale air from his nostrils, he took in the ancient sights. A chill ran down his spine, feeling the cold lifeless eyes staring into him. Lost for an eternity in its presence, he heard the words ringing in his head.

"Now!" The booming voice blocked out his senses.

Fazeen spun around, looking into the darkened face of his apprentice. "You startled me, boy." Dropping his guard, he placed his hand on the lad's shoulder and pressed past to inspect the mirror.

Rezerik felt the power flowing through him. Why it had chosen him, he couldn't say. One thing was certain though, Fazeen would have to go. The elder would only stand in his way. He clenched his fists, feeling newfound strength course through his arms. In a flash, he grabbed his master's tattered clothing and lifted him. "Your time is up. I serve a new master now."

The aged dreualfar struggled against the younger's grasp. Feeling his feet leave the ground, realization set in. He was at the mercy of his apprentice. A dread overcame him, setting the whispers into motion. The fears, the voice, everything the statue had told him— it was all true. He locked eyes on the mirror, the terrifying unknown ready to greet him. "Please boy, have I done you so wrong?"

"That's the last time you call me 'boy'!" With ease he launched Fazeen into the dark reflection, which swallowed him like a pool of water. The surface shimmered briefly, growing smaller with each passing moment like a pebble tossed into a pond. Smiling at the disappearance of his master, he drank in his new-found freedom. A wicked smile stretched across his lips, revealing rapidly pointing teeth. He turned to face his witnesses. Frozen in disbelief and confusion, they stared blankly at the murderous dreualfar.

He let the power burn to the surface, controlling them with sheer force of will. "You've seen what I can do. Don't give me reason to show you firsthand."

Unable to resist his unspoken command, one by one they fell to a knee before him. Like tendrils of an unseen force, his powers jumped from one excavator to the next, spreading its way from the pit and into the scattered populace. Across the ancient city it traveled, enslaving every last dreualfar to him, and by extension, his master.

Looking around the musty tomb, he glanced at the mirror one last time. "Get to work. I want the rest of the structure uncovered. Take what pieces you can find and construct a grand temple over this site. Let any who wish to bask in the grace of Izaryle do so. But mark my words, any who touch the mirror will suffer a fate known only to Fazeen!" He turned toward the fractured wall and stepped through, into the cloud-blocked sunlight.

Looking down at his tattered clothing, he let the energies residing inside him loose, altering the rags into the finest silk garments he could imagine. They erupted forth, covering his black skin with equally black cloth trimmed in gold. Content with his appearance he climbed from the hole and marched through the sea of dreualfar scrambling to obey his command.

Thousands of dreualfar stood in block formation, dressed in makeshift armors and weapons modified from farm tools and crude hides. A great many carried weapons made for war, but their number could not supply the army built for a single purpose. They stared in silence, looking up at the balcony stretched around the blackened temple overlooking the city. Light brown weeds wrapped their way around, clinging to the repurposed stone. Several strands of vicious barbs followed after, binding themselves into constricting bands. A single figure loomed over them, inspecting the ranks in silent judgment.

Rezerik stood at the edge of his balcony. The banister was ornately carved with thousands of tiny depictions of skulls forming the foundation to his empire. The polished dark oak reflected the rapidly passing clouds of gray. He could feel the mist in the air, ready to fall in large droplets at any moment. It was sorely needed, but it wouldn't help. His lands were too far gone. Running his finger across the tip of one of the jagged weeds that had wrapped itself around the railing, a light bit of green ooze burned into his skin from contact. Wiping the venom away, he stared out over his dying kingdom. Remorse filled him. How had he allowed it to come to this? Though it wasn't entirely his fault. The desolate wasteland before him was filled with once majestic stone and wood structures, now lying in ruin, collapsed under their own weight. The ground was dry and full of large cracks. The sparse vegetation was thin and twisted, forming bands that clung to the structures they engulfed. His empire lay before him, dead and over populated.

The armies held fast, awaiting command with eager anticipation. Men, women, and children comprised the ranks. No one was too young to wield a sword, one of the few traits remaining from their previous life. The commanders took position in front of their armies, bearing blackened armors and tarnished weaponry that was once elegant. Behind each formation stood a smaller group comprised of several hundred dreuki.

Rezerik looked upon their ranks with envy. Those few were exceptionally skilled with magics he couldn't hope to possess. Not that he didn't have his own type of power. In a fight between himself and their mutated form, he could easily win. He was blessed by Izaryle, blessed to set plans in motion and free his imprisoned lord. The dreuki were but a pawn in his evolving game, yet he couldn't help but envy their mixed magics. Even the youngest of dreuki had an unnatural ability to harness the most powerful of magics. There was something about the divine infused arcana. It left the body twisted between forms, allowing the agility and grace of an arachnid while retaining the torso of the dreualfar.

Feeling the water droplets break against his robes, he returned to the present. The rain fell increasingly fast, soaking everything within sight. With the wave of his hand, Rezerik pushed the water away and watched the beads splash against an invisible barrier that now surrounded him.

They joined together, pooling into larger beads before rolling down the side of the clear sphere. With a final scan of his forces, he extended his hands, preparing their multitude to receive him.

"Citizens of Eldarian, time has come for us to expand our empire. This land is no longer able to sustain our number. The world of our god slowly drains our resources, leaving us with little more than dust and crumbled rock. The time has come for us to spread out like a plague upon the land. We will first make contact with the hydralfar. Once our cousins have welcomed us into the heart of their lands, we'll breed them out until the dreualfar are all that remain. From there we'll resupply and have everything we need to ensure our survival throughout the ages." He smiled at the might before him, unrelenting savagery waiting to be released upon the world. And they awaited his order. "Commanders, move out!"

The armies erupted in cheers of excitement and bloodthirsty screams. The sound of battle horns filled the air with high-pitched squeals. The collected shouts of the commanders bled together, each group following their superiors. The armies roared to life shaking the dying ground with footsteps and chants. Clouds of dust formed with the rumble of boots against the dead earth, despite the falling rain unable to saturate the ground fast enough. The march sent vibrations through the earth, shaking it to its core. Several of the dilapidated buildings crumbled into huge piles of broken wood and weakened stone, fanning out to create more dust.

Reaching the dead ring, surrounding the city, the massive formations split apart and formed into four individual armies. Each one turned, aimed for a specific destination. The chants and war cries grew dull with the increasing distance. Only a last bit of dust and trampled footprints showed evidence of their existence.

Rezerik watched them disappear into the horizon above his dying empire of dust and rubble. A smile formed across his lips, proud of his creation, yet remorseful that he couldn't join them. It made sense. Each army had a job to do. If he were to interrupt, the whole plan could fall apart. No, he was more suited to remain here, awaiting the days when Izaryle would need a host.

"Dark God of Chaos, our plan has manifested. It shouldn't be long until you're released from your prison and the world feels your wrath once again. On that day your brothers will weep for what they've done to you. And you'll stifle their tears with the knowledge that they'll never be worshiped again."

Rezerik looked down at the broken pendant hanging around his neck. The split demonic face carved into the onyx sigil shook violently, as if it had a mind of its own. It pulled against the leather binding trying to tear itself free.

"What is it, Izaryle? Have I displeased you?" Confusion and worry began to set in. He'd followed every order. Why was he being punished?

The pendant shot up, ripping through cloth and leather. Rezerik reached to catch it, but it was too late. In the blink of an eye, it flew out of sight.

"No!" He mourned, feeling a loss greater than any he'd known. Fear and anger sparked inside him. He was powerful, more powerful than any living being. Maybe he could recall it. Forcing all of his will into the tiny black sigil, he tried to locate it, but it was nowhere to be found.

Frustration shot through him. *How could he do this to me?* With ease, he jumped over the banister, free-falling several stories. As if jumping from no more than a few feet, he landed, sending a shower of dust and mud out around him.

Questions and anger fueled his mind. He stormed around the corner and toward the sealed onyx doors. He braced himself for the drain the stone would inflict upon him. It was undoubtedly the reason it was used to create the tomb. The strange material had a way of draining his abilities unlike any other. It seemed the stronger the magic, the quicker the drain. If his had the same effect on his lord, he was undoubtedly weak from eons of exposure.

Throwing the doors open, Rezerik rushed down the winding stairs feeling his fear and anger rise with each step. He stepped into the sconce-lit antechamber and stared into the statue.

"Izaryle, why do you betray me so?" His voice cracked with the instant barrage pulling him toward the mirror. He had to brace himself against the booming voice coming from the statue. It was deep and raw, unlike any other he'd heard before. Overcome by the godly presence, he felt his grip waning against the edge of the statue.

Dust and debris fell from the shaking walls and ceiling with each word. "Your purpose has been served. In time your line will return the pendant to me. At that time, your destiny will be fulfilled and you will be granted a place of honor at my side."

"A place of honor at your side?" Rezerik scoffed. "I had a place of honor. I was ruler of the dreu. As King of Eldarian I had everything I needed to free you. And now you tell me it's my offspring that'll complete the task?"

A dark laughter echoed through the temple, chilling him to the bone. "You forget Rezerik, everything you are, everything you have, it all came from me. I can reclaim it anytime I choose."

His anger boiled with news of the betrayal. "You're imprisoned in another world. There's no way you can free yourself and exact your revenge without my help."

The mirror slowly began to swirl, creating a vortex of purple and blue. The colors twisted together and reached out toward the rebellious dreualfar like a mystical whirlpool threatening to swallow him whole.

Rezerik felt the whispers inside his head. They were less commanding, but more intrusive. In this state, he couldn't hide the simplest thought from his god. He felt his arms go limp, abandoning his struggle to stay firmly planted. He tried to scream out, but his mouth wouldn't comply. The whipping tether of purple and blue wrapped around him, pulling him toward the mirror.

"There you are correct, my devoted Rezerik. I'm imprisoned. And you've been a valuable agent in my plot. But you've served your purpose here. It's time you joined me. You'll be much better suited to help me in a position where I can adjust your opinions as I see fit. From this day forth, you'll no longer be known as the dalari turned dreualfar, Rezerik. Join me as the first Nightking. You'll command forces against those that seek to evade my influence. With an army of orcs and sharliets at your command, you'll serve me until such a time arises that your line frees me from this prison. On that day you'll walk with me as an equal as we reclaim your world. The heavens will weep the blood of gods upon my return!"

Rezerik spun uncontrollably faster, feeling the churning in his gut. The vortex had already swallowed him to his waist. He was running out of time. He had to do something. He was not powerless. Even with Izaryle's hold on him, he still had his power. He could use the black stone to slow him down.

Reaching out with his mind, he felt the edge of the statue. The hold was like that of a scalding pan clenched in his grip. It burnt as he held it, feeling his skin away in large chunks. He screamed out, realizing Izaryle was screaming too. With the dark god's hold over him broken for the moment he stretched as far as he could, hoping to escape certain doom. The air escaped his lungs. He glanced down, realizing he'd sunk to his shoulders in the spinning whirlpool of magics. He tried to breathe, but found it impossible.

There was no air. There was no light. Only a mixture of spinning color surrounding him. With his final burst of energy, before what was sure to be his death, he lunged forward, feeling the rough edge of that familiar purple cloak against his fingertips. It burnt, but not nearly as much as it had earlier. Clawing at the mineral, he felt a piece break away. His grip lost, he tumbled into darkness disappearing behind the blackened surface. The ripples smoothed away to nonexistence, leaving little more than a memory of the first dreualfar king.

The black stone statue stood erect in the center of an empty crypt, overlooking the entrance. A broken purple shard glimmered on the stone floor beneath, reflecting the glow from burning oil lamps.

Chapter II
The Monsters Beneath

The sun shone down over a deep valley. The rocky bluffs were lined in trees, deflecting the commotion within. Sounds of battle bounced off the jagged stone, echoing for miles. The choppy, torn dirt was littered with opposing armies, one black as night, while the other stood in stark contrast. The dark army was surrounded, choked into submission by the outnumbering forces around them. A deep crater lay open in the rock behind them, dark as the creatures at its crest.

"Hold the lines!" Kashien shouted to his brethren. His sword was drawn, ready to strike down the cursed foe. He parried a wide slash, thrusting his blade into the dreualfar's throat. Back stepping, he withdrew from combat, assessing the situation. Thousands of dreualfar stood defiantly against his armies. They were outmanned and outmaneuvered, with only one escape. He watched in amazement as his soldiers advanced into position, swallowing every inch of slack the enemy offered. He found it difficult to believe how easily they were bottled, falling perfectly into his trap. But here they were, the last of their kind. Genocide felt wrong, but it was necessary. They were an abomination of his race. A mistake that should have never been offered sanctuary. He pitied them more than anything. It could have just as easily been his men that fell to the corruption. Setting aside his personal feelings on the matter, he raised his longsword and readied his next command. Rolling the blade forward, he shouted across the battlefield. "Force these abominations into the darkness from whence they sprang!"

The dreualfar cursed and spit their altered tongues at their captors. They were losing ground and quickly. It wouldn't be long before they would be crushed beneath the heel of their ancestors. Surrounded on all sides they began to fall back, slowly escaping into the large hole in the earth. There they could regroup and claim victory with shadow games. Several thousand stood defiantly around the brim, awaiting their chance to follow without crushing those before them. Or worse, falling into the depths from the chaos. They readied themselves. It wouldn't be long before the dalari would be upon them again.

The dalari army shouted in unison beginning their march forward, choking against the surrounded resistance. They moved as one, flowing like a constricting wall, forcing the dreualfar to abandon ground.

The general marched behind the front line, moving them toward victory. Commands flowed from him, keeping his men moving. If the front slowed, those behind would trample over them unable to stop, forced from the rear. They raised their weapons, ready to swiftly deal with the shrinking army before them. The two met with a crash, littering the rocky terrain with a sea of blood. The explosion was great, sending several lines flying back on either side. Each man was replaced by the one behind him.

Ducking a scimitar swipe, the dalari commander slashed with his longsword. Spinning around he parried another blow, raking the edge of the blade into another of the cursed beasts. He dodged and ducked, using each action as preparation for the next, performing a dance of death that would have entranced any who paused long enough to watch. With a wide swipe, he thrust his free hand forward, blasting several of the black-skinned creatures back with an invisible barrier. They landed in piles, disappearing beneath the swarming horde. Kashien worked his weapon, keeping them at arm's length. Glancing at the thousands of dead or dying dreualfar before him, he quickly counted his own men. To his relief their superior numbers and keen tactics resulted in few casualties, though he could tell his men were tired. They would need rest soon if they were to make the trek home. "Where the hell are the alfar?"

His question was answered by a familiar voice to his right. "General, they've not been seen since our victory at Durnal Hill." The dalari beside him raised his sword up, deflecting an opposing strike. With ease, he slid a dagger up under the crude hide armor of the dreualfar and split him open. Disengaging the battle, he turned to formally address his commander.

Kashien withdrew combat. Dismissing the salute, he placed his hand on his captain's shoulder. "Trendal, I'm glad to see you made it. But why didn't the alfar come with you?"

"I don't know My Lord. They broke away when we left Durnal Hill. Haven't seen them since."

"It would've been nice to know they weren't going to join us."

"Aye, My Lord."

"The men are tired. We need to end this now. Take your men to the left flank. Send word to Razorius. I want his men to cover the right. We have to horseshoe them and close the distance. If we don't funnel them quick enough, the plan falls to pieces." Kashien jumped back, dodging another swipe from the dreualfar. With a lightning fast strike, he thrust his blade into his attacker's throat. Spinning to block another attack, the blade cut through, sending the dreualfar's head into the air.

Trendal nodded. "Understood, My Lord." Falling back, he disappeared into the ranks. Fighting his way through the crowded battlements he spotted the man he sought not far from the front line, locked in battle against one of the strange eight-legged hybrids. Without pause he charged, leaping into the fray. He drove his dagger deep into the creature's chest, feeling its loss of strength before he hit the ground. Picking himself up, he sheathed the blade and turned to face the younger dalari.

"Show off! You know, you're lucky I saw you comin' otherwise I might have mistaken you for one of these bastards."

He chuckled at the man's response. "You'd need your eyes checked if you mistook me for one so ugly." With a cunning smile, Trendal continued, "Razorius, Kashien asked you to gather your men and take the right flank. We have to end this quick. Blow your horn when you're in position. Don't advance until you hear mine. We'll have to move as one and quickly close on them."

Accepting the call to duty, Razorius snapped to attention, regarding his friend as well as his direct ranking superior. "Aye, Captain." With a salute, he turned and shouted orders to his unit.

Kashien felt the beads of sweat and blood run down his face. The afternoon sun was blistering hot in the thick leather, but it was better than the scars he'd suffer were he not wearing it. His slightly pointed ears twitched with the familiar sound to his right. A moment later, a similar tone echoed to the left. His men were in position and moving forward. He paused, catching a glimpse through the rows of soldiers. "Meaius?" The soldiers moved, blocking his view. The familiar profile was gone.

Shaking his head clear of the memories, he returned to his task. Forcing a smile, he channeled his energy through the sword, letting the athame do all the work. The metal began to glow red. Within moments it was so bright he found it hard to look at. Slashing out, the magical blade cut through his enemy with ease, charring their flesh before it even connected. Clothing and armor were no match, bursting into flame with the slightest touch. Even the occasional metal armor became useless against it, melting and searing its wearer. "Keep em' moving," he shouted, clearing the path in front of him. With a final charge, he thrust his sword into the air, firing a bright flash of red over the battle. It burst overhead, showering the area with a deep red glow. He set his feet, hearing the army move into position around him.

They roared with synchronized footsteps, quickly gaining ground against the unsuspecting dreualfar. The gap closed quicker than ever, with no leadership to oppose the advance. Within seconds they engulfed the encircled foe. The rear of the dreualfar army began to disappear, leaving a few thousand to stop the progression. Like a plow forcing snow over a precipice, his men surged forward. More and more of the enemy fell into darkness, their strength dissolved with each passing moment.

Kashien watched the last few take the plunge, disappearing into the earth. Cautiously, he stepped forward and peered down into the hole. If they had any ideas as to his plan their faces, blurred by distance, didn't show it. Beneath him, the thousands inside climbed against the rocky slopes, forcing the others to retreat deeper into the catacombs or be crushed beneath the weight. The walls were too steep to climb with any speed, not that escape was possible anyway. Feeling his pity return he stabbed his sword into the churned dirt and rock, leaving it to rest in the ground beside him. They scurried in the darkness like a hive of angry ants clawing to escape the flood that was about to wash over them.

Without a word he flipped the buckle on his belt pouch and pulled a tightly wrapped scroll. Breaking the red wax seal pressed into the seam, he unrolled it and uttered the words etched onto the page.

"By the power of your ancestors, you are condemned to darkness for the rest of eternity. Should you resurface, the light of the sun will char you to a crisp." The words were little more than notice of their fate.

Executing his plan he extended his hands, letting the scroll float slowly into the pit below. A bright light formed above the hole, stretching to the edges. It shifted into a wide disc and completely covered the entrance. Several beams of blinding light shot forth, illuminating the horde below. Screams bellowed up as they pressed deeper into the cavern in hopes to evade the burning light.

Watching the last dreualfar disappear from view, he turned, spotting a fearsome sight lining the clifftops. Legions of hydralfar stood along the ridge behind his men. It didn't take a military genius to realize they were in ambush position. Thousands of bows were drawn and aimed, ready to bring an end to his men. A familiar, celestial voice caressed his ears.

"Lord Kashien, by order of Emperor Jullien the Third, you and your kind have been pronounced human and are hereby stricken from our history. Your race is responsible for the foul abominations that have torn this world asunder and you must now pay for your crimes. We cannot allow your kind to flourish for fear of this, or another incident happening again!" Waving his hand forward, he gave the signal. "Fire!"

Kashien watched tens of thousands of arrows release, flying high into sunlit sky. The advancing shafts were ready to end the majority of his men in one fell swoop. For the briefest of moments he felt the burning sun leave his skin, replaced by the shadow of death. The wooden shafts rained down, plummeting into the army of unsuspecting dalari. He felt a violent thrust against his side, knocking him from his feet and covering him completely. Several sharp pains stabbed into him, but none felt deep enough to be life threatening. Pushing the form off of him, realization set in. *Why was I spared?* Pain and confusion filled him. Looking into Trendal's blood-coated face, he saw too many arrows protruding from his friend's body. A steady stream of fresh blood ran from his paling skin.

"General," Trendal said with his dying breath, "get home."

He felt a pain deeper than the arrows had plunged. Stealing a glance around, his army was no more, riddled with the wooden shafts. A few crawled from the massacre. Osirus was unable to claim them with the number of souls received, but they wouldn't live much longer.

The ground shook with the massive alfaren army breaking their halt. Drawing their battle glaives they marched down the steep paths and into the valley floor. It wouldn't take much to end the few survivors in a final assault.

Kashien felt the ground shake with the numbers advancing toward him. Crawling from the pile of bodies, he took in each of their faces, unsure how he would avenge his men. He knew if they reached him, it wouldn't be long before he joined them in death.

The alfaren commander scanned the extermination. He felt a pang of guilt for his betrayal, but his emperor had made the task very clear. To disobey would be considered treason. But what was the price for betrayal? The majority of the dalari were already dead and the rest would be soon enough from blood loss or the keen blades of his soldiers. Searching the valley, he caught a familiar figure where Kashien had been standing.

The dalari general crawled to his feet, knowing a second volley of arrows would result in death. Hoping the alfar would rush him with their blades, he spotted their commander, watching from the clifftop. If the traitor was going to pay, he'd have to taunt him into action.

"Keal'neaus! You've attempted genocide and murdered my men in cold blood, for what? So your petty emperor can save face? You and I fought side by side against the dreu. I saved your life time and time again and this is how you repay me? With the blood of my men. Your emperor is a coward and is unworthy of the blood we share. Or have you forgotten that my people created yours as well? I will not stand for this. Mark my words, your emperor will regret this day!"

Keal'neaus drew his thin blade and stormed toward the wounded general. Reaching the edge of the carnage, he shouted over the dead. "I regret having to give that order, but it comes from my emperor. I will not disobey."

A smile crept to Kashien's face. He was a superior swordsman, provided he hadn't lost too much blood from the shallow arrow wounds. "So be it. Your death will be as merciless as the one you offered my men."

The two generals charged in, their swords glimmering in the sunlight. Keal'neaus ducked a swing. Slicing low, he hoped to wound the dalari general.

Kashien lifted his leg, avoiding the blow. Bringing his pommel down on the alfaren commander's back, he shoved, throwing him off balance.

Keal'neaus quickly recovered, spinning to guard against another attack. He swung hard, hoping to catch the dalari off guard.

Kashien watched the alfaren general summon the strength for a powerful strike. Bracing himself, he readied to parry the blow. Using both hands he slowed the attack, sending it wide. Recovering, he spun around and drove his sword deep into Keal'neaus' shoulder. The wound wasn't fatal, but it would limit the use of his arm.

Keal'neaus felt the blade penetrate deep, rendering his arm numb. Realizing the tendons were severed, he focused his effort with his right arm. Picking up the pace, his alfaren sword danced with remarkable speed.

Kashien was having trouble keeping up with the speed of the lighter weapon. He gave up predicting the attacks, instead relying strictly on the movement of his opponent's shoulder. Fear began to creep into him with the increasing speed. He had to do something quick or it would all be over. He wasn't able to keep up. The arrows must have robbed him of more strength than he'd realized. With no other options he lunged forward, forcing the alfaren commander to readjust.

Keal'neaus took a step back, regaining his balance. His rhythm was ruined, forcing him to slow again. He swung, hoping to reclaim his speed but it was broken.

Kashien felt a bit of relief seeing the general take the bait. He easily deflected the next few strikes, sending each one wider until he saw his opening. With a quick jab he plunged the tip of his sword into the chest of his alfaren foe. Without giving him time to react he retracted the blade and spun around, letting his momentum carry the deadly edge. The longsword cut deep into Keal'neaus' neck.

The alfaren commander spun from the force, feeling the gaping gash in his throat. He felt cold. Raising his hand to inspect the wound, thick, red blood coated his fingers. Wide-eyed, he looked over his men before falling to the already blood-soaked, body and arrow ridden earth.

Remorse shot through Kashien, but there was little choice. The fact was had he not killed the man he'd fought beside for so long, he wouldn't be able to warn his people.

The encircling hydralfar rushed in like an army of ants to a bowl of sugar. Within moments he was completely surrounded, trapped within impenetrable walls. They held their glaives at the ready, poised to avenge their commander.

Kashien glanced at the keen edges ready to end him. He smiled and sheathed his sword. Taking a deep breath, he prepared himself. "Such is life!"

The front line swung, aiming to cut the dalari general down.

Feeling the first blade contact his skin, he let the energies release, engulfing him in an orange glow.

The alfar stared in confusion, searching the empty space between their solid walls.

Kashien materialized in the Arcanum. Its glass floor and high vaulted ceilings made it feel larger than it really was. The room was illuminated with hundreds of floating candles, mindlessly hovering in the air out of reach. Stepping from the suspended floor, he made his way into the elegant corridors of Dranar. His heavy footsteps echoed on the polished marble, leaving dusty tracks behind him. He could feel a trickle of blood from the alfaren glaive running down his cheek. Ignoring the minor wound, he rounded the corner and stepped into the grand hall.

The room was covered with ancient runes carved into the walls and ceilings. Even though a city of the mortal plane, the gods were known to frequent the ancient settlement. He took in the tales depicted in the runes, recalling the hundreds of times he'd heard the stories in his childhood. Several columns stood on each side supporting the cloudy vaulted ceilings. Hundreds of sconces hovered overhead, each one positioned perfectly between the others, illuminating the massive room. He glanced at the throne, spotting the oldest of his kind resting in his black elegant robes. Without delay he marched along the liner running the length of the room, stopping a few feet from the dais. Dropping to a knee, he locked eyes on the crimson carpet beneath his feet and addressed the eldest dalari formally. "My Lord, the alfar have turned against us. My army has been demolished and they've declared us human. I fear we're to be hunted until the last of our kind is exterminated."

The ancient dalari emperor motioned his grandson to stand. "My boy, you're young. Your emotions get the better of you. Our people will have difficult days to come, that's a certainty. But this is hardly the first time this world has lost its need of us. Worry not, we'll be restored when our kind is nothing more than a distant memory. On that day, we'll be reborn and Dranar will once again be filled with dalari." The emperor held a contented smile, reassuring the young prince.

Kashien looked into the eyes of his grandfather. "May that day come swiftly, for I do not know how we will last."

Levi Samuel

Chapter III
The First Dreuslayer

Constellations changed time and time again over the centuries. Some stars burned out, while others ignited for the first time. Despite their age and placement, this evening they looked down through the massive cloud cover over the Reinir Sea. Her waters boiled and churned, rushing over everything within sight. Of the tiny specks of light lost in the water's surface, one in particular remained visible.

The ship rocked violently with each wave crashing into the hull. The unending cascade of motion sent the men on board racing to secure the lines. The sails jerked and fluttered, catching the massive twisting winds.

Gareth's muscles flexed, straining against the wheel. He couldn't fathom how the single rudder could present so much resistance. Bracing himself for the approaching wall of water, he felt mist speckle his exposed flesh before the collision. The wave hit with a crash, knocking his feet from beneath him. He pulled against the spokes, locked firmly in his grip.

Getting back to his feet, he looked down at the crew below. He couldn't afford to be thrown overboard. Not only would it result in his death, but the lives of his crew hung in the balance. The heavy droplets of rain stung when they hit, like thousands of needles stabbing into his face. They pooled together and dripped from his bald head. His thick, red beard was drenched, streaming the salty liquid into his already soaked tunic. The white linen clung to him with the moisture, exposing the matted hair on his chest. With moments to spare before the next wave would hit, the grizzled captain surveyed the deck, hoping the storm hadn't claimed too much.

Their entire haul had been washed away, making the trip altogether a waste. Much of his crew were missing, most likely swept over the side, leaving their jobs to be filled by the remaining men. The gale winds blowing in each and every direction made it difficult to keep the sails taut.

There's no way to rescue them, they're at Corin's mercy. Half-lost in thoughts of his men, he fought the shifting current hoping his decision would save the rest.

"All hands on deck, drop the sails, we're more likely to break a mast than we are to get anywhere in this wind." His voice bellowed out over the howling sea and hammering winds. "Everyone else, grab an oar and start rowing." The exhausted captain steered the fishing vessel directly into the waves. The ride was much rougher, but there was less chance to keel over. He looked through the dark, rolling clouds to the tiny flickers of light beyond. He couldn't be certain without a clear view, but port shouldn't be more than a few days out in dry conditions. The storm would delay them greatly.

The ship started to gain speed, but the constant change in direction stifled their progress. The great currents, along with the wind pushing them off course, made the wheel difficult to hold steady.

He glanced down at the compass, watching the lubber's line. Correcting direction, he searched the horizon for any sign of familiarity. Last thing he needed was to run aground, provided he could keep her afloat long enough to make port. Without warning the wind picked up, nearly knocking him from his feet.

Several minutes it blew harder than ever before. Then, as quickly as the maelstrom arrived, it was gone. The choppy waters calmed leaving the ship to float gently across diminishing waves. The dark-gray sky began to clear, allowing the rising sun to burn through the thinning clouds. The beams reflected off the shimmering water, illuminating the lone vessel gliding gracefully atop the glassy sheen.

Relief washed over him. Checking the horizon, he tied off the wheel to keep her straight. Making his way from the helm to the upper deck, he overlooked the crew still rowing in unison.

"Captain on deck!" The first mate shouted, notifying the crew of his presence.

They locked the oars into position and jumped from the small wooden benches lining both sides of the deck. Awaiting his command they looked up, clearly relieved to be out of the storm.

Gareth surveyed the deck, saddened by how empty it was. Nearly a month's worth of work was lost in a few hours. His crew was nearly half the size it was the day before. The ship was battered, but she was whole. That was more than he could ask for. "Joseph, take two men and survey the ship. I want a list of everything lost, including sailors. We're not far from port. I'd like to be able to notify their widows when we arrive." He watched the three men jump from their station and rush below deck. "The rest of you raise the sails and stow the ship. We've lost too much to delay any longer. Helmsman, get up here and take the wheel. I'm gonna' find out exactly how far off course we are."

"Aye, Captain!" They sounded in unison. Watching him turn from the balcony, they scurried off to batten down everything lost in the storm.

With purpose, Gareth marched across the upper deck and stepped into his quarters. Stripping off his wet clothes, tossing them into a barrel, he grabbed a fresh set. Drying himself, he quickly dressed and grabbed a round leather case lying on the floor near his desk. The room was trashed. Nothing was where it belonged. Items had been thrown from their assigned places during the night. At least it was still on board, unlike much of his crew. Forcing his sorrows beneath the surface, Gareth unbuckled the straps and pulled the cap off the end of the deep-brown case. Removing the parchment within, he unrolled it exposing a large map. Tacking the corners down, he went to work discerning their exact location.

Night had fallen on the vast ocean, calm and peaceful with the gentle sounds of water slapping against the bow. The large vessel slid across the surface like a hot knife into butter. The mild breeze held the sails taut. Only the occasional flap could be heard when the wind changed direction.

"Land ho!" The watch shouted from the nest, signaling east.

The signal fire was little more than a speck on the horizon, flickering in the distance. The sun was just beginning to crest, making the growing flame all but disappear in its glow.

Gareth stood at the helm, arms folded across his body, watching the helmsman steer the ship ever closer to home. Even from this distance the sight was unnerving. *Something's wrong. This is the largest port city for at least a month in any direction. I've never seen fewer than twenty ships docked.* Reaching for the leather holster on his hip, he removed his sight glass. With a quick flip of the wrist, it extended. He brought it up, scanning the port. "After a storm like that, this place should be packed. Why's it so bare?" He thought aloud, unintentionally giving it voice. The thought sent a chill down his spine.

"I don't have answers any more than those you're already thinking, Capt'n."

A smile graced his bearded face. While the helmsman was blunt with his speech, he was always painfully honest. "Well put, Malakai." He watched the harbor draw ever closer. Timing their descent with the wooden posts that marked each side of the port entrance, Gareth bellowed out. "Drop the sails. Ready to make port, starboard side!"

The sails fell with a crash, removing the steady thrust. With clipped wings she drifted forward, carried by her momentum.

Malakai cranked the wheel, steering her into the bay. She groaned with the sharp turn, sliding sideways toward the dock. With a gentle bump, she rocked against the rawhide bumpers, coming to a stop.

The harbormaster stood on the wooden planks watching the ship roll in. With a quick glance he looked at his feet, measuring distance from the water. His two assistants stood near the edge, waiting to catch the moorings. A soft, subtle smile breached his lips. A heavy splash erupted between the hull and dock, soaking the lads. He grinned contently at the water line just ahead of his feet. A gentle reminder of what it was like to be inexperienced.

"First Mate, see the ship secured. I'm gonna go have a chat with the master." The captain waited for the gangway to be positioned before he stepped off. He took in the sight of the elderly man, standing tall in his fine tunic and embossed felt vest. With age alone, he was ready to relinquish his duties to someone younger. But he retained a good sense of spirit, something many his age had lacked for years.

"Captain Gareth D'Averon, I'm glad to see you made it through that mysterious storm." He placed his hands on his waistline.

"Master Merrick, why's the port so bare? Has something happened?"

The old man dropped his cheerful guise. Looking to his assistants, busy tying off the lines, he hesitated before speaking. "We— We were attacked. They came out of nowhere, from every direction. Like a swarm of darkness in the middle of the night." He shifted uneasily, searching for anything to change the subject. Darting his gaze around he found the young captain's eyes, forcing him to continue. "The guards were taken completely by surprise. It didn't take any time at all before they'd overrun the whole town. Several people were captured. We don't know how many were killed. Most of the boats set sail last night, to restock supplies. That and for fear of them returning."

Gareth hung on each word, intently listening for anything substantial. "And my family, do you know anything of them?" His voice cracked with fear.

"I'm sorry sir, we've been too busy repairing damages. We haven't been able to gather an accurate count of survivors. All I can say is I haven't seen—"

Without pause, Gareth turned, breaking into a full sprint toward his home atop the hill. The light brown siding was broken in places, revealing the wooden beams beneath. Several articles of clothing, broken candlesticks, and other common items were strung along the ground as if they'd been grabbed without thought, then abandoned in the dirt.

He reached the door, finding the frame busted leaving the two-story home open for all to see. Gareth stepped inside, seeing the broken pieces of door and frame scattered across the polished plank floor.

The common room was trashed. Lanterns had been knocked from their hooks, lying broken on the floor. Scorch marks scored the wood where the oil had burned. He was surprised the whole place hadn't gone up in flames. The candles had burned out, leaving long tails of wax hanging from their fixtures. The table was overturned, its ornaments scattered throughout the room.

Drawing his cutlass, Gareth slowly made his inside, looking for any sign of his family. Reaching the nursery, he peeked through the cracked door. The room was silent, save for his weight under the occasional loose floorboard. He pushed the door open, finding the cradle overturned. His heart pumped faster, beating inside his chest, sending fear down his spine.

Lying on the floor near the spilled blankets, he noticed a torn piece of his wife's favorite dress. It was bunched and discarded. A small amount of dried blood stained the wood next to it. Not enough to suggest death, but certainly injury. A pain erupted in his heart. Snatching up the light blue fabric, he clenched his fist around it. Bringing it to his face, he closed his eyes, forcing his fears aside. A rage grew in its place, unlike any he'd ever known. Overflowing with pain, a single thought echoed in his mind. The scent of the fabric filled his nostrils, sending memory of his wife into mind. A hatred burned inside him, fueling his desire for revenge. It didn't matter if they simply scratched her. They'd caused her pain and that was enough to evoke his wrath.

Tucking the ribbon into his sash, he opened his eyes and stormed up the stairs. Refusing to slow, Gareth lifted his leg and kicked the sturdy door, sending it off its hinges. It flew across the room, shedding bits of the wooden frame. He opened the wardrobe and looked inside, finding his quarry.

He snatched the gray leather armor from its wire stand and slipped it overhead. With a quick tug he tightened the pull cords along the sides and tied them off to prevent loosening. He recalled wearing it only once, the day he was named captain. His captain's words echoed in his mind. *'Every good captain needs a suit of armor. Ye never know what life's gonna throw at ya'. One day ye may be sailin' the seas. The next, ye have to sell 'yer boat and take up arms. It's always handy to have a good set of armor.'*

Forcing the memories, back he pulled against the hem, hoping the shoulders would abandon their training and form to his present shape. As he ran his hands across the brigandine, the numerous studs lining both sides scraped his fingers. The once shiny steel circlets were now dull and slightly corroded from years in storage. Brushing them one last time he adjusted the straps, making sure he could move properly. Opening the wardrobe drawer, Gareth removed a thick leather belt and strung his sheath and pouch on it. Throwing it around his waist, Gareth caught the tail. Looping it around the buckle, he tied a hitch knot and let the tail drop down between his legs. Adjusting his gear, he sheathed the blade and set off for the docks.

Resting in his high-backed oaken chair, the harbormaster glanced out the side window of the dock house. Fear crept into him with the sight of the armored captain. His stature demanded attention, and, more importantly, caution. Pushing against the polished armrests, Merrick got to his feet and grabbed his staff. Taking a deep breath, he made for the door to meet the clearly enraged captain. He'd taken pleasure in dealing with so many good men over the years. But situations like these made him dread his duties. Stepping out the door he silently prayed to Corin, hoping the encounter would pass easily. Pausing on edge of the dock, he awaited Gareth's approach. He had a look about him that would frighten the common man. There was something primal in his eyes. Something that told him to run. But he couldn't. It was his job to interact with the captains. Besides, there was no guarantee Gareth wouldn't give chase.

"Merrick, what'd the creatures look like?" Gareth demanded, dropping all formalities.

The old man was shaken by the tone. It was low and dangerous. His hair stood on end, sending chills down his spine. He tried to speak but the words couldn't escape his mouth. "Capt—"

Abandoning all tact, Gareth shouted louder than intended. "What'd they look like?" He could feel his anger rising.

"I— I didn't get a good look, sir. They were hard to see. Like they were always standing in shadows. Yo— You might ask Adrian Blakner over at the bakery, he barely got away from them last night. If anyone got a good look it'd be him."

It wasn't much of a lead, but it was better than nothing. Gareth turned and briskly marched toward the bakery. He passed several boarded up shops. The few citizens he passed along the way gave him a wide berth. Finding the small shop on the east side of town, he glanced at the charred siding. It seemed the place had caught fire at some point. The storm more than likely had some hand in putting it out. With little care for the people nearby, Gareth busted through the door, demanding answers. "Adrian, I need to know what the creatures look like."

The boy behind the counter was barely old enough to run the shop. He jumped at the loud bang, backing away from the large man barreling toward him.

Lost in his purpose, Gareth grabbed hold of his tunic and pulled him over the counter. "I need to know what the creatures look like."

The young man began to speak but was so frightened he couldn't get the words out.

Slamming him against the wall, Gareth hoped to jar the boy's memory. He had no time to wait for an answer. Pinning him in place he dropped a hand and slapped him across the cheek, more alerting him than causing pain. "Speak!"

"I— I saw th— them."

Gareth heard a trickle of liquid hit the floor. Glaring into the shop keep's eyes he spoke in a slow quiet tone, "What'd they look like, boy?"

He shook uncontrollably, choking on his words. "Th— They were black, their skin wa— was black. So— some of them had long hair, others had short. They had magic, th— they could disappear in the dark, like hide inside it— they used the night to get close and then they'd attack. They would appear and— and—" He started crying, uncaring that he'd wet himself. "They— They took my mother." He sobbed, letting the tears roll freely down his cheeks.

Gareth shook him, attempting to regain his attention. "What kind of weapons did they have?"

The young man looked puzzled at the question, staring into the anger-filled eyes. "They had all kinds of weapons, mostly swords but— but there were others."

"How many of them were there?"

He began to sob again. "There were— There were hundreds of them, they came out of nowhere, took what they wanted, and disappeared as quickly as they arrived. Please, tha— that's all I know." He begged, sobbing uncontrollably.

Gareth released him, letting him fall to the floor. Without a word, he turned and stormed from the bakery.

Chapter IV
The Last of the Dalari

Rays of sunlight beamed down through the trees on the edge of the small town of Winterhaven. Spring flowers stood tall through the dense grass, displaying a wide variety of colors. Each and every one stretched up in response to the sun's warmth. Laughter echoed across the clearing, finding its way to a boy standing at the edge of the forest road leading into the settlement.

Ravion waited patiently, watching over his siblings. His brother and sister played in the distance, paying no attention to the world around them. With a sigh, he felt the weight of his ten years. Instinctively, he rested his hand on the pommel of the dull short sword hanging from his hip. He couldn't explain why, but he enjoyed fondling the aged weapon. This was the first time he'd been allowed to carry it outside his training. It made him feel proud and slightly untouchable. Glancing over, he checked on the two younger children, recalling the days when he was able to play as they did. Instead his were filled with training in the ways of the sword. Any breaks he was allowed involved babysitting the younger two. It wasn't all that bad though, it gave him time to reflect on his training. Though too much reflection grew old quickly. He admired his sister, sitting among a patch of flowers. She split the stems, lacing them together to make a beautiful spring necklace among other accessories.

Despite her innocent appearance, she was naturally gifted in the ways of combat, as all dalari were. She had an aptitude with daggers unlike any he'd seen before. It wouldn't be long before she'd be required to sacrifice her play time as he had.

Shifting his attention to his brother, Ravion searched the forest's edge for the child, just out of his toddler years. The dark-green tunic was hard to see among the grass and leaves, but he found him. The child wandered the far edge of the grove, beyond the tree line. Ravion recalled the numerous times he'd marched across the grove to reclaim him, each time reminding him to stay in sight. He knew the youngling was testing his limits, wandering off a bit farther than he was supposed to. He was true to his nature. He wouldn't be dalari if he hadn't expressed a desire to explore the world. But he would have to be careful. He didn't understand how easily he could get lost in the forest. Calmly shaking his head, Ravion counted the minutes until he would have to retrieve him again.

Returning his thoughts to his training, he pulled the sword from its short leather sheath and stared intently at the blade. It was discolored from age, but held a brilliant, polished surface. He ran his fingers along the edge. It was rolled from years of use without sharpening, if it had ever been sharp in the first place. Several nicks were embedded in the forged iron, marred where it'd contacted another blade. Despite its less-than-ideal condition, he was proud of the simple weapon. And he vowed it would be proud of him one day.

A familiar sound echoed in the distance. The slightly pointed tips of his ears twitched, catching the noise. Sheathing the blade, he turned toward Winterhaven. Several pillars of smoke billowed from the wooden structures in the distance. Fear and excitement rushed through him. He'd trained since the day he was able to hold a weapon. If this wasn't the opportunity he needed to prove himself, he didn't know what would be. He glanced along the path ensuring the way was clear. It would take some time to get back, but if he ran he could close the gap in a few minutes. His mind made, he turned toward his sister, seeing her run toward him. "Alexzandra, something's wrong! Stay here and keep an eye on him."

Hearing his words, she froze and turned to head back to her flower patch. Glancing over at her younger brother, she retook her seat.

Ravion turned and ran as fast as he could. In the blink of an eye, he'd crested the hill and disappeared from the grove. Atop the hill the sounds of battle, an extremely large battle, assaulted his ears. He heard the familiar clank of swords echoing all around him.

Smoke rose from homes and shops. Bright orange flame licked the layered wooden shingles atop the sloped wooden roofs. They were turning black from the heat, ready to burst into flame.

He felt sick to his stomach, like he'd eaten something bad. The only home he'd known was under attack. He wasn't sure what he was supposed to feel. Ignoring the pain deep within him he moved forward, using the outlying buildings for cover. They seemed to be the only ones that weren't ablaze.

Several armor-clad figures, wielding graceful and well-balanced weapons, swarmed the far edge of town. They surrounded the townspeople, cutting them down with ease.

He was too far away to make out who they were, but they were clearly winning the fight. He had to get home and find his parents. Drawing his sword Ravion slowly made his way through town, hoping to avoid being seen. The tailor's shop was just ahead, having suffered minor charring along the siding. It seemed the fire had been put out before it consumed too much. He quickly made his way around the corner and stepped through the door. The building was abandoned. Everything remained in its proper place, suggesting the tailor and his family simply left.

Ravion grabbed a large patch of tan linen, noting the resemblance in color to that of the dirt roads outside. Throwing them overhead, he tied them off to wrap around him like an oversized robe. It would be too bulky to fight in, but perhaps he could get closer to home before they saw him. Testing his reaction time to disrobe and draw his sword, he carefully made his way from the shop and turned down the narrow alleyway. Inhaling softly, Ravion cleared his mind, the first thing he'd been taught. His vision began to focus and zoom. He was at one with his surroundings. He felt faster and stronger, like he was connected to the world around him.

Making his way from the alley, he spotted the attacking figures. They'd killed nearly everyone and now were checking for survivors. He'd have to make sure they didn't see him. Placing his back against the wall, he stood as still as his body would allow. The tall, slender aggressors resembled human, but their ears were severely pointed. Realization set in. He knew what they were and why they were here. He closed his eyes, attempting to force the story from his mind. His family's origins, and more importantly, their reason for living among the humans, wouldn't help him. He couldn't understand why the alfar hated them, or why they continued their manhunt for so long. But the real question found its way to the surface. How had they been discovered? And why was there no warning?

He felt his focus fading. He couldn't allow that to happen. Taking another deep, steady breath, Ravion calmed himself, returning his focus. Waiting for the intruders to pass, he slowly, carefully made his way through the village, avoiding those that would kill him for the mistakes of his ancestors.

Ravion made his way through the streets. His face paled at the sights before him. Dead and dying bodies of the town's residents littered the ground, left where they'd fallen. Their attackers had abandoned them and moved on to another part of town. This was no simple hunt for the last of the dalari. This was extermination of anyone they met. This was genocide.

He turned the corner, looking up toward the house atop the hill. He couldn't see it yet, but he couldn't see signs of fire, either. Much of the smoke had settled, leaving the streets foggy and dense. Hopefully the alfar hadn't bothered taking the hill. His father built their home with the intention of its defense in mind. Anyone attempting to take it by force would undoubtedly suffer heavy casualties.

He continued up the small hill, spotting the roof of the wood beamed cabin. To his relief it remained free of flame. A momentary victory faded, leaving worry in its place. Sounds of battle echoed overhead. They were louder than ever, increasing volume in his mind. Running toward the commotion, he saw several bodies wrapped in thin, yet sturdy leather armor lining the curved road. It was clear these were the casualties of his father's work, having fallen during their trek. Fletchings protruded from them in various places, matching those of his father's arrows. Emotions twisted inside him. Many of the alfar were lost in the approach, but from the sounds of the continuing battle at the peak, at least a few had to have survived.

Ravion hurried up the hill, assessing the situation. Frozen at the sight of a crowd gathered in front of his home, he realized they were encircled around a single man. A shocked gasp escaped him, realizing the lone man was his father, armed with a longsword, outstretched and ready to strike.

The elder dalari took in everything and nothing at the same time. Sweat glistened off his forehead. His long golden-brown hair was pulled into a tail at the back. He stood with his feet a short distance apart, hands placed one above the other, locked around the extended handle of his blood-coated longsword. He held fast, awaiting the moment to attack.

Several of the alfar rushed in, striking in perfect unison. Their target proved too skillful to handle one on one. If they were going to take him down, they'd have to strike as one and overpower him.

Ravion watched, frozen in fear. His father was everything. Nothing could best him. But against so many how could he hope to succeed? His fear settled as he watched the group fall before his eyes, their deaths a mystery to him. He hadn't seen his father move, let alone strike the outnumbering opponents. Another group followed, suffering a similar fate.

The remaining alfar closed on the lone dalari. Many of them suffered moderate wounds, but the blood loss hadn't affected their ability yet. They perished as quickly as they approached leaving just over half a dozen to finish the unharmed, but exhausted warrior.

Ravion moved closer. The attackers were too busy to worry about him. He kept his eyes forward, but made sure to listen behind him. He couldn't help his father if they were able to catch him unaware.

The battle shifted with the thinned numbers, leaving large gaps between the alfar.

His gaze darted to a body unlike the others, lying crumpled just outside the door of his home. His mother's cold, lifeless eyes stared back at him, void of the love she'd shown him for as long as he could remember. A fresh pool of crimson fluid ran in streams down the stone walkway leading from their door. "No!" Unable to stop himself, he charged toward his father.

The elder dalari brought his sword up, blocking a potentially deadly blow. "Ra'dulen, get your siblings and retreat!" Without pause, he spun the blade around and thrust deep into the attacking alfar's chest. With ease he redirected back to his neutral stance, ready for the next advance.

Ravion came to a stop several steps from his father. *Why did he tell me to retreat? I can help. I've been trained for this.* He didn't know what to do. He wanted to return to the grove as his father had commanded, but he also wanted to help against so many intruders. Taking another step closer, he froze, lost in the moment for an eternity.

Using the distraction to their advantage, the alfar rushed in, bringing their blades down in all directions. The familiar ring of steel on steel sounded out, echoing into silence. One by one the alfar dropped their weapons joining their brethren on the blood-soaked earth.

Ravion stared into his father's eyes, frozen at the sight. The silence was deafening. As if the drums of war were inverted and pounding in his chest. The long pause between beats consumed him. His gaze shifted to the blade protruding from his father's chest. A red stain soaked into the cloth, expanding around the wound. *Did they use me as a distraction? Why didn't I listen? Is this my fault?* He hadn't realized he was continuing toward his father. Stopping just out of reach, he felt the tears trickle down his cheeks. He felt numb. Reaching out, he saw a pain in his father's eyes. One he'd never seen before.

The elder dalari fell to his knees, helpless against his murderer. He looked up, pleading to his successor. "Teradun, please—" he coughed, blood spurting from his mouth, "Please, spare my son. He's just a boy. I know you're following orders, but allowing a single child to live cannot make much of a difference."

The alfar glanced at the boy. He didn't look like much. Scrawny and dirty with a dull short sword. *One child won't make a difference. But when he ages, with the training he's undoubtedly been given, he'll make a formidable opponent. Not to mention, he'll most likely seek revenge for this day. Is it worth having to look over my shoulder for the rest of my life? The dalari are near immortal and extremely resourceful. He may not find me for a thousand years, but one day he will.* Returning his attention to the dying dalari, he made his decision. "Don't beg, Marquel. It's unbecoming. Your family has evaded us far too long. Standing orders set forth by Emperor Jullien the Third, and reissued by Emperor Jullien the Fifth declare, 'All dalari must die.' You know this." A smirk stretched across his face. He was taking joy in his assignment. Placing his booted foot next to the embedded sword, Teradun gave a hefty kick, pulling the blade free. Timing it perfectly, he spun around, lowering the razor edge to the correct height. The sword passed through Marquel's neck with little effort causing a small amount of blood to spray from the wound, spattering across the boy's face.

Ravion watched his father's head roll from his body. It landed hard on the ground, bouncing a little before coming to a stop. His fist clenched in silent rage. He felt his knuckles pop in protest. He could not stand for this. His father, his mother— everyone he'd ever known was gone. They would pay dearly for this. He felt a cool breeze blow across his face. He didn't know why, but it made him remember his training. His father's words echoed in his head. *'Clear your mind. A clouded mind makes a reckless combatant.'*

Ravion took a deep, but controlled breath, releasing the anger building inside him. Revenge was not the way of his people, nor was justice. His people held balance above all else. The scales had finally tilted in his favor. Forcing all that was and all that was going to be from his mind, he exhaled slowly. The only thing that mattered was this one moment. The moment when he would have to kill or be killed. Pushing his thoughts and emotions aside, Ravion lifted his sword, ready to defend himself.

Teradun calmly approached the child. He wouldn't be careless. After all, the child was surely trained. He'd never met a dalari who wasn't. Stopping just out of the short sword's reach, he took aim, preparing to cut the boy down with his first strike. Like a flash of lightning he struck, the blade cracking out like thunder.

Ravion brought his training sword up at the exact moment. He didn't know how, but his dull sword acted as if it had a mind of its own. His reflexes responded of their own accord, rescuing him from the sting of the alfaren blade. He stared up at the towering hydralfar, sharing a moment of surprise by his actions.

Caught off-guard the alfar took a step back, keeping his sword at the ready. *How did he move that fast?* Pressing again he brought the blade down, adding strength and speed to the lethal attack.

Ravion felt his arms react. He brought the training sword up to defend as he had before. The weaker metal flexed beneath the force of the blow. He heard it snap, seeing the shattered pieces splinter toward him. Jagged shards flew past his face, leaving shallow cuts in his flesh. Staggering from the unexpected blow, Ravion dropped the shattered weapon, grabbing his cut face. Forcing his resolve, he brought his bloody hands way, seeing the red fluid drip into the dirt. Several fragments of his sword laid among the blood, informing him he was unarmed. Taking a step back, he wasn't sure how he was going to survive this.

Teradun smiled. "Your kind is nearly extinct. You no longer have the ability to defend yourself. And when I'm finished, the dalari will be nothing more than a distant memory."

Ravion stood defiantly against the alfar. He had to survive. He had to find his siblings and make sure they grew up. *'A clouded mind makes a reckless combatant!'* The words echoed in his head a second time, as if his father watched over him, guiding him in this fight. "Your task is for naught. You've spend your life in pursuit of my kind. I may not have been around when your emperor gave this order, but I will not stand by while you commit genocide against my people. I promise you, I'll survive and I'll find them, wherever they are. And when that day comes, we'll rise from the ashes and remove any trace of this outdated and idiotic order from both our histories. I don't know why you wish us dead, but I'll find out. I'm just sad your emperor will be long dead before that day comes." Ravion took a step closer to the alfar, purposely placing himself within his attacker's reach.

Teradun felt his blood boil with the defiant child's words. Unfortunately, he was too close to effectively cut him down. But he would not allow words against his emperor to go unpunished. Bringing his gauntleted fist down, he caught the child across the cheek.

The impact launched Ravion from his feet. He felt the impression of the hardened leather across his face. For the briefest of moments he was weightless, flying through the air. His face hurt, but it had to feel better than a sword cutting into him. He collided with something hard but forgiving, forcing the air from his lungs. Panic rushed through him, causing him to spasm where he laid. Focusing on his task he calmed himself, controlling his breathing. Looking around, he found a pile of alfaren bodies beneath him. Rolling from the mound of death, he searched for anything that could help him. The sight of his father's body drew him in. His gaze locked on the longsword lying in the dirt, a few feet away. Climbing to his hands and knees he looked around, locating his attacker. Teradun was over fifteen steps away, whereas the sword was just out of reach. Ravion smiled, he had plenty of time to get the sword before the alfar would be upon him again. He launched forward and grabbed the weapon. Continuing around, he rolled to his feet standing with sword in hand.

The alfar smirked, making his way for the armed child.

Ravion took a defensive stance, lifting the surprisingly light weapon. It weighed barely half what his training sword did. Raising the blade, he prepared for the next assault. A single heartbeat felt like a lifetime, watching the alfar tower over him. As before he reacted with pure instinct, deflecting the multitude of blows raining down upon him. He felt a bit of joy watching his attacker struggle against him. He didn't have much of a plan, but this was working. Each unsuccessful strike granted him more time for his next action.

Sweat poured from the exhausted alfar as he swung wildly, trying to get past the young dalari's defenses. Unable to find weakness in the miniature form, he was rapidly growing tired.

Ravion felt his strength growing. Even the sweat he'd felt clinging to his skin was beginning the fade. He took a deep breath, allowing the calm to flow through him. He was connected to everything and nothing. Like a bystander watching his own body, witnessing the world around him with superior knowledge of its events. The entire battle quickly played out before him. He watched in shock, reliving his father's death. Only this time his emotions remained in check. He reviewed everything up to his current point, but it didn't stop there. The battle was moving forward, revealing details that hadn't yet come to pass. The vision, as best he could figure, played to its conclusion. He knew he was still fighting, and judging by the fact that he hadn't felt any pain, he was still alive. Feeling himself sink back into his body he deflected a quick jab from the towering alfar, as his vision revealed. Each action played out exactly as he'd seen. The precise moment was coming fast.

Teradun swung hard, overextending himself.

Ravion watched the opening present a perfect target, just as he'd seen. Seizing the opportunity, he thrust the longsword up, straight into the leather plates. The blade sank deep with minor resistance. Surely he'd pierced a vital organ. Twisting the blade slightly he was rewarded in blood running down the polished steel, showering him in the crimson life-fluid.

The alfar fell to his knees before the young dalari, his bright red blood steadily pumping from the lethal wound.

Ravion pulled the sword free, taking a step back to keep from being crushed by the large opponent.

Teradun stared curiously at the child before him. *How could a child not only hold me off, but defeat me?* Unable to take another breath he fell to the unforgiving ground, his blood pooling beneath him.

Ravion watched the life fade from the alfar's dulling eyes. He stood as victor over the alfar responsible for his father's death. He watched the life leave his enemy, feeling no remorse, nor pride in what he'd done. It was simply something that had to happen and he was destined to accomplish it.

Hours passed, leaving the fading sun a soft glow on the horizon. Several fires burned brightly, illuminating the barren street.

Ravion knelt down beside the forest road, studying the tracks. There were clearly fresh hoof prints, but that didn't explain where his siblings were. The alfar didn't have horses as far as he'd seen, so it was unlikely they went to Eastwood.

"Alexzandra where are you?" His question was answered with silence. He felt the pain of losing his parents begin to grow within him, and now his siblings were missing. He searched the grove for what had to have been the hundredth time. The flowers remained where she'd been, trampled and wilting. A few drops of dried blood rested on the stems and petals, but not enough to suggest serious injury. Large, booted footprints covered the area in all directions, but they clearly came from town. Nothing suggested they returned with captives. Even if he knew who else had been here the tracks were too numerous to locate a single set.

Ravion glanced at the final slither of sunlight, disappearing behind the trees. "It's time," He admitted, knowing no one was around to hear him. Pulling a small stone from the pouch strapped to his side, he secured the torch he'd brought with him. Quickly, he struck the flint rock against his father's sword. The sparks danced to life, finding refuge in the oil-soaked cloth. It flared to life, illuminating the area. He raised it overhead and waved it back and forth, signaling the others.

A group of just over a dozen children, the oldest one looking to be a few years younger than Ravion, approached carrying what few belongings they could manage wrapped up in blankets and old packs. They stopped in front of him, awaiting orders.

"The path seems clear. If you walk all night you should reach Eastwood by midday. Tell the guards what happened and they'll make sure you're taken care of. Joshua, Carin, take these." Ravion handed two of the dull training swords to the oldest of the group. "Hopefully you won't have to use them, but it's better than nothing. Don't stop, don't split up, and don't leave the road. Take the torch. If you have to stop for the night use it to make a campfire off the road. You don't want to draw unwanted attention, but you also don't want to be caught unaware in the dark either. Good luck."

The small group set out, disappearing into the shadows of night.

Ravion watched their light shrink in the distance. He couldn't help but wonder if his siblings had already headed that way. Returning to town, he wondered if the children would make it to Eastwood. Short of going along, he'd given them every opportunity to survive. It was on them now. *It's for the best. They aren't in any condition to assist me anyway.* With a heavy sigh, Ravion lit another torch and tossed it into a pile of straw he'd layered inside the tailor's shop. The fire flared to life, quickly spreading to the walls and ceiling. Within moments it encompassed the bodies within. Watching through the inflamed doorway, he could see their flesh blister and char from the heat. It was a burden no child should have to bear. But he was the only one to carry it. The others didn't need to face this with him. They'd seen enough already.

Their homes were gone. The best he could offer them was a chance at survival.

Hiding his exposed flesh from the heat, he stuck another torch into the flame. Carrying it to another building, he tossed it in, letting the flame engulf the wooden structure in a matter of minutes. The alfaren bodies piled inside didn't deserve to be laid to rest with their victims. It'd taken the better part of the day to sort and pile them, but it was the right thing to do. Nearly everything he could find to burn was piled with them. It would take a great amount of heat to properly dispose of their bodies, and the fires would be seen for miles, but it was better than leaving them to rot in the streets. Leaving them to be consumed by the flames, he returned to the cabin atop the hill. His parents were wrapped in several layers of cloth and laid to rest peacefully in their bed. It wasn't quite according to tradition, but it would have to suffice.

The once beautiful village of Winterhaven was now barren and dark. The moonlight made the blood soaked streets glow and the numerous pyres coated the ruined village in ash.

Grabbing his father's backpack, he tossed a few sets of clothes into the bottom. It would have to be rearranged, but first he needed to load up. He tied a slightly larger pair of boots to the side. It would give him something to grow into. Rolled a thick woolen blanket inside his bedroll, Ravion strapped it to the bottom of the bag to save room. Searching every room in the house, he grabbed anything he thought he might need. The bag was nearly overflowing, but he continued packing. His father's whetstone fit perfectly into the side pocket, along with the flint rock. Pulling the drawstring taut, he heaved it over his shoulders, and made for his parent's room. He wasn't quite strong enough to carry the bag. But the supplied would run low soon enough. By them, maybe he'd be equipped for life on his own. Stopping at the side of their bed, he stared at the blood-soaked blanket covering their still forms. Laying the bag to rest at his side, he offered a warrior's salute. "Mother, Father, thank you both for teaching me the value of life and the responsibility of death. I'll uphold the traditions of our people as best I can and honor the balance entrusted to me by my birthright. If I can find our people, I'll do my part to lead us into a new era."

Pulling the blanket back enough to see their faces, he placed a silver coin over each of his parents' eyes. Lifting his pack, he turned to leave the room, snatching his father's belt and sheath on his way out. It was too large for small stature, but with a few simple modifications it would fit. Locating his father's leather tools, he quickly sized the belt and tossed the smaller tools into one of the size pockets on the pack. Sheathing the sword, he tested his draw. It was a bit too long to draw smoothly, but he would grow into it.

The last things he needed were food and coin. It would take some time before he could make either on his own. Stepping into the common room, he pulled a chair over to the hearth and climbed up. The small chest resting atop the wide ledge was filled to the brim with gold, silver, and gems. Provided he could manage it properly, he shouldn't have to worry about funds for at least a few years. Grabbing a leather pouch, he poured the contents in and tossed it in the pack. If he'd packed right, he would have just enough room for a month's worth of rations.

Rummaging the cupboards, he stuffed the last bit of dried meat, fruit, and bread into his bag and double checked everything, making sure he hadn't missed anything. Time was upon him. It would be daylight soon and he needed to get on the road. Hopefully Alexzandra and Demetrix would be waiting for him at Eastwood. Reaching the door, he paused, grabbed the oil lamp resting on the corner table. With a final look around, he memorized every detail. He'd never see this home again and such a memory would have to keep him going.

Sighing deeply, Ravion tossed the lantern as hard as he could. It shattered on the floor, spilling flaming oil all over the wooden planks. Smoke billowed and the flame climbed the walls. Within moments, the cedar shingles were ablaze, burning away his past. Ravion turned and marched toward the forest road, ready to face what tomorrow held. He didn't know where he was going, but if any part of his family was still out there, it was his duty to find them. It was a large world and he needed to search as much of it as possible. If nothing else maybe he could find and reunite the remaining dalari. His people needed to be led into a new age. Maybe he would be the one to guide them.

The sun was beginning to set over the high mountain peaks. Flakes of white blew all around, landing comfortably on the sleet covered ground. Several thin evergreens stood, waving in the breeze of the cool evening air. Among the rocky peaks and thinning trees, a man stood at the cliff's edge, overlooking the world below. He was young in appearance, but his demeanor held years beyond his appearance.

Over two hundred years had passed since a young child set out from a burning home in search of his people. Over two hundred years of journeys and quests in exchange for information. Over two hundred years of puzzles, all leading him to this one place. And finally, he was here.

Ravion stood at the mountain peaks looking into the wind. The frozen specks clung to his face, landing in dark contrast to his black cloak and navy blue garments. The sight before him filled his mind. He stared into the distance, feeling the snow and wind surround him. Pulling his cloak tight around his thin frame, he squinted through the clouds to the world below.

Several kingdoms rested as far as the eye could see, each one holding secrets of their own. A long wall stretched across the land, sealing the northern lands from the south with a single outpost in the center. He couldn't help but feel helpless at the sight of the lands stretching as far as the eye could see. But the rumors and information he'd gathered sent him here, to the birthplace of the dreualfar, to the ancient lands of his people before their mistake.

Ravion held the cloak tight, locking the chilling wind out. He took his first step into Dalmoura, making sure his foot was secure in the snow covered peaks. Again he stepped, each time moving closer to possible answers. His feet firm against the sloping, dangerous ground, he walked carefully, making his way into the strange new lands.

Near the base of the large mountain range he came across a weather worn sign planted firmly in the dirt at the side the winding mountain road.

"Tresengal sixty miles. Aldridge thirty miles" He read aloud, glancing both directions. It would take a while to reach either city, but closer was always better. At least until he gathered his bearings.

Chapter V
Wrath of Dragons

The sounds of slaughter echoed through the trees, announcing the smell of smoke in the air. It was just beginning to settle, catching the rays of sunlight and layering the grove in a thick cloud.

Demetrix covered his ears trying to block out the frightening noise. The screams lingered long after they'd stopped. He could barely see his sister through the smoke. He couldn't hear her words, but she was clearly screaming at him. A figure appeared behind her, more shadow than man. Demetrix lifted his trembling hand, extending his finger toward the man.

What's he pointing at? The nearing footsteps caught her attention. Alexzandra spun around to face the sun-gleamed edge of a sword hovering over her, poised to strike. The keen blade fell, sending a sharp pain through her chest. With a spray of blood, she fell, landing roughly in a patch of daisies.

Demetrix stood frozen at the spectacle. *Is she dead? Who is he? Why does he want to hurt us?* He glared at the man, unable to take his eyes off the tall figure.

The man stepped toward him, sword in hand, ready to cut the child down as he had his sister.

Demetrix watched in horror. The echoes of pain and fear began to fade, replaced by the sound of hooves. A rider appeared through the fog, moving quicker than anything he'd seen before. The horseman drew an unusual, dark-colored sword. As fast as he'd drawn it, he brought it down cleaving the malicious man in half.

The slender figure stood motionless for a long moment. He took a step forward and fell face first into the dense grass.

The horseman continued on, coming to a stop a few feet past the children. He jumped from his saddle and approached slowly. "Demetrix, do not fear me. My name's Meaius. I'm here to help." The horseman cleaned and sheathed his wide sword.

The dalari child stared intently at the weapon as it disappeared into the leather cover. He'd seen many swords before, but this one was different. It was made of a black metal and nearly twice as wide as his practice sword.

The blade firmly secured in its sheath, Demetrix studied the man himself. He wore black armor with an hourglass inscribed on the left breastplate. Despite his dark clothing and armor, the man had a familiar glow about him, almost white in color. Demetrix had seen such a glow before, but never white. The man's features were clearly human but he felt— different. "My sister." Demetrix gestured toward her limp form, half-buried in the grass a few feet from the dead assailant.

"I fear there's not much I can do for her, but I'll try." Meaius turned and scooped the girl up. Carrying her back to the boy, he laid her on her back and placed his gloved hand above her chest. Closing his eyes, he whispered a quiet chant. A glowing light radiated between the two, soaking into the wound. As carefully as he could, he picked her up and gently laid her over the horse. With ease, he placed his foot in the stirrup and swung, positioning himself in the black colored saddle.

Looking down, he extended his hand to the boy. "You coming?" He was a squat little thing, maybe four seasons. *If he only knew how important he was.*

Demetrix took the outstretched hand and felt himself fly up into the saddle. Wiggling into place, he positioned himself at the rear so he could hold his sister still.

Meaius gave a light prod, the dark-brown horse launched forward in a smooth transition. Moments later they were deep in the forest, leaving the boy's former life behind. Meaius looked back, watching the heavy plume of smoke grow smaller with the distance. Not much longer and it would disappear entirely behind the height of the trees.

The sun was setting on the horizon when the horse finally slowed to a stop. Demetrix felt his legs throb with the change in pace. His backside was inflamed from the trip. It wasn't often he'd been atop a horse, much less spent the better part of a day on one.

Meaius climbed down and helped the boy from the saddle. Kicking a pile of leaves together, he carefully placed Alexzandra in the make-shift bed.

Demetrix knelt down, searching the tear in her dress. It was discolored from dried blood, but he couldn't find a wound anywhere. *Did the man heal her? How is that possible?*

"You're both from a strong race. While her body has healed, the wound cut much deeper than flesh. If she's to survive, it'll be by her own will. There's nothing more anyone can do for her. At least until she chooses to wake up." Meaius reached into his saddlebag and grabbed a thin, leather pouch. Unrolling it, he removed a piece of dried meat and handed it to the boy.

Demetrix snatched the meat from his hand and took a bite. It was a bit tough, but it was food. He wasn't used to skipping meals. Truth be told, he wasn't used to any of this. Realization set in. *How long will it be until I eat again?* Slowing himself, he tore off a small piece and began chewing, stuffing the remainder in his pocket.

"I'm glad to see you have wisdom beyond your years. Your father has taught you well. But you don't have to ration just yet. We'll camp for the night. We're about a mile from Eastwood. It won't be a long trip in the morning. When we arrive, I'll make arrangements for you to join a caravan."

The boy stared up at Meaius. The man knew something he wasn't saying. "Why can't we go home?"

"I'm sorry but your home is gone. Your family was in hiding. I tried to reach your father before the alfar got there, but it was too late. Had he not asked me to get you as far away from there as possible, I would have helped him hold them off. Which brings us to the next point; your people are being hunted by the hydralfar. They saw me leave so I'd imagine they'll be searching for me now. When we reach Eastwood, we must part ways so I can draw them away from you."

"Why do they want to kill me? I didn't do anything to them."

Meaius shredded a few twigs and placed them in a pile. "Life isn't always fair. People tend to fear things they don't understand. That fear often turns to hatred, and before long they start making mistakes they can't take back." He paused for a moment, striking his flint. The sparks landed in the tinder and began to smoke. He gave a slow and steady breath, watching the flame flare to life, burning away the twigs. Adding a few larger sticks to the small ember, he continued, "Long ago, a small faction of your people made bad choices, which resulted in dark times for all of us. Unfortunately you're being forced to pay for those mistakes." The flame grew into a sustainable fire. "Would you like to do me a favor? Don't go too far, but gather some firewood, nothing bigger than your arm." Meaius gave a light smile, watching the boy step into the shadows.

The city of Eastwood bustled with merchants and travelers going about their daily lives. A steady roar of voices echoed in the air, preventing any one from standing out above the others. The stench of manure radiated from the steady supply of livestock and horses being led along the roads. Some pulled carts or wagons, while others were ushered into stalls for sale and trade.

Demetrix sat at the rear of the enclosed wagon, watching out the open gate. He mindlessly kicked his legs, dangling over the edge while Meaius negotiated their deal. The dark armored man had a way about him that the others respected, or possibly feared. He couldn't be sure.

The two men paused for a moment, looking over at the seemingly human child innocently watching them.

"You'll take them as far as Ickula?"

"Aye. Though I don't know why you'd send them there. Nothin' but thieves and cut-throats, since the alfar marched through."

"Don't concern yourself with that. Ozmodius works in mysterious ways."

"Whatever you say. I'm getting paid. That's all I care about."

"That you are. And extremely well, I might add. Don't let anything befall them."

"You have nothin' to worry about. I've made the trip three times this year. Not so much as a broken wheel along the way."

"Good. Give me a word with them and I'll be on my way."

"I've already been paid. Do what you want."

Meaius approached the boy with a half-hearted smile. "Are you ready to go?"

"I guess. I'm not sure why we can't stay with you. You could protect us."

"I've other duties to attend. Besides, you'd grow tired of me after a while. I'm quite boring once you get to know me." He ruffled the boy's hair, laughing.

"I don't think so. I bet you could defeat anyone that came after us." He nodded to the broadsword sheathed on Meaius' hip.

"I'd try at the very least. But I've found it more effective to try and talk to an opponent first. You'd be surprised how many problems can be resolved with a few sensible words. Besides, if words fail you can always fight afterword. That's one lesson I hope you remember, Demetrix. A premature sword slice cannot be undone. It's a warrior's duty to understand what he's fighting for and to decide if it's worth killing for. If you don't understand these two things, you're no better than the men you morally tower over. Nevertheless, take this. You never know when it may come in handy."

Demetrix took the dagger. It was made from the same dark material as the broadsword. Tucking it into his pants, he wrapped his arms around the armored warrior and hugged him tight.

"I'll miss you, too. Now, let's get you tucked away. It's a three month journey to Ickula and you'll need your rest." Meaius waited for the boy to lay back and close his eyes. "Safe travels, Demetrix. I look forward to our next meeting." He latched the wooden gate and unrolled the canvas flap to block out the sunlight.

His eyes shot open with the violent crash. *How am I supposed to sleep with the constant bumps and screeching wagon wheels?* He sat up and looked over at his sister, lying unconscious atop a pile of fur. She looked much better than she had, but he was beginning to worry she wouldn't ever wake up. Getting to his feet, Demetrix moved to the rear of the wagon and pulled the flap to the side. A brown horse with white spots trotted several feet behind them, attached to a wagon in tow. A human sat atop the coach, directing the horse.

"Be careful, boy. One wrong move and you'll fall. I doubt the wagon master will be able to stop before the horses trample you."

He glanced to the man on horseback beside the wagon. The man wore tan leather armor and carried a sword at his side. Ducking beneath the flap, Demetrix returned to his spot and laid down.

The wagon hit another bump, bouncing his head off the wooden sidewall. Anger shot through him. He sat up hearing the strangest sound he'd ever heard. The noises outside the wagon intensified. The shouts of men and the whinny of horses echoed through the thick canvas top. Some sped up while the wagons seemed to slow. The noise echoed again, chilling him to the bone. It sounded like a massive roar, wrung out over a great distance. A blast of wind hit the side of the wagon, threatening to tear the top away from its supports. Screams echoed all around. Demetrix jumped up and headed toward the flap. A powerful crash hit the side of the wagon, toppling it over. He crashed into the cloth liner, feeling it tear under his forceful weight. Sunlight flashed into his vision for the briefest of moments, replaced by shadow. He crashed through branches and leaves, landing hard in the packed dirt of the forest floor. Rolling several times, he tried to stop himself. His arms buckled under the motion, useless to him. Pain shot through his body, slamming into the base of a thick tree. His vision faded to black.

The sweet scent of rotting meat roused him. His eyes shot open and he searched for anything to tell him where he was. The ground was hard and jagged reminding him of the rocks along the edge of the river, though he clearly wasn't there. The air was cold and damp, but he didn't feel a breeze.

The cavern was larger than any he'd seen before. Discarded weapons littered the underground terrain, pieces of their owners with them. The stone floor was caked in a thick, soupy mixture of blood and dirt. Along the walls, piles of gold, silver, and gems were stacked perfectly into grand pyramids.

Demetrix heard a deep rumble from inside the cavern. He sat up, searching for its source. His head throbbed, but the cool air was slightly soothing, aside from the rancid stench that filled his lungs with each breath. He couldn't see as well as he was used to. Even the caves around the river weren't as dark as this one. It was expected for his kind to see in pitch-black. This wasn't natural.

Two thin yellow lines appeared at the far end of the chamber, rapidly growing into massive orbs several times larger than the child.

He peered up the massive glowing— eyes? A deep fear enveloped him, stronger than any fear he'd felt before. Yet somehow he was able to control it. He was scared, that much was certain. But it felt as if a stronger force pushed back. Something inside him was protecting him from it.

"Yes— Yes, there it is." The deep, gravelly voice shook the cavern to its core. "I knew I smelled a dalari among all those humans. Tell me, boy. Where were you going?"

He stared at the disembodied orbs, feeling the bass of the voice thrum throughout his body. *Should I answer? Why does it want to know?* "That's none of your business. Where's my sister?" Demetrix clenched his fists, demanding an answer.

Sinister laughter echoed throughout the stone chamber, knocking several of the stalactites from the ceiling. They crashed down, breaking against the equally hardened floor. "You amuse me, Son of Esoteric. Though do not mistake my amusement for patience. Why was a child of the dalari in the company of a band of human traders?"

Why do you want to know?" He squinted his eyes, hoping to catch a glimpse of the creature in the shadow.

"Again, you answer with a question. I'll make you a deal. Answer me and I'll let you go. You can return to whatever life you came from. You can even take as much treasure from this place as you can carry to ease you in your living."

He searched the shadow, studying the silence. *What can it learn from the truth? It's not like I have some big secret. And the treasure would help to find Alexzandra.* "How do I know you're telling the truth?" No sooner than the question escaped his lips the shadow moved closer, resolving into a huge scale-covered snout with four barbed horns curving around the creature's head. Two extended out and wrapped around like those of a ram while the other two arched up and back, lining the sides of its massive head. Hundreds of teeth, each one larger than his entire body, lined its clenched maw. Its nostrils pulsed, as if it were smelling him.

"Because, I'm a dragon. And dragons always keep their word."

Demetrix took in the sight of the great black. He couldn't understand how he was able to resist fleeing at the beast's sight. Every muscle in his body wanted to run as far and as fast as he could in the opposite direction, but he held fast trusting the feeling in his gut.

"Do we have an agreement?" The dragon cocked its head, awaiting response.

"Fine. I'll answer your question. But I want to know what you've done with my sister before I leave."

"You have my word. Now, let's see— Two bodies I have, though both joined in one. The longer I wait, the more I run. What am I?"

"But— That wasn't your question. You asked where I was going."

"I changed my question. Do you forfeit?"

"No— I— That's not fair."

"Who told you life was fair? Answer my question or you forfeit."

"Two bodies, one. Longer I wait, the more I— Is it a wagon?"

"A wagon? How would it be a wagon?"

"Well, if you have two people in a wagon, they become one. And if you're riding, then the longer you wait, the longer it runs."

"I weep for today's youth. Didn't your parents teach you anything about your creators? It's an hourglass. The symbol of Ozmodius. The king of the gods? Is any of this ringing a bell?"

"Nope. I still think it's a wagon."

"It's not a damned wagon!" The dragon snapped, slamming his clenched fist into the rocky floor. Calming himself, he returned his attention to the child. "But I'll set your mind at ease. I haven't done anything with your sister. Had I known there were two of you, she'd be right beside you."

He felt fear begin to overcome him. *Where is she? If the dragon didn't take her, what had happened to her? Is she alive?* He felt tears begin to steam down his face. "Why'd you bring me here?"

"Let's just say I have plans for you. Maybe not today, nor tomorrow, but one day you'll play a valuable part in the grand scheme of things."

"So I'm to stay here until you have need of me?" Demetrix reached down, wrapping his hand around the dagger Meaius had given him.

"Heavens, no. You're free to roam. I've no use for one kept out of touch with the world above. You need to be familiar with their customs."

"What if I refuse to help you?"

"You act like you have a choice. You answered wrong. Your life is mine now."

Demetrix glared his hatred at the dragon. "I won't help you. You can kill me a thousand times over. I'll never do anything you ask."

"I'm not asking."

Drawing the dagger, Demetrix flung it as hard as he could. Without pause, he charged toward the dragon. He'd escape or it'd kill him. Either way, he'd be free.

The dagger stuck, sinking to the hilt in the dragon's eye. It roared in pain, feeling the mythical ore pull at his core. He fumbled with the blade, trying to pluck it from his ruined eye. Anger flooded him. *How did I not smell he had darkstone?* Spinning around in the crowded cavern he sucked in as much air as his lungs could hold. Searching for the boy's scent, it was nearing fresh air. He was getting away. With tremendous force, he exhaled, shooting a nauseous cloud of green vapor into the passageway. "Run all you like, I'll find you, you little brat! It may take me a thousand years, but we'll meet again!"

Demetrix ran as fast as his legs would carry him, hoping the blade found its mark. He turned down one of the crossing corridors, feeling his feet leave the ground. His stomach churned with weightlessness. Splashing into a dark substance, the liquid forced its way into his mouth. He struggled against its swallowing surface. The cavern grew dark, and disappeared.

Water slapped against the muddy bank, echoing through the trees of the forested alcove. Crickets chirped along the edge, hidden from the birds flying overhead. The battered form of a child rested in the muck, his chest rising slowly with each breath.

Demetrix slapped his cheek, knocking a tiny insect from it. Groaning, he rolled over and pushed himself up. Clawing at the muddy soil, he took in the unfamiliar surroundings. He was still in a forest, but the trees looked— different. They seemed thicker, greener than the ones he'd grown accustomed to.

Getting to his feet, large clunks of mud clung to his dirty and tattered clothing. Attempting to dust them from him, Demetrix realized he was covered head to toe in the soupy mixture. Stepping into the river, he felt the cold surround him. As quick as possible, he washed the mud away and left the frigid water. The sun warmed his face. Closing his eyes, he took in its warmth, recalling the earlier days. *How had things become so complicated in such a short time?* Climbing the bank, Demetrix was careful to keep the mud from soiling him again. *The river was a few miles from home. If it's morning, that should be west.* He looked up past the trees to the yellow orb in the sky. It was half way between the horizon and midday, yet bright enough to be on the rise. Turning away from it, he started walking. If the gods favored him, he would find familiar terrain. A small sliver of hope filling his tiny body, he started walking.

Chapter VI
Born of Vengeance

The bright orange sun was half hidden behind the horizon. An ocean of purple and blue clouds stretched across the evening sky, giving a final day's beauty to the encroaching nightfall.

Gareth inspected the pile of discarded goods, forming a trail from town. Best he could figure, the raiders grabbed more than they could carry, and simply left whatever they dropped. The littered items were few and far between, but they'd led him this far. He crouched at the base of a large oak, peeking through the underbrush at the seemingly uninhabited cavern. Another pile of abandoned loot was scattered outside.

Hurriedly, he made his way down to investigate. The discarded linen was crumpled and tossed roughly on the ground. The scent of moist dirt and stagnant water radiated from the dark crevice in the hillside. Glancing toward the disappearing sun, he sighed heavily, drawing his cutlass. He was a few days behind his family. He wasn't going to save them by waiting around out here.

Stepping into the darkness he kept the rough, mossy walls in sight. The light was rapidly becoming sparse due to the falling sun and dark underground. He dove deeper, feeling his way along the wall. The last bit of light faded, leaving him in total darkness.

Like a torch being lit, his vision returned. To his surprise, the total loss of light triggered something in his eyes. They felt more open than he'd been used to, as if somehow they'd adjusted to the complete darkness. Somehow he was able to see, nearly as well as he could in the daylight. If it weren't in shades of gray, he would have thought it his normal vision.

Pausing his trek into the depths, he ran his hand in front of his face several times making sure he wasn't imagining it. *Corin must be lookin' out for me!*

Blessed with his new-found sight he continued deeper, feeling the change in temperature against his bare arms and bald head. He shivered, more from adrenaline than the cold. The smell of cave dirt made his nostrils flare. More so, in the cool underground he could smell something else. The faint scent of iron hung in the air. He hadn't noticed it before. Searching the dark cavern, he couldn't find its source. But it had to be here, somewhere.

The ancient passageways were beginning to shrink, leaving him little more than a shoulder's width to pass. The jagged rocks scraped against the sides of his leather, snagging the metal plates from time to time. He forced the memory of the bloody, torn ribbon into his mind, letting his rage drive him deeper. He would need the rage to fuel him. It somehow calmed his nerves. Passing the first intersection he'd seen since entering, Gareth froze, hearing footsteps around the bend. Stepping into one of the numerous crevices between the stone, he waited patiently, listening to the unseen beings move closer.

"Deruoved swa eno tsrif eht sa secaf rieht ees uoy?" One of the black-skinned creatures said, a wicked grin lingering on his face. He carried a bundle of torn and dirty cloth, ignoring the few pieces dragging the ground.

The other gave a sinister laugh, holding a clay jug in one hand and an unlit torch in the other. "Desu eb ot scigam hcus tcepxe t'ndid yeht."

The sounds grated against his ears, more vile hissing mixed with vocal clearing than actual words. He watched the two pass hoping to get a good look at what he was dealing with.

Their ears were elongated and poked through colorless hair, like those of the alfar he'd seen. In fact every aspect of their appearance reminded him of the woodfolk, save for the color of their blackened skin and the repulsive sounds they made.

Given the items they carried, they had to be responsible for the raid. That was all the evidence he needed. Without hesitation, Gareth raised his thick, curved blade and charged. He slammed his shoulder into the closest one, knocking it to the ground. Before the second could react he swung his sword, catching it in the throat.

The creature gargled, clenching the fatal wound. Falling to the cavern floor it hissed in protest, unable to form their twisted words.

Gareth spun around, seeing the first creature pick itself up. He leapt forward and drove his sword into its back.

It screamed in pain, buckling under the added weight.

Knowing he had to silence it before more came, he pushed his weight onto the creature, forcing its arms to give way completely. It face-planted in the rock-hard clay. Gareth ran his fingers into the long, stringy hair and pulled violently, yanking the creature's head up. Using every bit of strength his arms possessed, Gareth slammed the creature's head forward into the stone. It crunched beneath the force, splitting wide open. His fingers still entwined in the stringy hair, he pulled it up once again, dragging the edge of his blade across its throat. It sliced deeply, assuring the creature's death. Gareth glanced at the other one, slowly drowning in its own blood.

It stared blankly at him, those dull, red eyes refusing to blink. Its hatred burned bright. Convulsing uncontrollably, it weakly shuddered and fell still.

Gareth got to his feet and approached the dead creature. Distaste in his mouth, he spat on the corpse. Dropping to a knee he placed his cutlass beside its head and grabbed one of the long, pointed ears. Dragging the sharpened edge across the back side, the flap of skin and cartilage came free. Claiming his trophy, he ran the torn blue ribbon through the hole and tied it off. Glancing around, he placed the makeshift necklace over his armor, towering victoriously over the bodies, wondering which direction he should go. Spotting a jug laying on its side, he noticed a small amount of the liquid had spilled out. He gave the cork stopper a quick sniff and recognized the strong odor of alcohol. There was no way he'd consider drinking it. But perhaps it would come in useful. Snatching up the jug, he quickly searched the bodies for anything of use. Examining the corridors for cast-off items, he traced the passage of his defeated companions. Full of resolve, Gareth rushed ever closer to his family, or so he hoped.

The smell of cooked meat and burning wood wafted through the tunnel and into the large overhead cracks. He stared down from his refuge between two of the large rocks overlooking the underground city. In his travels he'd heard rumors of ancient dwarven cities, but these creatures obviously weren't dwarfs and their structures didn't match the descriptions he'd heard.

His head filled with questions, many of which raised more. The anger building inside him begged for release at the sight of the black-skinned devils. He didn't know what they were or what they wanted. Hundreds of questions raced through his mind. But among them all, a single certainty was loud and clear. Each and every one of these beasts was going to die. And he was going to be the noose around their necks.

He felt the pain in his backside, pressed uncomfortably against the jagged rock. His stomach growled with the smell of meat below. He couldn't recall how long he'd been in the underground settlement. Days? Weeks? Without the sun, he couldn't decipher time.

Taking the last drops of water from his wineskin, he watched another group enter from the far side. They made their way through the underground city, little more than a permanent camp. They passed several roughly thrown-together wooden shacks and canvas tents, torn and strung with mismatched rope. The entire scene appeared to be more of a joke than an organized band of raiders, though they clearly were just that.

He focused on the group making their way to the large building in the center of the cavern, the only building that seemed to belong. It was constructed of stone, with a level of skill applied to its molded shape. The group pushed small carts loaded with crates and supplies of all kinds. They piled them beside the entrance leaving them for another group to sort out. Weapons and armor were tossed into one pile, while food and supplies were sorted into another. The clothes and less valuable items were tossed roughly on the ground and gathered up by a couple of the weaker looking black-alfar.

Gareth studied their movements. If he was going to investigate, he needed to learn as much as he could. Nearly a hundred carts had been dumped before his attention was fully engaged. A group arrived, but instead of looted goods they escorted several women and children of varying ages. The occasional elderly man was tied up with them, but they were few and far between.

He perked up seeing the humans. This was a routine he hadn't seen before. They were beaten and starved, staggering against the ropes that bound them together, but they were still alive. A spark of hope ignited inside him. Two of the creatures walked ahead of the prisoners and another two behind. They were led through the city and forced into the central building. One by one, they stepped through the stone archway and heavy wooden doors. Gareth adjusted himself, hoping to get a better look. If his family was still alive, they were sure to be in that building.

Glancing around, he made sure he could move without being detected. Grabbing the mass of brown linen he'd collected and strung together, Gareth threw it over his bulky frame like a makeshift cloak. He knew he wouldn't be able to walk through without being noticed, being much larger than the slender beasts, but if his plan worked it would allow him to be overlooked long enough to get close.

Backed out of the tight crevice he'd positioned himself in, A sickness overcame him. He couldn't tell if it was due to the smell of the rags, his impersonation of the foul creatures, or his lack of food, but he was quickly growing weak. The bile built inside him, forcing its way out. Spitting the sour contents of his stomach onto the cavern floor, Gareth emptied the last drops of water, hoping to wash the taste out. It did little to sooth him, but he'd manage. Glancing at the tunnel leading into the city, he knew he had to act fast. If he delayed much longer, he'd be drained of energy before he had chance to find his family. Thinking through his plan one final time, Gareth reached down and grabbed the fist-sized rock he'd been eyeing since his plan's inception. Rearing back, he locked sight on his target and launched.

The stone flew a fair distance, crashing into the canopy of one of the nearby huts. The weight tore through, collapsing the weak wooden rods holding it up. The canvas collapsed atop the small fire at the base, and it flared to life. A thick cloud of smoke billowed up, and suddenly, the canvas ignited in huge gouts of flame. It licked the next hut, catching it almost as quickly. And another. In minutes, the entire section was ablaze.

The creatures scrambled to contain the leaping flames, but they couldn't put them out before they jumped to the next tent.

Seeing his moment, Gareth tossed the soiled cloth over his head and jumped down the overlook, behind one of the burning tents. Making his way through the chaos, toward the central building, Gareth was careful to avoid the rushing creatures. Sidestepping, he avoided one carrying a bucket of stagnant water. The smelly liquid sloshed out, soaking into his rags. Seeing the creature's face, he knew he was caught. The was no time. He had but one option. Bringing the clay jug around, Gareth smashed it over the creature's head and pushed it into the fire.

The creature ignited in flame instantly, screaming his torment for a few short moments. Tripping over the burning debris, it fell silent, refusing to stir.

Gareth didn't wait around for the others to check on him. Masking his way through the commotion, hoping no one had seen him, he took a deep breath, realizing how much stronger the smell was on the base floor. The whole place reeked of feces and sweat. His nose wrinkled in disgust. Focusing his thoughts, he scurried through the commotion and reached the large stone building at the center.

He was fairly certain he hadn't drawn attention to himself. And if he had, they hadn't acted upon it. Making sure he wasn't being watched, Gareth opened the thick wooden door, noticing the broken face embedded in the wood. It was unlike any he'd seen before. Elongated with antlers protruding from the crown. It reminded him of a demonic face staring from the center of a full moon. Shaking the uncertainty of the sigil off, Gareth stepped inside.

Strange chants echoed through the barren cathedral. It had a rhythmic pace to is, suggesting the creatures were performing some kind of ritual in one of the upper levels. It echoed off the walls chilling him to the bone, but at least it would cover the sound of his footsteps on the stripped wooden floor. Throwing the rancid rags off him, Gareth drew his cutlass and slowly made his way deeper into the unknown, keeping an eye out for any of the creatures.

The building seemed to be some kind of temple. Several broken pews littered the sides of the room, tossed roughly against the walls. The far end held a stone altar with a demonic face, matching that of the door, staring back at him. The stone was covered in torn cloth and soaked in what appeared to be blood. It made him feel uneasy.

Spotting a curved stairway to the side, Gareth followed it around and to the overlooking balcony behind him. Cautiously making his way up, the chants grew louder, closer, with each passing step. Reaching the second story, Gareth peered around the corner, finding a broken banister wrapping the balcony's edge. The far side of the temple held an outcropping, obstructed from view by a set of thick wooden doors.

He rushed across the open walkway, hoping he could reach the other side as quickly as possible. He knew he was along in the main chamber. But he still didn't want to be in the open if he could help it. Though what did they have to fear? Who would be stupid enough to infiltrate their underground complex? There was nothing they had to fear. At least not yet. Though all that was about to change. He was going to teach them fear, if it was the last thing he ever did. Approaching the doors, Gareth peeked through the cracked seam. Several of the devils stood together on the other side. They were dressed in black robes and performing some kind of ceremony. Human bodies were piled roughly in the center of their circle, appearing to have been mutilated and bled out.

Slowly opened the door to get a better look, Gareth noticed the new arrivals chained against the wall, awaiting their sacrifice. He searched their faces, feeling his rage grow. None were familiar. There were nearly twenty prisoners and his wife's face was not among them. He couldn't take anymore. Raising his sword, Gareth burst through the doors, letting them crash against the walls on either side. "Where's my family, you ugly sons of bitches?"

One of the robed creatures raised a blood-coated dagger and turned to face him. "Ereh eb t'ndluohs uoy!" It smiled, walking forward.

Gareth felt his anger spill out. Fury unleashed, he charged forward releasing a deep battle shout.

The creature collapsed against him, unable to withstand his larger bulk. Hitting the ground, the dagger skated across the blood-soaked floor.

Continuing past, Gareth slashed into the group. His blade danced with precision, slicing and hacking everything that came within reach. The rage inside him turned to pleasure with each kill.

Taking a deep breath, Gareth looked around the room at the mangled bodies surrounding him. They had little chance against his wrath. His shallow victory was short-lived. Glancing at the mixed bloods, his prey and their victims, something felt wrong about the black fluid tarnishing the spilled red. They deserved better. But was he the man to give it to them? Making his way toward the pile of bodies, Gareth marched over the limp forms of the dead creatures, stomping into them with each step. Granted they couldn't feel pain any longer, he took a small amount of pleasure feeling their bones break beneath his boots. A low, pain filled moan caught his ear. Glancing back, he noticed the first creature he'd charged, slowly crawling toward the door. Rage flooded him. Did this evil beast believe he'd be able to escape and warn the others? Was he so forgiving? That lesson needed to be taught. Slamming his boot down on one of the dead creature's head, it popped, spilling blood and brain matter on the floor. Gareth calmly approached the prone beast, ripping it up by its hair. Unlike the others he'd seen, this one had a slight brown tint to the stingy locks. Staring into its frightened face, Gareth shouted. "Where's my family?"

A wicked smile formed, revealing dangerously sharp, blood-lined teeth. "Doolb rieht knard dna staorht rieht tuc I!" Spitting its black blood in his face, it laughed.

"Wrong answer." Gareth rested the edge of his sword against the creature's ear, allowing the weight to cut into his flesh. Quickly jerking the blade, the ear came free. Gareth tucked it away for later addition to his necklace.

The creature screamed in pain, grabbing the hole in the side of its head.

To keep it from calling reinforcements, Gareth jabbed it in the throat, silencing the screams into muffled choking coughs. Pulling the creature's head back, Gareth thrust the pommel of his sword between the warped floorboards. It took a little wedging, but he was able to make it stay. Aligning the tip with the creature's chin, Gareth slowly pressed its head onto the sharp tip, watching it pierce gradually. It passed through its lower jaw and into its mouth. Hoping to inflict as much pain as possible, Gareth slowly guided the creature onto the blade. Feeling it go limp, his pleasure was minimized. The blade was embedding in its brain, killing all receptors. Leaving the beast where it laid, Gareth secured the hilt of his sword and ripped it free of both the floor and his escaped companion. The sharpened edge nearly cut the creature's head in half, leaving it to thud against the floor. Smiling his success over the beast, Gareth returned to the other bodies, where he quickly removed ears from each one. With ease, he added them to his collection and placed the lanyard around his neck.

Several begging cries reached him. He'd been in the moment, ignoring the constant pleas. Looking around at the chained prisoners, he couldn't find his compassion for them. He was here for his family. These few didn't matter. Ignoring them as best he could, Gareth surveyed each room in search of his family. Unable to find them he took a deep breath, regarding the pile of bodies in the center. He'd hoped to find them before having to look through it. Not only was it morally questionable, but if he had to resort to searching for bodies it meant his family was dead. He sighed heavily and lifted the first one, inspecting her face. The cold stare was unfamiliar. Pulling her from the pile, he laid her to the side as careful as possible. After all, it wasn't his intention to disrupt the dead. The next few were easily discarded. There was no reason to even inspect the males.

Halfway through the pile he uncovered a bloody, yet familiar fabric matching the ribbon around his neck. A high-pitched ring set in his ears, drowning out the cries of prisoners, still pleading his assistance. All tact vanished, Gareth roughly tossed the bodies from her, uncovering the blue dress as best as possible. Rolling her over, his heart shattered into a thousand pieces. His wife's fearful, blank face stared back at him void of color and warmth. Her dress was torn open revealing a broken and violated body.

His eyes were locked on the deep, purple marks lingering in her mutilated flesh. Her throat had been slit so deeply that only a small bit of skin held her head in place. Staring at her clenched arms, Gareth feared what was within them. He didn't want to see. But he had to know. Tears rolled down his cheeks. He knew his son was with her, but he had to confirm it. He pulled at her arms, trying to reveal what they held. Even in death, her grip was so tight, he had to strain against her grip. All sound exited the room. There was nothing. No cried, no sobs, so pleading for assistance. Only him and his wife, and their infant son. The image rang in his mind, drowning out his senses. Pulling the child from her constricting grip, Gareth looked him over. His skin was blue from lack of oxygen. Several bruises showed on his body, but they were few compared to those matching his wife's arms. She'd protected him from the most damaging blows, but it was her protection that ultimately killed him. He felt the tears stream down his face. His body wailed uncontrollably over them. The ringing intensified blocked all else. He couldn't even see beyond his family any longer, shrouded in black. Pulling them tight, he held them one last time. The cold of their skin washed away. He had nothing, no one.

The ringing was unbearable, reverberating in his head. It had to stop. He couldn't take anymore. *I have to make it stop!* The ringing continued. *Make it stop.* A drip of bright red blood landing on his wife's face. Wiping if from his nose, he shook, unable to ignore the ringing. *Like they stopped her life, like they stopped his life!* It got louder, burrowing into his head. *Make them stop! Make them stop! Kill them!* The pressure inside him grew, forcing his eyes to water. Blood trickled freely from his nose and ears. *Kill all of them!* It was so incredibly loud, he couldn't focus on anything but the mourning pain. "Make it stop!" He demanded, his voice echoing throughout the temple. "Make it stop!"

The ringing quit, leaving him in complete silence, save for the echo of his words in the near empty chamber. He felt the last tear roll down his cheek, splattering on his wife's forehead. Pushing their bodies from him, he stood, glancing around the room.

The prisoners pleaded his attention, but he couldn't hear their words. They spoke to him, but their mouths moved in silence. A slow heartbeat echoed in the room, like the beat of a drum. The steady yet slow pace told him what he had to do. Lifting his sword, Gareth started for the door.

One of the prisoners reached out, grabbing his arm. She jumped back, seeing a void in his eyes. Only then did she register the sword pointed at her throat.

Gareth trembled, his sword arm outstretched and ready to kill. He could narrowly contain the amount of restraint he had to apply to keep the blade away from her. It seemed to move of its own accord. Had he not stopped it, she would have surely fallen to him. He could see the fear in her eyes, not because of the blade. She was afraid of him. She retreated like he was one of the monsters that'd locked her in here. And that was fine. He needed to become a monster. That was how he was going to do what had to be done. Lowering his sword, he turned and casually walked out the door, his care for discretion gone with his family. Making his way toward the entrance, Gareth kicked the doors open, seeing the fires were nearly out. Listening to the wicked tongue in the underground city, Gareth felt a hatred unlike any other. It was an assault against his ears and it would be stopped.

Stepping into the open, there had to be more than a thousand in this city alone. A sadistic smile formed on his lips. "Come get me, you bastards!" Raising his sword, Gareth charged into their ranks, hacking and slashing with every bit of strength he possessed. His hatred burned like fire in the night. He was unstoppable, empowered to destroy them one city at a time.

Gareth stood at the upper deck of his ship, watching the last bit of cargo find its way into the hold. He stood tall with his armor in place and sword strapped to his hip. A long, blue necklace, full of severed black ears hung openly on his chest for all to see.

"Capt'n, we're ready to set sail."

Gareth turned to address Malakai. "Well done, First Mate. Have the crew oar into the deeps and raise the sails. There's a storm on the horizon and I've got a feelin' it's gonna hit us before we're ready for it."

Malakai saluted and turned to relay orders to the crew. Raising his voice, he let his words carry over the wind. "Alright, you lazy dogs. Capt'n says it's time to set sail. Weigh anchor and loose the mooring. Grab an oar and quit yer snorin'." He chuckled. "I made that up. Row to the deeps and prepare to raise sails."

The anchor chains clanked into position as the men pushed the ship away from the wharf. Free from the shallow waters the sails shot up. They flapped in the breeze for a few moments until the wind caught, pulling them taut with a loud pop. The ship lunged forward, picking up speed.

"Navigator, head due north."

"Aye, Capt'n."

The ship turned, leaving Everik behind. Gareth felt the sea breeze against his bearded face. The waves crashed gently along the side of the ship, giving it a majestic bounce. Making his way to the bow, Gareth leaned over, inspecting the keel. She was chopping the waters with relative ease. Finding peace in the tranquil bounce, he watched the waves wash against the hull, allowing the only two things he'd ever loved to erode with the increasing distance. A smile on the horizon, Gareth closed his eyes.

Kill them all, no exception!

Chapter VII
The Scholar

The darkened room of rock and petrified wood was filled with the scent of aged parchment and the stale odor of clay. The walls were crowded by multitudes of shelves in all sizes and conditions. What remained of the clear varnish coats were cracked and worn in most places, due to time and misuse. Thousands of tomes rested in their cluttered spaces, seemingly the only organization the dark room had to offer. The occasional rack of scrolls stood amidst the clutter, divided by wooden runners, each one bearing odd runes to identify their contents. A young dreualfar sat at the edge of one of the ancient slab tables, his hands locked against his forehead holding his long, silver hair out of his face.

Nezial stared down at the inscriptions smudged across the yellow page. Taking a deep breath, he turned to see another set, just like the ones before. Despite his restlessness, he felt a fondness for the dusty old collection. It was a home of comfort, far removed from the chaos right outside his doors. A loud crash roused him, demanding his attention. The sounds of battle echoed through the sealed, wooden barriers causing his ears to twitch. Frustration growing, he placed a small piece of polished bone between the pages and closed the book. Pulling himself up, Nezial stood with a heavy sigh. He walked toward the door, listening to the commotion grow louder, as if a war was being waged right outside. Cautiously pulling the door open ever so slightly toward him, he peered out.

Several dreualfar, not much older than children, blocked the wide passageway. Bloodthirsty cries of excitement escaped the gathering, urging the two in the middle of their number.

Nezial stepped out to get a better look. The two young black-skins stood facing each other, defensive and full of anger. A dagger was outstretched in each of their hands, ready to drive into the ribs of the other at the first chance.

One sliced in, narrowly missing the other.

The second jumped back, crashing into the crowd behind him. Unable to catch his balance he was aided by shoves and punches to his back. He tumbled forward and hit the ground. Rolling with the motion, he sprang back to his feet, colliding with his enemy. Staggering back, he glanced at the crude, unpolished pommel protruding in his gut. Blood began to drip from the wound. His gaze traveled, finding the panicked face staring into his. Taking a step backward, he pulled the blade free. Studying the blood coated weapon, his hand trembled. The chants reached him, telling him what he needed to do. Armed with both daggers, he locked his fingers around blood-slicked handle and charged. The small instruments felt heavy, unwieldy even. Rapidly losing strength, the boy tripped over his feet and face planted into the rocky floor.

"Finish him, finish him!" The crowd cheered, urging the unarmed youngling to make a move.

The weaponless boy glanced around, taking in the mob before him. Pride fluttered in his gut. He'd won already. He just had to finish the job. Forcing the butterflies in his stomach into submission, he approached the whimpering body. A pool of blood was beginning to form beneath him. The daggers were lying on the rocky floor scattered where they'd fallen. Reaching down, he secured the bloody weapon, knowing that one to be his, and took position over the dying dreualfar. Smiling his success to the crowd, he grabbed a fist full of unkempt, dirty hair and yanked the boy's head back. Exposing his thin, gasping throat, he closed his eyes and swallowed his anxiety. Pressing the dull edge against his taut skin, he drug the blade across, feeling it pop against the pressure. Listening to the final gasp, he released the boy's hair, letting his limp head hit the ground with a thud. Standing to his full height, he threw his arms into the air, claiming victory.

Nezial shook his head at the sight of the dead pup. *So much untapped potential wasted on a flawed ideology of keeping only the strong.* Refusing to watch a moment longer, he turned and stepped back into his study, closing the door behind him. *They fail to realize strength comes from more than just combat specialty.*

Recalling the trials of his youth, he made is way toward the table and retook his seat. He had always been forced to battle the stronger dreualfar. They always thought it was going to be an easy match, him being scrawny compared to most. But all that change the day he blasted that kid with a fireball. They pretty much left him alone after that.

Renewing his focus, Nezial opened the book where he'd left off and set the piece of bone aside. The contents of the passage played out in his mind, as if he was watching an ancient scene. He couldn't explain why, but this particular interested him. It took him back to his childhood, when he used to dream about walking the surface world.

The stories of their entrance to the darkness were fairly common, though he was certain they were wrong. The contradictions in the books pretty much guaranteed that. His people created the tale, playing the victim, when in fact it seemed to be the other way around. He didn't know when his people were banished, but he felt like he may as well have been one of the dreualfar forced from the light that day. He'd never gotten live in it. But that didn't stop him from thinking about it every waking moment.

Leaning against the backrest of his chair, Nezial broke away from the scribed passage and allowed his imagination to carry him out of the library. He found himself walking in the sun, wondering what it would feel like upon his skin. How pleasant it would be to be able to do so without pain. He'd felt its sting before. No, he wanted its gentle caress, like the surface dwellers enjoyed. He wanted the simple things in life. Like watching sunbeams burn through the green of the tallest trees, sparking bright patterns on the ground. The creatures of the surface would be so different from his own. They'd say 'hi' to each other and welcome new comers to the *town*, he believed that's what they were called. Whatever those small human settlements were. They'd help protect each other instead of plotting to overthrow their neighbor at the first opportunity. Nezial rubbed the scars on his chest recalling the villagers that greeted him the last time he tried to walk the surface. The burns lasted nearly a week, leaving him in a constant state of pain the entire time. Had it not been for the burning, he could have made his way through all those people unnoticed. It was no wonder they were scared of his kind. If he'd seen a figure sizzling in the sunlight, he'd probably be afraid of it too. Truth be told, his fear rivaled what he evoked in them.

Realizing he'd gotten distracted, Nezial shook the memories from his head. In a violent outburst, he slammed the book shut. "These thoughts serve no purpose! I'm one of the most powerful dreualfar in the Underdark. I need to find a spell that will allow me to walk the surface without fear of the sun, or those that live in it. But thinking about how nice it would be, isn't helping!" Taking a deep breath, Nezial pushed the tome away from him, letting his self-irritation evaporate a little.

Days turned into evenings, the hours drifting along, though in the underground it was difficult to discern time. The sunlight had no impact, therefore nothing was timed. Life simply drifted along as the mood called, or the whips of the elders, which ever came first.

Nezial slammed the tome shut. A scowl took form across his face, "I need no history lessons. I need evidence, this damn book doesn't contain anything close to its synopsis." He shouted, venting his anger. The heavy pages clapped together, sending a cloud of dust into the dank air.

Resting his elbows on the table, he laid his head in his hands and ran his fingers through his stringy, silver hair. Reaching the back of his head he locked them in place and leaned back. A long, deep sigh escaped him. He was exhausted. The continual study was tiring, but he had to find the answers.

Staring blankly at the shelves across from him, Nezial scanned the thousands of bindings staring back at him. He'd had the have read at least half of them already. Or ruled them out at the very least. Doubt began the grow with each cover he passed. None of them held anything close to the knowledge he sought. Shaking his head, he released his hold and stood, scooping up the closed tome before him. Carrying it to one of the shelves near the rear wall, he searched for its home. It didn't take long to find it. A perfect sized slot rested between the other books, free of dust where he'd removed it hours earlier. Gently sliding the book back into its pocket, he looked around, lost in the library's abundance.

Glancing across the dark chamber, a heavy sigh escaped him. The books were a never-ending puzzle. Some spoke broadly, other simplistic. Though none seemed to hold the answers he sought. *Why is it so difficult to find information on the curse?* It was as if the knowledge didn't exist. But that was ridiculous. Books were made for knowledge. One of them had to hold the key. The question was, which one? And would the author offer up his secrets? Would he open that window into his mind where his ideas flowed like water? It was the strangest form of telepathy, lasting distance and time. The author would write the world as they saw it. And hundreds, maybe thousands of years later, someone would read the words and understand exactly what the author meant. There were obvious exceptions. After all, everyone saw things in their own way. But the general idea was always there. If that wasn't telepathy, what was?

Nezial extended his arms, stretching his back in an arch. Instinctively, his mouth opened wide, releasing a deep yawn. On instinct, Nezial reached to his chin and gave a firm, steady push. Several loud pops echoed in the empty chamber, bringing a renewed flexibility to his neck. Repeating the process on the other side, his eyes caught a brief shimmer on one of the shelves. His attention locked on the overflowing rack, he rushed toward it hoping to catch a glimpse of the item that called to him. Moving to the left, he started at the top corner and quickly scanned each binding, hoping to see it again. He investigated three full rows before coming across a thin, black book, one he'd never seen before. A strange phenomenon in itself, considering it was on a shelf he'd already checked.

A slight golden sheen surrounded the book as if it were reflecting some kind of light. Stepping back, Nezial search for any sigh of light. He worked without candle or torch. Such items were useless when you spent your life in the dark. But the need for heat was a common enough concern that such items weren't unheard of. Finding nothing, he removed it from the shelf and returned to the large table in the center of the library. Placing it where so many others had sat, he loosened the buckle and took his seat.

The glimmering cover continued to flicker, inviting him to its contents. Nezial stared at it for several minutes, unsure if he should open it. Fear crept into his mind. *Will it contain another failure or, at last, success? And more importantly, what will either mean?* Swallowing hard, he reached for the edge of the cover and flipped it over, revealing the pages within. A sickness overcame him. He stared deeply into the aged parchment, blank as it could be. Not the slightest smudge could be seen on the coarse surface. Vigorously, he thumbed through the pages. No words, no marks of any kind, just blank sheets staring back at him, appearing to be made from a thick, dried skin.

"Damn it!" Losing himself to anger, Nezial slammed his fist down, feeling a sharp pain shoot through his knuckle. Fueled by rage, he glared at the wound, inspecting the broken flesh. A single drop of blackened blood pooled from the deep laceration, falling to the open book. Unable to stop it from splattering onto the page, several smaller droplets splattered around the initial impact. Nezial reached to wipe away the thick beads, but they disappeared, soaking into the flaky parchment before his hand reached made contact. He rubbed his fingers against the rough texture, unable to find the smallest trace of wetness.

Nezial stared in wonder. *Where'd it go?* Flipping vigorously through the pages, he searched for any evidence of the black life-fluid. The book remained free of mar. *This isn't likely.* On a whim, he grabbed his dagger out of his boot and pulled the leather sheath from the blade. Placing the edge against the back of his hand, he pressed in, letting the steel bite. Blood pooled around the blade, running freely from the wound. Holding his hand over the exposed pages, Nezial laid his dagger on the table and watched the beady fluid drip. It spilled onto the calcareous material, disappearing quicker than he could fathom. His heart beat within his chest, threatening to overcome him. He shook from excitement, unsure if it was the mystery of the book or the thrill of something unknown that had his curiosity peaked. Waiting patiently, hoping his blood would expose the secrets of the blank page, Nezial watched in anticipation.

Minutes passed. The page remained blank. Excitement leached away, leaving the bitter taste of failure in its wake. Lowering his head in defeat, Nezial took a deep breath. *Another waste of resources.*

Reaching across the table, he took hold of the cover, ready to close it and return to his search, he froze, unsure what he was seeing.

A faint message was forming in the center of the page.

His heart pounded away, threatening to leap out of his chest. Holding his breath, afraid to move, lest it disappear, Nezial watched the marks grow darker moment by moment. Finally, it was dark enough to make out the symbols written in what he guessed was his own blood. It was a strange language, unlike any he'd seen before, yet somehow, he knew it. A large smile spread across his face, understanding the first sentence.

To release the shadow, the ever-changing host must anoint the chosen in the reflection of worlds.

Nezial read the words again. His puzzlement over the meaning of the message diminished his pleasure in understanding the script. "How can I do this?"

The markings disappeared, leaving the page blank once again.

He waited several minutes, hand on his dagger, ready to feed the greedy book. Placing the blade against his flesh, he readied to sate its appetite. The iron bit into him a second time just as the new symbols appeared.

Returning the blade to the table, he picked up the small tome. "A key is required to free the ever-changing from the sanctum of void. Once free, there is no avoiding the path, for avoidance is the key to assurance." He read the words aloud, listening to them, tasting them on his lips.

They faded slightly, revealing a large symbol below the message.

A smile came to him. Nezial gently shut the cover and locked the buckle into place. "Thank you," He whispered to the slim volume, placing it in his satchel.

Returning his dagger to its sheath and stuffing it back into his boot, he flung the leather strap of his satchel over his shoulder and headed for the door.

The darkened chamber was built for intimidation. Its round walls place any visitor at the center of the chamber and at a severe disadvantage. The single entrance was sealed away from public eye, keeping the happenings inside out of scrutiny.

Nezial walked along the narrow isle, watching at the jagged border of stone at its edge. The other side was a sheer drop, disappearing into the depths of the Underdark. Reaching the center pedestal, He peered up at the towering chairs enwrapped around him at the far edge of the room.

The elders, each one wicked in their own right, sat over him, silently judging his arrival.

Dreualfar society was a meat locker. Only the finest made the cut. The rest were shaved off in battle or infection, despite their natural resistance to such. Nezial recalled the boy killed outside his library days earlier. Once the obvious fat was trimmed, so to speak, it was these seven that did the trimming of the rest. They were the elders, they had no equal. Each one obtained his or her position by replacing the former holder through trickery, seduction, and murder. Their entire system was shaped by this group, keeping only the strong and letting the weak die off systematically. If many of these elders had it their way, he would have been among the clippings, dropped to the floor and shoveled up for rat meat. Fortunate for him, he was stronger than they'd expected.

"Why have you called for us this time, Nezial? Have you found another enchantment which will allow you to exist comfortably in the sunlight?" One of the old dreualfar mocked.

Nezial absorbed the taunt. He'd been subject to their humiliation as long as he could remember. It didn't change anything. In fact, it made him push harder. One day he would be able to shove it in their faces. Their cold, dying faces that would look up rather than down at him. He waited patiently at their center, awaiting the laughter to fade away before continuing. He was used to being mocked and tormented by his people. They didn't understand his desire. Accustomed to their scorn, he chose to ignore them rather than respond. There was no sense in giving them ammunition. His gaze fixed on his aggressor, Khronis. The elder was nearing a feeble state. Soon he would start to weaken and his chair would be ready for a new occupant. Nezial always hated that wicked smile perched on his lips. He was unusually cruel, even for a dreualfar. Swallowing hard, ready to speak the words he'd rehearsed a thousand times over, Nezial let his feelings about the elder pass. He looked to each of the seven, erect in the chairs, some men, some women, some ancient, while others were slightly older than him. Studying their faces, he ensured they were ready to receive his words. "I've discovered something much more interesting than a simple enchantment." He declared, pulling the thin black book from his satchel, raising it for all to see.

Whispers filled the room at its sight.

An ancient woman rose from her central chair, naming her as the eldest of elders. With a gesture toward the others, she made the whispers subside. "Tell us what's been revealed to you." She leaned against her podium, anticipating his words.

Nezial recited the story, leaving no detail unattended.

The whispers resumed, growing in volume, yet too sporadic and mumbled for him to decipher.

"Interesting," The eldest woman commented. Her voice gained strength as she spoke, "We're aware of whom the book is referring. The oldest of our kind have always believed the unspoken one is responsible for our existence. We do not know what happened to him, all knowledge of that time having been lost or forgotten. We only know of him from an old tablet found thousands of years ago. If this book can tell us how to free him, then it's our responsibility to do so. There is however one thing you must do before we can provide the assistance you'll need."

Nezial listened carefully, hanging on her ever word. As far the elders went, she was the only one whom had never openly mocked him. That in of itself demanded his respect. He felt overjoyed that she believed him and even more excited that she would help him. "What do you need of me?"

"You'll need to travel to Eldarian, to the tomb at the center of the city. There, you'll learn everything you need to know." Reaching to her neck, she pulled a thin, black chain from her robes. "You'll need this." Tossing it to him, she returned to her seat.

Nezial looked over the amulet, noting the strange icon. He studied the stone symbol, cracked down the middle revealing half of a demonic face. It was an odd sigil, but perhaps its meaning would come to him soon. Placing it securely in his satchel along with his book, he returned his focus to the elder woman. "I'll return once I have this knowledge." Refusing to wait a moment longer, he turned and made his way from the chamber.

The ancient woman waved her hand, watching him exit the thick stone doors. Dust fell from the archway with the vibration of the slabs moving into place. Within moments the passage had opened, allowing his exit, and resealed itself, as if it had never been opened.

Nezial waited for the stone to settle. Spinning on heel, he placed his ear against the barrier. It was commonplace for the dreualfar to try and hear what was being discussed beyond those thick doors. Yet many didn't possess the ability to discern more than a faint echo through the stone. The voices were muffled and difficult to understand. Contorting his fingers, Nezial recited a quick chant to the stone and placed his ear against the slab. Instantly, the voices cleared, as if he was still in the room with them.

"Nadilia, do you truly believe he's capable of bringing him back?"

"He found the book. According to the markings we were able to translate from the tomb, only the one that can read the book can unlock the prison." The eldest woman responded.

"But Nezial? He's an accomplished magician and decent swordsman, I'll give him that, but he lacks the determination and blood-lust of our people, let alone how the legend describes the chosen one." Khronis burst out, challenging any who would oppose.

Nadilia responded, "Khronis, my old friend, I'm aware of his personality. I'm also well aware of the legend. However, the legend states the chosen one is unlike any other. He both found and fed the book. That in of itself means he's the only dreualfar that can read the tome in its entirety. When he returns I think you'll agree that he's quite different."

Nezial had heard all he needed to. Turning from the sealed doors, he let his spell dissipate. He needed to visit his personal chambers. There were a few things he was going to need if he was going to undergo this perilous journey.

Beans of sunlight pierced the darkness, creating an inverted tunnel ending in a blinding glow. Nezial shielded his eyes, hoping they wouldn't burn forever. One foot in front of the other, he made his way through the catacombs, rapidly approaching the end. His satchel was bulged to capacity, allowing his hands to remain free. He would need them if he came across any unexpected encounters. A polished sabre hung loosely at his side, sheathed and positioned for quick draw if needed. He preferred the light weight of a rapier but his fighting style was more fitted for the curved blade, using mostly slashes as opposed to the fencing posture the flimsy weapon required. Throwing the hood of his heavy cloak over his head, he took his first sanctioned steps into the sunlight. The heat burned through the layers leaving him in a constant state of nausea, but he was, in a roundabout way, doing what he'd dreamed of his entire life.

Hours passed and Nezial was still in the rocky canyons near the human settlement of Makshield. He was much closer than he preferred, but this was on the only path that didn't lead directly to the human stronghold. Peeking through the dense cloth, shielding him from the bright overhead orb, he was surprised at the resilience he was showing. It was as if something was protecting him from the burning rays. The book? The necklace? There was no way to tell. But that didn't mean he was completely free from harm. The brightness left a dull ache behind his eyes. Perhaps he'd grow accustomed to the glare over time. He could only hope. Listening to his footsteps on the dried, crunchy dirt and rock, Nezial recalled the maps packed away in his satchel. Their details were fresh enough he didn't need to consult them again. Glancing around, he searched for the landmarks he'd noted on one in particular. Seeing the abandoned, ancient tower in the rocks, he altered course and made for the river crossing. It was larger than he'd expected, but small enough to walk. Though he'd have to be careful of the current. It wouldn't take much to drag his legs from beneath him and wash him out to sea.

Slowly making his way across, Nezial reached the other side and turned north, looking into the misty hills far beyond the seemingly never-ending forest in the distance. Fear, excitement, hope— all of it burned into his stomach.

Miles of deep-green trees, tall and broad, sprawled across the land. An occasional patch towered over the rest. Those were areas he needed to exercise the most caution. The myrkalfar were notorious for building their cities in such places. Beyond the forest of Evinwood, the hills rose like mountains in the distance. Less rocky and equally covered in vegetation, but they felt more inviting. Perhaps it was due to the dangers between here and there, he couldn't say. There was only one certainty he could offer. His goal was there, somewhere, hidden beyond the alfaren borders. He'd have to be extremely careful. Not only were the villagers a danger, but there was the possibility of soldiers between him and his destination. Many carried a wide array of opinions in the world, and most weren't favorable of his people.

Aside from the common man and soldiers, he'd also have to keep an eye out for the other races of Ur. Some could be trusted, others not so much. In fact, it'd be safest to reserve trust for those who've earned it. He chuckled to himself at the correction. He would be crossing many borders after all, and his kind were enemies to most. For that reason alone, he'd earned a death warrant before he was even born. None of these concerned him as much as one specific group. Among all the threats he could possibly face, the most dangerous obstacle would be the Dreuslayers.

Nezial recalled the stories he'd heard when he was younger. They were ever a mystery to the dreualfar. Sprinkled throughout his people's history, riddled in their lore and myths, yet disappearing time and time again. Such a thing was nearly impossible as far as he could find in his books, yet no logical explanation offered advice. The Dreuslayers were the one thing his kind feared. They specialized in the destruction of his people. If not for their methods, they were feared for their tactics. They were the one force known throughout history that was known for standing off against an army of dreualfar on any terrain, above or below ground. Numerous cities of the Underdark had fallen to them in ages past, earning a permanent residence in their history. They were the nightmares the monsters dreamed about, their leader especially, who claimed an ear from each dreualfar he killed.

Nezial straightened his spine, letting the chills pass. He swallowed hard, forcing those thoughts from his mind. He didn't need to focus on them. Such a thought could cause him to see things that weren't there. His fear would dilute his focus. It was not productive to plan for their arrival. He needed only concern himself if they showed up. Closing his eyes he centered himself, bringing his purpose back to the forefront.

Staring through the distance, calculating his trip, Nezial guessed he had nearly another week's walk to get through Krondar. From there he'd continue north to the hot plains, which marked the border between the barbarian lands and Evinwood. There was no telling how long he'd be in the forest. Distance alone suggested another week, maybe two, but that didn't account for unexpected encounters or getting lost. He sighed heavily and took his first step into the open plains lands, hoping to reach the forest in the distance.

Several days passed, moving him closer to his goal. Nezial hid at the edge of a small section of forest along the eastern pass. The sun was retreating for the night, disappearing behind the mountains to the west. He wrapped himself in the cloak and hunkered down into a thick patch of leaves. Closing his eyes, he drifted off to sleep.

The rustling of leaves woke him. He instinctively wrapped his fingers around the leather wrapped hilt of his sword, ready to draw the curved blade. Opening his eyes, he could see an orange glow reflecting off the trees. A burly human staggered toward him, taking a rather long draw from his tan colored wineskin.

Nezial watched the hulking man. He clearly hadn't seen him. With any luck, that fact would remain true. He squeezed his hilt, contemplating his options. *I don't know how many there are. If I kill this one, the others are likely to come looking. I don't need a search party on my ass. Perhaps he'll continue on, without incident.*

The drunken man rested his forearm against one of the trees and pressed his head into the thick muscles along the back side. Fumbling with his leather breeches, he got comfortable.

Nezial felt the mist splash off the leaves, spattering all around him. If only the barbarian knew how close he was to death. Holding his breath he waited, letting the man finish his business. Clearly, the human believed himself to be alone.

Shaking the last few drops, he tucked himself away and spun around to head back toward the caravan.

Nezial watched him wander off. He needed to get out of here now. He'd grown too comfortable. Cursing himself for allowing anyone to get that close, he quietly picked himself up and slung the satchel over his shoulder. Making his way from the occupied woods he stepped into the moonlit plains, leaving the encamped humans behind.

He crossed several dusty roads, remembering the layouts as best he could. They were few and far between, but even one meant civilization. He was drawing close to the main pass to Heroes Gate. The moon radiated a dull white, leaving dots in his vision. It irritated him. He could see so much better without it. The massive glow was more a distraction than anything. It made shadows seem like figures, each one watching, waiting for him to relax. His vision played tricks on him. One moment a perfect silhouette would be standing. The next, a fallen limb or patch of wheat remained in its stead. Night travel was much harder than it seemed.

The crunch of dry grass and grain faded, replaced by hollow footsteps on crumbled earth. Despite his distorted vision, he could tell he was on a road. A main road, from the size of it.

While it would take him to his destination faster, it also increased his chances of discovery by hostile strangers. If there was a main road, there would surely be travelers. He looked up at the moon. It nearly sat upon the mountain ridge, following the sun's path earlier in the evening. He guessed he had about two hours before it would fade, allowing the sun to reclaim dominion. At that time he needed to be clear of the road, but a little distance gained wouldn't hurt him in the dead of night.

Morning light finally peaked over the tree line, illuminating the brown grass on both sides of the road. Nezial watched from the thickest patch of briars he could find. The sharp needles burrowed their way into his flesh as if his clothes were nothing more than a thin layer, easily punctured. He watched a detachment of soldiers march past, blue and silver tabards hanging loosely over their armor, marking them as weapons of Shadgull. The last thing he wanted was to draw attention to himself. If he tangled with these men, there was no telling what kind of wrath would be brought upon him. He watched them fade into the distance, refusing to move from the painful perch until he could be certain he was alone.

Hours passed with no sign of travelers. Wherever the soldiers were headed, it was clear they weren't coming back anytime soon. The thorns ripped free of his cloak as he wriggled out. It was nearly midday and he had to make up the time he'd lost. Time he so foolishly believed he'd gained by taking the main pass. He was back in the trees in no time, happy to be hidden once again. Krondar's northern edge was densely packed with forests. If not for the fact that he hadn't crossed the hot plains, it would have been easy to mistake this forest for that of Evinwood, but he knew that wasn't the case. Every account he'd read about the plains suggested they were impossible to miss. And the myrkalfar homeland seemed much more ominous than this.

Seeing a clearing ahead, Nezial rushed to the forest's edge. Looking out into a wide field of golden grain, the crops stood nearly half the height of the others he'd passed. Recalling the details, Nezial dredged up every memory he could of the fabled hot plains.

He scanned the tops of the grain, watching for any movement. Every now and then a small stream of water would shoot up. They didn't seem to have any pattern or design that he could see. *Surely such a small spray cannot be responsible for the reputation this site has gained.* Abandoning all caution, he stepped into the reputed, perilous field. A faint hiss echoed all around, reminiscent of a light breeze through autumn leaves. He continued along, smirking wickedly at the deception scribed in so many books. Halfway across, the hiss grew louder, sending a massive jet of water straight into the air not ten steps from where he was standing. The scalding mist rained down over the area.

Scalding hot droplets pecked at his cloak, burning their way to his flesh. The larger drops were likely to fall much harsher. Realizing he'd made a mistake, Nezial had to do something. Focusing his will he threw his hands overhead, thrusting his palms to the sky.

The water collided with an invisible barrier, splashing and pooling along the top of the hidden disc. It collected together and ran down around him. Letting the water cool he dropped his hands, allowing the shield to dissipate. A large splash soaked into his thick cloak.

He parted the stalks and found himself facing an odd figure lying half buried in the deceptively muddy earth. Sunken humanoid eyes stared back at him. An expression of shocked terror was burned into the cooked being. Glancing around, he noticed many more. These were victims that believed as he had. "I may have underestimated this place."

A newfound respect for the plains, formed inside him. But now was not the time for admiration. He broke into a run, hoping to escape the field before the jets erupted again. The hiss grew louder all around him. He was moving too quickly to determine its location. Slowing, he listened for it. It wasn't far off, but it wasn't right on top of him either. He felt a minor quake under his feet. *Am I too late? Did I make a mistake?* He lunged forward, bending his knees to jump as hard as he could.

The ground gave way a few inches, squishing water out around his boots and he took to the sky, feeling the thick stream erupt where he had been standing. The jet grazed his backside, burning its way into him. The pain was unbearable. Like a sting that continuously repeated itself. It soaked into his clothing, lingering on his already sensitive skin. He was glad he kept moving, allowing his momentum to carry him away from the majority of the blast, but it didn't make it hurt any less. His feet collided with the soggy ground, sinking into the muddy grass-covered dirt. Losing his balance, Nezial fell face first into the mud.

The geyser rained down upon him, burning deep into his clothes.

He cried out in pain, feeling the blistering water pound against his back. *Is this how it ends? Am I another victim to underestimate the field?* His cloak offered little protection to the scalding vapor.

No! I will not be defeated so easily. I've been tortured my whole life. It will not end this way! Biting his tongue, he picked himself up. He could see the tree line just ahead, marking the border to Evinwood. Hand over fist, he crawled through the mud. The water receded, raining the last bit down upon him. On hands and knees, he made his way to the forest edge, passing from the deadly field.

Reaching the trees, he buckled, falling into the leaves and dirt. The pain shot through his blistered back. He wanted to roll over, but it required too much strength. Forcing everything he had into the single action, he pushed himself to his side. Letting gravity do the rest, he plotted down on his back, wincing in pain from the sudden pressure. The young dreualfar lay there, looking into the blinding clouds of white and blue.

The moon was already out, ready to claim dominion over the night. Nezial lay there, watching the sun fade. Despite the annoyance of its burning beams, the transition was a sight to behold. All the shades of orange, yellow, and blue came together to sing a lullaby for the finished day. It was a painful price to pay for such a memory, but it was well worth it.

The sun faded completely, surrendering to the moon. Nezial gathered his strength. He had to find shelter before his body tensed further than it already had. Pushing himself up, he got to his feet and staggered into the trees.

Just past the forest's edge, he found a fairly secluded ravine. It slashed into the earth, protecting him on all sides. Of course it offered no escape if he was surrounded, but at least no one would see him until they were already there. Weakly, he slid his way to the bottom and stripped off his wet clothes, placing them over the low hanging branches to dry. He kicked the leaves into a pile and held his hands over the mound. Whispering a short incantation, he closed his eyes, focusing his magics into it.

The leaves began to shift, caught between a single entity and the pile they were before. They changed form, gathered, and solidified into a single mass.

He opened his eyes, looking down at the thin bedroll before him. Pulling the top layer away, he exposed a down pillow and thin liner. Unable to spend another moment awake, he wiggled into the roll and covered up. Silently praying his back would feel better in the morning, his eyes clapped shut and he drifted off to sleep.

Chapter VIII
Stolen Thoughts

Seasons came and went, years passing like the evening sun into the dead of night. Giant trees stood minus their leaves, scattered across the thawing ground, while the occasional crunch could be heard against the collection of fallen refuse.

A young man skirted across the frost covered road, disappearing into the dense forest. The dark-green and browns of his leather armor stood in stark contrast to the autumn surroundings, making his movement seem like a mirage, darting in and out of view.

Keeping an eye on the overturned wagon in the distance, he passed from one thick trunk to the next, speeding toward the wreckage. Demetrix approached without caution, experience telling him the danger had long passed. Coming to a stop at the broken frame, he surveyed the abandoned cargo. It clearly wasn't bandits. They avoided this part of the wood, in large part due to him. Moreover, nothing seemed to be missing. He'd seen the same damage many times over. Leaning into the debris, he checked the bodies, hoping there was at least one survivor.

The three victims were cold to the touch, clearly absent life.

Ripping a piece of the large, torn canvas from the wreckage, Demetrix covered them so he wouldn't have to look upon their still forms. Despite their fate, they were fairly lucky. They'd died before the beast fully descended upon them. Most of the others weren't so fortunate. Tucking the makeshift tarp around them, he carefully dug through the scattered cargo, searching for any supplies he might be lacking. It seemed a shame to let them go to waste, after all, nobody was coming for them. He found a hand full of salvageable arrows. Laying the collection on the broken bench, he checked each one, ensuring they were straight enough to fly true. Quickly stuffing them into his quiver, he grabbed a few other items and tossed them aside.

Content there was nothing further he needed, Demetrix piled the crates and shattered wood around the disabled wagon, ensuring the center remained open. He needed as much heat as possible at that point to dispose of the bodies. Anything less wouldn't allow an even burn. Positioning the last few pieces, he pulled the cork from a barrel of lamp oil and generously poured it over the wood, letting it soak for a few minutes. Certain the wood had soaked enough, he ran a line away from the wagon and struck a piece of flint, letting the sparks dance. They skated across the oil soaked ground, disappearing into nothing. It took a few moments, but the small flame caught and the oil and flared to life. The orange and yellow wave traveled away from him, reaching the piled wood. It whooshed, spreading to the entire mound in a matter of moments.

Demetrix waited in anticipation, watching the flame climb up the edges of the rough oak. It ate itself into the wood, growing before his eyes. Satisfied it would continue to burn, he turned and stepped back into the forest. Finding a thick tree with low hanging branches, he climbed up and positioned himself to watch the pyre burn away the remnants. It wasn't a proper funeral, but at least the animals wouldn't get to them. Pulling his cloak tight around him, Demetrix shut out the cooling evening air. The fire would keep him warm for the night, though the smell of burning flesh might make it difficult to sleep. Getting comfortable, he closed his eyes and listened for any sign of approaching trespassers.

Demetrix's eyes shot open at the first signs of morning light. He glanced down at the pile of smoldering ash, seemingly little more than a mixture of flaky powder and melted iron. Quickly scanning his surroundings, securing in his solitude, Demetrix threw his cloak open. The collection of frost and ash flew from the black barrier and gently fell to the ground. He gripped the rough tree bark and climbed from his perc. Approaching the smothered pile, he noticed the heat was nearly gone, buried beneath the layers of cremated mineral. It was probably safe to abandon, but there was no need to take unneeded risks. Kicking a mound of dirt around the edges, he quickly covered the site, ensuring it wouldn't reawaken and spread to the forest around him.

Certain the containment barrier was sufficient, Demetrix kicked his crude boots against the base of a tree, knocking the clinging ash and dirt free. He dusted the gray specks from his leather and stepped off the road, no destination in mind.

A familiar roar echoed through the forest, shaking the limbs free of their remaining leaves. That roar recalled him to his childhood. Drawing his bow, Demetrix strung and nocked an arrow in one fluid motion. The beast was close if he could hear the roar. Without hesitation, he broke into a sprint, hoping to reach it before it disappeared as it had a hundred times before. Such a creature would never expect to be hunted by him. That fact alone gave him a fighting chance at success.

Seeing the ground dip for a deep ravine, Demetrix sprung from his feet, locking his arms around one of the outstretched branches. Shimmying his way up, he got to his feet and ran along the wide pathway, jumping from one branch to the next. He could move quicker without the underbrush tearing at his cloak. His armor was a different story. He'd designed it to resist the briars and thorns. Truth was, he preferred the tree tops. While he had less cover, he was able to move quieter and faster. And the typical bandits he'd taken to stalking rarely looked up. Reaching the end of this tree's reach, he jumped to another, making little more sound than a squirrel. Had it not been for the iron spikes in the soles of his boots, such a feat would have been nearly impossible. But such was the way of life in this forest. One had to be resourceful to survive.

He could see a gap in the trees ahead. He didn't remember this part of the forest. *River, grove— rocks?* He questioned to himself, unsure what to expect when he reached the edge. Stepping into view, his instincts screaming at him to stop. He locked his leather boots, letting the barbed soles dig into the bark of the thick limb. Feeling his balance establish, he backed against the trunk and stared intently down his arrow at the behemoth before him. The feelings he recalled as a child welled up inside him, torn between fear and tenacity. He wouldn't run away this time. He'd kill the dragon, or it'd kill him. Either way, he was done running.

The dragon extended its neck, rearing its horned head to the tree tops. Its massive wings expanded, stretching out over the entire clearing. With an earth shattering roar, it flexed its many muscles, waving its head back and forth in the cool breeze. A powerful blast of green spray shot from its nostrils and into the sky.

Demetrix watched the sound wave escape the beast's snout. He couldn't imagine what a force like that would do to his body if he were caught in it. Unable to look away, he stared, fixated on the black, lost in its fearful beauty. It seemed much larger than he remembered, yet he was only able to see part of its head in the cavern's Underdark. How he'd escaped such a creature, he'd never know. His vision trailed down the black scales, shimmering in the sunlight, to the spiked horns running down it's back and tail. They glistened like the bits of broken glass he'd found in some of the caravans. Bracing himself, he carefully moved closer, keeping his arrow at the ready. Watching, waiting for a change.

The dragon's elongated nostrils flared, sniffing at the air. A familiar scent came to him. He scanned the tree line, searching for its source.

Demetrix froze, his arms quivering, ready to release. Fear intensified, spotting the ruined, glossy opal. *Did I do that? He'll certainly remember me now.* Lost in his thoughts, he hadn't noticed the large yellow slit of the creature's good eye locked onto him. *This was a mistake! How can I to kill it, if a dagger to the eye didn't?*

A booming serpentine voice echoed through the trees, threatening to tear him from his perch. "So you've returned to me, dalari? I knew you couldn't hide forever. Your kind never can."

Demetrix swallowed his fear, letting the wind carry his voice. "I've come to kill you, beast. You'll haunt my dreams no longer!" He heard the words leave his mouth, unable to stop himself.

A deep, bellowing laughter erupted. Holding his belly with his front claws as a portly human would, he shook his head and plopped to his hind haunches, wrapping his thick tail around like a perched cat. The earth shook with such weight being slammed around. "So you believe you're able to kill me? Many have tried, Child of Esoteric." Abandoning his humor, his nose wrinkled in disgust at the notion. "It took you two-hundred and eighteen years to build up the courage to die. But you came here with purpose. I respect that." The dragon stood, rearing his head back. With a powerful thrust, he unfolded his wings and flapped them toward the ranger.

Several gusts of deadly winds washed over him. He lowered his head in an attempt to withstand the force. *I have to get a shot off.* Releasing the bow string, Demetrix watched the shaft spin into the gale. The arrow twisted, its tail fanning out catching the cross wind. The arrow flew out of sight. That was his chance and he blew it. The winds were too strong. He couldn't hold on much longer. Feeling himself slide backward, his barbed boots tearing against the bark, he slipped. Weightlessness took him briefly. He saw the ground rapidly approaching. Bracing himself, the nimble scout rolled with the terrain, jumping to his feet the moment his knees hit the dirt. With blinding speed, he drew and nocked another arrow. Taking aim, he accounted for the wind and adjusted. With any luck, he could fire under their currents. Letting the string loose, the arrow launched. It's fletching spun, cutting through the gusts. In seconds the arrow sank deep into the corner of the dragon's scaled mouth.

It roared, more in irritation than pain. Lowering his wings, it licked at the slight trickle of blood from the minor wound. The tip of his forked tongue pressed against the shaft, dislodging it. "You're going to have to do better than that, if you hope to kill me."

Demetrix nocked another arrow and readied to fire. His feet left the ground, a hard force knocking his legs from beneath him. He hadn't noticed the massive tail whip around behind him. Landing hard on his back his arrow released. It disappeared into the clouds. Demetrix rolled, narrowly dodging the thick tail crashing into the ground beside him. Thundering steps were upon him before he could move.

The dragon approached, all four legs moving in sequence. Atop the young dalari, he raked his front claw over him pinning him to the ground.

The disabled ranger was completely covered, his head alone protruding between the huge, clawed talons. Demetrix struggled against the grip, unable to move. He watched the dragon's head lean in close. A rancid stench flowed from its mouth, burning his lungs. He felt vomit work its way up, settling in his mouth. Unable to roll over to spit, he swallowed the acidic substance, bringing the sickness upon him again.

Every bone in his body shook from the booming voice, so close to him. "I was going to kill you. You deserve it for destroying my eye with that darkstone so long ago. But I've had a change of heart. And, to be honest, you amuse me. Besides, dalari don't have much meat on their bones and my stomach is already full. It's time you paid your debt." The dragon plucked a familiar, dagger from between his scales, holding it gently with the tips of his talons. He displayed the black dagger responsible for claiming his eye so many years ago. "I really must thank you for delivering this. Though I would have preferred alternative means of securement." Careful not to cut too deeply, the dragon drug the blade's tip across the boy's left shoulder, splitting the flesh with ease. Crimson blood spilled from the wound.

Demetrix screamed in pain. It felt as if his soul was being ripped out.

"Hush now, it'll be over in a moment." Pricking one of his scaled talons, the dragon allowed a single drop of his dark red blood to spill over the open wound. Gently rubbing the two fluids together, he released the boy. He was bound by magic now. And there was no escaping that.

Demetrix felt a rush of energy flow through him. Whereas, the dagger was robbing him, this new power filled him. Lying on the forest floor he closed his eyes, unsure what was happening.

The smell of maple rushed to his nostrils. Shooting up, a damp rag fell from his forehead, landing on the thick blanket covering his legs.

"Easy lad. No need to be alarmed." A frail old man sat across from the bed, weaving a sweater from a bundle of gray yarn.

Cautiously searching the cabin, the question spilled forth. "Where am I?" It was cozy, but small. An iron kettle steamed inches away from the fireplace, radiating the sweet scent throughout the hovel. Daylight peered through the single window, illuminating the entire room.

"Nearest town is Farodun. Three days west. But I'd recommend you regain your strength before making any trips." The old man worked the needles, refusing to look up. "Got some oats ready if you're hungry."

The boy locked eyes on the kettle, feeling his stomach rumble at the thought of food. "Yes, thank you. How'd I get here?" He twisted, setting his bare feet on the cold wooden floor.

The old man laid the incomplete sweater over the arm of the chair and grabbed two wooden bowls. Ladling a scoop into each one, he placed them on the table, and poured a couple tankards of milk. "I was on my way home from a trade run when you wandered out of the woods. You were staggering every which way and clearly suffering from dehydration. You collapsed when you reached the road. I couldn't rightly leave you there, not with bandits on the loose and all. So I loaded you up and brought you here. That was three days ago." Taking a seat, he slid the milk to the far side of the table, gesturing toward the empty chair. "How old are you, boy? Fourteen, fifteen?"

Pulling out the chair, the boy took a seat. Staring at the thick mixture of grain and spice, he looked up feeling the realization set on him. "I— I don't know! Last thing I remember was being lost in the forest. I don't even know how I got there." A deep fear overcame him.

"Not to worry boy. We'll find your folks. Until then, you're welcome to stay here. It's been ages since I last had company. Truth be told, I tend to get a little grouchy in the solitude." The man chuckled, slurping a spoonful of the soggy oats. "You got a name?"

Silence filled his memory, struggling to recall the slightest memory. A cascade of tears formed, rolling down his cheeks. He tried hiding the evidence of fear but it wouldn't be staunched. "I— I don't remember."

Seeing the boy's obvious fear, the old man stood, placing his hand on his shoulder. "It's okay, son. Fear's nothing to be ashamed of. It's how you overcome it that defines you. Since you can't recall your name, we'll just have to give you one until yours returns to you. Any ideas?"

The young man gently shook his head.

"Well then— I've always been fond of Kane. You think that'll suit you for the time being? And you can call me, Mortimus."

Sobbing his agreement, the boy took a bite of the food, feeling his taste buds explode with sensation of flavor.

Sweat poured from his brow in the noonday sun. Kane lifted the wooden handles and guiding the worn plow through the field. The blade at the base sliced through the loose dirt, leaving it churned for seeding. The first time he'd tried using it, he wasn't able to make a single pass. Now he could cover two complete fields before he had to rest. Of course, it was the mule that did most of the work. But it was a chore nonetheless.

"Kane, dinner's ready!"

Finishing the row he was on, Kane pulled the blade from the dirt, setting the wooden pin to keep it elevated. Removing the harness from the mule, he guided it to the rickety stable and grabbed his white tunic off the edge of the fence. Rinsing his hands and face in the water trough, he shook the excess liquid off and pulled the tunic overhead. Approaching the cabin, he took the rag Mortimus was offering and dried his hands. "The plow's pulling left again. I think I need to sharpen the blade."

"You already sharpened it twice this week. Much more and there won't be enough metal to get us past the harvest." Mortimus chuckled at the young man's initiative. It was refreshing to see someone who worked as hard as he. More so, that he never asked for reward.

"Forgive me, I hadn't thought about that." Kane gathered his bowl and took a seat, digging in before he fully sat down.

"Don't be absurd. There's no need to ask forgiveness. Without you, I'd still be breaking up the dirt with a shovel. I think three fields in one season is more than enough to cover a new plow should we need."

A smile breached his lips with the old man's praise. He liked him. He was funny and always knew how to lighten the mood. "Hey, Mortimus?"

"I've already told you, I can't dress as the scarecrow and wait for the neighbors to pass by. They won't fall for it a third time." The old man smiled, taking his seat. "What's up?"

"I was stacking hay in the loft earlier today. I moved one of the bails and found a hatch that led into a room between the walls. I didn't go in, but there looked to be a bunch of armor and weapons in there." Kane stared curiously at the old man.

"I thought this day might come. I guess I'll have to leave in the mid of night and find another rundown farm to call home for the next thirty years." A smile slowly formed, betraying his ruse. "I'm just kiddin'. Eat your dinner. Tomorrow, I'll show you the remnants of a time long past."

The next morning they made their way to the barn and climbed into the loft.

Mortimus strained against the stiff wooden door. Pulling it open, he climbed down the ladder and disappeared inside the hidden room. Moments later, a soft glow radiated from the hole.

Kane watched from the top. The old man came into sight, holding a weathered lantern.

"Come on down. Nothin' but spiders and history down here."

"Which one are you?" Kane couldn't help but laugh. It wasn't often he was able to make a joke before his friend.

"Very funny. Just because I'm fuzzy doesn't make a spider. And as far as history— well just say they don't make things like they used to."

The boy climbed down the ladder, lost in the sight of the treasures within. Every wall was covered in racks of weapons, varying design and size. Many of them he couldn't begin to guess what they were called. A suit of armor stood in the corner, positioned upon a stand. The once polished steel was coated in thick layers of dust from time and neglect. It stood over the room like a watchful protector, ready to strike at the first sign of trouble. The shelf beside it was full of glass vials. Several colored liquids and scrolls were organized and marked by a different colored wax seals. A wooden plaque was mounted to the wall, above the shelf.

Inspecting it closer, Kane noticed the tarnished gold inlayed into the carved words. *In honor of commendable service to the crown, Sir Mortimus, Paladin of Corin, is recognized as Protector of the Realm and granted deed to one thousand acres of uninhabited land within the kingdom of Kaladrum. King Renair Kaldum the Thirteenth.*

Noticing the boy's interest, Mortimus offered explanation. "It was a long time ago. I grew tired of fighting other men's battles. When my wife and children were murdered as a way to get back at my king, I retired, letting my reputation die in absence. I haven't looked upon this armor in over thirty years."

Noticing a large sword standing beside the plaque, Kane approached and ran his finger down the etching in the blade. He couldn't read the letters but somehow knew what it said. "Kane?"

Mortimus watched the young man lost, in the runes upon the blade. A gentle smile came to his lips. "It seems she's tired of being cooped up in this room. Pick her up."

Kane looked from the sword to the man, wondering how he was going to lift such a heavy weapon. It appeared to weigh more than him. Finding reassurance on his friend's face, he grabbed the handguard and lifted the sword from its stand. To his surprise it weighed little more than a broom, most of the weight being in the handle. *How can something so large weigh so little?*

"If you're interested, I could teach you a thing or two."

Kane smiled, unable to contain his excitement. Extending the sword, he tried to hand it to the old man.

"She's no longer bound to me. Only the true owner can read the words inscribed upon the blade. She belongs in service to an honorable man. I lost that privilege when I locked her up in this room."

The town was much larger than he'd expected. People rushed in all directions, tending to the duties of their various lives. They didn't pay him any attention and he didn't feel comfortable approaching them. Kane studied their faces, wondering if any of them were his family prior to meeting Mortimus? Moreover, how would he recognize them even if they were? They'd searched for nearly three years with no success, having visited every town for a week in each direction. Kane shook the thoughts away. If he had family, they either didn't care about him, or were much further away than he could afford to travel. He passed one of the larger buildings, hearing to the commotion within. Glancing up at the wooden signpost, mounted over the door, he read aloud. "The Inn of the Drunken Monkey." Smiling, he tied the mule to the hitching post, making sure the supplies were covered and secure. He didn't have much spending money, but perhaps he could see what pub life was all about. All the best stories seemed to start in them, perhaps this was a chance for his own adventure.

Stepping through those magical doors, the stench of pipe smoke burned its way into his nostrils. It was nothing he couldn't tolerate, but it was certainly overpowering.

Several people occupied the large room. Most of them sat around tables, sharing joy with their companions. Others sat along the bar, resting their rear ends against rickety stools of wood and leather. A handful of attractive women rushed about the room, delivering drink in exchange for coin.

Carefully making his way through the crowded room to one of the empty tables, Kane took a seat.

The patrons didn't seem to care about the mass of people within earshot. They spoke freely, letting their opinions and ramblings of politicians and diplomats fill the room. A select few clung to the topic of current events. It seemed an unknown assassin was at large, bringing his suspected death count to just under sixty.

His listening was interrupted by one of the pretty women, stepping into his line of sight.

"What can I get for ya, doll?" She gave a slight bow, exposing her overfilled bosom to the young man.

"I— um— I'll try an ale." Kane blushed, unsure how he should respond to her action.

"Comin' right up, sweetie." She spun around and disappeared through the crowd.

Kane tried to find the man talking about the murders again, but he seemed to have left during his distraction. Getting comfortable, he listened to the others, awaiting the woman's return.

A few moments later, she came back with a wooden mug, filled to the brim with a foamy, bronze liquid. Placing it on the table, she stared down at him, a knowing smile on her face. "That's two copper, hun."

Kane handed her a couple copper pieces and lifted mug, taking a long draw. The sour concoction burned his tongue and threatened to dislodge his lunch. Spitting the disgusting liquid on the floor. "How do people drink that?" He asked, regretting his decision.

The barmaid laughed aloud, placing the two copper back on the table. "Perhaps you'd better run on home. This place isn't for the faint of heart."

Kane collected his coin and stood from his chair. "My apologies for wasting your time."

"Don't sweat it. When you're a little older and ready for the true pleasures in life, come back and see me. Maybe you'll be able to handle a little more then." She kissed him on the cheek and turned to return to her duties.

Making his way through the crowd, he stepped out the doors, hoping his water skin still had some liquid in it. He needed to get that taste out of his mouth. The bright sunlight burned spots into his vision. He hadn't realized how dark the pub actually was until he left. Approaching the cart, he felt anger rise inside him. The spotted fur hide he'd used to cover the supplies was lying roughly on the ground. The cart was near empty, only the most mundane of items remained. Picking the tarp off the ground, he wadded and tossed it in the cart. *I was in there for no more than twenty minutes. I hate this place.* His head hung low, he untied the mule and started for home, dreading the disappointment Mortimus was going to have in him.

Night was falling on the last leg of the three-day journey. It seemed to take forever. Not only was he growing hungry from the lack of food, but the knowing failure he had to offer was eating at him. It also didn't help that his mind was playing tricks on him. He passed what appeared the be the same fence post three times now. But that seemed unlikely. The single road didn't turn back anywhere as far as he knew. And Mortimus made sure he knew the road to take. He wouldn't have agreed to letting him make it alone otherwise. Yet something clearly wasn't right. He should have been home that morning. *I guess this just proves I wasn't ready for it.* "Screw this." Kane led the mule to the side of the road and tied it to the post. Grabbing some of the feed he'd purchased with his spending money, he poured into a basin and laid it out for the animal. Unpacking his tattered sleeping bag, he rolled it along the small wagon and got comfortable.

The next morning, he untied the mule and set off for the final stretch, haunted by his dreams. It seemed not even sleep could rid him of the guilt. Every time he closed his eyes, the images crept into his mind. The vague memories crept to the forefront.

He remembered being a man, dressed in black, tracking through the woods. Following the trail, he came to a small shack. Supplies littered the floor, some used, others sorted and awaiting transport. The man inside was asleep, unaware of his presence. He carefully restrained him, ensuring he didn't wake. Taking joy in his actions, he splashed water in the man's face, ready to execute his malicious plan. One by one, Kane watched a dark form of himself remove the man's fingers and toes, listening to his scream in pain, begging him to stop. But he wouldn't. He didn't want to. This man was going to pay for his wrongdoings. Even when the man begged for death, he refused. Not because he didn't want to, but because I wasn't finished.

Kane pulled himself from the memory of the dream. He didn't want to witness what happened next. A whiff of smoke hung in the air, forcing the final details upon him.

The man cried out in pain, his bloody nubs tied off, keeping him from bleeding out. He was little more than a torso and head, still alive, but ready for death. He stared down at the helpless man, smiling his delight in his torment. Lifting the blood covered lamp from the table, he smashed it on the floor, watching the flame spread across the floor. It climbed the bed post, singeing the man's hair. The smell of burning flesh and lingering screams echoed in his mind as he walked from the burning shack. Fear and remorse billow inside him. How could such thoughts fill his mind, even in dream? Sure, he wanted justice, but torture and murder were an extreme leap for simple thievery. Even without Mortimus' tutelage, he knew that was wrong.

Suddenly, he realized the scent of smoke wasn't just from his dream. It was hanging in the air, like a layer of fog around him. Kane froze, searching the sky. There wasn't much in this area other than fields and the farm. *The farm!* A thick cloud of gray billowed over the hill. His heart sank, knowing where it was coming from. Abandoning the cart, he broke into a sprint. Reaching the top of the hill, he looked down at the flames ravaging the small cabin. The house was nearly gone, collapsed in on itself. The flame was quickly spreading. It'd already burned half of one field and was starting the spread to another. He ran as fast as his feet could carry him, as close as the heat would allow.

"Mortimus, where are you?" A low moan caught his attention amidst the roar of the fire. Searching near the barn, he found his friend beaten and bloodied. He laid on his back, half buried by grass and ash. "Mortimus, what happened?" Kane felt the tears swell in his eyes. Pulling his friend close, he noticed the blood-stained shirt. He had several deep gouges across his stomach and chest. The realization hit him. It wouldn't be long before his only friend would leave him forever.

Mortimus reached up, weakly running his fingers over the boy's cheek. His lower jaw quivered. Lifting a trembling finger, he pointed to the barn. A deep sigh escaped him and he fell limp.

Chapter IX
Forging Bonds

Wind slapped against the sails, clapping the loose edges together. Birds chirped, collected along the top of the masts, looking down at the crew below. The ship glided gently across the sea, propelled slowly by the mild gusts.

"Land ho!" The watch yelled from the crow's nest, his sight glass extended to peer through the low hanging clouds.

Gareth glanced up, noting the man's signal. Spinning to mimic his direction, he pulled his own sight glass from its leather pouch and extended it to get a closer look. The darkening sky and heavy fog made it difficult to see, but sure enough, land could be seen in the distance. "Drop the sails and bring 'er in slowly, boys. Looks like we got rocks ahead."

The thick canvas fell with a thud, crumbling to the deck. The crew went to work collecting them for their next raise.

Standing beside the assistant navigator, Gareth watched him spin the wheel. The ship slipped between the jagged boulders breaching the surface. Their size was remarkable, most of them twice as wide as the hull. There was no telling how large they were beneath the surface. Though it had to have been impressive considering they shouldn't be close enough for rocks just yet. Gareth would have preferred Malakai to be at the helm, but the man had already given fourteen hours. He was entitled to some down time. And the boy needed the practice. The young captain glanced at the black liquid beneath them. It reflected like polished glass, barely making a ripple beneath them.

A resounding crash echoed below deck, shaking the ship violently.

Gareth caught himself, unprepared for the sudden jolt. "Cabin boy, report the lower levels!"

A young boy, barely old enough to be called a man, took off below deck.

Gareth looked over his beloved ship. He didn't need a report to know she was going down. The rails bowed already. It wouldn't be long before she'd disappear beneath the black. He calmly walked to the overlook and peered down at his men.

The boy rushed to the deck, waving to the captain. Shaking his head, he sealed the already known fate.

"Men, it's been my honor to be your captain, but those days are done. I doubt any of us can swim the distance to shore, and gods know what lurks in the depths beneath us. It's up to you lads. You can stay here and drown, or make a swim for it and hope to reach shore before The Dutchman finds you." Gareth finished his speech and gave a quick salute to the men. Turning away from the railing, he entered his room. It was customary to go down with your ship and he intended to join his wife and son.

The deck was chaos. Many of the men ran, jumping overboard. Some met their end upon the jagged rocks just below the surface of the dark waters. Others hit with a splash and swam for the faint outline on the horizon, disappearing long before they should have.

Gareth dressed in his finest garb. Securing his armor and cutlass, he pulled them into place and stared into his mirror. Running a wooden comb through his thick, red beard he gave a final adjustment and nodded to his reflection. His appearance was sound. There was no finer way to be reunited with his wife. Being under dressed for the occasion seemed sloppy. Solemn, he opened the door and stepped out.

Only a handful of men remained on board, preparing to meet their fate with their captain. Seeing the adorned captain, they stood erect, offering salute.

"May it be quick and painless, lads." Gareth returned the gesture, allowing his men to stand down. Marching to the helm, he took hold of the wheel, feeling it was his rightful place at the end.

Water crept over the deck covering the tar sealed planks. The men cried silently, refusing to let their fear dampen the mood. Clenched to their various religious relics, many of them Corin's trident, they stood defiant, disappearing from sight.

Gareth watched the sea swallow his men. It rapidly approached the helm, spilling over the top of his boots. He felt the icy chill of death upon his back, rising up to consume him. He was numb by the time the water reached his face. Time was lost. He needed to go quickly. Thoughts of his wife entered his mind. She was wearing her favorite light blue dress and holding their infant son. Smiling his content, he exhaled, forcing the air from his lungs. The dark water covered his face, blocking out the fading light above. He looked around at the darkness surrounding him, letting the memories of his family calm his mind.

Pipe smoke lingered in the air around the crowded tavern room. The collected noise echoed against the wooden walls, making more of a dull roar than a cohesive choir of voices.

Ravion sat in the corner of the pub, his dark blue pants and tunic stood in stark contrast to his tan vest. His red tinged hair hung loosely around his shoulders, swept back to display his forehead. His father's longsword hung loosely on his left hip, a dagger sheathed beside it, tucked nearly beneath the table but ready for use if required. He was still fairly new in these lands, but nobody questioned him. It seemed travelers were in steady supply in these parts.

A barmaid approached carrying a bowl of stew and a wooden tankard of cider. She set the objects down and waited patiently for him to retrieve his purse.

Handing her a silver coin, Ravion took a long drawl from the tankard. The cider burned its way down, but it felt good against his throat. The frozen mountain winds hadn't done him any favors. "The change is yours. Perhaps you could tell me, where might one procure lodging for the night?"

She tucked the coin away. "We have a few rooms available, though we're more suited for a brief stay. If you're looking for a week or more you'd be coin ahead to talk to Melvin. He's the keep at the Inn of Aldridge. They average one to two silver less over a longer span."

"Thank you for the information." Nodding his understanding, Ravion waited for her to leave. Spooning the hot, steaming bowl of stew, he watched the strands of mist float away from him. He was hungry, but fairly certain it'd burn his mouth if he got too eager. Looking into the mixture of sauce, meat, and vegetables, he noted a rather large turnip. His nose wrinkled of its own volition. Scooping the plump mass from his bowl, he laid it to rest on the saucer. *I hate turnips.* Ensuring no more of the dense vegetables remained, Ravion reached across the table and grabbed a handful of the dried bread the wench had set out earlier. Crushing it into crumbs, he sprinkled it over the bowl and mixed the two into a semi-thick paste.

The patrons moved in and out, filling the room with gossip. None seemed to care who might have been listening. Many different stories echoed, each one having some slight bit of truth, as pub tales always did.

Ravion spooned in the paste, listening intently to the rumors. Having his fill on both counts, food and gossip, he stood and made way for the door. The planked barrier swung open, allowing the cool, fall breeze to barrage him. It was interesting how such a simple device could have such a drastic effect. The chilling wind tore through his light fabrics. Shaking the shock away, he wrapped his cloak around him and stepped outside. He needed to procure a room and perhaps find some thicker clothes. These new lands were harsher than he'd grown accustomed. Survival would come from planning, rather than simple intuition.

Reaching the inn, he couldn't help but study the architecture. It was similar to the other structures of the area, but seemed more elegant in its design. The clay shingled roof was trimmed in wood and curved to deflect wind and rain alike. It was an interesting design. One he hadn't noticed on the other buildings. It seemed this one was the foundation for the others, yet the quality dropped drastically from structure to structure.

Passing through the single wooden door, Ravion stood in awe at the interior. Not so much as a chair seemed out of place in the common room. The walls were decorated with trophies of hunts long pasts. The fireplace was blazing with a chainmail curtain, draped to prevent the embers from flying out. And even more interesting, the patrons were quietly minding their own business. None seemed to care about the other. Instead they simply ate their food and drank their drinks in silent solitude. Glancing to the head of the pub, Ravion noticed a middle-aged man standing over the polished countertop along the left wall. A thick book laid open in front of him, occupying his attention.

Ravion approached the man. "Excuse me. Assuming this is the inn. What are you rates?"

The man stole a quick glance from his book, surveying the young-looking scout. Returning his attention to the book, he spoke. "Three silver a week, one gold a month."

"Here's three gold. Can you tell me where the tailor's shop is?"

Refusing to look away a second time, he reached under the counter and pulled an iron key with a thin chain linked around the back side. Laying it on the counter, he continued. "Upstairs, you'll be the second door on the right. Tailor's shop is two buildings north, though they're closed for the night."

"Thank you." Ravion snatched the key and headed up the stairs.

A thick mist spanned in all directions, glowing white from the overhead sun beyond the clouds. Dark columns stood alone in the enveloping fog, taking the form of massive trees. The lone warrior wandered aimlessly through the unending mist, lost as much in thought as he was in his solitude. Weeks had passed since he'd last sat in civilized company. His pack was light and his stomach rumbled from hunger.

"Come on Kane, it can't last forever." He told himself, forcing the doubts from his mind. He was unsure where he was headed, but instinct told him he was facing the right direction.

A single beam of sunlight shot brilliantly through the dense fog reflecting against his chrome breastplate. The bright glare burned into the shadows of the misty undergrowth. It blinded him as much as it helped to see anything in the thick blanket. A thin, black cape was attached firmly at the shoulders of his armor, serving more as decoration than actual function. The name of his mentor was carved into the collar of the freshly tempered steel, and a coiled dragon was inlaid across the belly giving the smooth metal a textured feel. It was perfect in every way. Though its price was too high. Mortimus had had it made for him while he was away. If only the old man had lived long enough to show it to him himself. Instead, he'd found it on a stand, similar to that of the tarnished armor, in the room between the walls of the barn.

A sudden snap ripped him from his memories. Kane spun, gripping the sword's handle in searching of the unnatural commotion. He listened intently to the breaking twigs and crumbling leaves all around him, testing his sanity with the volume alone. It sounded as if it was right on top of him. But where? Unable to wait a moment longer, he drew the great sword and readied himself for battle. Standing defiantly, ready to strike down the first opponent to present itself, Kane squinted into the misty sheen.

A huge shadow formed in the fog. It was three times larger than the average human, and growing larger by the second.

Tightening his grip, Kane's fingers stretched around the leather-bound handle, his knuckles popping in protest.

The figure loomed over him, making its way closer to the defensive boy.

His stomach tightened, watching it move closer with deadly purpose. The rumbled of footsteps in the leaves filled his mind. He found himself wondering how big it had to be to make such commotion. His heart raced, thundering inside his chest. His skin was sticky, pockets of sweat forming on his brow. Fear on edge, tempting him to flee, Kane trembled in uncertainty against the over-sized shadow. Feeling he could take no more, his target sliced through the fog, revealing itself to him.

A white rabbit with tan spots hopped into view, presenting its menacing presence to the embattled warrior.

A sigh of relief escaped him. Kane lowered the sharpened blade, chuckling at his foolishness.

The startled rabbit hopped away, equally frightened by the armored man's presence.

Shaking his head, Kane continued through the fog, hoping he'd find a town soon. He was ready to rest. His fear of shadows being all the proof he needed.

Hours passed and the mist began to thin, revealing an old dirt road and a weather worn signpost stuck firmly in the ground. Tattered words were carved into the mossy wooden sign, hanging loosely from a single, bent and rusted nail. He read the words aloud, listening to them as he spoke. "Aldridge two miles ahead." Stepping onto the path, he altered course and made for town.

The streets where just coming to life when Ravion stepped from the tailor's shop, pausing just outside the door. Staring down his sleeves, he admired the new, thicker garments. They were much heavier than he was used to, but once they were properly broken in they'd function just the same. *Well, I'm going be here a while. I suppose it's time I learn the lay of the land.* Throwing the heavy cloak over his shoulders, he secured the ties and stepped into the cool, autumn air.

Ravion traveled north with seemingly unnatural speed. In truth, he wasn't moving any faster than a seasoned athlete, he just didn't tire nearly as quickly. It'd taken him nearly two decades to build up his stamina. Seeing the first signpost since leaving town, he noticed the words etched into the wood. *Heroes Gate*, he silently read. The name intrigued him. From what he'd learned about the landmark it was the only known gateway in the ancient wall that split the continent in half. It was rumored the ancient citizens of Shadgull constructed it, and it supposedly was built during some massive civil war thousands of years ago, but not much else could be said about it.

The sun was nearing peak height, creating a comfortable warmth on the ground. Though the occasional dense cloud or strong gust of wind was certain to remind the world of the chilly morning air.

Ravion reached the top of one of the few hills. Looking above the patchy trees in the distance, he could see the outline of the massive wall. The details were far from visible, but the image was shocking to say the least. Considering the stone structure towered over the trees lining the east side of the road, the term massive was putting it mildly.

Continuing closer, the iron portcullis took shape before his eyes. He couldn't tell how far away he was, but if such a structure was made to limit troops it must have been one hell of a force to begin with. Ravion slowed, hearing a commotion in the trees beside him. Placing his hand on his father's sword, he stepped off the trail and careful made his way into the forest. Following the unusual sounds, he stepped through the trees. Reaching the overlook on the other side, Ravion froze, lost in the sight before him.

Chirping seagulls and crashing waves echoed along the coast. The shore was lined with large jagged rocks, save for a small, sandy patch. A thick forest spanned from the east, wrapping to the north. And the western horizon was filled by a towering mountain range.

Gareth awoke to the chill of sea water rushing over his body, threatening to cover him completely. Just as it reached his face, it receded back into the ocean, only for another wave to take its place. Opening his eyes, the blaring sun burned into his clouded vision. Shielding himself, he rolled over and wiped the salt out as best he could. Pushing to his hands and knees, he glanced around, hoping to see how many survived the shipwreck.

Rocky canyons towered on either side of the sandy beach. Ocean to south, and a thick forest to the north, it seemed he was all alone. Searching for any evidence, Gareth noticed a large road along the edge of the forest. It turned and cut a thin path into the dense woodland. Surveying the terrain, he felt a sorrow for the loss of his men. If they weren't here, they were most-likely swallowed by the sea. And yet again, he was the sole survivor, as if the gods continued to curse him. Getting to his feet, he turned toward the sea. To his surprise, his ship's mast was nowhere to be seen. The waters must have been deeper than he'd thought, despite the numerous rocks breaking the surface. Watching over the watery grave, a silent goodbye echoed inside him. *By Corin's grace, sail the eternal seas, my men. May your longing be at an end and your hearth always warm. For the life of a sailor, while wet and cold, is one of exuberance and adventure. Many go their lives without really living. You, my men, did something many never will. You truly lived.* Snapping to attention, he gave a final salute and turned toward the forest road.

Reaching the top of the sandy bank, Gareth noticed a group of horsemen riding along the small road.

Breeching the forest, they abandoned their single file and staggered into an arrow formation.

Gareth was certain they saw him. They would have had to have been blind had they not. Hand on his sabre, he assessed the five horsemen, unsure if they were friend or foe.

The group slowed, signifying their desire to talk.

Close enough to make out details, Gareth looked them over. The first and largest of the group was adorned with a silver helm covering his face. A long tuft of blue fur flowed from the crest, dancing in the wind. His tabard was blue and silver, emblazoned by an odd symbol across the chest. A silver rapier hung on his left hip, graceful in all ways. The man on the right was helmless, but wearing similar garments. Instead of the single finesse weapon, a short sword was sheathed on each hip. These two stood out among the rest, dressed in court garb, while the other three appeared brutish in nature. It wasn't so much their frame or facial expressions, as it was their armor. These three were clearly knights, dressed in thick armors and sporting an assortment of heavy weapons and shields. Though they still displayed the silver and blue sash matching that of the first two.

The group came to a stop several feet away, keeping enough distance to prevent aggression, but close enough to communicate. Large man at the head removed his helm, revealing a mass of flowing golden hair. "Greetings, friend." A friendly smile adorned his face, overlooking the stranded captain.

Gareth waited a moment, studying the man's choice of word. "As I've never met you, I believe the title of friend has yet to be earned." He stated coldly.

The lead man looked the shipwrecked man up and down, allowing his smile to fade to little more than a smirk. "I cannot dispute your logic. However, as I do not yet know your name, it seems as fitting a title as I can muster to show you that we mean no harm. We only wish to assess your situation and offer aid." He paused a moment before continuing, "My name is Master Remle De Leon, Commander of the Heroes and Lord of Shadgull. This is my second, Sir Erik De Leon," He said, gesturing to the younger man on his right. "And my Lieutenants, Sir Victicious

Hovay, Sir Jem Asray, and Sir Kald Eirwan." Remle pointed to each of the men. "And you are?"

Gareth glanced over they, measuring each on in his own way. Returning his attention to the large, blond haired man, he replied. "My name is Gareth D'Averon, Captain of the *Merratin*, sadly resting at the bottom of the sea. We were a fishing vessel from the port city of Everik off the northern coast of Negield. My ship was lost among the rocks, my crew along with it."

Remle adjusted uncomfortably in his saddle. "Not all of them. One was found wandering the roads a few miles north of here. He informed one of my soldiers of your ship not long ago. We dispatched to see if there were any more survivors. It seems you may be the last. But we'll keep looking."

Gareth felt a slight bit of joy hearing one of his men yet lived. "Did you happen to catch this sailor's name?"

Remle looked at the exhausted captain feeling remorse for all he had lost. He seemed to have suffered more than the loss of his ship and crew. Something deeper troubled the man, something that made him feel lost yet resolved at the same time. "Yes, his name was Malakai Torne. He was taken into Shadgull City where he regained his stamina. From there he caught a ride to a town called Aldridge."

Gareth looked upon the men. "I thank you for the information. Would it be possible to barter a ride to this Aldridge so I may find this man? I have little to offer, due to Corin's need to sink my ship. But I don't mind working off a debt. May I repay the service with service?"

Remle thought about the offer for a moment. Glancing over the man's appearance, quickly assessed his abilities. He was exceptionally well dressed for a man washed ashore. His gaze locked on the blade resting peacefully in its scabbard. "Are you any good with that?" He gestured toward the bound weapon.

"I hear the pointy end goes in the other guy." Gareth smiled, refusing to boast his prowess. It was too soon to trust these men. If they turned on him, it was best they underestimated his ability.

Remle chuckled. "Well, my friend—" He paused at the thought of using the title again, "I have a problem with a young dragon attacking caravans on the road to Heroes Gate. Unfortunately, my men have been busy with more local matters. If you would agree to take on the task of slaying this beast I would see you not only to Aldridge, but with a small fortune to pay for expenses and to accommodate you while you're in these lands."

Gareth felt a small trimmer of success hearing the matter of coin arise. "I'll accept your terms."

Remle pulled a large blue bag from his waist and tossed it to the sailor. "Jem, see this man to your saddle."

Gareth climbed atop the horse, securing himself to the rider. They set off at a gallop, disappearing into the forest.

The fire crackled and sparked, sending tiny sprites into the night sky. Several men laid around the fire. Some lost in its dance, while others were fast asleep. The gallop of a horse echoed closer, halting just out of their camp. A lone voice echoed from the darkness.

"Get off yer' asses and come take a look at this!" The lowly human climbed from his horse and pulled a frayed burlap sack from the saddlebag. It was packed so tightly that the seams stretched, threatening to burst open and spill its contents. It hit the ground, ringing out like chain links.

The others roused themselves and slowly approached.

Heaving the bag with rushed, small steps, the man moved toward a crude wooden table hammered between a pair of trees. Coin and small trinkets spilled from the newly formed hole in the bottom.

"That's a good haul, Kelly. Where'd you get all of this?" A man with a wide scar across his face asked, watching him pour it into a large pile.

"I got a lead on a big score. This was the proof. There's a lot more. A whole room in fact." Kelly smiled smugly at the others, his superiority evident by his expression.

They stared in awe at the amount of gold, silver, and gems resting on the weathered table.

A large half-orc towered over their shoulders, admiring the collection. Rubbing the sleep from his eyes, he pushed through, hoping to get a better look. "That a lot of loot."

"Ya plannin' to hit it tomorrow?" The scarred man asked, shooing the half-orc away. "Go lay down, ya oaf. If we need something smashed, we'll let ya know."

"Sorry, Sean." The green-skin yawned, flexing his arms and back. Turning around, he sauntered off toward his cozy blanket near the fire.

"Yeah, tomorrow's the best time. I'd hate for my informant to give the details to someone else and have them beat us to it."

The scent of cherry floated in the air of the crowded pub. A dull roar echoed from the patrons minding their own, while others laughed and joked with their companions. The room was lit from above by a large basin suspended from the rafters and a flickering flame spouted from the oil within.

Kane leaned back in his wooden chair, listening to the legs creak against the unusual weight. He watched the sparks dance inside the blazing fireplace. An occasional ember skipped through the chainmail curtain blocking the fiery oven, only to go out when it hit the floor. Stretching his arms, he flexed the muscles in his back, allowing it to pop several times before relaxing them. Returning the front legs of his chair to the floor, he watched the barmaid hurry over, remembering the last time he'd visited the pub.

The barmaid carefully set the tankard on the table, keeping the contents from sloshing too wildly. Staring at the armored young man, she waited expectantly.

Fumbling with the leather binding on his coin pouch, Kane pulled it open and snatched a two copper pieces from the bag. Handing it to her, he watched her bow, revealing a deep crevice at the top of her corseted blouse.

A knowing smile breached her lips. Giving him a good, long look, she spun and rushed off to tend to her other duties.

She's cute, but unlikely to have interest in me, Kane thought, watching her form through the fitted dress. Retying the pouch, he stuffed it under his armor, making sure it found its pocket. Lifting the heavy mug, he sniffed the golden liquid, savoring the sweet scent. Placing it to his lips, he took a careful draw, hoping it was nothing like the ale. The taste of fermented honey filled his mouth. "No wonder they call it the nectar of gods." He stated to no one in particular. Laying the drink to rest on the table, he noticed two men stepped through the doublewide door.

They wore thick, layered armor, mostly covered by matching blue and silver tabards. Marching across the tavern room, they approached the barkeep, actions full of purpose.

Kane watched intently. He'd never seen soldiers such as these. And they clearly had some business here. One of the men pulled a rolled piece of vellum from his pack and laid it on the counter. The other laid a small brown bag beside it. Judging from the size and shape, it was most likely full of coin. The first one leaned over the counter, speaking a few words through the echoing voices behind them. He tried to hear them, but the patrons were too loud.

The barkeep nodded, watching the two men leave as quickly as they arrived. Seeing the doors close, he broke the seal and read the missive.

Feigning a long draw of mead, Kane watched the barkeep pocket the bag and disappear into the room behind the bar. He guessed it was the kitchen, but there was no way to tell without drawing attention to himself.

A few moments later, the barkeep returned with another scroll. This one was crude compared to the original. Carrying it over to a large board nailed to the wall beneath the stairs, he tacked it to the mass of existing bounties. Returning to the counter, he started wiping the same area he'd been cleaning when the soldiers approached.

Curiosity peeked, Kane slammed the remainder of his tankard and wiped the excess away on his sleeve. Setting the wooden mug on the table, he stood, feeling the effects in his legs. Careful to retain his balance, he approached the board and read the notice.

Wanted notifications of criminals, heroes, or simple help crowded the soft wood, filled with pin holes. Even a few requests for ritual sacrifice or intimate encounters were posted for all to see.

Kane reviewed the board, noting the name *Craig* carved along the top boarder. Looking over the numerous items, he found the newly tacked parchment.

Attention weary travelers, the road north is being accosted by a dragon. Any attempting to travel to Heroes Gate should seek an alternate route. Those who wish to rid the world of this beast, meet at the north edge of town at first light, tomorrow morning. Reward will be given for any who assist in the assault.

Reading the message once again, assuring he understood its meaning, Kane shook his head, clearing the fuzzy sight that was starting to plague him. "Perhaps it's worth investigating." He said to no one in particular. Rubbing his eyes, he turned to leave. His feet frozen at the sight of a stranger passing through the doors.

The man wore ornate brigandine armor and had a short, curved blade on his left hip. His head was freshly shaven, reflecting the orange glow of the fire light.

Kane felt a strange sensation wash over him. It wasn't the man's appearance that halted him. It was something deeper. Something familiar— yet unknown. Frozen, unable to look away, Kane watched the man approach the barkeep.

"I need a room for the night." Gareth tossed a silver coin on the counter. He glanced around the room, locking eyes with a young man near the stairs. A strange glow radiated from him. It wasn't a solid aura. While that was rare, it wouldn't be the first he'd seen. No, this man's glow was cracked and faint. Like it both was and wasn't at the same time. This truly was a first. The sound of metal sliding across the counter roused him. Glancing down, he snatched up the small brass key. Refusing to delay a moment longer, he headed for the stairs, nodding to the young man as he passed.

Kane stood frozen, trying to understand what he'd just seen. Surely the mead hadn't made him see things. Shaking the thoughts from his mind, he made for the door. *Glowing red men are too much for one evening. And if I'm going to aid in this dragon hunt, I'll need to prepare myself.*

The brilliant moon beamed into an enveloping fog, hanging low in the sky. It illuminated the lantern lit streets in a dull white glow, blocking vision for more than a few feet. It was remarkably quiet considering the number of people still out, but most of the population was indoors for the evening.

Ravion passed the signpost at the edge of town, lost in his thoughts. *It wasn't very big. Little more than a juvenile, I'd wager. But it's still too much for me to handle on my own. I need to find someone skilled enough to combat the beast, and preferably wealthy enough to pay me for services. Maybe if the man's gullible enough to believe the search was his idea, I can score an added bonus.* Rounding the corner, he heard the first real commotion since he returned town. Altering his destination, Ravion followed the shouts to the pub he'd first visited. Approaching the doors, he jumped back, narrowly dodging the wooden barriers.

A man flew head first through the double doors, landing hard on the dirt road. Small bits of dust flew into the air, coating him in a light layer. He groaned in pain and rolled onto his back.

Ravion watched two men march from the tavern.

One threw a sword and belt atop the man, while the other tossed a cavalier hat at him. Spitting in the man's general direction, he turned and marched back inside. His companion at his heels.

"Rough night?" Ravion asked, kneeling beside prone man and extending his hand.

"You might say that. I've been shipwrecked, robbed, and now thrown from a pub because I caught a man cheating at a game of cards. I can't rightly cut him down since it seems every man at the table was loyal to him." He reached up, accepting the offer.

"I see— Well, there's always time for retribution another day. Come on, I'll get you a drink." Ravion pulled the man to his feet and snatched the dirty hat off the ground, handing it to him.

The man took it, patting it off against his equally dirty leather armor and loose-fitting clothing. The stench of salt water radiated from him. Placing the hat atop his head, he grabbed the belt and tied it in place. "Name's Malakai by the way. Malakai Torne."

"Ravion Santail," He stated, giving a graceful bow, rolling his hand in kind.

The two made their way for the Inn of Aldridge and took a seat at the corner table.

It was much louder than Ravion remembered. Instead of a slow evening, as it had been the previous day, it was now just like every other pub he'd ever attended. Crowded and full of conversation. Signaling the barmaid, Ravion laid a few coins on the table.

She appeared a moment later carrying two tankards. Laying them to rest, she snatched up the coin and disappeared again.

"So— I see you carry two blades. Is it safe to assume you're skilled with them?" Ravion casually took a swig, sucking in much less of the liquid than he let on.

Malakai grabbed the other mug and tipped it back. "One might say that. I've spend the majority of my life on the sea. Most recently I served on a fishing vessel from Everik."

"Interesting. Though I must admit I'm curious. What kind of fishing vessel requires a swordsman?"

"That's a good question. We were a fishing vessel, though it's been months since we've caught any fish. The port we hail from was attacked, leaving many of our families murdered. I was fortunate, my family died years ago. I didn't have to witness what much of the crew had. We set out in hopes of finding more of the creatures responsible. Maybe we could help some folks like no one did for my mates. But not all tales have a happy endin'. Our ship ran into rocks a about a week's ride south of here. I woke up on the shore near a forest road. Started walkin' until I met a patrol. And I eventually ended up here. Been tryin' to decide what to do ever since. I'm lucky—" Malakai paused, "Armor's rarely worn on a ship. When it gets wet, it gets heavy and tends to pull you down. Captain told us we were going down. I dressed in my best figurin' it was my time. I laid down in my bunk and next thing I know I'm lost, wandering aimlessly down a road."

Ravion listened to the confusion and sorrow in the man's voice. He couldn't help but feel for him. Having shared a similar bond, it was always hard to say goodbye. Or worse, be denied a goodbye. But he'd never suffered a shipwreck. His departure from the sea was much more favorable. A bald man wearing brigandine armor caught his eye. He had an aura about him, reminding him of his own people, but this was different. This man couldn't be dalari. He didn't feel right.

Gareth looked around the pub, spotting a familiar silhouette sitting with his back to the stair. He seemed to be in conversation with a young man, maybe in his early twenties, though he had a much older stature. Not to mention the light blue glow radiating from him. He'd seen similar effects before. The man probably used some form of fancy magic, though he wasn't dressed as a typical caster.

Ravion watched the man approach. Locking eyes, he raised a finger to silence his companion. Hoping the gesture would prevent him from carrying on in the stranger's company. "May we help you?"

Malakai glanced behind him, spotting the face of his captain. He jumped to his feet, nearly spilling his tankard. Without hesitation, he snapped to salute.

Gareth smiled. It was good to see one of his men yet lived. "Relax, Malakai. The ship's gone. I'm no longer your captain."

Malakai dropped his arm, nodding respects to the stout man. "You'll always be my capt'n, Capt'n."

Resting his hand on the sailor's shoulder. Gareth continued. "I'm glad at least one of my crew survived, and I'm fortunate it was you. I'm in need of your tracking skills. I can pay for the service. And your new friend here, if he so desires."

Ravion stood extending his hand, "Greetings, I'm Ravion Santail. And while I haven't been in this area long, I'm known as the finest scout for days." *Doesn't matter who knows me as that.*

Gareth smiled, shaking the tall, skinny man's hand. He felt a kinship to him. He was familiar— yet unknown. "Well, I'm gonna' go see if I can find a few men capable with a blade. I bid you gentlemen goodnight. I expect to see you on the north edge of town in the mornin'. We're tracking a dragon so be prepared." Before they could ask any more, he turned and made for the door.

Chapter X
The Tyrant

The early morning sun beamed through the trees, glistening off the layered dew. A snapping branch echoed through the forest, accompanied by the crunch of leaves.

Nezial rolled over and opened his eyes, careful to keep from blinding himself. Listening intently to the echoing sounds, he whispered a quiet incantation. His clothing disappeared from the overhead branches and fell into place around his body. Getting to his feet, he waved away the summoned bedroll. It reform into the pile of leaves he had been before. Throwing his hood overhead, Nezial grabbed his satchel and cautiously climbed from the ravine. In search of the commotion, he dove deeper into the alfaren homelands.

Movement passed through the thick brush up ahead.

Making his way closer, new sounds echoed into his ears. Nezial recognized a voice. Its owner was unknown, but the language seemed familiar. A smile crept to his face. Language meant intelligence. And intelligence meant purpose. Taking in the guttural pitch, he tried to recall a spell that would allow him to understand it. It clearly didn't belong to the myrkalfar. Their tongue was musical in nature, like listening to the elements sing to one another. No, these creatures were trespassers, same as him. That meant there was a chance for an allegiance.

Without a sound, Nezial moved closer, stopping on the edge of a small clearing in the now dense forest. Inside the grove, three large creatures stood, arguing among themselves. Recognizing the beasts, their language rushed into his mind. He felt foolish, having missed it before. He was little more than a child the last time he studied the brutish culture, but it seemed the knowledge stayed with him. Watching from a distance, he studied the creatures. It wouldn't favor him to give away his position prematurely.

They stood nearly seven foot tall and had thick tusks protruding from their lower jaws. Heavy hide armor protected their chests, while lighter leathers and furs wrapped around their forearms and legs. The exposed skin of their faces and hands was stained brown. That meant they were from the eastern clans, Nezial recalled. That lot was mostly hunters and gathers, but they had relations with the northern clans which constantly required them to pass through the alfaren forests.

The lack of wrinkles and scars on two of their number lad him to believe they were young. Whereas the third, stood nearly six inches taller with long white hair and a battle worn face to match.

Each one carried a large weapon, nearly as tall as its bearer. The thick wooden handles were decorated with leather and carved markings, meaningless to those outside orc society. A thick axe head protruded from one side, wide enough to chop a human in half with a single blow, and a heavy mallet stuck from the other.

Nezial had never seen an orc before. He knew their race only from the stories he'd heard and the books he'd read. These creatures, while large and brutish in appearance, were much more than they appeared. He couldn't help but wonder how much timber these three could clear if they turned their axes to labor rather than combat. *This forest probably wouldn't last long against an army of lumberers.*

But such tasks were rarely mentioned in his books. The orcs, even the brown ones, lived in a constant state of battle, whether with other races or among their many tribes. Over the past thousand years, they'd focused their ferocity against the myrkalfar. Holding the woodland race responsible for their ostracism to the north. Nezial gave himself a light slap, forcing him to abandon his entire recollection of orcish history.

The orcs spoke their guttural, deep tongue, unaware they were being stalked.

He quietly watched, unsure how to approach them. If he wasn't careful, the wrong action could result in his death. Coming to a decision he stepped from the dense trees and revealed himself, ensuring he had enough distance if they decided to charge. Dropping the hood of his cloak, the sun beamed brilliantly through the thin canopy, burning his flesh instantly. He forced the pain aside, hoping it wouldn't show to the proud warrior race.

The largest of the three grunted, raising his axe to a defensive position.

The younger two followed suit.

"I'm not here to fight." Nezial announced, contorting his tongue to form the brutish words. "I know of your feud with the alfar and I do not wish to interrupt that. I do however need to travel deep within these lands. If you can help me, I will aid you against them."

The large orc lowered his axe slightly, but kept it ready. Replying in Undercommon his deep voice echoed, having trouble forming the words around his tusk. "Why I need your help?"

This commander was much more than he'd initially thought. It he under the language of the Underdark, he was traveled and educated. That spoke volumes about the warrior race. His mind racing, Nezial continued, sticking to orcish. "Because— I have problems with the alfar, same as you. And I have something you don't." He let a smirk come to his face.

The large orc cocked his head slightly. "And what would that be?"

Nezial lifted his arm, facing the palm of his hand toward the trees.

The two younger orcs jumped in fear, seeing a cone of flame burst from the young dreualfar's hand. It sprayed out, engulfing one of the large trees. In a heartbeat, the ancient wood was completely ablaze. The autumn-brown leaves turned black and rolled up to be carried off by the wind.

Nezial knew it wouldn't take much to ignite the entire forest. Keeping his hand pointed at the tree, he whispered a different incantation. A jet of water shot forth, soaking the fiery tree and drowning the flame to little more than a cinder.

The large orc smiled, his lips stretched tight around his tusks. "Maybe we have use for you. Prove your worth and we'll help you reach your destination."

Forcefully returned the smile, Nezial hoped he could trust the brutish creatures. It would be dishonorable for them to betray him, honor being the one law their culture held most sacred. Still, he would have to be careful. Trust must be earned, never given.

Late into the day, the group traveled deep into the forests heart. The air was thick and sticky from the lingering heat of the warming climate. They followed the river as closely as they could. It cooled the air and kept them on track, though it had to be abandoned some hours back due to the increasing number of alfaren outposts and patrols.

Nezial trekked along behind the orcs. He was growing tired of their rapid pace and refusal to take a break. He couldn't blame them. Their numbers meant they could be found much easier than a lone traveler. But it didn't change the fact that they were conditioned for such strenuous travel, where as he was still adjusting to it.

The orcs led him to a well-traveled path deep in the forest heart.

"This is Evinwood. We have to keep our eyes open now. The alfar here aren't like the others we've encountered. Here, they travel in large groups and will attack on sight."

"I thought we were already in Evinwood."

"The alfar like to claim the whole forest. But no. The southern forests belong to my people." The orc leader demanded.

Nezial nodded his understanding to the lead orc. The alfar they'd encountered hadn't offered much resistance, being eliminated before they could call for help. But that didn't mean it wasn't difficult rooting them out. His magic had proven invaluable in their advancement, having caught the scouts off guard. But as far as he was concerned, it was more a matter of luck than skill. He felt a rumble in his stomach. If the myrkalfar were more organized in these parts, what chance did they have to make it through without having to deal with the whole populace?

Nezial was beginning to feel a strange sense of belonging, something he'd never truly felt before. He didn't know if it was because the orcs so far had respected his abilities, or simply because he was traveling with them as an equal. Either way, he was glad to have the company. He still didn't know if he could trust them, playing every possible scenario in his head. But trust and respect didn't have to be mutually exclusive. *I'll be prepared if they turn against me. If they don't, I'll still be ready.*

They traveled for nearly four days, leaving the ruins of Eldarian just under two days from their grasps.

Nezial couldn't help but think of everything that stood between him and the knowledge he sought. *Trees, alfar, orcs, unknown obstacles, vicious animals— Something's not right!* Pausing, he searched the trees.

The orcs marched through the forest, unaware of their companion's halt.

Three distinct swishing sounds echoed from the trees overhead, followed by just as many thuds. Nezial tried to call out, but it was too late. One of the younger orcs dropped his war axe and fell to his knees. The heavy mallet smashed hard into the ground, landing with the axe head pointing straight up. Three bloody arrowheads protruded through newly formed holes in the back of his hide breastplate. Small streams of blood ran from each of them. The lethally wounded orc fell face first to the ground, his head landing directly on the sharp edge of his axe. It split in two.

Taking a defensive stance, the orcs scanned the forest in search of their unseen attackers.

Nezial knew he wouldn't be able to warn his comrades, nor locate the alfar without help. Closing his eyes, he recalled a spell he'd learned from one of his many books. Finding the words, he looked into the tree tops and slammed his hands together.

A wave of energy expanded away from him. Like a strong wind, it blew debris in all directions. Trees ripped themselves from the ground, through huge mounds of dirt into the air. Forcing its way past the orcs, it knocked them prone.

Nezial watched his sonic blast clear the forest in all directions for nearly fifty feet, leaving the once hidden alfar to pick themselves up from the forest floor. He counted over a dozen of the long-eared, majestic creatures scrambling back to their feet.

The orcs recovered, gripping their weapons to slaughter the exposed alfar. They rushed to the right side of the now cleared area, bringing their weapons down as quickly as possible. The closest alfar was cut in two before his sword left its sheath. The superior numbers had to be whittled down or they would be overrun.

Nezial saw the anger on the large orcs face, certain some of it was directed at him, having been affected by his magics.

The large orc swung his war axe, crushing one of the alfar between the heavy mallet and a toppled tree. The distorted body broke against the roots, flying uncontrollably through the air.

The younger orc took position behind his commander, keeping his back protected by his own. He swung fiercely cutting down another, dancing as he'd been trained.

The pair tore into the still recovering alfar, hacking and slashing at all within their reach.

Nezial looked around. The orcs had the largest portion covered, but there were still several of the slender, would-be assassins all around them. He saw a group to his left, their weapons drawn and headed toward him. He thrust his hands forward, sending energy into the air. It wrapped around the approaching group, solidifying and forcing them together. Contorting his fingers he made the proper gestures and recited the words, calling the power to him. A cone of bright orange and yellow flame shot from his fingertips, the same spell he'd displayed to the orcs upon their meeting.

Screams echoed from the flaming figures, slowly being devoured in their prison. They ran into each other desperately trying to escape the invisible walls containing them. Continuing to move after death they crumbled into a heap of charred meat, nothing left but smoldering bone and soupy gore.

Nezial scanned the area. The few remaining alfar joined the battle against the orcs, attempting to surround them.

Drawing his sabre, Nezial stealthily moved behind the group, hoping to avoid the broken branches and debris on the forest floor. His plan would fail if he couldn't remain silent. He moved into position and thrust his sword into action. A series of quick slashes and stabs laid waste to them, cutting the remaining alfar down before they realized his presence.

The battle was over quick, leaving the dead to litter the forest floor.

The large orc glared at him, choosing his words before speaking. "I'm grateful you exposed their location, but I expect warning before you act. I cannot anticipate chaotic decisions." His deep voice echoed between breaths. He was exhausted, but clearly trying to hide it.

Nezial felt regret hearing the commander's words, but it was meaningless. Forced to make the same decision, he had no doubt he would have done nothing different. "I'm sorry I caught you off guard, but I couldn't think of a better way to force them out of hiding. It was that or risk losing the element of surprise."

The old orc placed his large hand on Nezial's shoulder, the size made him look small in comparison. "Overall, I'm glad to have you on my side." He allowed a bestial smile to tighten around his tusk.

They piled the bodies in the center of the clearing, away from the now shattered trees and foliage.

Nezial held his hand over the pile, channeling his energy. The bodies burst into flame, burning to ash in a matter of minutes, leaving nothing but a few charred remains.

Entangled vines and vicious barbs stretched from tree to tree, far removed from any remnants of a trail. The overgrown brush was nearly untraversable, slowing them to a near stop. The orcs heaved their axes, tearing into the brambles more than cutting. Several hours passed, carrying them long into night. The moon loomed overhead blocked out by the thick canopies, leaving them in near darkness.

The three continued onward, their eyes accustomed to the lack of light.

Nezial studied the faint outline beyond the trees. It looked like the top portion of an ancient temple, but it was still too far to tell for certain. Even at this distance it towered over everything around it, leaving him to wonder how such a landmark could remain unexplored for so long. *It's not like its location is unknown. So why has there always been such mystery surrounding it?* One thing was certain. Those questions would be answered very soon.

They traveled into morning, watching the sun illuminate the forgotten city before their eyes. They passed into the lands that were once streaming with his kind, the dalari before them. Nezial stared in wonder, excited to be so close to his ancestral home. There was something about it that called to him. Something that made him feel powerful. Something that made him feel as if he could snuff out the sun with a single thought. The power was so intoxicating he almost hadn't realized the absence of all life in this once populated site. Listening, he could hear nothing but the sounds of his companions. Not even the chirp of a bird nor the fiddle of a cricket sounded in the desolate city, leaving an eerie silence over the dead lands.

They continued in, chopping their way through the overgrown brambles. The dry wood cracked and broke into several pieces, unnerving them further. It was so different from the resilient vegetation they'd traveled through moments before.

Nezial could see the forest edge just ahead. Excitement filled him, growing with each step toward the large clearing.

They crossed into the cleared landscape, lost in the sight before them. A dark shadow loomed overhead blocking out the sunlight, leaving a perpetual gloom. Several ruined structures towered throughout the city, left to the elements. Many of the large stone structures had fallen, nearly buried by time and dirt. The ground was barren, free of weed and grass. Only dry, cracked earth covered the floor in all directions. Even the trees branching over into the clearing were dead, their limbs petrified and jagged.

"Welcome to Eldarian, the birthplace of my people." Nezial passed the orcs, leaving them to take in the sight. He thought it strange considering the amount of overgrowth not a hundred feet away, yet the city itself was void of all life save for his group. He walked toward the center, eyes locked on the one structure that remained untouched by time and elements.

The orcs followed slowly, their axes ready for the unexpected. Such a place was unnatural. It was best to be prepared if anything remained.

The tomb stood tall, jutting into the sky like some kind of dark temple. It was made of black colored stone, appearing to have sprouted from the ground. A dark cloud wrapped around the peak of the spire, hiding it from view. The occasional bolt of lightning flickered from within, but the its absence remained steadfast, entrapped by the gloomy shadows blanketing the area.

Nezial watched the other clouds drift past. *Strange that one defies!* He approached the thick stone cover embedded in the side wall. Several chiseled symbols marred the obelisk, half worn away by time. Running his fingers over them, he felt the rough texture and indentations. They grew bright beneath his touch, burning to the surface, as if they'd been there forever, only hidden from view. Understanding their meaning he read aloud, listening to the story flow from him. "Tides clashed against the shore, unleashing new revelations. In that time, the youngest was split, as all things are. Creation sobbed, her tears unheard. Only the three could restore what was lost. But ignorance is a curse, even among gods. In their opacity, they sealed their fates. Beyond this door, lies their greatest betrayal."

The ground roared and shook violently. The vibrations rattled and pulled against the spire, tearing the earth at the base. A crack splintered through the stone, shooting out like a spider web. It fell to pieces, littering the damaged ground beneath it. Obscured by dust, the outline of a large doorway remained.

Nezial fanned the dust from his face, hoping to get a better look at the sealed door. Waving his hand, he let his magic flow forth to embrace the obviously heavy stone. To his surprise, it didn't work. He was certain the magic had taken effect, but the door didn't budge. He placed his hands against the seal, feeling his magic flow into the dark structure. "That's odd?"

"What's wrong?" The orc commander watched, uneasy over the entire situation.

"It's my magic. It's like the stone is absorbing it. I've heard a few myths of such an ore, but never found evidence to its existence. That is, until now." He pressed lightly, feeling the seemingly heavy slab rotate with ease. Studying its construction, he guessed it was pinned and counter weighted. *How else would something so heavy move so freely?* "I need to go inside alone. When I return, we'll continue to your destination."

The old orc nodded his acknowledgment and turned to watch the perimeter.

Nezial stepped through the doorway and into the shadows. Instantly, his eyes felt better. The bright sunlight had left him with a mild headache for days now. The darkness seemed to have relieved the pressure. He marched through the narthex and looked around the open chamber.

Several doors lined both sides of the room. The ceiling was beyond sight, but surely the height of this place wasn't wasted on the three layers of balconies he could see. Crossing the nave, he reached a shrine at the far side of the room. The symbols held a familiar presence, but he couldn't place them. Reaching into his satchel he retrieved the broken amulet, feeling an energy that wasn't there before. It led him to one of the side rooms, containing a stairwell and little else. The amulet nearly buzzing with energy, he stepped onto the stairs. His vision faded, leaving him in total darkness. "Um— This is new?"

No sooner than the words left his lips, both sides of the ancient passageway flared to life. Every several steps a sconce was secured to the wall. A glowing purple flame danced from each one, omitting all heat. Stepping into the unnatural light, he traveled down for what felt like forever. The narrow passageway opened into a single chamber, revealing a large statue standing in the center.

The figure was shaped like a man. It was wearing heavy armor and a shiny purple cloak, made from some kind of living mineral. The thick, jagged armor was molded perfectly, covered in places by the cloak. The raised hood concealed much of the facial features, obscuring the figure's race. Its hands rested on the pommel of a large sword, the lower portion buried beneath the stone base. It peered down, its lifeless eyes watching the entrance of the chamber.

Nezial approached. Looking under the hood he tried to see any detail of who or what it may have been. An overwhelming sense of dread washed over him. Unable to turn away, he stared into the figures consuming eyes. An unbearable desire to flee overcame him, but he was too scared to move. His will consumed he forced himself to break contact, forcing the dreaded desires to abandon him. Avoiding eye contact, he noticed something hidden beneath the living stone cloak. A pendant was dangling below its neck, as if it were held by a chain. But no such device was present. He moved closer, attempting to get a better look. The sight of the broken sigil shocked him. The familiar emblem called out, begging to be rejoined. His clenched fist raised of its own accord, displaying the broken piece dangling from the thin, black chain. It twisted and aligned, revealing the complete symbol to him.

Ripping free of his hold, it sealed itself against the other piece, becoming whole.

Curiosity gripped him. Nezial stepped toward the statue and lifted the assembled icon. It came free. He heard a whisper in his mind. *Put it on!*

Cautiously, he laid the thin chain over his neck, letting the sigil relax against his chest. He wasn't sure what was going to happen, but the urge had to have come from somewhere. Glancing up, he was much closer to the figure than he'd realized. He tried to move, but it was too late.

The statue lunged forward and grabbed him.

He struggled against the large stone gauntlets clenched to the sides of his head. He could feel warm blood running from its grasp. It pulled him closer, forcing him to stare into those cold, lifeless eyes. A purple glow burned into him, melting away his mind with each passing moment. He flailed his legs, trying to reach the ground. He couldn't feel it. He tried to pry against the stone fingers. They were too tight. His body betrayed him. His resistance drained, he fell limp.

A pain unlike any other shot through his head, dwarfing the melting purple light by comparison. The chamber, the statue, the glow, all of it faded from view, leaving him a calming serenity to settle over him. Even the pain he felt burning throughout his body took the form of pleasure.

He was lying broken in the desert sands. Two extremely powerful beings towered over him. He felt a kinship toward them. A connection he'd never known. They were brothers. His brothers. He was beaten, unable to stand. His mind rushed with the desire to lash out, desiring to kill the two beings, both frail looking old men. But he also loved them. Why would he raise a finger against them?

The older was well dressed, wearing robes black as night. He held his weight against the long handle of a wickedly shaped scythe made from bone and steel. His bright blue eyes fell on him, full of conflict. They showed disappointment and support.

The other held himself against a tall staff, weathered in places, but constantly renewed. His face was wrinkled by time, his eyes full of youth known only to an infant. He couldn't help but feel lost in them. The bronze robes surrounding his ancient form were trimmed in a black stone-like material. He could feel its effects, pulling at him like the stone door.

"Ozmodius, Osirus, my brothers, nothing you do can stop me. I will return and when I do, your followers will be lost to you." Nezial heard the words escape his mouth but he didn't know why he said them.

The two men looked down on him. He could feel their thoughts. They smelled of remorse and pity.

A strange energy grabbed hold of him, pulling him from their presence. He tried to fight it, but it was too strong. He closed his eyes, screaming his anger at his brother's betrayal. Opening them, the pull disappeared. He stared out over a dark new world, watching legions of followers drop to their knees at the mere mention of his name. Though it wasn't his name. It was the name of his god, Izaryle. It was good they knew their place. Unfortunately there were many in the south that evaded his influence. They would suffer like no other had.

He felt the power flow through him. Spreading his wings, he shot into the heavens, ascending to his rightful godly stature. Flying over graying clouds, he soared to the south. Positioning himself over the heretics, he focused his will toward their destruction. Conflicted emotions filled him. He wanted to kill them. But he also wanted them to live. To his surprise, his magics wouldn't obey. Like they were trapped between realms. He could still feel them, but they couldn't affect the mortal planes. Screaming his discontent, he cursed his brothers one last time. If he was going to crush these infidels, his followers would have to do it for him. But they deserved a fair chance at redemption. They were, after all his children.

The world shifted again. The lands were decimated. Armies of gray orcs marched through the people of the realm, slaughtering any and all within their path. They were commanded by men clad in black robes and armor. Several strands of a wicked purple and black energy flowed from him and into the armored men below. They redirected the energy into his will. No, not his will. Their will, but conveyed by their commanders as his will. He was having trouble understanding. There were so many conflicting emotions. Returning his focus to the soldiers, he could tell who held complete faith in his divine right and who doubted his presence. The strands couldn't lie. Within minutes the world was his leaving only the persistent southlands beyond his rule, protected by a collection of alfar, men, and dwarves.

Again the world shifted, and again, each time filling him with knowledge. He witnessed an eternity of events, watching each one as if he was the source. He felt his sanity slipping away, replaced by bits of knowledge. Knowledge too great for any living being to possess. And suddenly, as quickly as he'd disappeared, he was back standing over a crumbled statue at his feet.

He fell to the stone floor, feeling the last bits of information settle into place. The fading purple glow of the seeming living mineral disappeared from sight. It was all inside him now. All that power. All that magic. It was all his. No, not all of it. Nezial took a deep breath, seeing a single piece of the glowing mineral intact and holding strong. He reached down, picking the shard from the rubble. Inspecting it, it appeared to have been split from the statue years before as a light layer of moss was beginning to claim the rough break. He felt power rush through him, flowing into the fractured piece. Shifting before his eyes the jagged piece elongated and thinned, retaining its wavy curves. A moment later, a purple blade with a black hilt sat idle in his hand. Admiring the kris dagger, he felt the remnant energy flow through the blade, trapped inside the material. Fingering the hilt, he spotted a broken setting where a gemstone once rested. *Now that's annoying. Why give me the key to limitless power only to have it crippled by an incomplete bridge?* Nevertheless, it belonged to him, and he to it.

Urgency called to him. He glanced at the mirror, knowing what secrets remained on the other side. Recalling his purpose, Nezial shook the thought from his mind. He had to find the other one. Izaryle would be freed. Stuffing the dagger into his satchel, he turned and rushed up the stairs.

The two orcs waited patiently outside the dark temple, looking into the deserted city around them. The little sunlight that pierced the dark clouds faded when their companion stepped from the chamber.

Nezial locked eyes on the orcs, patiently awaiting him. They seemed much smaller than he recalled. He glanced at the darkening sky. It felt good to stand in the sun without the constant pain. Dropping his hood, he felt the sparse rays on his flesh.

The larger orc stepped toward him. "You look different. Find what yo—" His words fell short.

Nezial placed his hand on the old orc's breastplate. A smile crept to his lips. The thick hide began to contort and turn black under his touch.

The orc screamed, feeling his body burning beneath the armor. He tried in vain to get the straps loose, but they burnt him further. He fell to his knees with the loss of muscle. He tried to take a final breath, but it would not come. Falling forward, his charred body crashed into the ground with an explosion of ash. A discolored husk was all that remained of him.

Nezial glanced at the younger orc.

He stared in horror, watching his commander's body blow away in the wind. He raised his axe and charged the traitorous dreualfar. Bringing the thick blade down with all his strength in that single blow, he hoped to cut the mage in half.

Nezial's smile grew wider at the inexperienced orc's attempt. Clapping his hands together, he caught the thick cutting blade moments before it would have bit into his skull.

The orc stared in confusion. *How can such a small creature stop the strength of an orc?* His shocked expression turned to worry. Fear crept into him, feeling the pain take hold of his arms. He tried to release the axe, but his hands wouldn't comply. He felt it flow into his chest. The orc watched his flesh turn to stone before his eyes. It passed into his legs and moments later he was fully engulfed, vision locked on the smug dreualfar less than an inch from the edge of his axe.

Nezial looked into the fading sun. He took comfort in its inability to harm him. With a final glance at the eternal orc, he turned and disappeared, leaving the living statue all alone in the abandoned city.

The young orc silently wept, unable to give his fear voice. He stared blankly at the open tomb wondering if he would ever see another living being.

The dark passageways were full of dreualfar, each one avoiding him. They cowered when he was near, moving away as quick as possible, keeping watch until he was out of sight.

Nezial marched through the catacombs. The smell of dirt and fear caressed his nostrils. He wasn't sure why they feared him. *Maybe due to the power that flows through my veins? It doesn't matter, I have a job to do and they'll help me or be swept away by my prosperity.* He rounded the narrow corridor, spotting the elder's chamber just ahead. Approaching the sealed slabs, he released his power.

The heavy stone exploded, leaving the chamber door open for entry.

The elders were sitting in their chairs, surprised by the intrusion. Many jumped to their feet, watching him storm into the room.

"Nezial, what's the meaning of this interruption! Do you think these actions will go unpunished?" Elder Khronis jumped in a fit of rage at the intrusion.

"I've returned as I said I would." A wicked smirk formed on his lips.

Nadilia smiled. "I see you've succeeded in your task. This is good, I'm glad that you've accepted the mantle set before you."

Nezial felt a fondness for the vicious old woman. She was just as dangerous as the rest of them, but she had a vision similar to his own. The rest of the elders were petty and acquisitive. He had no purpose for them. "I've discovered a great many things since I last stood before you. I now know who I'm searching for and what I must do to free him."

The chamber filled with whispers, each one attempting to conceal their thoughts from him.

Nezial found it amusing, the efforts they took to hide their motives. The attempt was fleeting, he knew what they were going to say before they did, but it was still entertaining. They were schemers, each one scheming against him, all except Nadilia. The old witch sat quietly, waiting for him to continue.

"It might behoove you to know that I've also learned something none of you were aware of." Nezial interjected, silencing their whispers. "Well, that's not entirely true. I've learned a great many things none of you were aware of. But there's one thing in particular I wish to share." He looked over the feeble, so called, Elders, letting his words sink into their ears. "You see, I'm not the scared little pup I was when I left. You might say I've matured. I've gained more knowledge than this entire council combined and I now have the power to escape age. These two details have made me more than any of you will ever be." His hand danced, creating an expanding disc of purple energy over the void beneath him. Pacing far beyond the narrow platform, he added to his insubordination. "I guess what I'm trying to say is, it's not me, it's you. By the rites of our people, I hereby disband this council of elders." Nezial gave a sadistic smile to each of them. "You're dismissed!"

The once whispering elders stood, outraged by his insolence. As one, they demanded his respect. Of all their voices, one in particular rose above the rest.

"What's the meaning of this betrayal?"

Nezial glared at Khronis. His taunts and mockery lingered in his memory. "The meaning of this, old man, is you're no longer needed to lead our people." The wide smile held steady on his face. Snapping his fingers, Nezial watched the inflated ego of the abusive elder take hold. Khronis' head grew nearly twice its original size. With a sickening pop it exploded, sending bits of skull and brain matter against the wall behind him.

The elders, save for Nadilia, panicked, rushing for their personal exits, trying to escape their doomed fates.

Nezial slaughtered them, one by one, taking pleasure in each kill. All but the eldest laid dead on the cavern floor. Appearing on the high-rise platform, he approached the woman, still sitting calmly in her chair. "Nadilia, you're a smart woman. Serve my purposes and you'll be around much longer than you intended. The commanders are loyal to you. Bring me their obedience. We march for Maradar Keep within the month." Nezial turned, stepping over the bodies littering the floor. "Oh, and Nadilia, I know you were the one responsible for sending me the book. You have my thanks for that. But just so we're clear, I'm the sole ruler of our people. I'll remain so until someone emerges to take that status from me."

Nadilia nodded, her expression solemn and absolute. "As it should be, My Lord!"

Chapter XI
Booty and the Beast

The sweet scent of decay lingered outside the wide cavern entrance. Sunlight beamed through the trees, melting the light layer of snow at the mouth. The white contrast against the black, rocky wreath ebbed warning. Five figures looked upon the entrance, lost in the darkness within.

"What do you reckon's in there?" Sean asked, fumbling with the crates stacked neatly inside the small wagon.

"Treasure. Lots of treasure." Their leader replied, hiding his fear behind his excitement. "Krenin, go on in and check it out. Let us know what you see."

"Why Krenin have to go first?" The half-orc questioned, studying the nervous humans.

"Cause unlike us, you can see in the dark. Now get your ass in there and tell us what you see." Kelly shot an angry glare at the brute. "Unless you're scared." He quickly added.

The half-orc puffed his chest at the challenge. *How dare they accuse me of scared?* "Krenin not scared of anything!" Raising his axe, he marched toward the opening and disappeared inside.

They others watched in anticipation, awaiting word, be it screams of terror or otherwise.

A moment later, Krenin stepped back into the light, axe dangling limply from his side. "Nothing in here!" He shouted, hearing the echo reverberate around him. He turned and stepped back into the shadows.

The others, still on edge, followed after, guiding the single horse and dilapidated wagon inside.

The scent grew stronger at the mouth, carried by the warm air exiting the cave. The snow at the entrance had melted long before the rest, erasing any evidence of other trespassers. One by one they stepped into the darkness.

Krenin watched his friends slowly make their way forward. *Ha, they call me scared. Looks like they the scared ones.* He glanced at the scattered remains lying about the moist floor, mostly animal carcasses, but many were unidentifiable to his eyes. He couldn't help but feel small compared to the deep gouge marks along the stone walls and floor. "Look like claw marks." He stated to no one in particular.

"What?" Sean jumped, searching for the half-orc in the void. "I can't see anything. James, light a torch." He rubbed his scar. It always seemed to hurt when he was nervous.

Krenin saw the first bright sparks ignite from one of the men's flint. He shielded his eyes, knowing the pain that would follow if he didn't. The torch flared to life, illuminating the dank room. The humans stood relatively close to one another watching every nook and cranny in search of the most evil of foes. Wandering near the far wall, Krenin glanced back at his companions. "What made them ain't here." He assured.

Searching for the marks he was referencing, Kelly froze, spotting the deep scores. "Just keep your axe ready. We don't want nothin' jumpin' out at us."

"You the boss, Kelly." Krenin raised the dull weapon, wandering deeper into the underground chamber. He needed to keep the light to his back so it didn't affect his vision. The shadows grew dark, fading in the distance. He followed the rough wall, realizing it was a tunnel, twice his width, but nearly a foot shorter than him. Craning his neck, he slowly made his way along the passage, pausing at the entrance of the next room. Before him laid pile upon pile of gold and silver. He couldn't imagine ever seeing that much loot in one place. Yet here it was, waiting to be claimed. "Found the treasure!" His deep voice echoed along the corridor, resounding much louder than he'd intended.

"Quiet down you idiot. Last thing we need is visitors when we're tryin' to get out of here."

"Sorry, Kelly!" He shouted back, forgetting what he'd just been told.

Kelly spoke just over a whisper. "First chance you get, get rid of him. Every damn job, he finds some way to fuck it up."

Sean nodded his understanding. "Consider it done."

They rounded the corner, finding the half-orc lost in the sight. "Well, don't just stand there, you oaf. Get to loading the crates. The wagon can't fit back here. Someone has to carry it." James jabbed him in the ribs, extending an empty sack.

Krenin lumbered forward and scooped handfuls of coin and jewels into the bag. It quickly filled to the top. Setting it aside he loaded another, and another. Before long he had nearly twelve full bags.

A deep roar shook the walls, causing the unstable piles to vibrate and tumble downward.

"What the hell was that?" Sean asked, ducking low, as if somehow it would shield him.

"Sound like a roar." Krenin raised his axe, searching the enclosed ceiling.

"No shit! Where'd it come from?" Kelly drew his sword, leaning in to whisper. "Now's your chance. Use him as a distraction. The rest of us can get out of here with what we can carry."

Sean nodded and turned to face the half-orc. "Krenin, help me get these bags to the wagon. We need to move before that thing finds us."

Krenin hung his axe from its leather strap and heaved four of the bags at once. He ducked under the low ceiling and waddled toward the cart. A sharp pain erupted in the back of his head. Unable to turn around to see what hit him, another blow connected, dropping him to his knees. The bags spilled out, echoing throughout the chamber. He glanced back, seeing his friend standing behind him with one of the half full bags, ready for another swing. "Why?" The bag collided a third time, busting open against the side of his face. Krenin collapsed to the floor.

"He's down. Help me tie him up before he comes to."

The others rushed in, securing the half-orc. Dragging him into the treasure room they bound and shackled him against the wall, sinking the spikes deep into the stone.

Another roar echoed through the room, much closer than the first. They froze, unable to move from the fear of what crawled through the opening.

A wispy, serpentine voice surrounded them. "You trespass in the home of Autzumo. You seek to claim my treasures? Tell me why I should allow you to leave here with a single piece."

"I— I—." Kelly shuddered over the words, unable to get his thoughts out.

Sean rushed forward, letting fear fuel his words. "We caught this trespasser trying to sneak away with your treasure. Had we not stopped him, he might have made away with a large majority of it. Surely this is worth our freedom and a small amount to claim as our own?"

Autzumo reared his scaly head in laughter. "It took three of you to stop one trespasser? I find that unlikely. Even if he is a half-breed." His laughter subsided. "But I suppose I can let you have one trinket, for your valiant efforts."

His wicked scar stretched across his face, contorting into an awkward grin. Feeling eased by the young dragon's words, Sean glanced at the piles around him. Eyes searching for his prize, an odd, black orb, inlaid with golden runes grabbed his attention. He carefully lifted the orb, displaying it to the young black. "I choose this one."

"That's a fine choice. The Stone of Rezerik, First King of the Dreualfar. It's said to contain his emotion, cast away into the stone in order to lead his people to victory. Take it. It's yours."

Sean greedily stuffed the fist-sized object into his pouch and glanced at the others, still frozen where they stood.

The scaly head shot forth with lightning speed, snapping shut around the greedy human. Autzumo's thick, jagged teeth tore into flesh ripping his frail body in half before his screams were silenced. Swallowing the top half, he whipped around to face the others. "Who else would like a piece of my treasure?" A wispy green mist rolled gently from his nostrils, forming into a thick pool around them. It floated through the air like a heavy fog, collecting at their feet and engulfing their bodies.

Kelly felt the poison burn its way down his throat. He coughed, seeing blood escape in clotted chunks. His knees hit the ground, sending coin scattering about. His vision was fading quickly. Watching the black-horned head hover over him, its gaping maw opened, revealing hundreds of needle sharp teeth and a thick, forked tongue. It flicked once and snapped around him. A sharp pain erupted in his numbing body. And then he felt nothing.

Krenin awoke to the rumble of stone and the clinking of coin. He tried to move, found the task uncooperative. Opening his eyes, sight of the large beast filled him with dread. It was sitting on its hind haunches, sprawled out like a chubby orcling sorting his favorite pebbles.

The piles of gold were moved, organized and stacked high once again. The creature plucked a single coin between his deadly talons, inspecting it thoroughly. Laying it to rest atop one of the piles he grabbed another. "Did you steal my treasure?"

The voice was unlike any he'd heard before. Realizing the question was directed at him, Krenin responded. "Define 'steal'."

"Did you leave here with my treasure?" The dragon laid another coin down, inspecting another. His head didn't so much as glance in the direction of the subdued half-orc.

"No. Was going to. But didn't get that far."

"Then explain to me why I have four-thousand and seventy-two pieces missing." The dragon shot up, scattering several piles from their neatly organized stacks. He paused inches from the half-breed's face, awaiting an answer. "I could kill you in a moment's notice. I wouldn't think twice about it. But your friends and their horse have temporarily sated my appetite." Autzumo backed away, keeping his beady, dark eyes locked on the half-orc. "I've counted my treasure several times. I do not make mistakes. Tell me where my treasure is and I may let you live."

Krenin pulled against the irons, hoping he could dislodge the stakes. "They buried it at camp. Only one bag."

"Good." The dragon reached into the now mess, pulling a single, clear gem from the treasure. Holding it in front of his face, he gently blew. A cloud formed inside the clear prism, displaying an array of color. "Do you see this gem?"

"Yes."

"I've trapped your life essence in it. I'm going to release you and you're going to retrieve my treasure. Bring it back to me and I'll give you this gem. Your life will be your own, to do with what you please. But trust me when I say if you skip out on a single piece, not only will I know, but I'll crush this gem and your life along with it."

Krenin watched the beast for a moment, considering his options. *Can he do that? Nobody has that power. He don't know where it is. Wouldn't ask if he did.* Defiance in his voice, he made his decision. "Crush it. You not have power over Krenin. Krenin the only one who knows where treasure is. You kill me, you never find it."

A deep roar echoed through the cave. "Insolent half-orc. You'll bring it to me. Days, weeks, it doesn't matter. You're stuck here. Eventually you'll get hungry enough that you'll agree, or you'll starve to death. It makes no difference to me." Autzumo flung the stone across the room and spun around.

Krenin felt a breeze wash over him. He was blinded for the briefest moment. Glancing around, only the tip of a spiked tail could be seen, slithering out the small tunnel.

Night had fallen on the town of Aldridge. The lanterns were lit and the usual fog had rolled in.

Gareth stepped out of the general store, cinching the leather strap on his overstuffed duffle. A coiled rope and several sized bear traps dangled from the side. He tossed the sack over his shoulder and turned toward the inn.

A familiar face caught his attention. The warrior from the tavern skirted across the road, headed for the edge of town. He looked young, almost too young. But the expression on his face said more than enough. He'd see things most wished to forget. That was seasoned enough in his experience. He seemed small in stature. The massive great sword strapped to his back didn't help that appearance. Perhaps he'd not yet reached his adult years? Or perhaps he'd simply chosen a life he wasn't physically built for. He was of fair height, though short by human standard, by a few inches at least. And he wasn't overly heavy. His body just didn't fit his gear. Like he was a warrior made for finesse, but for some unknown reason, he relied on strength.

Gareth watched him. There was something familiar, something he couldn't place. Deciding silently, he strode for the boy. "Oy, lad!"

Kane stopped, turning to see the broad man headed toward him. He waited patiently for him to reach talking distance, not that he had anything to talk about.

"You any good with that sword?" Gareth asked, surveying him.

"Depends on your purpose, you may find out first hand." Kane stated coldly, hoping he wasn't going to have to fight.

A smirk found his lips. "Easy son, I've no quarrel with you. I'm looking for a few men to assist in the slaying of a dragon. I thought you might be up for the challenge."

Kane studied the man, recalling him from the tavern. He carried a cutlass on his side and his gray armor was adorned with several pieces of metal. The leather was thick and looked to be finely crafted at one point, though it was worn and weak from years of misuse. Nevertheless, he wore it well and it would protect as designed. What was more curious was that red aura he'd seen earlier. It persisted after the drink had worn off. There had to be something more to this man than met the eye. Magic or otherwise, he was unlike any he'd seen before. "I suppose you're going to tell me to meet you at the edge of town at first light?"

Gareth nodded. "You've seen the poster then? Very well, if I see you there, it'll be a welcome sight. If not, safe travels!" He offered salute and turned the way he'd come.

"Hey!"

Gareth froze, glancing over his shoulder and the young man.

"The name's Kane. And I'll be there."

"Good!" Gareth continued on his way, stepping into the rolling mist.

Kane watched the large man disappear, leaving him to his solitude. Returning to his path, he made for the edge of town. Finding a small clearing inside the tree line, he dug out a pit and lined it with rock. Piling tinder, he struck his flint and watched the sparks dance to life. The twigs began to smolder and moments later, a small fire flared up. He stacked slightly larger sticks around, hoping it'd burn for a few hours. He didn't need something he'd have to tend to in the middle of the night. But he also didn't want to draw too much attention to himself. Mostly he just wanted to keep warm for the cool, autumn night.

Pulling his bedroll free of the pack, he unrolled it. Stabbing his sword into the ground, he unbuckled the metal armor and draped it over the hilt, allowing it to serve as a makeshift stand. Lastly, he tossed his clothes over the polished metal to prevent the morning dew from rusting. Lying down, he curled up under his blanket and drifted off to sleep.

The mist was thick, obscuring sight beyond a few feet away. Even the buildings of the well-populated town were difficult to see in the dense blanket. Lanterns hung from posts, attempting to illuminate the streets but they offered little more than a faint glow in the early morning.

The sun was threatening to peek over the horizon when Gareth, Malakai, and Ravion made their way to the town's edge.

Kane stood, great sword in front of him. The tip was stuck in the dirt, allowing him to rest against the pommel. His armor had an unnatural glow in the heavy fog, proudly displaying the coiled dragon engraved in the belly. It stood in stark contrast to the polished chrome breastplate. He stood erect flipping his sword up to his shoulder, watching the others arrived.

"Good morning." Gareth offered, coming into sight of the young man. "I'd hoped a few others would have shown, but it seems not all men are cut out for the slaying of dragons."

The others inspected Kane, as he did them.

Gareth offered introductions. "Kane, this is Malakai."

Malakai lifted his sabre in salute.

"And this is Ravion. Gentlemen, meet Kane. It seems he's gonna' be our meat shield during this little adventure."

Ravion locked his gaze on the young warrior's aura. He had to be at least part dalari. It was present, but faded, a strange attribute of his heritage. There were no half-breeds as far as he knew. The dalari blood always seemed to overpower the mixture. *This man could prove useful.* He gave a gentle bow using his sword to salute, allowing his knowledge of nobility and grace to flourish in the morning light.

Kane returned the greetings, distracted by the large pike in the bald man's hand.

Gareth noticed his gaze and offered explanation. "The beast we're going after, while young, is still a deadly opponent. This'll help us pin 'em down without getting too close. If you'd like I can fetch you one as well.

Kane chuckled. "No, thank you. I'm quite comfortable with my sword."

"As you wish. Well, this beasty ain't gonna' slay itself. We'd best be on our way before the sun tells every creature between here and there of our intent."

The group set off into the dense forest. The morning mist was still extremely thick, as it was every morning. It began to fade with the sunrise.

Ravion took the lead retracing his steps of the previous day, feigning his tracking skills as if he'd picked up a trail. They didn't need to know he'd already found the monster. He moved as quietly and gracefully as possible. Not even the sound of his boots could be heard on the forest's floor.

The others were a different story. Gareth sounded as if he wasn't trying to mask himself whatsoever. The crunch of foliage under his feet crashed through the trees. And branches cracked and snapped against his wide form. Even the jingle of his sword echoed.

Malakai wasn't overly loud, but could still be heard in the thick vegetation, mostly due to the panting from his fondness of pipe tobacco.

Kane was surprisingly quiet despite his heavy gear. The occasional noise came from a protruding branch gliding off the breastplate, but otherwise he stepped as light as the ranger.

They progressed closer to the dragon's lair, slowing their pace in the passing moments. It was easier to be quiet at a slow speed.

Ravion threw his hand in the air for all to see. Taking position at the top of the ravine, he waved them forward.

They carefully made their way to his side, looking into the clearing.

"Your dragon's in there." He pointed to a wide cavern entrance, hidden by the valley. "If you find yourself in further need of my services, I'll be at the tavern." Denying chance for refute, he turned and started the direction they'd come.

Gareth felt a slight irritation. Reciting their arrangement in his head, he faced the realization. *Damn it! I paid him to track and lead me to the dragon. We never discussed combat.* "Wait! If you stay and fight I'll double your pay."

The ranger spun around, correcting his step and fell in line. "Shall we?" A satisfied smirk formed. He cautiously stepped past the group and made his way down the hill.

They made their way into the clearing, weapons at the ready.

Kane took lead, marching into the dark cavern. He was surprised by how well he could see in the dank passageway. Broken pieces of wood littered the ground, remains of what looked to be a wagon at some point. The stench was nauseating, but not unbearable. It reminded him of a butcher's mart on a hot summer day. Though this was less sticky.

Malakai had a bit of trouble seeing anything past the entrance. Only the reflecting sun off the young warrior's breastplate told him which direction to go. But that was rapidly fading. Soon he wouldn't be able to see anything.

A serpentine voice echoed from the void. "More visitors come to seek death?"

Gareth replied with forceful presence. "Your reign of terror has come to its end, snake!"

"We shall see!" The dragon retorted, whipping its tail from the shadows.

Kane felt the impact against his right side. It launched him off his feet sending him crashing into the cavern wall. He slammed hard against the jagged rocks and tumbled to the ground.

Gareth and Ravion readied their weapons, preparing for another attack.

Malakai closed his eyes. They were useless in here. It was best he let his other senses take over. Listening for the impact, he charged what he guessed was the fallen warrior. Taking a defensive position in front of him, he stood as ready as he could be. "Is that you, Kane?"

Large bouts of air rushed into his lungs, threatening to send panic in their wake. Realizing he was breathing too hard, he exhaled slowly, forcing his body to comply. Malakai had taught him well. Getting his body back into submission, he answered. "Yeah. I'm okay. Can you see?"

"Nope. And there's no time to light a torch."

"Alright. I'll try to guide you as best I can."

Autzumo extended his scaly neck. The muscles flexed, preparing to spew his acidic breath over the group of would be slayers.

Kane reached to the small of his back, drawing a dagger. With the flick of his wrist he launched the blade, striking the beast in the underside of its jaw. The blade sank to the hilt, spewing a green ooze from the wound. He felt several of the droplets spray against his face. They tingled his flesh, like a fly landing for a brief rest.

The dragon choked, abandoning his deadly breath weapon. A mighty roar escaped him. Whipped his tail in protest, he batted at the trespassers.

Malakai felt the droplets hit him. Burning into his clothing, he quickly ripped away the tainted sleeves, listening for any sound of movement.

Ravion rolled, easily avoiding the wild tail. Springing to his feet, he lunged at the out-stretched appendage a few feet from him. The tip of his blade scratched into blackened scales, splitting a small section.

Gareth thrust the pike, forcing the dragon to retreat toward the cavern wall. It roared against the shaft, fighting to keep ground.

"Jump!" Kane shouted, attempting to defend the blind man.

Malakai tried to move, but it was too late. The thick tail collided, knocking his feet from beneath him. His legs buckled against the force, and he hit the ground. Throwing his sabre out in defense, he narrowly deflected a crushing blow from the forceful whip.

Kane wiped the spray from his face, noticing the toxin eating into his clothing. Pulled from his observation, he spotted the tail headed toward him again. Prepared for the assault this time, he brought his great sword around, allowing the force to amplify his swing.

The dragon roared in pain, feeling the last several feet of his tail become severed from the rest. "You'll pay for that!" Autzumo howled. Fighting the pike, he was limited to his claws. Batting at the swords and numerous attackers, he tried to land a solid blow against at least one of them Though he was having trouble. There were too many to defend against.

Ravion narrowly dodged the lethal, foot long talons. He noticed a green ooze seeping from the tips.

Using the distraction, Kane grabbed hold of Malakai's arm and pulled him to his feet. Feeling the lightly armored warrior take his own weight, he spun and charged, hoping to finish the beast.

Autzumo calculated his options. His movement was severely limited. If he pushed forward too much, the steel head of the pike would tear through his beautiful scales. And with his tail damaged, he was unable to keep them at a distance and under a disadvantage. Catching movement out of the corner of his eye, he saw the armored man that'd severed his tail charging. His sword was raised and ready strike. He swiped at the warrior, hoping he could tear him into pieces before he was able to raise the enchanted weapon.

Kane fought the claws, his strikes full of ferocity. Swinging the oversized weapon as if it were the weight of a feather, he struck with unnatural speed, deflecting each swipe.

The sword was chipping away his talons, piece by piece. It wouldn't be longer until they'd be too weak to pierce hide.

"Hold!" Gareth shouted, hoping the others would follow suit. Gaining proper footing, he knew he couldn't be moved. With renewed force he thrust hard, watching the steel tip pierce the dragon's scales.

Kane spun around, putting everything he had into a single, solid attack. How he could withstand the beast's strength was beyond him. It didn't matter. He needed to find weakness if he was to end this.

Autzumo roared in pain, feeling the spearhead sink into his soft innards. Blood seeped from beneath the scales where the pole-arm had penetrated. He was on limited time. *Did I make a mistake? Did I get sloppy by staying here too long? Where's my flight?* The final thought awoke something inside him. *My flight! I have been forsaken!* He hissed at the slayers, striking at the armored warrior with everything he had. How did he not smell it before?

Ravion took advantage of the dragon's distraction, counting the time between attacks. Waiting for Kane to deflect the next blow, he ducked beneath the swipe and rolled his blade.

Malakai listened to the sounds of battle. They had the upper hand. Hearing the deflection, he charged, flipping his rapier in-hand. The tip pointed down, he jumped and stabbed as hard as he could. It passed through scale and sank to the hilt.

Autzumo hissed his pain. The betrayer had been chipping his claws, distracting him. He hadn't noticed the thin one roll into range. Sticky fluid dripped from beneath his scales. He stared at the severed claw, cut smoothly from him. His leg was pinned to the ground by the other one's sword. To his surprise, it didn't overly hurt. In fact, it still felt like it was attached. He tried to pull his leg free of the rapier, but it wouldn't budge. His other front leg was useless, lying detached on the ground. Only a few pieces of torn flesh dangled around the bone. The spear tip shot in, awakening the pain inside him. Extending his neck, he howled louder than ever howled before.

Seeing his chance, Kane spun, letting his sword swing wide. The tip passed through the beast's throat, neatly severing its windpipe.

Autzumo's strength began to wane. His fight evaded him, replaced by the need for air. Panic took hold. He was dying. *What's this dreaded feeling— Fear? So that's what it's like.* His body too weak to resist, he laid his head down, the scaly eyelids too heavy raise. It was no matter. He didn't really want to see his final moments. His entire existence was a betrayal. Expecting death to claim him soon, he counted his gold one last time, feeling lost four-thousand and seventy-two times over.

Gareth knew the fight was won, but the beast had to be finished. Gathering his strength, he thrust deep, sending the pointed head into the dragon's heart. It pierced with a *pop*, spurting a thick liquid from the enlarged wound.

Autzumo gasped his final breath, feeling the pounding of his ruptured core slow to a stop.

Kane reached down and pulled his dagger from the creature's jaw. The metal was pitted, nearly useless. Tossing the ruined weapon to the ground, he felt a hand against his shoulder.

"Well done lad." Gareth smiled, admiring the successful hunt.

Chapter XII
A New Friend

Krenin jumped, hearing the first sounds of battle. Had his friends come to rescue him? *No, they betrayed me and left me here to die.* The realization washed over him. He didn't have any friends. If they returned, it was for the purpose of killing him and claiming the treasure. If it wasn't them, who knew about the treasure? And who would be willing to face the dragon? He pulled against his chains, testing their strength for the thousandth time. He was growing weak from lack of food, relying on the small bits of moss and fungus he could reach. "I have to get out." He calmly stated to himself, letting the weight of the chains fall to the ground.

The half-orc search for anything he could use as a weapon in the event it would be needed. The room was littered with jewels and gold, glowing like a beacon in the low-lit cavern. It was odd. He'd craved such wealth his entire life. And now that he had it, it wasn't worth the price. Crawling toward the pile in hopes of finding something he could use, the shackles reached their end, yanking against him. He didn't need to see them to know the thick bands were cutting into his wrists. He could already feel the deep red bruises forming in his green-tinted flesh. Scooting on his rear, letting his arms extend behind him, the tendons tensed from the odd angle. It hurt, but it was a small price to pay for freedom. His feet were just within reach. Kicking at the pile, he uncovered a few trinkets and treasures not previously seen. Coin spilled around him, threatening to cover his legs. Again he kicked, feeling something sharp cut his foot.

Withdrawing his leg, he bent it to see the bottom. A shallow gash laid across the calloused heel. *Sharp means a weapon.* He felt relief for the first time since awakening in the cavern. Carefully sticking his feet into the pile once again, he swept the treasure away, hoping to find the item that cut him.

A weakened roar echoed off the walls, telling him the battle was nearly over. Worry set into his stomach. He was running out of time, he had to act fast. He could feel the edge of the item, but it was too heavy to dislodge. He needed to uncover it. looking around for something, anything, to dig it out, Krenin spotted a decomposing body not far from him. The remains were unrecognizable aside from the fact that it was human. The skin and meat was nearly gone, leaving the majority of a shattered skeletal structure intact. Only a few pieces of rotting meat held it together.

He took a deep breath and pulled himself from the heap. Moving toward the body, he grabbed hold of one of the arms. Twisting it above its head, he felt the dried tendons snap. Pulling as hard as he could, using his other hand to secure the rest, it popped and the ball separated from the socket. The arm came free in his hand.

Moving back into position, he extended his reach, using the bone hand as a scoop. Shoveling the treasure away, he saw, for the first time, what had scraped him. Lying there amidst the scattered loot was his battle axe. He smiled his fortune upon the lost weapon. Knocking it closer to him, he discarded the arm and lifted his long-lost friend. His only friend. The leather wrapped handle felt good in his grip. Like a favored toy that had been misplaced long ago.

He listened for the sounds outside the entrance of his prison. The battle had all but subsided. All he could hear now were voices— human voices.

Krenin spun the axe in hand, facing the blade away from him. Pulling against his shackles he put as much pressure on the stakes as possible, hoping they wouldn't ring out. He smacked the sides with the flat of his axe, working it back and forth. Within a few moments, he was free.

"Correct me if I'm wrong, but in the stories I've heard, aren't dragons usually accompanied with tales of treasure?" Malakai asked, looking deeper into the cavern. His eyes squinted in search from the flicker of his torch and a nefarious smile lingered on his lips

Gareth wiped the thick blood from his cutlass. He looked down at the dragon's freshly severed head as proof of the creature's death. "I've heard such tales. So long as we have the head, there's no harm in exploring a little further. Especially if there's treasure involved."

Ravion lifted the blood-soaked pike, plucking the tip from the dragon's heart. Flipping it around, he quickly thrust it forward, impaling the head upon the long shaft.

Kane turned, hearing the sickening pop. He watched the slender scout lift the bear-sized trophy. The shaft flexed against the weight, staining to hold it up.

Ravion carried it to the wall and laid it to rest where the blood could drain without soaking the handle. Glanced at the young warrior, noting his interest, he offered explanation. "It makes transportation easier and offers a slightly more intimidating means of displaying victory to one's enemies."

Nodding his understanding, yet still sickened by the supposed tradition, Kane turned to accompany the others deeper into the cavern.

The group slowly made their way into the unknown, following the contours of the moist and jagged walls. The sound of footsteps and jingle of gear echoed all around them. The torch flickered against the faint breeze, creating shadows on the far side, leaving all on edge and anticipating ambush. The ceiling lowered, forcing them to crouch down or risk hitting their heads. Moving little faster than a crawl, they found a narrow passageway just large enough for two men to stand side by side. How a dragon, be it a small one, could move through such confined spaces was a mystery in its own right.

One by one they stepped through the narrow passageway and into the large chamber glowing from the orange flame. Pile after pile of gold, silver, and gems stood illuminated. Even in the darkness, they could see how large the room truly was. It was far from full, but it looked to go on forever in the darkness.

They stood in awe, lost in the sight of the treasure before them.

A coin hit the ground, ringing out in the silent room. Gareth leaned closer to his companions, whispering as quietly as possible. "We're not alone."

The half-orc ducked behind one of the piles, watching the torchlight flicker off the walls. It messed with his vision, made it hard to see the men headed toward him. Squinting against the blinding light, he watched them step into the open, lost in the sights before them. He leaned in, getting a good look at their faces. They were human by appearance, except for the tall one, maybe. He had the look of a the alfar. Maybe half? There was no telling with their kind. It was so difficult to see anything with that accursed torch. In his quest to get a better view, he hadn't realized how much he was leaning against the pile. He felt it shift beneath him, several pieces sliding from their perch. Adjusting his position, he removed his weight, halting all that he could. His heart sank, hearing a tiny coin bounce off the stone floor. It rang out, betraying his position. He closed his eyes, silently cursing himself.

Tightening the grip on his axe, Krenin readied to defend himself. *Today not the day I meet Osirus!* He waited for them to charge, surprised at their lack of action. Perhaps they didn't hear the trumpet-like coin that betrayed him?

He glanced over the pile, stealing a quick look. They were still there, admiring the loot before them. The one carrying the torch stepped closer. He had a foreign look to him. His mustache twisted and curled toward his nose and the dark red leather on his shoulders and arms didn't match any style he'd seen before.

"How do you reckon we get it out of here?" The foreigner asked, turning toward the others.

"A cart at a time, I suppose." The heavy, bald one announced scratching his head.

It seemed he was in luck. They clearly hadn't heard him. This meant he had a chance to get the first strike before they could recover. And with any luck, the short one's armor looked like it might fit him. Lifting his axe, he exhaled a hearty battle shout and jumped from his perch, aimed to cut down the man with the torch.

A cool breeze carried the scent of pine through the air. Birds chirped from their nests, and squirrels frolicked around the sides of the massive trees.

Kane took another exhausted step, listening to the crunch of leaves beneath his boot. The sun beat down on him, draining his energy with each step. Sweat poured from his pores, dripping into the linen tunic beneath his armor. He wished he could admire the orange and brown leaves littering the forest road, but he was preoccupied. The dragon's head weighed a ton from atop the pike. Why they had to transport it that way seemed silly, but the others insisted. His footsteps were muffled by the commotion behind him.

The half-orc grunted. Sweat beading down his green-tinted flesh. His small tusks jutted from his lower jaw, displaying his gritted teeth between them. A thick rope was draped around him, securing his arms to the twin poles dragging the ground behind him. He pulled hard against the overloaded gurney. Gold and silver were piled high on the crude contraption, held in place by a patchy, canvas tarp.

Gareth, Malakai, and Ravion marched on all sides of the orc, keeping him in line.

"That's enough grunting, you green-skinned bastard. You don't have that much farther to go." Gareth taunted, keeping the half-orc's anger constant, but controlled. "You've been given plenty of water. Another mile and you're good for all the bread and water you can stand."

Krenin pulled hard, dragging the small portion of treasure behind him. His rage kept him moving, kept him strong. The thought of escaping the bald man and biting down on his throat made him smile. The sweet taste of blood in his mouth offered hope.

"What the hell are you smilin' about? You failed. You attacked too early. You could have also done without that weak shout before rushing us. You might have gotten a blow in before we captured ya'."

His words were infuriating, but he wasn't wrong. As much as he wanted to kill him, he was kind of likable. *He's kind of like orc.* Krenin shook the thought from his head. *No! He the enemy. I was defeated and he not kill me. This not go unpunished.*

Ravion hid his smile, knowing exactly what Gareth was doing. He had to keep him fueled or he would die from lack of food. Never mind the fact that he would have made the trip much easier if he weren't being used as a mule, though it made sense. The half-orc was young. He attacked prematurely. For that, he had to be subdued. His only saving grace was that he hadn't hurt anyone. But using him as a slave seemed wrong.

Gareth glanced at the scout, reading the concern on his face. "Ravion, run ahead and announce our arrival. Let the people witness the fall of their dragon. They should celebrate after they've feared for so long."

The ranger picked up the pace, surpassing the young warrior at the head. He crested the hill and looked back, timing their speed. It was amazing how quickly a wider step could advance your position with no more or less energy consumed. Calculating their arrival time, he turned and made for town.

They could hear the commotion before they reached the forest edge. The smell of meat and wine lingered far and wide. Reaching the clearing, they heard the cheers of joy erupting from those who saw the dragon's head. More and more people rushed to the road hoping to see the heroes responsible for the beast's death.

Kane felt the eyes upon him. It was a wondrous feeling, but he wasn't sure he cared for it. He smiled passing them, hoping to reach the pub and get inside as quickly as possible.

Ravion stepped in front of the group, rejoining them. He didn't care for the attention, but Gareth wasn't wrong. These people needed cause to celebrate. Perhaps it was for the best.

Krenin lugged the treasure past the wall of humans. He hated being placed on display like this. *Why they not just kill me? They want to do it public? Why so happy? I'm nobody. Not like Thievesmaster Zanthin.* He kept his eyes straight ahead, walking where the bald man directed. If he was to die, he'd go out fighting. But now was not the time.

Smoked meat, pipe tobacco, and the smell of wine radiated from the tavern. Bards played their music, and patrons cheered their joy into the wee hours of the night. Every seat was filled, leaving a large number standing throughout the common room.

The largest table at the center was littered with cooked boar, fruit, bread, and the finest ale, mead and wine of Shadgull.

Master Remle De Leon sat at the head, rocking his tankard back and forth in tune to the music.

Gareth sat beside him, content with his roasted turkey leg and ale, while the patrons scrambled to be near them, each one trying to make themselves known to the heroes.

Kane sat back in his wooden chair, feeling the effects of the mead in his head. He laid his tankard to rest on the table, the light brew within sloshed against the sides. Grabbing a piece of bread, he took a bite hoping to regain his composure.

Ravion sat properly, refusing drink. His sword hung at his side, ready for use if needed. His eyes darted about the room, cautiously scanning the crowd for any would be aggressors. His elongated pipe rested in his hand, a light waft of smoke slithering from the bowl. He took a puff, blowing the solid white cloud into the air.

Malakai spoke through the food in his mouth, retelling the story of the battle and how they narrowly escaped the dragon with their lives. He was careful to add as much excitement and detail as possible to keep the listeners interested and on edge. His hands moved with embellishment, his tankard in place of his sword, small amounts spilling out as he stabbed and slashed, reenacting his part.

A loud crash shook the walls, silencing the music. Hearing it stop the crowd grew quiet, listening to the muffled outside world. The warriors jumped up, grabbing their weapons. Many of them too drunk to stand, let alone fight.

The pub doors burst open and an unnatural darkness spilled into the room.

Gareth stood, letting his chair fall behind him. Drawing his cutlass, he glared at the void. "I knew I'd find you here, you dark-skinned bastards!"

His tone was low but deadly. Spring into the darkness, he disappeared from sight.

Ravion drew his longsword. "Dreu?" He questioned himself. Sword at the ready he casually stepped into the night, following after the impulsive warrior.

The darkness rolled in like a wave, devoured over half the room. Patrons disappeared inside it, heir screams echoing all around. The unnatural shadow moved as if it were alive. It traveled across the area leaving a wake of dead where cheerful citizens stood moments before. Blood poured from the fresh wounds, seeping into the cracks of the wood planked floor.

Lifting his great sword, Kane charged, ready to halt the strange shadow. Swinging with all his might the blow struck home, sinking into something solid but soft. He twisted and shoved deeper, hoping the wound was fatal. Withdrawing, he spun around, ready to attack again.

The darkness in the room faded, leaving a black-skinned alfar in its place. Its body laid motionless on the floor, a thick black ichor seeping from the fatal chest wound.

Kane stared into its fading eyes, feeling something familiar but unknown in the wicked being.

The barred cell was growing chilly in the night. It was bare, save for a wooden cot and an empty bucket resting in the corner. Krenin laid on the wood and canvas bed, his feet overhanging the small structure. He wished they would have at least left him a blanket. Hearing the screams echo from the single overhead window, he shot up.

Several shadows rushed past, reflecting in the outside lanterns. He watched as best he could, seeing the light disappear. An unnatural darkness to wisp through the small portal, flicking about the iron runs, as if it were searching for something. There was something unsettling about it. *The darkest night not hinder my vision. But this— mist? I can't see through it.*

His fear grew seeing a similar shadow seep through the cracks of the jailhouse door. It licked at the keyhole, threatening to come inside.

Krenin stepped to the door of his small cell, pulling the bars with all his might. His strength was returning, but he was still far from peak. And worse yet, now he was completely unarmed.

The door burst open spilling darkness into the room.

He braced himself, ready for his death to swiftly follow. But he wasn't going to go down without a fight. Raising his fists, he stepped back, watching the shadow approach the cell. He could hear something alive inside it, something intelligent.

A familiar click echoed from the door and it creaked open. The void engulfed the door and floated closer to him, leaving no place to escape.

Krenin felt the wall at his back. He was out of space. Clenching his fist, he roared and leapt into the shadow. His fist beat down, colliding against something— soft? He felt it give with his first swing. Again, he struck. A warm sticky liquid clung to his knuckles, though it wasn't from him. He swung again, and again. He hadn't realized, but the shadow had faded leaving a frail, black-skinned creature beneath him. He felt its skull give way, the mush inside spilling onto the floor.

Lost in the black gore covering his hands, Krenin wiped them on the creature's clothing and stood. Grabbing the crude, rusted sword it had been carrying, he stared out the open door to the chaos beyond. The handle was too small for his large hands but it would have to suffice. Seeing another shadow in the doorway, he knew he had to act. This one wouldn't be so easy.

It rolled toward him with blinding speed, engulfing everything in its vicinity.

Timing his attack, Krenin swung the blade in defense. To his surprise metal rang out, telling him it was locked against another sword. Refusing to give the enshadowed creature another chance, he slid the blade down letting it glide against the parried weapon. Reaching the cross-guard he twisted and thrust deep, feeling the tip sink into the obscured figure.

Ripping the sword free, the second monster fell from the shadow and landed hard on the wooden floor. A pool of black ooze spilled out.

Armed with two blades, Krenin rushed through the door. *I no longer a prisoner! That means I have to die. But I not die unless I die fighting!*

Chapter XIII
Order to Chaos

Darkness enveloped him. He couldn't tell where one ended and the next began. Swiping wildly, Gareth felt his cutlass bite into one of the foul creatures. Spinning around, he connected with another. The shadows were starting to fade allowing him to see the moonlight through their swarming mass. Glancing back at the dead dreualfar in his wake, he lunged forward, feeding the numbers. A sticky, black liquid dripped from his face, splattered here and there. He didn't have to look down to know that he was covered in the soupy substance. *It's not the first time, it won't be the last!* Another creature fell before him, releasing an overwhelming sense of pride. A satisfied, wicked smile glowed bright in the enveloping darkness, seeming to burn away the shadow.

Ravion spun around, twirling his longsword between thrusts. To the untrained eye his actions were sloppy and misguided, but to a seasoned combatant, each strike was a calculated step in his overall plan. He danced through the shadow, gracefully avoiding the unseen attacks. There had to be hundreds of them. Yet, they couldn't close in on him, not while he was moving. They seemed afraid of his dancing blade. Ravion swung, the sharpened steel unhindered by resistance. One would fall and another would take its place.

A sadistic laughter echoed through the darkness, reaching his ears. The tone rang familiar. Making his way toward it, felling several of the black-skinned, cloaked creatures as he went, Ravion stepped into the moonlight, able to see for the first time since exiting the pub. Gareth's face lingered among the black. His wicked smile revealed a monster in hiding, taking pleasure in the death of others.

Gareth stabbed his cutlass into the blood-soaked earth and knelt beside his freshest kill. Retrieving his dagger, he neatly removed one of its ears and tucked it into his pouch. Glancing at the approaching scout, he picked himself up. "Ah, glad you could make it." Ripping his sword from the earth, he spun around, decapitating another.

Dark fluid ran the valley at the center of his blade, spilling over and dripping to the floor. The shadow faded, revealing another of the beast. A woman cried at its feet, her rose colored dress, torn and blood-soaked. The sticky cloth clung to her, but she appeared unharmed, if a little shaken up.

Kane extended his hand and pulled her to her feet. "Get to the rear. Others are already back there."

She rushed toward the back room obeying his instruction.

He shot a glance to Malakai, pulling his sabre from one of the dead creatures. Several bodies littered the ground, human and devil alike, but the pup was finally free of shadow.

Stealing a glance to the barkeep, peeking from the barricaded kitchen door, Kane nodded to him, silently giving the command to seal it. All the patrons were either dead, or already in there with him. Approaching the fair-haired lord, cleaning his rapier and dagger, Kane prepared for the worst. "Lord Remle, what are you doing?"

"These creatures are in my lands. I won't sit idle while they attack my people." Remle stood to his towering height, gesturing toward the door. "I aim to march out that door and confront them head on."

"My Lord, if I may?" Kane paused, adding the illusion of request. "You don't know how many are. This town has suffered enough this night. Do not allow it the chance to claim their lord as well. My friend and I will go out and fend them off to our last breath. I would request you remain here as a last defense, should we fail?"

The towering lord thought through his options. Sighing deeply, he had to admit the young warrior stance. "I suppose you're right. And while I don't like it, I'll remain here. If you're able, my men are stationed a mile south. Any way you can reach them, do so. We need all the reinforcements we can get."

"Understood, My Lord." Kane gave a respectful bow and spun around, searching for the swashbuckler.

Malakai stood beside the door, cleaning his fingernails with a dagger. "You ready?"

Kane nodded, grabbing hold of the bronze latch. Pulling it open, he stepped into the night.

The door clicked behind them. Raising their weapons, the fight already upon them, they took a defensive stance. As a pair, they swung and dodged, using each other's style to defend their openings. One would swing, the other would block. Together they fought their way into the unending veil, hoping to fell as many as possible before they met their ends.

The chill of death lingered on the back of his neck. They swarmed all around, encircling him. Gareth dodged a wild swipe, pushing the scout out of the way. The man could clearly handle himself, but his fancy style made it difficult to anticipate. Last thing he wanted was to get the man killed by failing to watch his back.

Ravion caught himself, glancing at the broad warrior. Had it not been for the shove, an unnoticed scimitar would have bit into his spine. For that he was thankful, though the warrior clearly wasn't used to fighting with a unit. Ravion plunged his sword into one of the revealed beasts, using the momentum to send him into his companion. Despite his calm, sweat beaded down his face. *How are there so many? More importantly, where did they come from?*

Gareth felt one of the wicked, curved blades bite into his arm. It wasn't deep, but it would be an annoyance for a while. Grimacing the pain, he grabbed hold of the crude weapon, pulling its wielder close. Bringing his head forward, he slammed it into the dark-skin's nose. It crunched beneath the impact. Refusing to wait for him to recover, Gareth stabbed him in the stomach, letting gravity carry him off the sword.

Unable to see an end to the assault, a heavy sigh escaped him. Exhausted and ready to rest, Gareth lowered his guard and closed his eyes, expecting to join his wife and son. The brief moment felt like an eternity. He waited, hoping for the longing sting that would be his end. A familiar shout roused his curiosity. Peeking into the night, the half-orc slammed into the group, disorienting them.

Krenin slashed wildly, tearing into the unsuspecting foes. Their shadowy spheres faded with each death, granting more light.

Seeing the half-orc jump into the fray, excitement coursed through him. The thought of a challenge rejuvenated him. Renewed vigor rushing through his veins, Gareth raised his cutlass leapt into the dissolving swarm. "You damned, green-skinned dummy. You ain't claimin' all the glory for yourself!" Gareth crashed into another group, launching them back several feet. Taking position behind the half-orc, he deflected a swipe, running his sword into its deliverer.

Ravion tumbled toward the pair, thrusting his sword into an exposed back. Landing on his feet, he took position in their rank, ready to end the fight.

They fought, protecting each other, slowly making their way toward the pub. Each step twisted their stance, cycling them around with the movement. It kept them refreshed and always ready for the next attack. One by one they caught a glimpse of the tavern doors. Kane and Malakai had taken position just outside them, defending with all their might.

Nearing the pair, they spread out, the two groups becoming one. Five men stood, their backs protected by the others, forming a deadly pocket of hope in the midst of an outnumbering army.

The dreualfar washed against them, unable to break their resolve. They fell in troves, piling up around the defenders' feet. Regardless of how many they outnumbered them by, they couldn't break them. A high-pitched horn echoed in the night, calling the dreualfar to a halt. They stopped their attacks and slowly backed away, granting a moment of reprieve for all.

Gareth lunged forward, slashing as many as he could reach. To his surprise they didn't reengage him.

The darkness faded, returning the town's post lanterns to sight. Hundreds of dreualfar stood in the open, surrounding the already entrapped warriors. The impenetrable wall looked upon them, an unquenchable bloodlust in their eyes.

The five stood ready, weapons held high, anticipating attack.

Ravion glanced around, hoping for a miracle. They were surrounded on all sides, save for the sealed pub doors. Hundreds stood against them, ready to cut them down, each one with a city full of bodies worth of reason to do so. *Why do they hold?* His question was answered as if he'd asked it aloud.

A wide path opened, allowing a single dreualfar to pass through the ranks. He looked older than the rest, his long, stringy, white hair was pulled to the back and braided. Blackened leather covered his equally black form, highlighted only by his features. A silver clover design inlaid the edges, offering minor glow in the moonlight. An ornate rapier hung at his side, radiating a faint glow even through its scabbard.

"Enim si taht gnihtemos evah uoy!" He hissed, stopping a short distance from the resistance.

Gareth aimed the tip of his cutlass at the creature. "Speak that vile tongue at me and I'll cut it out!"

The dreualfar commander smiled, his elongated canines showing for the briefest moment. A smooth, collected voice echoed from him, seemingly misplaced by the harshness of his previous words. "As if your threats have any effect on me. You're only alive because you have something that belongs to me. And I want it back."

Gareth spat at the creature, the stringy saliva falling several feet short. "I was disgusted before I knew you were capable of intelligent speech. Now that I know you are, it just makes me want to slaughter you that much more."

The creature smiled. "You doubt our intelligence? If you had the slightest idea, you'd throw yourself upon your own sword just to escape our wrath."

Ravion placed his hand on Gareth's shoulder, hoping the gesture would calm the disgusted warrior. Stepping to the front of the group, he spoke. "What item do you believe us to possess?"

The black-skinned alfar looked over the young dalari. His interest was evident, but his motives remained hidden. "You're something unseen for quite some time. Perhaps I'll keep you as my own personal pet once this is all said and done."

Ravion smiled, letting the notion hide his thoughts. "The item?" He repeated.

"Oh, it's nothing much, just something a friend was holding for me. You took it from him earlier this day. I want it back."

The sea of dreualfar opened, allowing the dragon's severed head through, still mounted upon the pike.

"There were many items among the dragon's treasure. Perhaps if you told us what you're looking for, we may be able to say if we have it or not."

"I have a better idea. Why don't I just kill you one at a time until you tell me where all of it is. I'm sure I can find it myself at that point."

"Not gonna' happen." Gareth spat, ready to spring into action.

The commander smirked at the warrior's words, licking his lips. "You're so full of hate and despair. I think I want to keep you as well. I'll make you my plaything. There's nothing quite like a well broken stallion." He raised his hand, facing the palm toward the group. "Bring me the mouthy one."

The dreualfar rushed in, encircling tight around the group. They had no chance to fight. There were too many of them. Two of them grabbed hold of Gareth, securing his arms.

They tried to fight. Tried to move. Tried to perform the slightest action, but it was impossible. Some unseen force was holding them stationary.

Gareth screamed his discontent, annoyed further at the lack of sound. He struggled, kicked, bit, clawed, nothing worked. His body was not his own.

The dreualfar pulled him from the group, dragging him before the commander. He was on display, open for all to see. Kicking the back of his legs, his knees buckled. They set him on his knees and stepped away, leaving him unattended.

The commander smiled at the kneeling warrior. Slowly approaching him, he spoke. "You see, sometimes puny, rebellious humans have to be taught a lesson when they interfere with beings beyond their understanding." Grabbing his crotch, he pulled his armor to the side.

Gareth felt a pressure in his jaw, forcing his mouth to open. He stared in horror, unable to resist.

The dreualfar commander continued toward him, dropping his leather breeches to his knees. Erect and demanding attention, he moved ever closer to the defeated man.

Gareth wanted to close his eyes, hoping to hide from what was to follow. They wouldn't obey. He was being forced to watch his own sodomy. Something flew past his head, ringing out with a thud. A sickening scream echoed from the commander. Unable to comprehend what had happened, Gareth saw the handle of a crude scimitar protruding from the dreualfar's exposed growing. It bounced from the force of the hit and sudden movement. Finding his body responsive, he lunged toward the wounded creature, taking hold of the hilt. Forcing all his strength into it, he thrust the blade deeper, driving it straight through the commander. The curved steel caught on the pelvic bone, glancing upward into his stomach.

Gareth twisted the sword, letting the dull spine rip his body open. It was too kind to kill him quickly. He wanted to force as much pain as possible. Watching his would-be rapist drop to his knees, the dark face white from blood loss, Gareth took in delight in his torment. Content with the weakening screams, he ripped the crude, rusted weapon free. Standing to his full height he grabbed the dying dreualfar's head and drug the metal across one of its pointed ears. Assisted by the semi-sharp blade, Gareth tore his trophy free and placed the tip of the blade into the exposed ear canal. He thrust the blade hard, watching it explode out the other side of his head. Gareth let go of the sword, watching the body fall to the earth.

The assembled dreualfar hissed, unsure what to do without their commander. Confusion took hold. They scurried to escape, trampling one another in the effort. Some retreated into the darkness from once they sprang, while a select few charged, expecting a fight. Those few were cut down in moments.

Gareth turned, finding his companions outside the door. Looking them over, he noticed the half-orc held but one sword. Its twin lodged in the commander's head. Walking toward them, he placed his hand on the half-orc's shoulder. "Thank you for saving me from that."

"Not suitable for anyone. Krenin hope you do the same if it was me."
Gareth nodded his understanding.

"Permission to speak?" Malakai stated more than asked. "You must be blessed by Corin. After all, you nearly took a mouthful of dreu cock and the one person who helped you was the one who had the least reason to."

Krenin leaned in whispering louder than intended. "I aim for his head."

"Looks like you got it!" Ravion laughed.

Gareth shook his head, looking to the group of warriors around him. "Do me a favor and never speak of this again."

Ravion retrieved his sword. Placing it into its sheath. He glanced at the carnage around them. "I can't make any promises. Though I think it'd be wise to figure out what they were after and safeguard it. We can't risk failing next time."

The patrons stared at the half-orc, breaking their gaze when he made eye contact. It was strange to see such a large, barbaric brute wearing such finely crafted clothing and sitting at a table full of respected warriors.

Krenin liked the way the silk felt against his skin. It was much softer than the twill he'd been accustomed to. The ale was weak, but after several tankards he was beginning to feel its affects. The food was much better. Everything was sweet, from the meat to the bread. It tasted as if it had been made with the purpose of enjoyment, something far greater than to simply survive. He glanced out the north window, seeing another caravan of stone and lumber make its way up the hill. Leaning in his over-sized chair, compared to human standards anyway, it creaked under the shift in weight. "You think they be done soon?"

"No Krenin, it'll take several months for them to finish the keep." Malakai answered.

"What take so long? Orc homes built in days, not months."

"Orc homes are much simpler in design. Imagine building hundreds of orc homes into one large home with many layers."

"I see. Still, it take so long."

Malakai looked at the others, hoping for assistance. Realizing he was on his own, he sighed. "It must be nice to have such a simple outlook."

"I already look, they not done yet."

"No, I mean— Oh, never mind."

Ravion busted into laughter at the sailor's failed attempt. Resolving himself, he pulled a large piece of parchment from his satchel and laid it upon the table, careful to keep it off the food.

The map showed the area for months in each direction, outlining the southern shores all the way up to the orc lands of Tulgar. Several rocky areas were marked with a circular stamp, embedded by a trident in the center.

"These areas have been inspected and we haven't found any evidence of dreu activity. There are several more locations to search north of Heroes Gate, but as it stands, Southern Dalmoura seems free, aside from the few cave entrances we haven't found yet.

"What's the news on the lowest level of the Keep?" Gareth asked, paying close attention to the map.

Ravion pulled a scroll from his satchel and handed it to Gareth. "The lowest level is complete. The vault is in place and the prisoners are well secured."

"Have the locks been placed on the vault?" Gareth opened the report, deciphering the coded words.

Kane leaned forward, joining the conversation. "The stones are in place. Nobody can get into it without one of us being present."

Ravion glanced around, making sure nobody could hear them. "Moreover, the contracts have been carried out. The only people that have any knowledge of the vaults existence, let alone the locking stone, are sitting at this table."

Gareth sat back, content with the knowledge. "Very well."

"The guards have been asking when the tabards are going to be ready." Kane added.

"I'll be picking them up from the tailor tomorrow afternoon, along with the flag." Malakai offered, taking a swig from his tankard.

Gareth sat up again, resting his elbows on the table. "Good, it'll be nice to see The Order's colors on the chest of our men. I'll be taking a small detachment into the catacombs in the morning. Hopefully we can find it this time."

Chapter XIV
The Fall of Maradar Keep

The full moon faintly illuminated his army. Their dark skin blended into the existing darkness, little more than their glowing eyes and sparse features to be seen in the night. Those gifted with white hair, like their ancestors, were more visible than the rest.

The cool night breeze felt good against the back of his neck. He'd suffered an unnatural temperature since he claimed the ancient power of his god. An unpleasant side effect, perhaps? He couldn't say for certain, though if that were the case, a mild fever was well worth wielding ultimate power. Nezial looked upon the unsuspecting keep. His army was ready to march upon his command. The humans inside were fully unprepared for what he had in store for them this night.

The sound of footsteps roused him from his thoughts. Preparing himself, he gripped his sabre, daring the on comer to try something. He knew many disliked him. And if any one of them caught him unaware, it wouldn't take much to claim command. *But who among my army would have the intestinal fortitude to attack me?*

"General Nezial, the army is in position." The captain declared, stopping just out of threat range.

Nezial nodded, spinning around to look upon the frightened dreualfar. The stench was bittersweet. It was good they feared him. But fear made them weak. It meant they weren't ready. The whole lot of them needed to be conditioned, but time for that had passed. They had no choice but to fight, fearful or not. They would do as he commanded or they would die. "You're dismissed."

The captain rushed off as quickly as he could.

Nezial glanced down the left flank, then the right. A smile came to his lips. They were in position and awaiting his command. All he had to do now was give it. *It's a shame the young captain didn't try anything, that would have shown the others I'm not to be trifled with.* Surveying the army again, proud of the mass he'd forged, he looked into the sky. It was time they served their purpose. They'd trained in preparation for this one night for years. And still, they weren't ready. But they'd have to suffice. The tables had shifted. The dreuslayers had stepped into the open. He couldn't afford further delay. Mentally running through his plan one final time, ensuring all pieces were in play, he counted them off. The outlying villages were cut off. The garrisons had been destroyed, disabling any chance for reinforcements or escape. And the signal fires at Heroes Gate were under his control, ensuring no assistance from the south. These humans were defenseless. His smile grew wider. Every route has been covered. His victory was assured. He had but to take it. *These humans have no chance of survival and it is all due to my plan, my perfect, flawless plan. That is unless these idiots find some way to muck it up.* Feeling his anger start to rise, he glanced around once again, feeling the wind on his face. "Let's do this." He quietly whispered to himself, throwing his right hand into the air.

The army roared, breaking their halt. The sound of boots and the echo of war-cries shook the foundation of the very walls they were about to crush. Like a swarm of marbles rolling down a hill, they collided against the thick barrier.

Nezial watched them race toward the unyielding stone and mortar. They battered against it, numbers constantly renewed. The walls began to crumble, weakened by his magic. Seeing the first break, his horde seeped through the fallen barricade and into the courtyard.

Following after them, keeping a leisurely pace, he slowly walked toward victory. He was in no hurry. The keep would fall. It was inevitable.

Reaching the shattered walls, Nezial cautiously stepped over the crumbled stone. The courtyard stood defenseless, its protectors crushed beneath the fallen rubble and long past boots. He smiled at the carnage before him.

Dead and dying soldiers were everywhere, their bodies trampled and broken. A few of his dreualfar had fallen among them, their twisted and mangled frames mixed with the humans. It was obvious these few hadn't trained enough. They proved they weren't worthy of remaining among his elite.

A maniacal laughter erupted from deep inside him, echoing through the courtyard. *They thought they were invulnerable inside their capital. I've shown their folly.* He made his way through the courtyard and into the inner bailey. The grass was coated in fresh blood, soaking the hems of his leather plated robes. Everything was going according to plan. Soon he'd impregnate the keep. And then nothing could stop them.

Lost in thought, he hadn't noticed a human guard headed straight toward him. Spotting the lone attacker, he shook himself from his thoughts. In a single, fluid motion, Nezial reached across his body and grabbed hold of his sword. He drew, swung, and sheathed it in the blink of an eye, refusing to slow for the distraction.

He moved so quickly the human didn't even see him draw the blade. Locked in his charge, he overshot the wandering dreualfar. Unable to stop himself he arched, turning just enough to watch his enemy disappear around the corner. He slowed to pursue the trespasser, feeling an immense amount of pain overtake him. Searching his chest and stomach, no stab wounds were present. But something was clearly wrong. His body quit responding to him. He tried to take another step. It wouldn't comply. The pain subsided, leaving him numb. Lost in the fading awareness, he glanced down a second time, seeing a thin red line form across his chest. Pressing his fingers against the mark he lifted them, inspecting the fluid on their tips. The bright red blood clung to his bare skin, its contrast shocking and surprising. The comfortable numb turned to senseless. He could hear his heart beating inside his chest, pumping faster each passing moment. The line expanded, growing thicker with each beat. He fell to his knees, realizing his tunic cut. His left arm hit the ground, severed just below the shoulder. Staring at the lost appendage, unable to process what was happening, fear, pain, worry, it all escaped him. He was already dead. He just didn't know it yet. Grabbing his arm, he felt the world spin. He impacted the trampled snow and mud, realizing his bottom half remained where he'd fallen. He was a severed torso, lying at the base of his collapsed legs. The human closed his eyes, drifting into death.

Nezial chuckled, listening to the man's final moments. Calmly walking toward his destination, he couldn't help but wonder what it would be like, death. Would it be quick and painless, or slow and drawn out? Either way, it was a lesson he didn't expect to learn for quite some time.

Rounding the corner, Nezial found his army bottle necked at the reinforced wood and steel doors. They battered against it with one of the courtyard trees. Its limbs had been viciously chopped away leaving just enough to grip.

The doors were buckled slightly, but appeared to be holding against the impromptu ram.

Marched through the army, hearing whispers alert those in front of him. They glanced back, quickly jumping out of his path.

The gap grew wider, giving their terrifying master plenty of room for his tricks. They dropped the make-shift ram, stepping aside. It landed with a thud, cracking the cobblestone street where it'd fallen.

Within moments all was clear from his path, giving him direct access to the doors. Nezial studied them for a moment, running his fingers across the wood grain. Stepping away, he pulled his oversized sleeves up, revealing his blackened arms. Clapping his hands together, bits of dust flew from his leather gloves. As if they were cold, he rubbed them together. Exhaling slowly, he thrust them forward, shoving his open palms toward the sealed barricade.

A bolt of purple and black energy shot forth, striking the seal. It crackled and popped, following the intricate design of the grain. The wood groaned and twisted, distorting its resilient nature. A massive shock wave erupted from the barriers. It rippled outward, stretching the reinforcing metal to its limit. As if reacting in reverse, it slapped together, ripping the wood apart. The ancient doors shuttered and flexed, exploding into thousands of jagged pieces, launched all directions.

Dust and debris clouded the area, settling to reveal the open passage. Several humans laid dying on the back side of the now ruined doors, their flesh pierced and slashed from the explosion.

The army roared to life rushing into the inner city, their numbers resisted only by the width of the shattered frame.

Nezial waited for his army to pass. Watching from the rear, the dreualfar broke into several groups, flooding the streets and buildings. Screams echoed from the unsuspecting, like music to his ears. Breeching the shattered gate, he spoke, magically amplifying his voice. "Find every man, woman, and child. Drag them from their homes and slaughter them in the streets. Don't leave so much as a wagon unmolested. If it breathes, kill it. I want the streets of this city to run red each time it rains. Tonight, the citizens of Maradar Keep will learn to fear the dreualfar!"

Stepped over the broken barricade, scanning the central road, Nezial took delight in the destruction. *Wherever they hide, we will find them. Every human of this city will perish this evening, save for one.* He scanned the distance, searching for his prize. The keep stood high above the other structures, like a beacon to his desires. Its archers were in position, wasting arrows on scavengers. He smiled at their folly. *By the time we advance on the keep, they'll be spent.* He wandered down a side alley, watching the carnage play out before him. Only one path mattered. That was the path he was on.

Battle horns echoed across the city, alerting him of their success. The city was theirs. The inner curtain had been breached. The only thing left was the defenseless throne. *And they doubted me. Can't be sacked!* He mocked silently. *I've proven my worth. This victory will bring the others to my call.* Floating on success, he launched his hands into the air, firing several bolts of energy into the night sky. They exploded in arrays of purple and green, illuminating every detail of the defeated capital.

He listened to the rhythm of boots marching along the pitching, feeling the vibrations in his own. It was time to finish this. He sauntered onto the main road, following the army of dreualfar headed for the city's heart.

Reaching the shattered doors, Nezial glanced at the belvedere. The archers were absent, either dead or fallen back with their dwindling ammunition. His men rushed past him, anxious for the taste of blood. He didn't pay them any mind. They were following orders.

Nezial stepped over the ruined barriers and into the keep. Recalling his books, he recited his knowledge of human architecture. Making his way through the labyrinth of hallways and corridors, he passed into the great hall. Sounds of battle echoed off the walls, resonating in the stone and wood. It was difficult to tell which direction the conflict originated. Following the clink of swords as best he could, he sought his prize.

Rounding the corner, several of his men were locked in combat against twice as many humans. He watched intently, certain his men would fall to this small band of surface dwellers. It was good to study their actions. It would tell him everything he needed to know about them.

The humans washed over the small band, locking their sights on the lone commander. They cautiously stepped toward him, weapons at the ready. His laughter was unsettling. As if he knew something they did not.

Nezial drew his sword, thrusting it straight into the closest man's throat before he could blink. The blade shot out the back, sending a stream of blood onto the face of the man behind him. Twisting the blade, he spun. A gout of blood spattered just before the gore covered blade tore into the next. Nezial smirked, watching four men stagger to their deaths from his first strike. They clearly weren't prepared for one of his caliber.

The remaining humans paused, taking a step away from the lethal dreualfar. Centering themselves, unable to retreat for honor's sake, they swallowed hard and raised their weapons.

Their hesitation amused him. *These are the best Maradar Keep has to offer? What a jest. Perhaps they require more assurance?* Daring them to advance, Nezial twisted his wrist and spun around, leaving himself open for attack. Arching the tip of his sabre, he plunged it deep into the wooden floor, letting the thin blade sway back and forth. He raised his hands disarmingly, holding them out as if he were going to allow them to capture him.

They glanced nervously at one another, unsure if he was surrendering or deceiving them. They cautiously approached, swords at the ready.

Nezial kept his hands up, allowing the human to get closer. He watched the first one step into threat range. It was too easy. If I struck him down, the others would hesitate. No, he needed to dispose of them all at once. The wicked smile stretched across his lips, staring intently into the approaching human's eyes. It was too late for all of them.

Slamming his hands together, a resounding clap echo from his leather gloves. A light bit of dust flew into the air in front of him.

They jumped at his sudden movement, expecting his expert swordsmanship to dance to life.

Nezial grinned, finding amusement in their fear. The stench was so strong. Peeling his hands apart he cupped them, catching the airborne particles. They landed in light brown and gray speckles against the black covers. Raising them to his face, he gently blew them toward his audience.

The dust disappeared, lost in the dim light. Unaware of his plan, the humans inhaled the unseen particulates, being little more than common, everyday debris. After all the ability to breathe was one of instinct, not training. They froze, unsure what was happening. On edge, they turned, hearing one of their number gasp. Panic set in. Their chests grew tight, swelling like an overfilled bladder. The flesh covering their bodies stretched and contorted, displaying shallow purple veins beneath thinning layers. Like an animal carcass left in the sun for too long, they split wide open, spraying bright red blood from the ruptures. Their flabby skin wither and dried. Flaky hide chipped away into the dust they'd ingested. The more they struggled the quicker they deteriorated, falling into dried hunks on the floor. Blood seeped from the drying cracks like yellow puss in an infected wound. Desperately, they attempted to comfort themselves. They struggled several minutes against the inevitable, finally falling silent. Nothing remained but their dehydrated carcasses, shriveled upon the floor.

Nezial waited for the last one to draw his final breath, a sense of satisfaction on his face. Retrieving his sword, he stepped from the room, feeling their remains crumble beneath his boots, dusty clouds taking flight with each step. "I pray you aren't the best this city has to offer." He turned and made his way up the staircase. The lord was nearly within his grasp.

Nearing the top, his soldiers lined the walls, awaiting his arrival. They scurried to the side, allowing him access. No one lingered for fear of delaying his path to the front of their mass.

The large decorated doors leading to the great chamber were busted, announcing his complete success. Watching his men nod their respects, he passed, refusing to return the gesture. They were beneath him. Not worthy of his acknowledgment. Nezial stepped into the lord's council room feeling victory wash over him.

The highlord and his advisers stood captive, removed of their weapons. Each one stood bound and gagged, held in position by his officers. Such a task was too important to have sullied by an incompetent grunt. The lesser nobles laid dead on the floor, blood trickling between the cracked floorboards.

Nezial marched toward them, making eye contact with each of his officers. They had to know he was in charge. He passed three of them, finding one who refused to break the gaze. Drawing his sabre, he stabbed it deep into the dreualfar's face, letting the soldier collapse behind his prisoner. Another stepped into position, securing the man.

Reaching the head of the room he noted which among the humans wore the finest garb. Finding the man, held by one of his captains, he approached and took position in front of him. He gave the captain a gentle nod.

The dreualfar ripped the gag from his mouth, letting it fall around his neck.

Nezial amplified his voice, letting his calm and chilling tone carry throughout the keep. "You thought you were safe behind your thick walls and armed turrets? You thought you could keep us out? You should have known better!" His tone was low but demanding of attention.

Every human standing in the room cowered at the words, trembling against the grip of their captors.

Locking his gaze upon the man before him, he surveyed him. His composure and custom-tailored undergarments betrayed his status. Had he been smart enough to use a double, he may have delayed the inevitable. But these humans clearly weren't skilled tacticians. It took him less than a day to infiltrate their northern capital. With that level of incompetence, he could probably overthrow their entire empire in a matter of weeks. And with this success, and the joining of the other lines, that was entirely possible, provided his plans took him that far.

Returning to the now, his gaze narrowed on the middle-aged human. "Highlord Kashus, you know what I've come for. Give it to me and I'll ensure you have a quick and merciful death. Defy me and you'll experience more pain than any one person should ever know."

Kashus jerked his shoulders away from his guard, taking a step forward. He stopped directly in front of the dreualfar commander. "You may have crushed this city and killed every person in your path. And you may do the same to me. But I will never help you." Finalizing his statement, he spat his defiance into the commander's face.

Nezial calmly wiped away the saliva. His defiance was admirable, but folly. He nodded to the captain once again.

The captain shot forward, securing the human at the base of his spine. Digging his elongated nails into the fleshy collar bone, he forced him to his knees. Towering over him, he twisted his shoulders, ensuring constant discomfort and forcing him to keep his attention on the commander.

Nezial leaned in, placing his mouth inches from the subdued lord's ear. He could have licked the man if he so desired. "I was hoping you'd say that." His wicked smile revealed his sharp, dagger-like teeth. Wrapping his fingers around the hilt of his sword, he pulled fast and hard, bashing the highlord in the face. His nose crunch beneath the pommel.

Kashus stumbled, falling unconscious to the wooden floor.

Nezial slid his blade back into its proper position and straightened himself. "Search him."

The captain knelt down and riffled the man, finding a golden chain tucked beneath this tunic. Pulling it free, a small silver key was revealed. He ripped it free and handed it to his commander.

Nezial stepped over the body, holding the key up to the stained-glass window overlooking the room. Aligning it with the designs, he smiled and tucked it into his satchel. "Take him to the chamber of pain and secure him. He's going to learn that I'm no liar. As for the others." He glanced around the room. "Kill them." He held his hand up, gesturing a small loop with his fingertips. Bringing the invisible ring around him he disappeared, hearing the screams follow him through the portal.

Chapter XV
An Unwelcome Shadow

The golden fields outside of Shadgull City were speckled with tabards of blue and green. Soldiers struck in unison, mimicking the actions of their instructor.

Gareth felt his sweat drenched tunic cling to his back, warmed by the midday sun. He couldn't recall the last time he'd truly broken a sweat and now he was covered in the salty substance. He swung his pike outward striking with the butt end, watching his students follow suit. It was a simple task. Train the new recruits and separate the pikesmen from the shieldsmen. Service to the Shadgull army was demanding, but he found it to his liking. And it offered a fair amount of coin as a freelance.

"Master Polearm!" A young and out of breath voice called from behind him.

"At ease!" He watched the men shoulder their staves, taking rest. Stabbing the butt of his weapon into the dirt, he spun around to find a young man in his late teens standing in salute. A dark green tabard marked with a black trident across the chest burned its contrast into his eyes. Gareth glanced at the man's waist, searching for the circular badge emblazoned upon his sash. "What have you got for me, Initiate?"

"My Lord, the scouts have returned. Arborlond was attacked. We have proof it was the dreu. Reports say they're headed north."

Gareth took in the man's words, feeling his rage grow with each syllable. Refusing to let his emotion show in front of the man he gave a restrained nod. "Keep me posted. I want to know the second they move south of the gate."

The messenger offered salute a second time. "Yes, sir!"

Gareth waved off his salute, giving a half-assed return. "And have Ravion prepare an envoy to Evinwood. We need to know why the alfar allowed the dreu to attack so close to their border without alerting us."

The messenger nodded and returned to his horse. Climbing up, he positioned himself in the saddle and urged the steed onward. It sprang into action, carrying him out of sight.

Gareth pulled his pike from the ground and returned his attention to the men. "Fall in!"

The wilds of Evinwood were a sight to behold. They were rumored to be the most beautiful place in all of Dalmoura, and thus far held true to that. Flowers grew in abundance, animals frolicked in their instinctive lives, and the massive trees loomed over the world offering shade and comfort to all beneath their canopy.

The band of humans pushed through the luscious forest, ignoring all penalty from the natural defenses of the land. Their green tabards cried in protest against the sharp barbs and ridged branches, ripping free of the layered linen. The snap of a bowstring drew their attention. Weapons at the ready they took position back to back, searching for the source. To their surprise, they were surrounded by a ring of arrows standing vertical, their heads buried in the dirt. Not only were they surrounded, they were outnumbered.

A smooth, yet commanding voice echoed through the trees, sending an unsettling chill down their spines. "Why do I have five men traipsing through my forest? I've not received so much as a message announcing your arrival."

They searched for the unseen speaker, feeling helpless, but resolved to their training. Cowardice was not acceptable, especially on assignment. It could send the wrong message for The Order as a whole. Clenching their weapons, they waited, unsure if they should speak or not.

"I see you're men of Marbayne. Tell me, where is your commander, for I desire to speak with him? Ravion? Kane? I find it unlikely they would send men into my realm without first contacting me." The slender figure stepped from the trees, revealing his presence to the entrapped men. He stood several inches taller than the average human and carried a superior gracefulness. His armor appeared to be forged from the trees themselves, layered with oak leaves and reinforced plates of bark. Upon closer inspection it was clearly made of finely crafted leather with an expert's tooling, each detail carved to perfection. His hair was tied in a bun at shoulder length and a bow was strung across his back. Twin swords rested upon his hips and a narrow quiver of arrows hung below his kidney.

They were lost in the sight of the myrkalfar, so entranced by his majestic stature that they hadn't seen the others step into view, their bows drawn and aimed to kill. "Ma— My Lord!" One of the scouts gave a respectful bow, finding his tongue. "We were sent by Kane. He ordered us to investigate the silence from Tresengal. We haven't heard anything from them since before Arborlond was attacked."

"You seem to have gotten lost. Tresengal is north of Heroes Gate. You've found your way into the lands of Evinwood. But where are my manners? I am Aldulrien Quetalious Denarie, King of Evinwood and lord of the myrkalfar." He gave an exaggerated bow. "As for your assignment, I fear things are worse than your lords realize. The dreualfar have returned to the surface. They've amassed an army bred for war and I fear my people alone cannot hold them off. Maradar Keep has already fallen to a fraction of their number." He looked at his men, still holding their aim. Motioning them, they lowered their bows. "But I assume you'll want to confirm this for yourselves." He raised his hands, giving a gentle wave.

The trees behind the scouts groaned and flexed, bending at their trunks. Vines of ivy and barbs crawled away as if they were alive, revealing a clear path through the dense forest.

"Make haste, for the path will not last long. Once you've reached the wall, you'll find a crack large enough to crawl through. Tresengal lies just on the other side."

In the blink of an eye, the king and his men were nowhere to be seen, leaving the scouts to their solitude. Sheathing their weapons, they turned down the path laid out for them.

They reached the wall in no time, more than likely some kind of alfaren magic, they suspected. As promised, there was a break in the thick stone, just wide enough for a single man slip through. One by one they crawled to the other side, finding a different world. Where the forest had been warm in the midday sun, this new realm was cold and dark, as if somehow night had fallen while they were inside the thirty-foot stone barrier.

Aldridge was beginning to slow for the evening. It'd been a hot, sticky day in the summer heat, but the cool evening air was beginning to settle in for the night.

Kane stood at the edge of town watching the forest road, not far in the distance. His breastplate shined in the fading sun, displaying a brilliant symbol upon each shoulder, announcing his affiliations. The right side was an engraved smoked colored trident, trimmed in emerald, while the left radiated a faint red glow of a bricked tower. The second burned above the metal, seemingly applied through magic rather than alteration.

His patience was wearing thin. "They should have returned nearly four hours ago." He fumed, concerned by their absence. Glancing at the fading sun, watching the final slither disappear behind the horizon, he had to admit to himself that they weren't returning. *I can't wait any longer.* Sighing heavily, he turned and made his way for the tower. *Perhaps the magi will be able to scry and explain the reason for their tardiness.* A glimmer of hope growing inside him, he passed through the large iron gates set into the red brick walls. Continuing up the winding walkway he stepped through the red stone archway, feeling the power of the boss wash over him.

The haze filled grounds cleared, illuminated by floating orbs of various colored light. The towering structure shot into the sky as far as he could see, disappearing into the rolling clouds above. The tower's front entrance stood open, inviting him.

Kane stepped through the perfect sized opening, watching the breezeway expand before him.

A row of templar stood along each side, awaiting need of their services. Catching sight of their commander they snapped to attention, raising their pikes to form an archway.

The armored warrior paused a moment, giving them time to perform the unnecessary ceremony. He stepped through acknowledging each man, silently reciting their names and family status. It wasn't a common practice, but he felt it an important one. Even if he didn't put it into words, it showed the men that he cared about them and would personally see to their families' wellbeing in the event of their death. Wars could be won or lost with the loyalty a man felt for his commander, and he wasn't going to fall short.

He reached the opening at the far end of the entrance and stepped through, taken back by the sight, as always.

The chamber went on what seemed like forever, unconfined by the outside walls. The main room, a greeting area for visitors, was filled with rugs of the finest quality covering the floors. Their extravagant colors splayed out, intertwining with each other in the most fantastic ways. Large tapestries hung from the towering, red walls, displaying wondrous depictions of mighty wizards and battles long past. Frames hung here and there, their occupants moving about and interacting with the world around them. It was quite a sight to behold. Servants and apprentices alike rushed about, obeying the requests of their masters. It was utter chaos in the most organized way imaginable.

He passed the dancing colors and turned to face a well-fed woman sitting on the back side of a large oaken desk. She wore a fine blue dress with white lace. Her spectacles were crescent shaped, barely covering her eyes, and her long, brown hair dangled over the large tome resting in front of her.

She glanced at the man overshadowing her. "Good evening, Master Kane. How fares the heat outside?"

"It's cooling off a bit, but I fear it'll return in the morning. I don't mean to be rude, but I must speak with Relavin immediately. Can you tell him I'm on my way?"

The portly woman gave a half-hearted smile. "Not a problem, I'll inform him right away."

Kane stepped into a small archway off the side of the room. There was no floor, nor ceiling, just an empty room void of all save for a strange illumination that caused the walls to glow a light blue. Both the floor and ceiling were black as a starless night.

He envisioned the mage, focusing all his will into the man's image. The blue light radiating from the wall pulsed and twisted. Within a moment it shifted to a bright orange and began to spin.

The greeting room faded from view, surrounding him in the dizzying orange. His stomach churned with the changing color, growing more intense by the moment. Just when he thought he was going to lose himself, it returned to its calm blue, revealing a different room where the first had been. Taking a heavy breath to settle his stomach, he stepped into the large study.

The room was packed full of shelves, overflowing with books of all colors and sizes. There was a large oak table in the center with a single matching chair. Racks and curtains hung in various places, leaving much of the floor open but cluttered. The far end was draped by a large white curtain, dividing the study from the bed chamber, magically hovering in place.

A slightly overweight human appeared through the hovering barrier, as if he were a ghost. The dangling cloth remained stationary, despite his passing. He wore a white sleeping robe and had a matching tapered hat on his head with a single puffy ball at the end. His short curly hair was golden brown and his pale-white skin contained many freckles.

A hearty yawn escaped him. He stretched, flexing his back. "What can I do for you this evening, my friend?" Relavin asked, wiping the sleep from his eyes.

"I'm sorry to wake you. I know you have much to do and sleep can be a rare commodity, but I have a terrible feeling that something big is about to happen."

"Generally, when one feels such emotion they are rarely wrong. The question is rather, where and when this big event is to take place?" Relavin cracked a slight smile, knowing the man hated how the magi turned the simplest of statements into the most detailed philosophies.

Kane gave a weary smile, realizing his friend was picking on him. "I sent a group to scout Tresengal. They should have returned hours ago. We've received several reports of dreu activity, but we can't dispatch the armies until we have solid evidence that they're headed this way. I can't get any of them to mobilize until I have something substantial. And thus far I have nothing but aftermath."

"Kane, I'm a wizard of the tower, I do not require schooling in the customs and regulations of the union. Part of my wizardry responsibilities is to maintain and manage these relations."

Kane sighed deeply, realizing his friend's accuracy. "I'm sorry, Relavin. I traveled with you how long?"

"Six years." Relavin interjected

The warrior placed his hands on one of the small tables, feeling it creak beneath his weight. "Yes, and in those six years I learned your responsibilities very well, as you've learned mine. I ask you, in that time, how often were my instincts wrong? I assure you something is happening and I fear this absence is directly connected to it."

Relavin flicked his wrist, walking toward the sturdy table decorating the center of the room. "Very well, my friend. I trust you. If it'll make you happy and allow me to get back to sleep, I'll scry on them. Alive or dead, we'll at least discover what information they carry."

A thick tome with a dark brown binding flew from the shelf and landed softly on the table in front of the mage.

Relavin opened the book as if the correct page was already marked. He grabbed a bowl of sparkly dust from the one of the shelves and sprinkled a small amount over the exposed pages, reading the incantation. "Sterces ruoy em wohs!"

The room faded black, revealing a circular light over the book. Inside displayed a meeting between the scouts and the alfaren king. The scouts stepped onto a clear path and disappeared. The light followed the king and his men to a secluded grove, deep in the forest's heart.

"The dreualfar are a taint upon this land. They must be stopped!" Aldulrien demanded, spitting on the ground.

For an alfar he seemed very human in trait, save for his pointed ears and his affinity for natural looking garments.

"I have a favor to ask." The myrkalfar king continued.

"You have but to name it." The man's face was concealed by shadow but his voice sounded familiar.

"Do all within your power to gather the human lands. Make them aware of the threat we face. My men will keep an eye on the dreualfar movement. When time comes, the myrkalfar will stand with you in battle."

The two spoke as equals in the privacy of the grove like chamber.

The scene faded, returning to the scouts at the wall. One by one, they crawled through a hole in the wall, disappearing into shadow. It was as if they were trapped in a dark room, unable to see the slightest detail. Their fear radiated through the spell, drifting into the scrying chamber.

Kane caught the scent of sulfur and honey, a yellow mist disappearing into his nostrils. He watched the shadow bubble from the book, spreading into the room.

"Army of dreu. Searching for something." The words didn't sound like those of his men. He could feel their pain, their inability to breathe. There was no way they could have said the words. It was more like their emotion, their fear, their combined thoughts forming the message.

The dark presence sent a chill down his spine.

Without warning the book exploded, sending small pieces of burning paper in all directions. The magical flames hovering over their sconces brightened, illuminating the room enough to burn away the remaining shadow.

The two stood over the ruined book watching the last bits burn to ash.

"That was strange." Relavin stated with a perfectly calm demeanor, refusing to show the least bit of concern.

"You think?"

"It seems my spell was cut. We should have seen everything that happened to them, including their deaths, if that were the case. It shouldn't have ended like that."

"I would have guessed your book shouldn't have exploded like that either." Kane added.

"Yes— Well, generally that doesn't happen."

"Is there anything we can do?" The armored man asked, more concerned than before.

"Not that I'm aware of. What's happened here is beyond my knowledge. I must meet with the Magnis. If anyone knows anything, it would be him. Continue your duties, I'll send for you when I've something new to share."

Kane nodded and turned toward the archway as he had once before. The blue lights swirled and the room faded.

Cheers of excitement echoed through the trees surrounding Dreuslayer Keep. The courtyard was full of servants, visitors, and trainees standing around the outer ward, watching the sport before them.

Malakai sliced in with his battle rapier, spinning around to block with the short sword in his other hand. The blows were solid and forceful, yet no harm was intended in the strikes.

Krenin twisted the newly forged great sword, deflecting the slice. Rolling his wrist, the large blade danced around for a secondary attack. The ferocity of his strike knocked the sword from his friend's hand, overpowering him and nearly catching Malakai in the side.

The swashbuckler jumped, avoiding the potentially deadly blow. His offhand weapon skated to the other side of the arena. Adjusting his style, he positioned his feet and reengaged the half-orc. Holding his reinforced blade in front of him, he paused, letting Krenin advance again.

Krenin adjusted, knowing the single blade would be much faster than the dual-blade style. He rushed in bringing all his might to the powerful strike. Continuing forward, his shoulder collided knocking the swashbuckler from his feet.

Malakai forced the air from his lungs, feeling his feet leave the ground. Sucking through his nose, he controlled the intake, keeping himself from taking too much and panicking with its loss. He flexed his legs, letting them absorb the impact. Landing on his feet, he bent and sprang toward the larger combatant.

Krenin brought the newly forged sword in front of him, locking it against the smaller blade. It flexed under the pressure, groaning in protest. Had it not been reinforced for the purpose of such blows, it surely would have snapped. He looked into Malakai's eyes, seeing the exhilaration in his expression. It made him enjoy their exercise that much more. "You gonna lose!" He stated defiantly, fueling the fire.

"Not today, I'm not!" Malakai hooked the half-orc's leg, shoving against him, using the locked weapons to balance himself.

Krenin stumbled backward, feeling the obstacle behind his leg. Ripping his blade free, he twisted and disengaged.

"Cease battle!" The voice echoed over the chatter of the audience, reaching both the combatants.

They lowered their weapons, glancing toward the bailey. Kane hurried down the steps toward them.

The armored warrior stepped into the courtyard, rushing past the spectators. He stepped into the arena, stopping between the two warriors. "We're needed. An urgent meeting has been requested between Remle, Aldur, and the other lords."

"We're all needed for that? Don't you and Ravion usually handle that kind of stuff?"

Kane spoke in a hushed tone as to not rile the listeners. "Typically, yes. But this is different. This time, we prepare for war!"

Chapter XVI
Pain and Gain

Several candles illuminated the dank cavern room, flickering off the roughly chiseled walls. The air was cool and smelled of earth.

Nezial reached across the table, securing a bucket of water. Moss had grown to the wooden slats and a thin layer of film floated atop the stagnant liquid. "I hate when they pass out, it takes all the fun out of their punishment." He spoke aloud to no one in particular. Overturning the bucket, he poured the slimy contents onto his guest's head. "I hope you didn't expect me to kill you so soon. I made a promise and I intend to keep it."

Highlord Kashus' eyes shot open on response to the cold splash. His body was drenched and shivering. Blinded by the multiple lights, he blinked several times, letting them adjust. He attempted to sit up, finding himself unable to rise. His vision cleared, revealing a large mirror mounted to the ceiling overhead. He laid upon a stone slab, secured at each joint by a thick leather strap. His eyes darted between the mirror and what little he could see in his peripherals. Fear rose in his gut at the sight of the dreualfar commander, that cruel smile lingering upon his face. Attempting to fight his restraints, memories of days past rushed to him. He recalled the mutilation of his body, rendering him non-recognizable. His torturer thus far, had only used his vile magics to punish him, pulling at his insides, burning him beneath the flesh, twisting his soul until he felt pleasure. But each morning he awoke renewed, forced to live it again. Never in his life had he experienced anything like it, and it was only going to get worse. Swallowing the memories, he turned his head as far as the straps would allow, acknowledging the commander. "Let's get this over with." His voice was weak, but defiant.

Nezial pulled against the straps. "As soon as I make sure you're secure. It'd be a shame if you flinched and forced me to cut too deep. That'd be no fun at all." His wicked smile burned into the man's soul.

Kashus straightened his head, staring straight into the reflection, awaiting the pain that was sure to follow. Why they'd gone through the trouble of installing the speculum was an unknown mystery. Best he could figure, its sole purpose was to display the horrors to befall to him.

Nezial leaned over the slab, obstructing the man's view. Grabbing hold of the small, wooden table overloaded with various instruments and devices, he drug it closer, pressing his weight into the human's midsection.

The unexpected weight crushed Kashus, making it difficult to breathe. He tensed his stomach muscles, hoping it would offer some resistance.

The dreualfar wiggled the table a bit further, glancing up to ensure it was visible in the mirror. "Can you see that alright? I'd hate for you to miss the show."

"Could you move it a few inches to the right? I can only see half of the saw." Kashus weakly chuckled his rebellion, feeling the previous day's ache.

"Absolutely." Nezial dug his elbows into the man, shifting the table slightly. "It that better?"

Kashus groaned in pain, closing his eyes to block it out as best he could.

Smiling at his prisoner's defeat Nezial stood, grabbing an iron instrument. It resembled a pair of shears with narrow flat metal pads on each end. He opened and closed them, revealing the small spikes inside the pads. "Hold still. This may hurt a bit." Securing the highlord's arm, Nezial pressed his hand against the stone, forcing it flat. Carefully, he inserted the sharp tip under the edge of his fingernail and gently separated the soft skin from the nail. The gray metal glided easily, seating near the root. Nezial squeezed the handles, locking the pads around the nail.

Kashus couldn't see much of what was happening, but he could feel the cold metal inside his finger. It took every ounce of will to keep from crying out in pain and anger.

The dreualfar commander glanced at his prisoner's face, smiling his wicked smile. "Are you ready?" Refusing to wait for a response, he rolled the tool backward toward the secured wrist. The nail flexed briefly and then split away, ripping several strands of white nerve endings with it. He pulled the detached nail away, hearing the last bits of skin pop in defeat.

Kashus lost his battle, screaming the pain away. It was nearly unbearable, as if the bone was being torn out.

The first nail free, Nezial held it over a glass jar resting on the table. Opening the bills, the small piece came free and landed in the bottom. Wasting no time, he secured another nail and promptly removed it.

Kashus watched curled bits of him ping across the bottom of the jar. The salty tears burned his eyes, adding to his pain. His fingers and toes bled from the torn roots, throbbing in-time to his racing heartbeat.

Nezial dropped the last toenail into the jar, directing his attention to his captive. "See, that wasn't so bad." He patted the man atop his head, glancing at his table. "What to do now? Oh, I know." He grabbed a small razor with a leather wrapped handle. The leather was blood stained and blade slightly rusted, but it remained extremely sharp. Stabilizing the man's wrist, Nezial positioned the tip.

"Let me guess. This is going to hurt?" Kashus cried through the words, trying to find his resolve.

"Extremely. But worry not. You won't die." Watching the man's eyes, Nezial pressed the sharpened instrument into the side of his finger, feeling it hit the bone beneath. Carefully, he drug it down to the tip. The skin split easily, revealing meat and bone the length of the appendage. Repeating the process on the other side, he wrapped around, joining the two.

Kashus cried out, unable to escape the scalpel. He closed his eyes, hoping he could retreat into his mind.

Nezial laid the blade on the table and lifted the bills he'd used before. Clicking them together, he cast a disappointed glare at the highlord.

"Open your eyes! I didn't go through the trouble of lighting this room and giving you a mirror if I didn't want you to watch."

Kashus grimaced, but slowly looked upon his captor. Finding his rapidly fading spark of rebellion, he weakly spoke. "My apologies. Boredom was luring me into slumber." It hurt, cracking a smile, but it was worth it. If he could anger the dreualfar, perhaps he could die quickly.

"Oh? I'll take care of that." He jabbed needle like jaws into the tip of the wound, closing it on the meat and flesh. Pulling slowly, careful to prevent tearing the flesh, while evoking the most pain possible, Nezial peeled the finger like a banana. Once he'd finished with each finger, he moved onto the hands, and finally the arms, using the loose meat and skin to pull the rest.

Kashus' arms and legs were little more than bloody sinew and torn muscle, displayed in the mirror of torture. He was horrified by his visage, gripped in agony, but unable to look away.

Nezial laid the pliers aside and grabbed a pair of long nosed tongs and a wooden plank, notched on the ends. Laying them on the stone slab, he observed the tormented soul before him, content that he hadn't looked away. "Now, let me ask you again. Where is it?"

Kashus coughed, feeling his body jolt from the instinctive action. Pain shot through him, crippling him further. "I'll never tell."

Nezial sighed heavily. It wasn't nearly as fun anymore. "I have things to do. Yet you continue to defy me. Very well. Your tune will change soon enough. Mark my words." He grabbed the blood-soaked scalpel and cut a small slit in the highlord's lower abdomen. Spreading the hole, he reached in with the tongs and secured a small section of intestine. The rubbery hose was slick, coated in a clear, thin fluid. He slid the plank under the squishy cord, setting it in the deep notches. "Are you sure you won't tell me?"

Kashus glared at the mirror, refusing to answer the question.

"As you wish." Nezial twisted the plank, coiling the intestine around it, pulling the bowels out further with each wrap.

Screams echoed through the underground cavern, calling all dreualfar within earshot to investigate the source of the disturbance.

Nezial didn't mind. It showed his people what he was capable of, kept them inline and ready to obey his commands.

Overflowing with torment and tears, Kashus closed his eyes hoping to block out the pain.

Nezial felt his anger rise, noticing his toy's retreat. He laid the plank across the open wound, letting the coiled hose stick together with the lack of pressure. "I told you to watch the show!" Snatching up the razor and flat tipped bills, he encircled the alter, shaking his head. Coming to a stop above the highlord's head, Nezial glared his disapproval. "You're being disrespectful!" Losing all composure, he slammed his fist down beside Kashus' head, knocking one of the ceramic jars to the floor.

It shattered, sending bloody chunks of skin, tendon, and glass in all directions.

He straightened himself, regaining his calm. "Although, truth be told, I'd hoped you'd look away." His vile smile returning, Nezial leaned over the subdued man and slipped the flat pad under his eyelid. Squeezing the handles, he pulled, stretching the thin layer of skin away from the eye. Dragging the razor over the stretched lid, it came free. Quickly moving to the other, he smiled his satisfaction.

Kashus tried to turn his head, a feeble attempt to protect his face, but the straps prevented it. He screamed, feeling the protective layer leave his eyes vulnerable to the cold air and dust of the underground. He could already feel them drying out from lack of moisture, the steaming blood doing little to sooth his discomfort.

Nezial laid the tools to rest where they had been sitting and tossed the two pieces of severed skin on the table with them. "Now that I have your attention, may we proceed?"

His eyes burned from the pool of blood and tears. He could no longer escape to the shadows of his mind. He'd lost everything. Everything, but his one secret. *No, I'll not tell him!* "Go to hell!"

Nezial's lips tightened, wrapped into his familiar smile. "You're already there." He returned to his position at the man's side and finished coiling his intestines on the slotted plank. They slid through the small slit with ease, leaving a trail of film to run down the wound. Nezial wrapped several times, overlapping the rubbery hose. He didn't want to get too zealous. That could result in a tear or rupture and that would rob him of his fun. No, this was going to last as long as he could make it.

The pungent odor of innards began to fill the room. There were no flies or other insects so deep in the underground to risk infection, but the exposure to the dank air was quickly drying him out, turning the pinkish cord to a yellow-brown.

"You should have answered me. This next part is going to be rather painful." Nezial lifted a medium sized hammer. The head was polished and perfectly flat. Not so much as a mar stained the hardened metal. Heaving a wide piece of iron, equally flat, with a forged handle on the back side, he placed the dolly on the bottom side of Kashus' foot. Ensuring the skinless, mutilated toes were pressed firmly against the cold steel, he lifted the hammer and brought it down in a single, fluid motion.

A sticky red and white paste shot from between the two pieces of hardened iron, ringing out from the impact.

The highlord screamed, feeling the already sensitive appendage explode. He glanced down at the ruptured nub. Shredded strands of meat were all that remained. Kashus sucked air between his clinched teeth, watching the dreualfar reset the dolly against his foot.

One by one, Nezial crushed his toes, turning them into a soupy paste. He laid the bloody tools on the table and bent over, grabbing the sides of a large sack on the bottom rack of his cart. With a groan, he lifted the burlap, setting it to rest on the edge of the stone slab. Opening the top, he reached in and scooped a large amount of the loose grain into his hand. "I don't want your wounds to get infected. This will help. Though I fear you'll experience some minor discomfort." Eyes full of pleasure, he slowly poured the large crystals of salt over the restrained captive's limbs. It began to melt, sticking to the bloody appendages. Grabbing another scoop, he gently rubbed it into the missing toes and flayed skin. Working his way up, Nezial massaged the damaged areas, allowing the salt to burn its way into his guest. Reaching his face, he paid special attention to his lidless eyes, careful to keep the sticky mixture out of his orbs. It wouldn't serve to have the man blinded so soon.

Kashus screamed, feeling the salt burn into his mutilated form. It absorbed much of the blood, allowing it to somewhat dissolve and travel deeper into his wounds, drying him much quicker than before. Even the few grains spilled on his stomach burned. If only there were some way to end it all. He bucked as hard as he could, feeling the damaged sections of his body tear open with the movement. It was painful, but worth it. He watched the coil of his innards fall from his midsection and hit the slab. If he could knock it off, perhaps the weight would damage them and he could die. Bucking again, his hopes dissolved like the salt in his wounds.

The blackened arm shot out, catching the roll, carefully returning it to its proper place. "Now be careful, Kashus. Such an accident could rob me of my fun. And we can't have that." Nezial snapped his fingers, letting his magic do its job.

A thick leather strap shot up from beneath the table and coiled itself around Kashus' waist. It tightened, cutting into his hips, preventing even the slightest movement.

"We're done for the day. Rest well and think about your choices. Tomorrow we'll try something new." Nezial walked out of the chamber, leaving the tools where they laid.

Kashus watched two dreualfar rush into view. They were much cleaner than he expected, as if they'd just bathed. Probably an order from his captor.

They carefully cleaned the wounds, leaving as much salt in them as possible. Uncoiling the sticky intestines, they tucked them neatly into the hole and stitched the wound closed with a dull needle and waxed sinew. Bandaging the restrained human, they ensured the blood loss wouldn't release him from bondage any time soon.

One of the dreualfar pried the man's mouth open, while the other poured a milky substance from a tiny glass vial.

It tasted of chalk and had the texture of syrup.

Massaging his throat, the dreualfar securing his neck ensured he swallowed it.

The two dreualfar wiped the tools off and returned them to the table. Grabbing their supplies, they disappeared out the door, leaving him to his solitude.

Screams echoed through the underground corridors. The flicker of candle light danced on the cavern wall, opposite the opening.

Searing pain tore through his senses. The fresh skin he'd grown overnight was raw from the bandages and covered in thousands of blisters and welts. His wounds were sealed, but the fresh burns went deeper than flesh. The muscles beneath were stiff, cooked like a well-done steak.

Nezial brought the wood handled brush down the man's chest. Thousands of sharp wires comprising the bristles, cutting into him. They tore through the soft skin, leaving a trail of thin, bleeding lines.

The raw skin was the least of his concerns. He could feel an added pressure in his stomach. He couldn't remember the last time he'd relieved himself, and his intestines were tangled and knotted inside. He cramped, unable to curl from the pain. It wouldn't be long until his death resulted from his clustered bowels.

One full day he suffered through the burns, until the dreualfar commander left him for the evening.

The following day he found himself covered in ice, freezing what was left of his senses. His body was little more than a wasted mass of bone and desecrated tissue, his mind being the one thing that remained intact, but that wouldn't last much longer in this infernal place.

Kashus lay strapped to the table, his face blue from the icy spells and frozen water. After the other forms of torture, the ice seemed to kill his senses, bringing a slight amount of comfort. But even that was beginning to give way to pain.

Nezial took a step toward him, the sadistic smile ever-present on his lips. Commotion echoed from the dark hallway and a pop echoed in the room. Nezial glanced down, seeing an arrowhead erupt from his stomach. He let out a howl of pain and fell over the wounded highlord, before collapsing to the floor.

Kashus stared into the mirror, shocked to see the three arrows protruding from the now dead commander's back. The thick leather straps that held him in place prevented him from seeing who fired the shots but if they killed the commander, perhaps they would free him.

Sword rang against sword, announcing an unseen battle.

Kashus searched his limited view, trying to catch sight of who stood in the room with him.

Three figures approached. Their features hidden by shadow, unseen in the flickering candlelight.

"Lord Kashus, your wife hired us to rescue you." The large man in the center announced. "Our men have the remaining dreu on the run. Let's get you out of here before we lose this opportunity."

The man on the right placed his hand on Kashus' chest. A faint green light sparked to life, widening and soaking into his body. Kashus felt the warmth flow through him. His skin itched, healing before his eyes. The burns faded, disappearing from view. The open wounds pulled shut, strands of skin jumping from one side to the other, sealing them completely. He felt his crushed toes reform. It was painful, feeling the bones sprout through the healing ends, but it meant he'd be able to walk again. Looking in the mirror, skin wrapped around the digits and they settled in their rightful place, solidifying the renewed bone and muscle. Kashus wiggled them, unsure if he was dreaming. To his surprise, they responded to his request. His stomach churned, but it wasn't in a sickly manner. He could feel his insides moving, getting reoriented to their proper location. Within moments he was whole again.

The man who'd healed him went to work unstrapping the leather bindings, while the one on the left pulled a set of clothing from a brown, linen sack.

Released from his binds, Kashus sat up with assistance from his saviors. His eyes had trouble adjusting to their features, having been in the dim light for so long. He swung his legs off the slab, knocking the buckets of unnatural freezing water to the floor. A light amount of steam floated into the warmer cavern air. He felt his heart jump, seeing their faces clear into his vision. The dreuslayers stood before him, ready to lead him to salvation. "I thank you for your willingness to retrieve me. Many would not dare enter this forsaken place."

Gareth looked the battered man up and down. He was lucky to still be alive. "Thanks would be better offered in coin when we make it out of here."

Kane pulled the tattered clothing in place. The man's bluing skin was cold to the touch and needed to be gradually warmed to prevent shock.

Ravion helped him to his feet, certain he was going to have to learn to walk again.

Taking his first step, Kashus stumbled. He'd lost track of how long it'd been since he last stood. He quickly secured the rags around him, tucking the tension bands out of the way. They were by no means the clothing of nobility that he was used to, but they would offer a little protection in the cool cavern air. He stepped over the fallen commander, feeling comfort in his death. "Get me out of here."

The dreuslayers escorted him from the small room and into the corridor.

Passing from the light, darkness overtook him. He couldn't see so much as a shadow in the pitch black. Holding his hands out, searching for anything, Kashus felt lost, abandoned in the dark. "I can't see anything."

Ravion's calm voice echoed, calming him. "Worry not. We can see just fine. We'll guide you."

He felt one of the men grab hold of his shirt, directing him through the tunnels. He had no idea how far they'd traveled. The absence of light made it feel eternal and brief at the same time. He could feel the walls enclose around him, narrowing into a single passage, told only by the echo of shuffling steps. The packed clay and rock felt to incline slightly and he felt the lingering warmth of the stone ceiling not far above.

The battle continued to echo all around. He didn't know how far away it was, or even if they were going in the right direction. But these men had made a name for themselves. Perhaps they could see him to his family. Trusting in his rescuers, he moved when instructed and slowed when required.

They moved forward several paces, stopping long enough to fend off the unseen attackers, and continued again.

How they knew where they were going in the underworld of the catacombs, he couldn't answer. The fact they had the ability to see in the Underdark was a mystery in of itself, but it served him. That was reason enough to keep quiet. Kashus recalled the rumors of their formation. They were supposedly the only beings, other than the dreualfar, to have successfully navigate the unnaturally dark passageways. Kashus followed, unable to fall behind or move ahead. After what felt like hours, he could see a faint glow in the distance.

They led Kashus toward the sunlight, growing with each step. He felt it greet his face, leaving the catacombs behind him. The bright light was uncomfortable, but it was better than what he'd grown accustomed to.

His eyes adjusting, Kashus glanced around, knowing he was somewhere south of the Krondar border. The coloring of the stone and dirt told him that much. It was much dryer than back home. He was used to the brown soil, usually covered in a light layer of rain or snow. This soil was more of a red clay. A land just as harsh as its occupants. It took several minutes for his eyes to fully adjust to the light. They stood in a secluded grove, the cavern entrance behind them, and large stones surrounding on all sides. A familiar voice reached his ears, bringing a long-forgotten comfort to him.

Kashus turned to see his wife and children appear between two of the large boulders.

They gracefully walked along the trail, breaking into a quick jog at his sight. His two sons, one twelve and the other seven, broke free of their mother's grip and charged, wrapping themselves around his waist. His wife smiled her precious smile, carrying their infant daughter in her arms.

He caught his sons, hugging them tight. Picking them up, he carried them a few steps closer to his wife. They were too heavy for his weakened form to carry for long. Reaching her, he opened his arms, pulling his family close, never wanting to be apart from them again.

"Kashus, I was afraid I'd never see you again." His wife mourned in his arms. "Where'd you hide the stone? That's what they're after. We have to make sure they don't find it!"

He felt the tears rolling down his face. "It's safe, my dear. I haven't told them anything. I thought for sure the dreu had killed you when they took the keep. I'm relieved to see you and our children are safe." Kashus held them for several minutes, afraid to let go.

Gareth approached, clearing his throat to gain their attention. "Our arrangement is complete. Although we've learned what they're after. We need to get out of here and move the stone. I can't risk it falling into their hands."

"Yes, yes. I switched it with the Jewel of Shadgull months ago. No one knows it's there."

"Good. We'll take care of it. For now, we need to get out of here. My men will keep your family safe. I suggest you take them to Marbayne so we can—" Gareth's words were cut short seeing the army of dreualfar swarm from the gap in the rocky outcropping. "What the hell?" He stared in confusion. "How are they in the daylight?"

The dreualfar continued through the hole in the ground. Already there were over a hundred, and many more filing out.

Kashus watched both Ravion and Kane fall to the mass of dark-skinned alfar.

Gareth charged into battle. Several crude scimitars stabbed into him, silencing his objections.

The ever-growing horde of dreualfar cheered their victory over the dreuslayers, headed for his family next.

Kashus glanced around, his wife and sons were several feet away. He rushed toward them, seeing their distance grow with each step. The dreualfar surrounded them, hacking his sons to pieces. When they had finished all that remained was a pile of bloody gore on the stone and dirt covered ground. His daughter was ripped from her mother's arms. One of the dark creatures began chanting over the infant girl.

Her features began to change. Her skin became dark, matching that of the dreualfar. Her ears elongated to a point and her short brown hair turned long and white.

Horrified, Kashus watched the vile beast change his baby girl into one of them.

His wife was forced to the ground, her clothes ripped away, revealing her naked breast. Several of the dreualfar restrained her while the others took turns ravaging her body. Having their fill, they beat her to a bloody pulp, leaving her violated and dying.

The highlord tried to look away, but his body wouldn't comply. He tried to reach her, straining to fight, but he couldn't move. He was trapped, watching his family's destruction. He screamed his failure. He couldn't save them. He couldn't slow them. He couldn't move. His wife's voice echoed in his mind. "You're a coward. You can't save me. You can't save anyone! You're a broken man with little more than a title! A man unworthy of being called a lord!" Frozen in fear, he watched his family suffer his blight.

One of the dreualfar grabbed his dying wife by her long brown hair. He ripped her nearly limp form from the ground, exposing her throat. Taking a rusty dagger, the dreualfar stabbed through the side of her neck and yanked the blade forward. Her lifeless body hit the dirt, tearing what was left with the impact. Her head rolled free, coming to a stop in front of Kashus. An expression of disappointment stared deep into his eyes.

He tried to fight, tried to yell, tried to move but found all impossible. He couldn't do anything other than stand there and watch, unable to process what was happening.

Nezial made his way from the dark cavern, his wicked smile burning through the daylight. He walked over, picking up the once-human baby girl. Continuing toward the highlord, he played with the child as if he had some dark sinister purpose for her.

His voice echoed deep into Kashus' head, a voice mixed with power, malice, and humor. "You thought you could escape me. You should know there's no escape for you." He playfully bopped the infant on the nose, withdrawing an innocent laugh from the corrupted baby.

Kashus screamed, he couldn't help himself. He tried to move, even to comfort himself, but was unable to do so. Looking deep into the mirror stationed above him, he was strapped to the stone slab. He could think of nothing but his family being slaughtered. His daughter being taken by these evil creatures to be raised as one of their own.

The commander stood over the tormented man. His body was broken and now his mind was as well. A smile came to his face with the location of the stone revealed.

Kashus screamed, the illusion of time eluding him. He couldn't tell how long he'd been here, he didn't even know where here was anymore. The visions that were forced upon him had taken all sense of placement. He wasn't sure of anything. He retreated into himself, reliving his failure again and again. He didn't know where he was. He didn't know what was and wasn't real. He wasn't even sure if he was himself, the reflection in the mirror looked like him, but it was so twisted and mangled he could have been mistaken for anyone. All thought abandoned and flooded him, entangling his mind. He was lost, broken. Broken in his soul, broken in his mind. All hope was gone. It all changed so much, so often, he couldn't decide if anything was real.

Several days later Nezial stood in silence, watching his soldiers position the large wooden wedge next to the stone slab where the man softly whispered to himself.

It was simply a section of tree trunk that had been cut at an angle and flattened to stand on end. It stood just over three feet tall, angled downward with the dull tip pointed straight up. The wood was stained with blood and other fluids from years past, but there was an excitement in finally using it.

Nezial had never seen its effects. But his books told him what to expect. The council, before his rise, reserved its use for traitors and general threats to their power. He no delusions, they would have used it on him, had he not claimed power when he did. He certainly proved himself a threat to their rule. But none of that mattered. He was in charge and they were dead. All but Nadilia, whom was confined to her chambers until he had need of her. And now he was going to get to see what this archaic tool was all about. The truth was, he'd grown tired of playing with the broken highlord. The man was of no use to him any longer.

Nodding to his soldiers, agreeing with their placement of the large device, Nezial unstrapped the broken man and removed him from the stone slab.

Kashus was limp, unable to fight even if he wanted to. His muscles were destroyed, leaving him at the mercy of his host. He was of no use to himself, of no use to anyone.

Nezial pulled him to the edge, and waited e guards to take him.

They grabbed the weak human and easily lifted him from the slab. Placing him atop the wedge, they made him straddle it, dangling one leg down each side.

Nezial tied a small rock to each ankle. It wasn't meant to pull, but to apply a constant pressure. There was no threat of him going anywhere. He didn't have the willpower. Turning to his men, Nezial waved them out. Following behind, paused just side the door. "Keep watch. I want to know when he's close to the end." Accepting their blank stare as acknowledgment, Nezial disappearing into the dark corridor.

Kashus stared into nothing. His mind danced with memories of life. Visions of the past, present, and future, none of which were true, but he didn't know any different. He wiggled, searching for a comfort that wouldn't come. Slumped down, his once rigid spine may as well of been a cooked noodle. Lost in nothing and everything at once, he sat there, unaware of what was happening to him.

Over the course of three days gravity pulled him, slowly tearing his body in half. The first day his hips began to separate, splitting him slightly. Blood and fecal matter rolled down the sides from his destroyed colon. The second day reached his stomach, allowing his bowels to drape, undamaged, but free.

He moaned incoherently, lost in pain, but unable to do anything about it. Even if his mind were intact, he didn't have the strength to move. The one thing he did know in his broken state, he would die soon.

The third day, Nezial sat in his study, reading the contents of his glimmering, black book. The secrets it held were his and his alone. No one would dare read from it, not that they could anyway. He was chosen.

A knock at the door roused him.

"Enter!"

The door creaked open, revealing one of his watchmen. "Commander, it's time."

Nezial tossed the book aside and jumped from his chair. He didn't want to miss the final moments. Rushing toward the torture room, he rounded the corner and stepped inside.

The guard took his post outside the door.

Looking upon the man, Nezial was amazed by the damage the simple device had inflicted.

The highlord was draped down both sides, his body nearly in two pieces. Yet he was alive, still looking around, tears of pain in his eyes. His innards had fallen from his body, functional but unprotected. There was a fair amount of blood and other bodily fluids, but clearly not enough to kill the man. Though his time was extremely limited.

Nezial watched in earnest. He heard the resounding pop of the highlord's collar bone collapse under the pressure. The final breath escaped his toy, lying in two piles on each side of the wedge. A wicked smile breached his lips. "At long last, the highlord is dead." The dreualfar commander turned and left the chamber, satisfaction radiating from him. Stopping outside the door, he addressed the two guards "Clean up this mess and prepare for our next guest. The Lord of Shadgull deserves our finest hospitality."

Chapter XVII
Dreuslayers

Thick patches of moss clung to the ancient walls of the Underdark catacombs. Most of the low hanging stalactites had been broken off, leaving a jagged ceiling just above head level. The floor was solid, the dense clay and stone worn down from centuries of travel.

Gareth and Ravion made their way through the dark corridors, listening to the echoes off the seemingly natural walls.

Ravion led the way. His light steps were unheard compared to the clanking of metal from Gareth. The thin dalari scout wore his usual dark blue clothing and tan leather vest. He carefully made his way forward, searching for any presence in the deep tunnels.

Gareth continued on, not caring if the vile creatures heard him. In fact, he hoped they did. It'd give him an excuse to kill the vermin. His large shield was slung on his back and a heavy mace hung from his side. His twin cutlasses were sheathed on each hip, waiting to be drawn.

Ravion stopped, throwing his fist into the air. Reaching across his body, he grabbed his longsword and prepared for battle.

Rolling his shoulder, Gareth flung his shield around and locked his arm into the strap. Grabbing his mace, he readied himself.

Several careless footsteps echoed down the dank passage, carrying the stench of feces and body odor. Unintelligible chatter bounced back and forth, announcing their numbers. It was clear they didn't know about the trespassers awaiting them around the bend.

Ravion stepped to the side, wedging his back into a crevice. He smiled at Gareth, knowing his companion would gladly play the bait. That would give him the perfect chance to ambush the creatures when they charged.

Two dreualfar walked casually down the passageway, carrying on their conversation. One ran his fingers along the rough wall, listening to the other talk. They rounded the bend, freezing at the sight of the broad warrior in the middle of the way. The man was stocky and of average height. He wore tattered armor and held a large mace, the head pointed toward them menacingly. A spiteful grin burned in the dark, taunting them into action.

"Come get some, you black-skinned bastards!" Gareth dared, slamming his mace against the shield. It rang out, echoing along the walls. It was possible the noise would summon more. And he desperately hoped for it. That meant more to kill. Knowing he had some time before they'd pass Ravion, lying in wait, he charged, daring them to do likewise.

They drew their crude scimitars and hesitantly rushed toward the large warrior.

Gareth purposely took half steps, allowing them to close the distance. Seeing they were nearly upon him, he jumped back, throwing off their perception. Bracing his shield, he prepared for the impact.

The first dreualfar slammed hard into him, dropping his sword from the unexpected change in distance.

The bald warrior brought his mace around, crushing the dreualfar's head. It popped, splattering brain matter and blood across the metal device. The now dead dreualfar fell to the rocky floor.

Ravion stepped from his veil, quickly moving behind his unsuspecting prey.

Gareth threw his shield out, easily blocking several swipes. He had no chance of getting past it. He was nothing. Just a simple grunt, armed for no other purpose than patrolling the tunnels.

Ravion calmly positioned his longsword, placing the tip against the unaware dreualfar's spine. Wasting no time, he plunged the sword downward, sinking over half of the blade. The dreualfar buckled at the knees, his life gone before the blade came to a stop. Falling forward, gravity retracted the blade.

Gareth took the opportunity to kick the bottom of his shield, slamming it against the dead creature's face. He heard the neck snap, whipping the head backward. The body spun from the impact, landing roughly in the dense clay.

Ravion knelt and wiped the tainted blood on the tattered clothes of his kill. He stood, sheathing the ancestral weapon. "You just had to get your blow in didn't you?" Shaking his head, unconcerned with the answer, Ravion turned and continued down the passageway.

"Of course! Now when he reaches Osirus, he can tell all his kin that he died at the hands of Gareth Dreuslayer! I'll bet he gets grand honors for that." Laughing at the notion, Gareth reached down and cut an ear from each of the fallen dreualfar. Quickly adding them to his necklace, he rushed after Ravion. "Besides, you can't say I didn't set it up for you perfectly. That means he was half mine."

The sun hung low in the sky, retreating toward the horizon. In a few minutes, night would claim dominion and the city of Shadgull would slow for the evening.

The streets were wide, laid with the finest brick. Not a single stone was out of place in the fading light. The buildings were fantastic, made of stone and wood, each one with a blue shingled roof. The blue and silver banner of Shadgull hung in every direction. A lantern post stood every thirty feet, alternating on each side of the road, allowing merchants and citizens to find their way in the dark.

Kane sat atop his horse, taking in the sight of the grand city. He'd been here before but it always made him feel small in comparison. It was by far the largest city he'd ever been to. And here, the people knew his name. *I am Kane, High Templar of the Tower of Magi.* He chuckled at the title. It was such a frivolous thing. Little better than a waxed stamp on a note. It spoke of position, nothing more. Though he couldn't deny its use. Such titles had a way of granting access to audiences normally out of reach. Returning to the task at hand, he recalled his reasoning for the trip. The words played in his head once again. *Army of dreu— searching for something.*

In the distance, he could see the outline of an amazing fortress. The shadows of the fading light made it glow like a beacon of hope. Spurring his steed, he closed the distance, urgency in mind.

The fortress had a large wall built around it with several sentries patrolling the ground. Two armed guards stood on each side of the barbican. The drawbridge was lowered, granting access to the structures on the other side. A heavy portcullis stood open, serving as a secondary gate comprised of a steel lattice. The heavy gate rested between two layers of stone and was held up by large iron chains, keeping the massive steel from sealing itself into the ground.

Kane reached the wood planked ramp and slowed his horse. While it stood open, he didn't need the guards attacking him over a simple miscommunication. "I bring message from the Tower for Master Remle De Leon." His horse fidgeted, unhappy with the sudden stop.

One of the guards waved him entry.

Kane obeyed and led the horse through the grand opening. Continuing up the road, he came to a stop at the fortress doors. He dismounted and handed the reins to the groom in waiting. Straightening himself, making sure his armor was aligned and unmarred, Kane marched the stone stairway toward the barred doors at the top.

The guards stood erect, waiting announcement of intention.

"I am Kane, Sheriff of Aldridge and High Templar to the Tower. I require audience with Master Remle De Leon."

"This way, Master Kane." The door creaked open, allowing him entry.

One of the guards led him through the doors and into the reception hall.

"Master Kane, I'm afraid I must ask you to disarm and wait here." The guard rang a bell mounted to the wall and turned back the way he'd come.

Kane nodded his understanding and unbuckled his weapon belt. Hooking it on one of the many racks, he ensured both his short sword and dagger were easily accessible if required, though such thoughts were foolish in such a place. He unhooked the leather strap, securing his great sword, and laid it beside his belt.

A moment later a thin man wearing a blue robe with silver inlay stepped into sight. "Master Kane, I presume?"

"Yes?"

"The Tower sent word of your arrival. This way please."

So they can send a message that I'm headed this way, but they can't relay the information themselves to save me a trip? He silently vented his frustrations, but followed after.

They passed through several hallways and large rooms until they finally reached the grand hall.

The floor was comprised of silver marble slates, and a thick, blue rug ran the length of the room. Matching tapestries hung from the walls, and the far end had a four-tiered dais, alternating between silver and blue. The top was set with an aged throne of what appeared to be polished oak. It was encrusted with several gems arching over the back rest and along the ridged frame.

Remle sat in the throne, his blonde flowing hair radiated the last glimmers of sunlight through the stained windows above.

Kane followed his escort toward the throne, stopping several steps away.

The court mage bowed low before the city's lord, holding pose in wait for the warrior to follow suit.

Realizing his mistake, Kane quickly gave a respectful bow and stood, waiting for permission to speak.

The mage stood and announced his guest much louder than required. "Lord Remle, may I present Master Kane, Dreuslayer, Sheriff of Aldridge, and High Templar to the Tower."

Without word, the mage turned and disappeared down the blue carpet, leaving Kane alone with the large lord and the several servants silently performing their various task along the sides of the room.

"It's good to see you again, Kane. What brings you to my city?" Remle asked, his fingers interlocked in front of him. He peered down at the man, recalling their previous encounter. It seemed much had changed for the boy since that night in the pub those few years ago. He was hardly a boy any longer, though he was still surprisingly young.

"My Lord, a group of scouts were sent to Tresengal to discern the motives behind the dreu assault on Maradar Keep. We received one message but it was cut short. 'Army of dreu, searching for something,' was all the magi were able to discern." Kane took a step closer. "My Lord, may I speak freely for a moment?"

The fair-haired man nodded his approval.

"What troubles me more— they were able to storm the capital in under a day. Even if they were attacked completely by surprise, they should have been able to hold for at least a month until reinforcements could arrive. That tells me two things. The dreu are extremely well organized. And they have something at their disposal that we haven't seen before. And now, My Lord, a question I pose to you. What's stopping them from directing their attention here?"

Remle leaned against the back of his throne, keeping his hands in position. "I understand what you're asking. I'll prepare my army for war and have them at the ready if these vermin should crawl from their hole in the ground. You may inform your brothers, Shadgull stands with them."

Kane bowed once again, dismissing himself. The last rays of light gleamed through the skylight, reflecting an emerald green gem set in the top of the throne. He paused, inspecting the stone. It was just like the others, but there was something different about it— something inviting. Shaking the thoughts from his head he acknowledged the lord once again. "It will be done, My Lord." Respectfully, Kane half turned to prevent presenting his back to the ruler. It was a long ride back to Marbayne and he needed to return as quickly as possible.

The heart trees of Evinwood stood taller than all the forests of Dalmoura. The smallest trunks were nearly twenty-foot-wide and the undergrowth between them was thick and constricting. The sheer size of the vastly unexplored lands made it easy to get lost. Even the canopy, far overhead, blocked out direct sunlight making direction hard to navigate.

The two soldiers pressed on, careful to prevent damaging the overgrown vegetation as best as possible.

Krenin squeezed between the low hanging vines, stepping into a patch of moss. He searched in all directions, amazed by the sights around him. He'd never traveled through Evinwood before, making the trip a completely new experience to him. The thick growth hindered his movement due to his thick, muscular frame, but he managed, amazed by the next strange looking plant he stumbled upon. "Malakai, look at this one!" Krenin knelt beside the large pod, resembling an open pistachio shell with several thin whiskers protruding from the edge. The inside was a deep pink pedal, covered in tiny bumps that smelled of fruit. He pressed his meaty finger against the whiskers, pulling back just in time to see the plant slam shut. A child-like giggle escaped him, watching it slowly open up again.

Malakai was somewhat less enthused. He'd encountered the myrkalfar on many occasions. Their pompous attitudes made him dread meeting the tall, slender folk. While he was able to travel the small trails much easier than his larger counterpart, he still found the forest cumbersome compared to a cleared road. Or even a stag trail for the matter. But they had neither. He desperately wanted to pull his blade and chop a path, but if they came across the treefolk—. It was one thing to hack your way through a familiar forest. But to do so in alfaren territory was asking for trouble. Malakai watched the half-orc poke the plant again, lost in glee with its response. "Leave that thing alone. You don't know if it's poisonous. Last thing I need is to be draggin' your ass through this forest."

Krenin stood, wishing he could play with it one last time. Following after his friend, he glanced around in search of other unseen wonders. "You see anything?" His short tusks made the common tongue hard to pronounce.

"Trees!" Malakai replied, clear annoyance in his tone. He stopped, staring dead ahead.

"You not lookin' hard enough—." Krenin walked into the back of Malakai, cutting his words off. The sudden stop startled him, causing him to jump back. His feet got tangled around one of the many vines littering the forest floor. Losing his balance, he crashed down, landing in a patch of briars. "Ouch, why you stop?" Krenin rolled over, trying to get up without the thorns digging in.

"What business does a human and a half breed have in the forest of Evinwood?" The brown haired myrkalfar stared down his arrow, trained on the swashbuckler. Three others stood at his side, their bows drawn and ready to fire.

"We bring word from Marbayne. Kane of the Tower asked us to speak with your king about the recent dreu threat." Malakai replied, trying to keep his irritation from showing.

The myrkalfar lowered their bows. "Follow us. We'll lead you to our commander. He'll decide if you have audience or not." They turned and easily passed through the trees showing no trouble in doing so whatsoever.

Malakai rushed after them, slowed by the foliage. He had no idea how they were able to move so nimbly. One moment they were there. The next, they were gone. He raced after them, catching a brief glimpse just long enough to enforce proper direction. His irritation grew. He knew they were toying with him. There was no doubt he could have seen them at all unless they desired it.

Krenin ran to keep up, finding it hard to stay on his feet. The forest was conspiring against him and his hurried pace. Tripping for the third time, he barreled through, letting the vines and ivy obstructing his path tear against his larger form. He slowed seeing Malakai just ahead.

The swordsman stepped through a rather thick patch of brush, disappearing into a grove of sorts. It still had its growth, but it would be much easier to travel than the forest itself. He spotted the myrkalfar at the far side waiting for them, clearly annoyed by their lack of respect for the forest and their slow movement.

Malakai and Krenin traveled unhindered for quite some time, following the alfar to a small clearing. The trees remained thick and tall, forming a natural wall around them. The canopies offered a great amount of shade, but allowed plenty of light through. It was as if the area was grown to perfection. Even the forest floor appeared as if the leaves naturally fell someplace else, leaving the bright green grass to flourish in the grove.

The brown haired myrkalfar reached behind him, pulling a thin, white horn with a leather strap attached to it. Pressing it to his lips, he blew, angling the opening toward the sky. It echoed out sounding more like some kind of animal call than a horn.

A few moments later another myrkalfar stepped through the trees and into the grove. He wore black leather armor with several studs placed to give the appearance of dragon scales. He spoke in a language neither of the dreuslayers could understand.

Malakai couldn't help but get lost in the unknown tongue. It reminded him of an ancient song of loss and sorrow, with a brief flicker of hope.

The others nodded and stepped through the veil of greenery, disappearing from sight.

The dark armored myrkalfar approached the two, giving a slight bow of respect. "Greetings, I'm Jaklus Motin Afar, Captain of Evinwood. My men tell me you bring word from Kane of the Tower. Judging from your garments, I wouldn't assume you to be in the Tower's service. This means you're more likely Dreuslayers." He cocked his head, curiously, seeking validation.

"You're correct. I'm Malakai Torne and this is Krenin. Kane asked us to meet with your king to discuss the recent dreu incursion. As I'm sure you're aware, they recently attacked Tresengal and have abducted its lord. We sent a group to discover what the dreu are after, but they were apparently killed before they found much."

Jaklus nodded, "I know of the men you speak. They passed through here not long before the Reaping of Maradar. Aldulrien has already declared that the dreu must be purged. Order has been given and if your people are going to march, you may count us among your number." Jaklus turned to leave.

Malakai reached out grabbing the alfar's arm.

The myrkalfar captain glanced at the hand securing him, warning evident in his eyes.

Realizing his error, Malakai released him, gesturing apology. "I'll inform them upon my return. Which I was hoping you might be able to help us with. My friend and I have been having a bit of trouble trekking through your forest. With your aid, there's less risk of breaking anything you hold dear."

Hurried footsteps echoed through the fortress of Shadgull. Servants, advisers, and lords alike turned toward the entrance of the great hall in search of the commotion.

A scrawny messenger entered the room, running as fast as his feet could carry him. His brow was drenched in sweat and his tunic flopped from the movement. "Master Remle! Master Remle!" He shouted across the chamber, continuing toward the seated lord.

"What is it Reginald? Catch your breath." Remle looked upon the man. His messenger's excitement was never this vocal. Something big must have happened. Remle only hoped it wasn't news of the dreu breaking their defenses. Such a feat would prove disastrous. He deferred suspect, patiently awaiting him to continue.

Out of breath, Reginald came to a stop at the base of the dais and bowed awkwardly. "Master Remle— The Coalition of Countries has decreed that you are to be crowned Baron of Dalmoura. They're on their way here now to deliver the coronet." He panted heavily, unable to contain himself.

"Baron is it? Well, I suppose we should prepare for their arrival." Remle clapped his hands, giving the silent order.

Servants went to work preparing the throne room for a banquet.

"You're dismissed, Reginald. Stop by the kitchen and get yourself a meal and drink."

The messenger bowed a second time, holding position. "Thank you, My Lord." Reginald stood and turned to leave.

Remle listened to the footsteps softly approaching his right side. A familiar voice flowed forth.

"Baron or not, are you sure it's wise to hold celebration when our outlying towns are being attacked?" Erik made his way around the dais, stopping in front of the throne. His freshly pressed silver and blue tunic sparkled in the beaming sunlight through the overhead windows.

"My son, you'll learn one of these days that even the most dedicated soldier needs time to unwind every now and then. A man fed on duty alone, while valuable, will eventually fall prey to his passions. In simpler terms, a man pushed too hard will deteriorate over time, leaving the shadow of the man he once was."

"Forgive me, Father. But I don't believe it wise to leave such things to chance. Keep the men happy, yes. But why push them to that point when there are other options?"

"To what options are you referring? We're at war. The only options we have are to fight or flee. And I've too much invested in this land to simply abandon it. My father, and my father's father, and his father before him sat upon this throne. As will you, one day. It's our job to ensure our people have a safe home. That's what it means to be a hero. Heroes Gate wasn't built by the men from the north. It was built by us, by our bloodline. When the options were much as they are now. Our ancestors chose to stand and fight, that's the only reason we have this home. That's what being a leader is all about, Son. It's choosing to build a shield so your people have the protection they deserve."

"I understand. But what if we find a trinket? One that will help."

"What kind of trinket?" Remle stared at his son. He clearly wasn't ready for the throne. Chasing such foolish notions of magic treasures was proof enough.

"I've heard rumor of a dagger that has the ability to give its owner unlimited power. Something like that could ensure the kingdom's survival throughout the ages." Erik reached into his pouch, retrieving a worn piece of parchment.

"Son, sometimes I fear my position here has clouded your understanding of the common man. Magic is not the answer. It has its uses from time to time, yes, but it's not us. We come from simple folk. To go gallivanting off on some crusade for some dagger that probably doesn't even exist would place our lands in further turmoil. Especially now that the dreu attacks have moved so close to our front door." Remle pulled his golden locks into a tail and tied it off. "Think on it, Son. I'm sure you'll find the answers you're searching for." Remle placed his crown atop his head and signaled the steward.

An aged man approached, wearing nobleman's garments of the house colors. "Yes, My Lord?"

"Have the stable boy prepare my horse. I feel like going for a ride."

Erik glanced at the crumpled sketch of the wavy dagger. Taking a deep breath, he wadded it up and stuffed it back into his pouch. *One day, old man. One day I'll have the crown and you'll listen to what I have to say.*

Shadows darted through the darkness, dancing in and out of each other. The clanking of swords echoed off the mossy cavern walls. Hundreds of dreualfar swarmed, trying to get at the trespassing figures amidst their ranks

"You'd think you'd insulted their mothers with the way they're coming at us." Ravion complained through labored breaths, deflecting another blow from the constant barrage.

"I did!" Gareth laughed. The spike on the bottom of his shield was planted, holding firm against the wave of dreualfar. Swinging his mace wildly, the large warrior knocked the encroaching mass away from him.

The two battled with an unnatural presence against the seemingly unlimited number.

Ravion yelled across the clank of swords, knocking the attacking blows away. "Do you ever think before you make your presence known? I mean, it's not like we're out numbered or anything!" Sarcasm was heavy in the air. He countered for another strike.

Gareth bashed the head of another dreualfar, spinning to look at his friend. "Usually? — No, it doesn't matter how many there are. I'm gonna to kill every last one of em'."

"And me along with them." Ravion retorted.

"Nah, you're too pretty to fall to these ugly bastards." Gareth chuckled, tightening the grip on his shield. He yanked the spike free, kicking the metal barrier outward. It collided with his closest attackers, launching them into the approaching sea. Several other rushed forward, filling the void created by the swipe. Gareth stabbed the bottom mounted spike back into the ground, making sure it was set. He dropped his mace, letting it swing from the leather strap around his wrist. Reaching under his shield, he pulled a clay flask from its leather band. "You may want to shield your eyes, pretty boy!"

Ravion sliced through three dreualfar at once. The words echoed into recognition, telling him what was about to happen. He swiped wide, letting the dreualfar easily deflect the feint. They got tangled and fell into one another, buying him a brief moment. Using the distraction to his advantage, Ravion fell back, covering his face with the baggy sleeve of his shirt.

Gareth squeezed the hardened clay, feeling if crack beneath his grip. He threw the weakened container as hard as he could, watching it disappear into the sea of black-skinned monsters. Wasting no time, he ducked behind his shield and covered his eyes.

A bright light erupted, revealing hundreds of dreualfar in the wide cavern hall. The explosion incinerated those closest to it, burning them to a crisp in mere seconds. Several others screamed in pain, trying to escape the lingering discharge. Those furthest scrambled to escape the effects, fearing another blast.

Popping up from behind his shield, Gareth swung his mace, bashing the stunned few in front of him. They tumbled to the ground in their death throes, their blinded senses rendering them unable to defend.

Ravion glanced into the rapidly darkening cave, seeing the dreualfar retreat. He lowered his blade, but kept it at the ready. It wasn't like them to flee, unless they took out the command. Which was possible. The sunstones were vicious.

Gareth lowered his weapon, securing it to his waist. Slinging the shield to his back, he glanced over at Ravion. A big smile clung to his face. "That was fun!"

Ravion sheathed his sword and pulled his dagger from one of the dead dreualfar. "Next time I suggest we find a spot a little easier to defend." He stepped over the piles of scorched bodies, making his way toward the blast site. The numbers were thinned drastically, leaving charred remains at the center. Little more than crumpled ash littered the worn floors where the broken flask rested. "It seems the sunstones are effective." He studied the distance, silently judging the damage the simple device had inflicted. It was nearly too much to consider morally right. Such a tool needed to be regulated. Shaking his head at the destruction he stepped over the remains and continued down the passageway, leaving Gareth to claim his ears.

"Aye, good thing too. I wasn't sure how much longer we could hold out, if they hadn't." Gareth replied, beginning his ritual.

A partial moon could occasionally be seen through the rolling clouds but it was much too sporadic to count on. Tonight, it was the stars that lit the darkened world. They seemed brighter than usual, glowing through the heavens and illuminating the surface. Tonight, those tiny little dots in the night sky were all that pierced the veil.

Kane stood at the forest's edge, watching the eastern road. It was the quickest path to Evinwood and his brothers were due back any minute. He heard a twig snap from the shadows beyond his vision. Instinctively, he placed his hand on the pommel of his sword, ready for any threat that might present itself.

Malakai and Krenin stepped into sight. The swashbuckler held the look of annoyance, while the half-orc wore a smile. He clearly didn't mind the journey. Spotting the young warrior, patiently awaiting them, they quickly made for the town's edge.

Kane watched them cross the clearing. He wanted to wait for them to get closer before speaking. There was no sense in sharing information with any bystanders. "I assume your meeting with Aldulrien went as expected?"

"Not quite." Malakai replied. "But we spoke with his captain. They're with us. Though I couldn't help but feel that decision was made prior to our arrival." He stopped in front of the templar.

"We'll count that as a lucky blessing. It's good they're willing to help. This war is going to be a great trial for us all. I'm pleased our allies have enough sense to realize that."

Malakai nodded. "Aye. That is good." He reached out, laying his hand on Kane's armored shoulder. "Now, my brother, Krenin and I must prepare for these trials— at the tavern." His smirk was accentuated by his coiled mustache. Dropping his arm, he stepped past the armored warrior and followed the road.

Krenin followed in silence, letting his closest friend speak for him.

Kane turned to watch them leave. "Your devotion to duty is admiral, gentlemen."

Malakai spun around, correcting his step to walk backward. "As is my devotion to you, so— if you require anything, anything at all. I'll be in the tavern, fortifying myself with a drink and a woman. Maybe two of each." He gave a knowing wink. Spinning around, Malakai returned to his proper footing and caught up with the half-orc who had passed him when he spun.

Kane shook his head, watching his brothers disappear into the small city. Marbayne wasn't overly large, but it had all the pleasantries one could hope for. Were he less duty bound, perhaps he could enjoy the simplicity the tavern offered, the pleasures his friends sought. But as it were, he was sworn to valor. He couldn't afford such luxuries. A cool evening chill ran down his spine. Shaking it from himself, he glanced into the darkness, feeling something amiss. The dreualfar were known for their ability to hide in the shadows. But this was something different, something closer. He rubbed the chill off his arms, watching the steam roll from his breath. Not finding anything, Kane exhaled, hoping the feeling would leave soon. It was getting late and he needed to get some rest.

Stepping onto the road leading back toward the gate, Kane felt a lingering presence around him. Like he was being watched. Ignoring it, he made the short walk, seeming to take longer than ever. Reaching the city walls, Kane passed through, making sure the guards were at their station. Everything was underway. He had no reason to fret.

Unable to shake the feeling, Kane navigated the small city, glancing up the hill to the keep at the apex, accented by the mountains in the background. He followed the winding road to a large portcullis. Passing through, a sense of dread washed over him. Whispers echoed in the darkness, calling out. The unknown presence lingered at the base of his neck. A voice rank in his ear.

"You need the jewel of Shadgull. You should take it. Claim it for yourself."

Kane's gaze darted, searching for the speaker. It was an eerie voice, almost a nefarious whisper.

"Don't be a coward! It's yours, take it. Take it back!"

"I'll do no such thing!"

"My Lord?"

Kane stared into the face of one of the guards, his green and black tabard proudly displayed over his armor. "My apologies." Passing through the archway, he stepped into the keep.

"If you won't take it, I'll just have to take it for you!"

"Get out of my head!"

Servants stared blankly at him. Their gaze interrogating, judgmental.

Abandoning the main corridors, Kane darted down the side hall and stepped into the hidden passage that lead to the upper levels. Quickly skirting the guards and servants, he stepped from behind a tapestry and into the living quarters. Finding his room, Kane stripped his armor and draped it over the empty stand. Laying down, he could no longer deny the voice was in his head. He was all alone, and yet it persisted. Sighing heavily, he closed his eyes. The coming days were going to be challenging. Suggestive voices wouldn't make it any easier.

The waist high grass brushed against his thick, black breeches. He darted across the fields of Shadgull at an unnatural pace, refusing to tire. His silver chainmail and studded, black leather reflected the moonlight, popping in and out of shadow like a mirage. His heavy, black cloak floated on the breeze, carried by his rapid pace.

Lythus shot across the open field, unseen by any in the starless night. Only a partial moon lit the way, hiding all but the keenest of sight. Reaching the forest, he stepped in and traveled down a deep ravine. The river bend cut through the center, leaving steep, muddy banks on both sides.

He slowed at the crossing, staring at the waters below. It wasn't deep by any means, but the night was young. There was no sense in getting wet so early. Summoning himself, he brought his arms back and threw himself across, letting the outstretched cloak catch as much air as possible.

His boots collided and sank into the slick bank on the others side. Stabbing toes inward, Lythus kicked and pulled himself from the ditch. Voices carried in the breeze, spoken in hushed tones. He couldn't tell what they were saying, but the tone said plenty. Slowly approaching, like a shadow in the night, he moved ever closer.

A soft glow flickered in the trees. He could see several figures sitting around the fire. A motley crew, they were. Comprised of orcs and men. Even a few goblins and a half-troll sat among their number. These were the men he sought. Lost, lonely, nothing but a few coins to their name.

Lythus slowly crept toward the fire, careful not to alert anything or anyone to his presence. Studying them, it was clear one of the humans led them. He, still being a bandit by appearance, was dressed nicer than the rest. His sword was polished, and his boots were clean. If this weren't enough evidence, the others ate every word he spoke.

Convinced of his target, Lythus stalked forward, making his way around the camp. Hidden by shadow, he approached, taking position behind his unsuspecting prey. Choosing his words carefully, they echoed menacingly from the darkness. "With a group such as this, you might be a little more cautious. If I'd desired your death I would have already claimed it."

The human jumped, reaching for his sword. To his surprise, it was in the cloaked figure's hand.

The many creatures around the fire jumped to their feet, ready to attack if called to action.

"Who are you?" The human thief demanded, trying to peak under the hood.

"No one of import. I'm here to offer something you desire. Unless you're not the fabled Zanthin, Master of Thieves, I've heard so much about." Lythus mocked.

"You've found the right guy. But you have yet to tell me what you have to offer." Zanthin replied. He was intrigued, but the shadow's demeanor left him feeling uneasy.

"Money, power, women— pretty much anything you desire. I have the ability to make it happen." Lythus flipped the stolen sword around, handing it over, pommel first. "Let's sit and discuss your future."

The brigand king took his sword, returning it to its sheath. Carefully, he sat, unsure if he could trust the cloaked man or not.

Seeing their leader sit, the others returned to their rest.

"It seems you're having a bit of trouble getting around the patrols and eluding the guards of this area." Lythus stated knowingly.

Picking his words carefully, Zanthin replied. "It would seem. Every time we set an ambush we're runoff by those stinkin' guards."

Lythus chuckled at the man's choice of word. "Coming from you, they must smell horrible."

"Huh?"

"Never mind. What I'm offering is more than just know-how and training. With me, you can fill the pockets of every man under your banner." Lythus said smugly.

"And what would you ask in return?"

"Oh, very little really. I simply require you to come when I call. And believe me, when I call, it'll be well worth your while."

Dark ichor dripped from the cavern walls onto the already soaked floor. Dozens of bodies littered the tunnel and even more were piled outside the carved archway.

Sweat dripped from the bald warrior, hunched over to remove an ear. Gareth stood, taking in the carnage around him. A prideful grin formed with the sight. He approached the entrance of the large room, blocked by one of the piles. Grabbing one of the dead dreualfar, he pulled, letting them topple down.

Ravion studied the numerous shelves standing freely about the room. The ancient constructs were petrified with time, seeming more like stone than wood. He ran his fingers over the items resting on them, each once unique in its own right. They varied in design and function, but shared one common bond. Each one was stolen and tucked away in the underground cache. Most of the trinkets were of little to no value, but the occasional treasure laid there collecting dust. He lifted a rather mundane looking chalice, inspecting the smoothed contours, free of design. It seemed out of place considering the ornate nature of the other items around him. Setting the cup back where it had been, he moved onto the next shelf, loaded with books. Grabbing one, he flipped to the center pages.

Gareth stepped into the room, finding his companion. "I only have one sunstone left."

Ravion clapped the book shut, feeling small bits of dust fly into his face. Returning it to its perfect sized gap, he glanced at bald warrior. "Well, let's hope we don't encounter any more large groups." Walking to another shelf, he picked up a strange dagger, made of some kind of blackened ore. It had a spectral feel to it, like it was pulling at his core.

"Gah! This is pointless. What the hell are we doing here? Dreu don't make plans or think like normal people. They slaughter and kill with no care for anything else. That's what they're bred to do."

Ravion raised the blade toward his face, inspecting the mineral. "Please don't tell me you truly believe that. You should know better than most that they plot and scheme. If they didn't, we wouldn't be in this place searching for their archives— again."

Gareth exhaled deeply, letting his shoulders drape with acceptance. "I know. It's just— I don't care what they're hiding or planning. I want to kill them." Pressing his booted foot against one of the abandoned shelves, he kicked, watching it topple over with a crash.

Ravion stuck the dagger in his belt. He couldn't explain what drew him to the strange weapon but he felt a connection to it. "I'll look through some of these books real quick. Whether I find anything or not, we'll head back to the surface. Maybe next time Kane or one of the others will want to come."

Gareth sat on the only table in the room, placing his hands on his knees. "You know I'll be here anytime we come to this place. I just don't like sitting here when we've got dreu to kill, out there."

Ravion smiled, seeing the frustration on his friend's face. He quickly scanned tome after tome before stopping on a leather-bound book with a strange marking on it. "I know this language!"

Gareth stood, walking over to his brother. "Looks like gibberish to me."

Ravion glanced at his friend and back to the binding. "No, not gibberish. It's eldar. My father was teaching it to me before he died."

"Maybe it's like all of these other things and was stolen in a raid." Gareth offered.

"I don't think so." Ravion flipped through the pages, skimming each passage. "At least, not in the traditional sense. I don't recall much of the teaching I received as a child. But I remember my father telling me about a corrupt sect of our people. He didn't give me specific details, as I was still fairly young. But he did say they went to war and were eventually forced underground. This book talks about that banishment. If I had to guess, I'd say this book was written by one of the dalari of that era. If it was stolen, it would have had to have been a millennia ago or longer." One page in particular caught his eye. Scanning through the ancient words, Ravion read aloud. "Locked away, the faceless host with hair of azure and crimson awaits the time of the shattering. Born of war, the breaker of walls walks unseen, without sound. A silver jingle marks his target, for its chime shall be the throes of death. His release will come when the eldar of equals has tasted the blood of his oppressor and walked away unscathed."

"Sounds like a damned ghost story. What do you think that is, a book of faerie tales?" Gareth laughed.

"It doesn't seem like it. It reads more like a book of prophecy. Regardless—" He flipped the book shut and stuffed it into his pack. "—we need to get back to the surface and find out who all is going to help in the coming war."

"You go ahead. I think I want to explore a little more."

"Are you sure?" Ravion asked, uncertain if he should leave the vengeful warrior to his solitude.

"Yeah. I'll head back once I've found something of interest."

Chapter XVIII
The Catacombs

Perrimen stumbled through the unknown wilderness of Vale. The voices screamed at him, none standing above the others. They blended together, preventing him from picking a single voice in the garbled mess.

"Would you all please shut up!" He screamed, grabbing a fist full of his long, unkempt hair. He looked around, gazing at the wonderful woodwork of the castle interior around him.

Servants fluttered about, performing their daily task, ignoring his presence.

The aging wizard stood in the middle of the large grassland. The grain stood to his waist, tiny barbed hairs snagged his linen pants in the light wind, ripping the seeds away from the stock.

"Excuse me, ma'am. Can you please inform your lord that Perrimen Sarandar is here to speak with him about the birds in the library?"

The sapling stood just taller than him, swaying in the breeze.

"Ma'am, I must insist." Perrimen declared. "Why are you ignoring me?"

A dark cloud floated overhead, forming a bulbous shadow on the ground.

Perrimen tensed, turning to see the dark form behind him. "At last, you've found me. But I must inform you, I'll not go without a fight!" Red energy crackled around his fingers. He flicked his hand toward a small shrubbery, launching his power at the unsuspecting foe.

The bush exploded, ripping its roots from the ground.

"That should teach you. Next time, make sure you know who you're dealing with." The aging wizard turned in search of the keep he was in moments before. To his surprise it was gone, replaced with the most unsavory of fields. "Who would put a grassland in the middle of nowhere?" Sighing heavily, he stumbled through the weeds, unaware of where he was headed.

An unseen force snagged his foot, sending him toppling into the overgrown field.

Perrimen glanced at the mettlesome trap, seeing a golden mask lying at his feet. "You don't belong here. Why have you come all this way?" He snatched the mask up and got to his feet.

The voices intensified, their ramble more chaotic than usual.

He closed his eyes trying to quiet them, but it didn't work. They just grew louder. Excitement filled his mind, but it wasn't his own. "Shut up!"

The voices silenced, leaving him to his solitude.

He turned the golden cover in his hand, inspecting the faded scratches along the sides. It had no straps or buckles of any kind, simply a golden emotionless face with eye holes. The nose and mouth were formed, but held no expression.

A single voice rang out, booming in his head. "Put it on!"

The insane wizard slowly placed the item against his face. Quicker than he could react, it shifted, forming itself to him. Perrimen felt the insanity of his years in solitude wash away, leaving him whole again. For the briefest moment, he was himself.

A brown leather duster formed around him, replacing the tattered and dull robes. A blue and red jester's cap with silver bells sprouted from his tangled, unkempt hair. The mismatched tendrils danced around like twin serpents in search of something unseen.

He stood, looking around the empty wilderness. "That was a hell of a way to spend the last decade." With a chuckle, he snapped his fingers.

The air around him began to swirl. The wild plains were no longer in sight. An orange glow formed around him, engulfing everything he was. As quick as he wished it, he was gone.

Kane stood defiantly at the edge of Aldridge staring at the map, calculating the distance from Heroes Gate. It wouldn't be long now, he thought, glancing back at his men, anxiously waiting behind him.

They shivered, standing in formation, whether from the cold, autumn night, or nervousness of the impending battle, he couldn't tell.

Dusk had fallen, and the sun's glow faded from view.

Returning his attention to the northern road, Kane rolled the parchment and stuffed it in his pouch. His great sword stood in front of him, the tip several inches in the ground. He wrapped his hand around the pommel and lifted the blade, heaving it to his shoulder. Squinting in the distance, he took a deep breath. It was time. "To arms, men. We're under attack!"

The dreualfar filed out of the darkness, showing their number against the hand-full of soldiers.

They'd made it much closer than he'd realized. "Form a wall. Keep the flanks open."

The soldiers squeezed together, locking their shields against the next. Several men stood behind the line, ready to thrust their spears into the approaching enemy.

Standing several steps ahead of his soldiers, Kane searched the force, ready to impart his final orders before the attack. "Beware the dreuki! As a rule, they tend to be spell casters. If we can kill it, we may break their resolve."

His men shouted in confidence, taunting their attackers.

The dreualfar roared forward, trampling the first few who weren't quick enough to stay ahead of the group.

Readying himself, Kane let loose a mighty swipe, cutting the first three in half. Spinning around to keep them at a distance, he prepared to attack again.

The dreualfar swarmed, surrounding the lone warrior. The others washed around, slamming into the shield wall. Several fell to the spears, but they continued to pour forward.

The soldiers planted their feet, holding their shields between themselves and the enemy. Many took turns, stabbing whatever weapons they had over and under the wall, hoping to fell as many as possible before the shield would have to drop. Several of the shieldsmen fell, letting the enemy pass through the openings. Absorbing the fallen, they closed ranks, entrapping the few dreualfar. It took nothing for the spearmen to dispose of them.

Kane spun around, letting the weight of his blade do the work. The dreualfar were afraid to move on the young warrior, fear of being chopped down by his agile fighting style evident in their eyes. Mid-swing, Kane dropped his left hand, leaving his right to control the large weapon. Grabbing hold of one of the clay flasks from his waist, he threw it as hard as he could toward the largest group of dreualfar. Regaining control of his blade, he ducked and shielded his eyes.

The bright flash exploded, sending several of the dreualfar into a panic. They rushed about, trying to escape the burning light, leaving nothing more than bone and ash to be carried away in the wind.

Kane felt the ground shake beneath him. Looking up, he saw eight, hairy, muscular legs stomp toward him. They reminded him of a giant tarantula. Though that didn't help to ease the concern. Lifting his sword, he prayed the fight would not be his last. The dreualfar still had him surrounded and his men were a bit preoccupied.

The human soldiers held together, keeping the dreualfar from entering the town. Several of the men lay dead around the wall, leaving less than two dozen to hold the line.

The dreuki stalked forward, flexing its thick legs with each step. It stopped just out of reach, extending its hands toward the armored warrior. Palms facing up, it's twisted dreualfar face hissed their vile tongue. "Taht rof yap ll'uoy!" The creature flexed its arms, displaying the hulking muscles beneath flesh. It slowly squeezed his hands into fists, locking them around some unseen object.

To Kane's surprise, two short blades formed in the creature's grip. It towered several feet over him, smiling wickedly. Rubbing the summoned swords together, the seemingly hardened material crackled with energy. Swiftly, it lunged, aimed to kill.

Kane swung his sword in defense, blocking the attack. It glanced off the steel great sword, going wide, leaving a trail of static down his blade. He could feel the hair on his arms stand on end.

The dreuki thrust with the other, whipping its rear around. The foot long stinger stabbed in, narrowing missing the armored commander.

Kane dodged the second attack, but the third made him stumble backwards to avoid the deadly sting. The surrounding dreualfar would most-likely run him through if he fell into their ranks. Realizing he had one option, he fell to his back. Timing the impact, Kane rolled, hoping he could get back to his feet.

The creature jumped, landing atop the prone combatant. The stinger plunged many time, leaving a green ooze in the dirt with each stab, unable to connect.

Kane kicked the oversized abdomen, launching himself a few inches at a time. It wasn't much, but it allowed him to avoid the deadly punctures. Trying to maneuver his great sword was impossible, the several legs of the creature and its size made the weapon a hindrance. Abandoning his sword, he drew a dagger from his waistline and narrowly dodged the arm-sized spike. Slicing quick and shallow, he felt the dagger connect against one of the hairy legs. That told him where he needed to aim. Repeating the process, he slashed hard, tearing into the spiderlike appendage.

It hissed, moving its other legs to compensate for the injured one.

Kane rolled, slamming all his weight into the injured leg. It collapsed from the impact, allowing him a small hole to escape. He squeezed through, crawling from beneath the beast and narrowly avoiding the crushing abdomen. Kicking hard, he twisted, letting the momentum carry him to his feet.

Realizing the human escaped his trap, the angered dreuki stomped toward him.

Kane grabbed the pommel of his short sword, drawing the small weapon from its scabbard. He adjusted his style and prepared for the incoming attack.

The dreuki locked its gaze on him. "Siht fo hguone dah ev'i!" It straightened its legs and hunched its abdomen toward the warrior. The bulbous, hair covered rear convulsed, ejecting a stringy spray of green across the field.

Kane dove to the side, dodging the thick stream.

Several dreualfar screamed, feeling the acidic liquid eat into their flesh. The others stepped aside, hoping to avoid a similar fate.

Kane glanced back at the screams, seeing the small group of dreualfar melt into a chunky pool of black and green ooze. His eyes widened. *Great, it can spray acid.*

The other dreualfar broke into cheer watching the spectacle.

The soldiers were beginning to gain ground. Their flanks horseshoed out, encompassing the attacking dreualfar. Even the spectators were beginning to fall to the advancing protectors.

Kane focused, knowing he would have to get much closer to injure the beast.

The dreuki hissed, angered by the miss. Stomping forward, ready to strike the human down, his deadly gaze locked on the warrior.

Kane waited for the creature to close the distance. Counting steps, he timed his attack.

The dreuki sprang into action, aimed to strike the troublesome warrior.

Knowing his failure would result in death, Kane lunged with the short blade. Training prevailed. Unable to close his eyes, he saw the tip plunge deep into the dreuki's chin. Refusing to leave it to chance, Kane reacted on impulse and brought the dagger around. It slammed into the side of the beast's head. Both blades passed easily, crisscrossing in its skull. The sword erupted out the top of its head, while the dagger narrowly escaped the other side. They were covered in black and pink ichor.

The summoned blades flickered and dissipated into nothing. The unarmed hands scratch harmlessly against the polished, yet dirty breastplate, unable to penetrate it.

"Meet one of the dreuslayers." Kane whispered into the creature's destroyed ear. He watched it draw its final breath, eyes going dull. Ripping his weapons free, he spun around to face any attacking dreualfar.

Unprepared for the loss of their muscle, the dreualfar screamed in shock and panic. As if an order for retreat had been given, they scrambled into the darkness.

"Follow them. Cut them down before they can escape!" Kane heard the words escape his lips. *I'm spending too much time with Gareth.*

Knee-high grass danced on both sides of the dirt trail, swaying in the breeze. A dense forest stood in the distance, and the mountain range was to the east. The sun beamed down causing beads of sweat to form on Krenin's green flesh.

The orcs lived on the northeastern edge of Krondar. They were known to be difficult to deal with, but with any luck, perhaps he could get through to them.

Grace was not his specialty, Krenin stomped as he walked, kicking up dust from the barren path. Wore tan leather breeches with an oversized red tabard, and leather armor comprised of multicolored scales in various browns and reds. The mighty half-orc carried his drastol great sword with a row of throwing daggers across his chest, and his trusty battle axe hanging from his side.

Krenin spotted the dusty pathway leading off the main road. Shifting direction, he trekked for nearly an hour before seeing the domed structures in the distance. Making his way closer, Krenin recognized them for what they were. He'd found the elusive and nomadic orcs of Krondar.

Making his way into their village, Krenin felt small under their glares of disapproval. It didn't help that the smallest among them was nearly half a foot taller than him. He wasn't accepted here, no more than he was accepted outside of Marbayne. But he had a job to do. It didn't matter if they liked him. They would hear what he had to say.

Approaching one of the armored males, Krenin stared up into his green face and spoke in orcish. "I need to speak with the clan chief."

"The chief does not need to speak with you, puny half-breed." The orc retorted, measuring the smaller abomination. The orc was nearly a foot taller, but had much less muscle despite his potency.

"You're mistaken." Krenin corrected. "I traveled here with intent to speak with him."

The larger orc backhanded him, nearly knocking him from his feet.

Krenin caught himself against the side of the crude, wooden hut. Reaching up, he wiped the liquid running from his lower lip. Inspecting his fingers, the bright red blood clung to them. He spat a mouthful onto the dusty ground, feeling his rage build. Abandoning all reason, Krenin charged the orc, hitting him in the gut.

The large orc didn't have time to react, falling to the ground with the half-breed atop of him.

Krenin punched, left, right, left, left, right. He could barely recognize the face beneath his fist any more. Stopping himself, he stood and glanced at his blood covered knuckles. The skin was split in several places, making it difficult to see how much was his.

Several other orcs surrounded him, spears and axes ready to end him.

An old orc with braided, gray hair approached the group. He pressed firmly against his walking stick, balancing himself with each step. "Let him pass." The voice was calm, but commanding. The elder turned and slowly made his way back toward the large, fur covered hut in the center of their grounds.

The orcs lowered their weapons, moving to give the half-breed access to the largest hut. It was clear they weren't happy about it. But no one would go against the shaman's orders.

Krenin passed between them, feeling their anger on his skin. He approached the large hut and lifted the fur covered flap. Stepping inside, the musty scent of herb and smoke burned his nostrils.

The floor was lined with animal pelts. A large log was cut lengthwise and smoothed, making a bench large enough to seat three full-sized orcs.

The aged orc had a long, braided beard, matching color to his equally lengthy hair. His olive-green skin was beginning to wrinkle and turn to ashy in places, but he looked as if he could still fight if required, despite his need for the cane. He gestured to the wooden bench, waiting for the half-orc to sit.

Krenin plopped down, hearing it creak beneath the sudden weight.

"What brings a half-breed to the lands where he is considered an outcast?" The elder orc grabbed a large gourd and pulled the wedged cork free. He placed it to his lips and took a long draw.

"I was asked to speak in regard to the dreualfar threat. They escaped the underground and already crippled Tresengal. If we don't band, they can overrun Dalmoura."

The chief spat the liquid on the ground. "Dalmoura— a name given by humans! It has no meaning here. Nor does your concern of dreualfar.

They concern only myrkalfar. As far as I am concerned, let them wipe each other out."

"The threat is bigger than the rivalry of two races. If you do not heed my warning, they will be here soon."

"Your words are noted. If they come, we will deal with them. If not, they are not my concern." The elder orc said calmly, replacing the cork and laying the gourd to rest.

The flap of the hut opened, allowing daylight to drift into the large, smoke filled shelter.

"Chieftain, Kalgar is dead." The newcomer glared at Krenin, his eyes full of hatred.

The shaman waved his hand in dismissal, watching the flap fall shut. "Unfortunate news. He was able. Served this clan proud. I am afraid you must settle his death."

Krenin looked from the chief to the door flap. "I apologize for his weakness. But I must return and inform your decision."

"That is no longer your concern. Kalgar had family. Without him they will have a difficult winter. The clan helps, but not enough. You must take care of them now. In Tulgrimm, you will work to feed his family. Once settled, you will be released to continue your path."

Krenin felt the rage growing inside him once again. He could crush this frail old orc with ease. Nobody could stop him. And that's exactly what he would do if they tried to overtake him.

The aged orc waved his hand, letting his energies flow.

Krenin reached for his weapon but it was too late. Several vines shot from the ground, wrapping tightly around his body. He struggled against them, unable to reach his axe. The need for air was becoming precious, against the constricting bands. He fought to get free, fought to breathe, but the vines were too tight. Accepting his doom, Krenin felt his fight drain away. Staring at the frail, old orc, blackness overcame him.

Mushrooms grew in thick patches, hunkered together in the cracks and crevices along the cave walls. They put off a soft glow in the Underdark, illuminating the tunnels like tiny torches every so often. The floors and ceilings were rough, layered in thick mineral deposits. It was clear these passages hadn't seen visitors in quite some time, if ever.

Nezial casually walked around the protruding stalagmites, their unique beauty lost upon him. He had one job, to free Izaryle. Beauty was a commodity he could no longer relish.

The ancient energies called to him. They were close, yet so far away. Feeling a change in their disposition, Nezial froze, turning to study the jagged walls. He placed his hand against the cool stone, listening for the response.

The glowing fungus dimmed, the rubbery stocks flexing to avoid his touch.

"I'm on the wrong damn level!" Nezial's anger boiled. He'd wasted so much time trying to find this specific tunnel, far below the known territories. Yet now it seemed he hadn't found the right one. "It matters not! I'll find it either way!" Determined, he threw his other hand against the wall. The energy flowed from him, burning deep into the stone. He watched the layers meld together and start to recede, leaving a deep crater where he'd touched. The corner of his mouth tightened with his success. Forcing his will into the spell, he pushed further, allowing his magic to cut through the earth, digging deeper, seeming never to stop.

He felt like it had no end. Every time he started to tire, renewal washed over him. It was Izaryle calling him home. It had to be. What else had the ability to rejuvenate a man such as he? His smile grew wider with each passing breath, reassuring his victory. The humans and alfar didn't stand a chance. Even if they rallied against him, his army was too massive. They were restricted only by the hole they crawled from, but the constant mining and new openings eliminated that problem. Shadgull was days from falling and the dragon stone was hidden in plain sight. Even if they knew what it was, there was no way they knew he sought it.

The last bits of rock melted away, revealing a perfectly smooth tunnel angling deeper into the Underdark.

Nezial had trouble seeing the distance, but there appeared to be some form of structure at the base. He lowered his hands and stepped into the newly constructed tunnel. The walls were slick like glass, all traction burned away by his spell. He slid down the perfectly round hole, careful to keep his footing.

Reaching the bottom, he couldn't help but feel lost in the sights before him. It wasn't so much the perceived beauty that caught his attention as much as it was the expert craftsmanship of the— cathedral? Every inch of its towering presence was engraved and smoothed, removing any evidence of tooling. It was as if the strange, black stone had been grown into its current shape and harvested to fit perfectly among the others. Even the fabled dwarves he'd read about didn't have that amount of skill.

Nezial stood in the shadow of the monumental underground complex, feeling his master's call from within. He marched around the side, finding an ancient road set in the cavern floor. It was made of the same onyx mineral, equally ornate and seamless. Which seemed odd considering it was simply a road. What purpose did it serve other than to travel upon?

Following the flawless pathway, he found the entrance to the antiquated structure. The doors were polished to a mirror finish, reflecting the looming cavern behind him. A thick layer of dust had settled over the surface, leaving a haze in the image. He approached the towering doors. They were much larger than required for any creature he'd ever heard of. By this scale, even the eldest of dragons would have had plenty of room to enter, not that a dragon would willingly come this far underground.

Lifting his hand, Nezial faced his palm toward the sealed seam. To his surprise, he couldn't see himself in the dusty reflection. Like a lost toy you didn't realize was missing until you searched for it. Dismissing the notion, Nezial channeled his energy, letting it soak into the mysterious ore. To his surprise it felt like the doors were absorbing his magic, pulling more than he desired to release. He tried breaking the spell, but it kept pulling, threatening to drain everything he had.

"No!" He couldn't let it take it all. He had to do something. His will focused into a single action, Nezial siphoned off what power he could hide from the demanding tether. Building it as quickly as he could, Nezial released it into one massive burst, exploding out in all directions.

Collapsing to his knees, a sigh of relief escaped him, feeling the siphon break. Panting heavily and near exhaustion, Nezial picked himself up. It was clear his magic wasn't going to work here. "Well shit, it looks like I'm going to have to do it the hard way."

Smoke rose from the center of camp, fading into the moon lit night. Embers danced among the rolling wisps, turning to ash and floating off. Twelve men sat in silence around the fire, staring into its hypnotic draw. Each well dressed, less than noble, but more than peasant. It was clear these men held great wealth, recently obtained, judging by their attire and trinkets. They held respect for one another, but played a silent rivalry. It was their intention to surpass the others, while not knowing where to start. From an outside perspective, they looked foolish, wearing their most expensive garment and effects to a private meeting in the woods. Were these men not the ruling leaders of thieves and bandits, this party would have welcomed such.

Lythus watched from the shadows, sizing the men. They displayed their weaknesses proudly, unaware of their broadcast. It was time. Stepping from the shadows, he revealed his presence to them. "I'm glad to see you all made it." He marched to the center of the villainous group, placing him back to the fire.

They were startled by his sudden arrival, unaware how long he'd been watching them.

"Enough games! You've called us here. Reveal your face so that we may look upon the man that has lined our coffers." A man with a tricorne hat and thick woolen coat demanded with a laugh.

"As you wish." Lythus slowly lowered his hood, revealing a bleached mask made from an orc skull. The protruding cheekbones reflected the moonlight.

They stared in confusion. "Why would he drop his hood only to be hiding behind a mask?" Whispers erupted among the group, growing in volume at a rapid pace.

"Silence!" Lythus demanded. "My identity is irrelevant. You're here for one reason only. The one thing you in common."

"And what is that?" A bearded, portly man asked, interrupting him.

Lythus moved with such speed, the man was caught off guard. "You like to interrupt when someone more powerful is speaking." Lythus whispered to his dagger, lodged in the man's ear. Pulling the blade free, he wiped it on his shoulder, watching him collapse. "And you all piss yourselves when confronted with your demise." He continued, increasing volume so they could hear clearly. Returning to his place near the fire, he started again, scanning each of them. "Now, as I was saying, if there are no more interruptions—," Lythus paused, daring them to step forward.

The band of brigands shook their heads, hoping to avoid the wrath of the disguised figure.

"—you seek easily obtainable wealth, but you're too stupid to obtain it by yourselves. You hold command over low-lives, savages, and scum, making your combined forces one to rival the armies you oppose. Prior to my arrival, you were met with resistance from the knights of Shadgull. But with my assistance, you've amassed a great deal of wealth. Your men are happy, and you have enough gold to rival the lords you seek to steal from." Lythus paced back and forth in front of the assembled leaders, lost in his words. "The one thing I've asked in return was that you come when I call." He looked around the group, locking eyes on each man. "And looking around, you have. It's time to repay your debt."

The leaders followed him, hanging on each word. He wasn't wrong. Profits had dwindled for all of them prior to his arrival. If it hadn't been Shadgull's nobles, it was the new band of protectors from Marbayne, a group called 'Border Wardens'. They served The Order, acting as protectors and bounty hunters for Dalmoura as a whole. Fortunately, their numbers were still fairly small, preventing them from establishing a solid hold in the highlands. But that would soon end if they didn't slow progression. The constant shuffle of armies also didn't help matters. While it was easy to infiltrate the larger units, soldiers didn't have much.

Lythus pointed to the south, continuing his speech. "In two days' time, the gong of Shadgull City will sound. She'll be without her lord. She'll be without her knights. And she'll be without her army. Each of you will gather your men and impregnate the bitch. You'll have nothing other than a few guards to deal with. They'll be easily overcome by your numbers. Once you've entered the city, I don't care what you do. Rape the horses, pillage the treasure, and plunder the women, whatever it is your type likes to do. I don't care. What I do care about, however, is a very special emerald that is set in the center of Baron Remle De Leon's throne. Retrieve this emerald and I'll consider your debts paid. If you fail me, I'll slaughter you. I'll slaughter your families. And I'll slaughter your men. Am I understood?"

They nodded agreement, fearing his unnatural speed and swift execution when questioned.

"And one last thing. You'll have three hours from the sound to acquire my gem. Any longer, and you risk the return of Remle and his band of ass hats. I'd recommend being gone before then."

The fire flashed, blinding them for the briefest of moments. Searching the opening, the cloaked tactician was gone, disappeared into the shadows.

The unfamiliar walls were covered in thick patches of moss. Glowing fungus clung to the crevices, displaying a variety of faint blues and yellows in the rocky passageway. The ceiling was moist. Thousands of water droplets gathered, ready to fall to the floor below, leaving tiny bits of mineral behind on their jagged columns.

Gareth cautiously walked along the natural formations. Chunks of blood and gore dripped from his shield, leaving a trail behind him. The glowing tunnel was eerily quiet, alerting him to the absence of his hated foe. He didn't recognize the passage. And judging by the unmolested walls around him, the dreualfar didn't frequent this place either.

Truth was, he only came this way because they were guarding it. Had they paid it no mind, he wouldn't have bothered. But they were, so it had to hold value. Gareth continued forward, spotting a change in design. A perfectly round hole was inset against the otherwise jagged wall. He approached to inspect the unnatural find.

It was a tunnel leading deeper into the Underdark. The stone was smooth, like it had been drilled away with the finest precision. As far as his eyes could tell, it didn't dip, or slant, or curve in any direction. It was simply a perfect hole, leading straight into the unknown. Whatever they were guarding, it had to be at the other end of this hole. Slinging his shield, Gareth stepped into the mouth. Subtlety was not his strong suit, but it was required in this endeavor. Checking the width of the tunnel, he pressed his shoulders and arms against the low ceiling and tight walls.

Content he could slow himself, he leaned back, allowing his hide soled boots to slip against the glass-like surface.

Within minutes he reached the bottom, seeing an ancient structure carved into the underground mountain. He guessed it was a dwarven city. He'd never met a dwarf, but from the stories he'd heard, he thought he would get along with them quite nicely.

Gareth followed the walkway, rounding the ancient complex. A large set of steps lead to what he guessed was the entrance. A huge set of blackened stone doors stood open to the empty cavern, inviting him into the complex.

Gareth stopped just outside the massive doors, dwarfed by their size. Continuing onward, he stepped inside, lost in the imagery. Each stone was carved and molded to fit perfectly against the others, leaving no trace of a seam between stones. Each was made of the same material as the doors. Not a single pebble was out of place, revealing the magnificence of the craftsmanship. He saw no sign of dust or debris, a miracle in its own right considering the age and size of the place. That thought was troubling. Clean, meant occupied. But where were the residents?

Carefully, Gareth walked down the darkstone stairway, keeping his eyes open for any movement. The hair on the back of his neck stood on end in the looming darkness. The solitude was almost worse than finding his enemy.

Reaching the bottom of the stairs, Gareth passed through the wide archway at their base. Several pews rested in the grand hall. A pathway remained open in the center and along the sides. The far end held a domed chamber with a large altar as the centerpiece.

Marching across the cathedral, Gareth walked the bare floor between pews, listening to his echoing footsteps. The craftsmanship was exquisite, much like the structure itself. These benches were made from the same stone as everything else, but appeared mechanical, like they could shift form. He inspected a bit closer, realizing a pattern to their design. Three rows made a complete set. The first row was immovable, while the second converted to form a table. And the third, the backrest rotated and seated on the opposite side of the seat. It was amazing how such a simple design could convert it from a church to a dining hall in a matter of minutes.

Glancing around the chamber, twelve towering figures stood over the room. Six per wall. The stood like columns, stretching up the ceiling. Black armor covered their form, everything but the faces. Near twenty-foot tall swords reached from their overlapped hands to the equally dark floor. Gareth peered at the stone face, unable to discern what he was seeing. Each time the features settled, it would shift to another, as if they were in constant fluctuation. He couldn't explain his reasoning, but he knew the twelve were protectors. Not just of him, but of the entire realm.

Shaking the vastness of their purpose from his mind, Gareth noticed the many thresholds along the wall between the column-like figures. All but one of the magnificent doors stood sealed for an eternity. Eyeing the single open door, Gareth resolve drove him toward action. That was where he'd find his enemy.

Gareth cautiously approached the open doorway, his hand locked around his mace. The dark room was bare, save for an open passage to his right. It looked as if the portal was once hidden behind the stonework, now busted and scattered about the floor. He stepped through the rubble and into the opening. A single chamber lied beyond with a partial hole in the floor. He could see the top few wedge-shaped steps, disappearing below. Quickly traversing the winding corridor, Gareth paused, seeing the flicker of fire light. The dreualfar didn't require light to see. This raised more questions. Slowly stepping forward, Gareth peeked through the archway.

A slender dreualfar with long white hair stood in the center of the room, his back to the entrance. He was dressed in elegant robes made of a royal blue with pearl colored runes around the cuffs and neckline. It stared into a large mirror, set in the far wall. The function seemed misplaced in the large structure.

Gareth couldn't help but notice it wasn't reflecting as it should. Where the contents of the room, dreualfar included, were clearly visible, it also showed the inside of a crypt. Gareth's attention shifted back to the dreualfar. Searching him up and down, he noticed a sabre strapped to his left hip and a brown leather satchel hung from the right. There was something unsettling about the creature. Something dark and dangerous, more so than his kind usually were. Gareth slowly made his way behind the beast, lifting his mace. If he could get close enough to strike before it realized he was there, it would be over quick. But did anything ever go as planned?

Nezial stared deeply into the ancient mirror, studying the magics flowing through it. He couldn't begin to understand the mysteriously woven strands, intertwined and layered unlike any he'd seen before, save for the speculum's twin. It was as if they didn't belong to any of the arcane schools, yet held elements of them all. But it was more than that. His knowledge of divine magics, while sparse, suggested they had a hand as well. But there was so much happening he couldn't comprehend. This mirror was something else, something forgotten.

A sweet scent drifted past his nostrils, a familiar flavor, coppery and dark. Dreualfar blood. Nezial's face contorted, stretching his wicked smile across his lips. "The commander of the fabled dreuslayers has come to pay respects. I must have done well to gain such honor." Nezial turned to face his would-be killer.

"Your kind has no honor!" Gareth spat, his mace at the ready, raised and ready to deliver the killing blow. Knowing he was too close to do much else, Gareth rolled his shoulder, flinging shield from his back and around his arm. Snatching the grip, he locked it into place and brought the mace down.

Nezial casually waved his hand, letting his power flow. It erupted in a violent burst, exploding into the blackened walls.

Gareth felt the flood of energy wash over him. His feet left the ground and he flew back, slamming into the far wall. *What the hell was that? Did he misfire?* Gareth had never seen like that before. Picking himself up, he watched the wild remnants of magic soak into the walls. Maybe this place, this stone, was warded against magic. Maybe that was why the spell reacted as it had. Though that was more maybes than he preferred to work with.

"This place is becoming increasingly annoying." Nezial demanded, his amused smirk faded slightly.

"It seems you can't get it up. Don't worry, it happens to the best of 'em." Gareth taunted, letting his rage build. Kicking off the wall, he launched himself toward his target, ready to deflect the explosion if it came to that. He brought the mace down, aimed for the slender creature's head.

Nezial's hand shot out with unnatural speed, catching the head of the mace. The swing halted, unable to advance another inch. "I don't need magic to kill you." Nezial forced the thick weapon back, letting the human's own weight do all the work.

The blood-coated handle slipped from Gareth's grip. The impact shot pain to his core. He staggered back, clutching his face. Shaking his senses back into place, Gareth noticed the bright red droplets splatter on the onyx floor. "Alright, you wanna play that way— let's play!" He spit the blood from his mouth, glaring his hatred at the creature. Tossing his shield to the side, he drew his cutlasses.

Nezial smiled, discarding the stolen mace. Sliding his sabre from its scabbard, the metal drug across the enclosed sharpening stone and echoed through the small chamber. He flipped the weapon around, gently grazing the floor with the razor-sharp tip. It left a mild scratch in the polished surface. Flipping it around a second time, he arched the blade and plunged straight down, embedding it into the stone floor. Taking a step back, Nezial revealing his empty hands, inviting a clear shot. The curved blade wobbled gently from the forceful thrust.

The dreualfar's confidence was shaking. If he was willing to offer a free shot, there was no telling his level of skill. And unfortunately, Gareth hadn't seen him fight. Accepting the challenge, Gareth charged and swung his right blade, while preparing to block with the left.

Like a bolt of lightning, Nezial shot out, snatching his sword from the floor. Rolling his wrist, he easily sent the first attack wide. Spinning, his back connected with the dreuslayer's and he wrapped around, carrying his original trajectory. Seeing the opening, Nezial danced around the sloppy block and stabbed inward. His saber buried itself deep into the Dreuslayer's left shoulder.

Gareth winced in pain. Growling his irritation, he hooked his left sword, keeping the piercing weapon in place. Using his footwork, he retracted himself the blade. Gareth pushed the sword from him, realizing his options were limited. Wildly swinging his wounded arm, hoping to distract the superior swordsman, Gareth redirected and attacked with his right-side cutlass. It was a narrow window, but just maybe he could get past the dreualfar's defenses.

Nezial knocked the feint wide and brought his sword across to parry. Using the blocked attack as leverage, he stabbed the tip of his sword into the wounded shoulder once again, careful to keep from tearing the wound further. He took pleasure in the anger growing in his opponent's eyes. It gave him something to strive for.

Gareth's rage intensified with each miss. He was nearing exhaustion and hadn't even broken skin yet. Something had to change, and soon. Otherwise, this abomination would have bested him. And that was unacceptable.

Nezial chuckled at the pathetic human's attempt. He was so slow and his strikes were easy to predict. It was his rage that made him such an easy opponent. Surely this wasn't the man of fabled repute. There was no way he'd killed so many with these tactics.

Gareth turned red, his anger overflowing at the dreualfar's laughter. He sent barrage after barrage, but nothing connected. It was as if every attack was announced by trumpets before it arrived.

Nezial deflected the wild swings, losing his patience. "I'm done toying with you." Bringing his sabre around, the strike was quick and full of purpose. It caught the dreuslayer just above his right eyebrow and sank through the socket, stopping in his cheekbone.

Gareth dropped his swords, grabbing his ruptured eye in pain. He couldn't see anything. Just a red glow in the darkness. It burned to his core, the rage and pain pumping through his body with each heartbeat. It thundered inside him, like the rhythm of a drum, recalling him to the day he found his wife. Staggering backward, Gareth tripped. He stumbled and spun around, his knees impacting the black stone floor. Tears and blood ran down his face. Gareth sucked the dusty air through his nostrils, trying to calm himself. Rage overflowing, a coolness settled in the air, surrounding him. His pain soothed. The bottled anger manifested itself into something else. Something that was no longer him. Blinded, yet aware, Gareth could feel the shadow approaching him. The dreualfar was ready to land the killing blow. He couldn't have that. His work wasn't finished. Gritting his teeth and clenching his fist, Gareth focused his hatred on the creature. He wanted to strangle him, wanted to feel his body go limp beneath his grip.

Nezial smiled at the defeated dreuslayer. His eye was severed beyond repair. Even the strongest of magics had no chance of restoring it. A sense of satisfaction overcame him. It was time to end the threat this man posed to his people. Approaching the kneeling man, Nezial raised his sabre, prepared to land the final blow. Caught unaware, a powerful grip wrapped around his throat. He struggled against the unseen force, searching for the energy. It wasn't magic, he would have felt that. But what else could it be? His smile faded, confidence turning to concern. His feet left the ground, dangling him several inches in the air. It was becoming increasingly difficult to breath. And still, he couldn't find the spell responsible.

Gareth squeezed, hoping to strangle the evil creature. He felt his fingers wrap around the vermin's throat, though his fist were nowhere near him. He couldn't see what was happening, but he knew he was in control. He could feel it. Hear it. Sense it.

Nezial knew he had to act fast or he would fail. His vision was beginning to fade to the crippling grip. Focusing the last of his will into a single action, Nezial let his power explode. As before, they expanded in all directions, flowing straight into the walls. But it served its purpose. The grip was gone and air was returning to his lungs.

The energy blast slam into him, breaking his concentration. Gareth flew backward, landing on his back and sliding toward the wall. Something was wrong. He felt sick, like he'd eaten something bad. Only it was more than just illness. He felt as if something dark had crawled inside him, tainting his soul. Pressing his knuckles against the cold floor, Gareth pushed himself up. His good eye was beginning to adjust, slightly. He could see the torch light through the teary opening. Movement caught his attention. It was him, in the mirror. Only it wasn't him. A wounded dreualfar stared back, one of his eyes missing and clotted. A yellow fluid ran from the puffy, ruined socket. The facial structure and clothes matched his own, but it wasn't him. It couldn't be him. Confusion took hold. Gareth jumped, doing the only thing he could do. Charging the imposter, he tripped over the dreualfar commander and slammed face first into the reflective surface. It reverberated, knocking him back.

Nezial heaved from the floor, trying to regain his composure. How the human had gotten past his defenses was a very serious question that would have to be answered. What was more concerning was how did he absorb the blast? He could see a piece of himself inside the frightened human, though such a feat should have been impossible. Struggling for breath, Nezial forced his words out his bruised throat. "How's it feel to be one of us?"

Gareth felt the hoarse words resonate inside him. It couldn't be true. He'd never be one of them. Death was a preferable alternative. But those cards were stacked against him. Glancing at the reflection again, it didn't lie. Somehow, he'd become one of the creatures he'd hated for so long. Scrambling to his feet, Gareth wiped the tears from his good eye. It was already feeling strain from its new dominance. Glancing at the prone dreualfar one final time, Gareth spoke. "I'll never be one of you!" Reaching down, he snatched the loose satchel lying beside the downed commander. Whatever was in it, would be better suited out of the dreualfar's possession. It wouldn't be long before the beast would be on its feet again and he didn't have the strength to finish him now. Gareth made for the stairs. He needed to get out of the catacombs and heal up if he was going to continued his obsession. He only hoped his new appearance wouldn't cause too many problems for him.

Chapter XIX
The Dreu War

Moonlight blared across the grassy plains of Shadgull. Light fog slowly drifted over the land delivering a calm, but potentially deadly night to the people of Dalmoura. Armies stood throughout the massive grasslands, assembled and awaiting orders. The myrkalfar were split into several battalions and positioned among the humans. Colors littered their mass, displaying blues, greens, reds, and orange. The southern nations had come together for the first time since the construction of Heroes Gate. Or as the stories went anyway. The races of myrkalfar and men stood ready. Their archers at the rear awaiting the command to rain death upon their enemy.

The dreualfar army spanned as far as the eye could see. They made no attempt to hide their number, lining the far side of the field by the thousands. Shouts echoed across the vast plain, preparing the formed units for the night's adventures. Several dreuki marched behind the soldiers, awaiting orders from their commanders.

Drums of war bounced along the flat terrain, delivering a steady tune of death and despair to both sides.

Ravion, Kane, and Malakai stood at the head of one of the large formations. The men behind wore the symbols of the Tower and the Trident, their red or green capes flowing in the night breeze.

Ravion glanced at his brothers. "It appears war is finally upon us."

"So it would seem." Kane replied, stating the obvious. "Have you heard from Gareth or Krenin?"

Shaking his head, Ravion glanced at the grass beneath his feet. "No. Gareth has yet to return from the catacombs and Krenin hasn't been heard from since we asked him to speak with the orcs."

"Maybe the orcs will arrive with him shortly." Malakai interjected his hope.

"It's possible, but unlikely." Ravion rebutted. "I've had a few dealings with the orcs of Krondar. I doubt they'll be much help considering their relationship with the alfar."

They nodded their agreement.

"I would have thought Gareth to be here. It's rare for him to miss an opportunity like this." Kane added, scanning the massive force ready to charge across the field.

"Aye, but remember, he was in the catacombs. I'm sure he's having his own fun there." Ravion sighed. "Once we're done here, I'll search for him."

"I'll join you. Two heads are better than one. That is unless you're fighting a hydra. I've heard that's not much fun." Malakai chuckled, accepting he was the only one who found humor in the joke.

The three took a final glance around, steeling themselves. All hell was about to break loose. And they were at ground zero.

The battle horns sounded, alerting Osirus to prepare his reapers. Both armies charged toward one another, the echo of their footsteps and battle cries drowning out the deep, rhythmic drums. Archers fired their load, launching a volley of flaming arrows into the dreualfar forces. Before the wooden shafts hit the ground, they had another set ready and lit.

The dreualfar did the same, returning unlit arrows to catch the surface dwellers off guard.

Ravion dodged and ducked the wicked shafts, making his way toward his enemy.

Kane was nearly struck, an arrow glancing off his thick breastplate. Another inch and it could have struck home.

Malakai felt the iron head bite into his flesh, leaving a shallow but painful graze across his arm. He glanced at the minor flesh wound, growling his irritation at the approaching army.

They collided with an explosion of bodies and blood. Neither side yielding to the other.

Ravion cut and dodged, avoiding strike after strike.

His brothers did likewise.

Within minutes the field was swarming with soldiers of the two sides. Each one in all out combat, fighting for their lives. The archers of both armies continued firing, choosing single targets in the chaos.

Kane dodged a scimitar, realizing his great sword was too bulky for the close quarters combat. Tossing it to the blood-soaked earth, he drew his short sword and dagger. Slicing into one of the dreualfar, he ducked another. To his surprise, it was remarkably easy to hold the wicked curved blades at bay. Almost as if they weren't trying to claim ground.

Malakai spun, stabbing his sword into one of the dreualfar's back. Retracting the battle rapier, he threw his shield up, shoving another attack away from him. Pushing off he brought the protective barrier down, breaking the arm of the dreualfar in front of him. It was one thing to hide behind the steel, quite another to turn it into a weapon. Seeing an opening, Malakai stabbed his sword into the chest of the broken armed dreualfar and released the blade. He reached under the metal and wood barrier and flung a small, balanced dagger into another dreualfar. Before it could fall, he ripped his sword free.

The three held their own cutting down foe after foe, but the battle was young and thousands more dreualfar flooded toward them.

The glowing fungus faded into memory, returning to familiar walls and known territory. Gareth felt the beads of sweat running down his face. His hatred exhausted, but lingering on edge, he struggled to keep moving. He needed it to survive. And right now, he hated everything. It was directed at more than just the dreualfar. He felt an equal hatred for himself. He felt the pain inside him, his body begging for rest.

Unable to take another step, Gareth leaned against the cavern wall. His legs buckled and he slid to the hardened clay floor. Pulling the brown, leather satchel to him, Gareth inspecting the bag. Flipping the wooden button through the small loop, he opened the flap and peered inside, feeling his remaining eye burn from the salty tears and sweat. A shimmering black book stared back at him, begging for attention. Gareth removed it and unbuckled the binding. Flipping it open, he was taken back by the blank pages within. "Why the hell do I need a blank book?"

A mixture of blood and sweat rolled from his cheek, speckling the flaky page.

Gareth watched in wonder, seeing it spring to life. While it was faint and hard to read, he could see words appear in the red writing, scribbled across the page. Reading the once hidden secrets, Gareth couldn't help but notice, it was an answer to his question. The book was explaining, in great detail, why it was blank. And more importantly, why it was written. Quickly growing bored with the technical information, He flipped through the pages, in search of pictures, or at the very least, something entertaining. Gareth ran his finger over faded, red scribes, wondering how a single drop of blood could reveal so much.

Footsteps echoed down the corridor, returning him to the now. Gareth shoved the book back into the satchel and slung it over his shoulder. Pulling himself to his feet, he reached for his swords, realizing he'd abandoned them. Their absence hadn't been felt until now. And that hurt nearly as much as losing his family. Snarling, Gareth took a defensive position. *I may die, but I'm gonna take as many of those bastards with me as I can!*

Several dreualfar stepped into sight, freezing at the sight of the lone dreuslayer.

Gareth charged, welcoming his impending doom. He slammed his shoulder into the first dreualfar, grabbing its sword and ripping it from grip. He spun around and punched the next closest, letting the poorly crafted scimitar slice into a third.

The dreualfar surrounded him, their shock wearing off.

Gareth chopped and hacked with the crude and unbalanced weapon, catching another in the neck. Something slammed into his side, launching him from his feet. Gareth fought to get up, trying to hold them off. But they were too quick. He was surrounded, with nowhere to go. A sharp stab burned through his leg. It went numb in an instant. Gareth tried to fight, but it was no use. He harder he struggled, the faster the numbness spread. His body was shutting down. Each beat of his heart left him more and more helpless. His chest was getting heavy, then his arms. Gareth watched, a prisoner in his own body, unable to act. Staring blankly ahead, he couldn't blink. His eye watered, burning its discomfort. A familiar hair covered legs step into sight. Suddenly Gareth knew what had happened.

The dreuki straddled him, snatching him off the ground. It went to work wrapping the paralyzed man in a thick, sticky web.

The dense silk encased him. Gareth tried to call out, but it was too late. The thread covered his face, obstructing the horrifying sights around him.

The dank air of the underground began to shimmer and swirl, revealing a rip in the fabric of reality. It expanded, shifting to a jagged oval of orange and black. The faint scenery of a grassy plainland appeared in the black. The tall stalks of grain swayed in a light breeze. A figure appeared in the opening, wearing a brown leather duster. His face was covered by a golden, expressionless mask and the blue and red jester's cap danced atop his head, searching as always. The silver bells on the ends jingled with each movement.

Perrimen stepped through the portal, sealing it behind him. A sense of purpose guided his every step, carrying him deeper toward his destination. He glanced at the smooth, black plates lining the walkway. He knew exactly where he was going, though he'd never been here before. The voices in the mask told him where to go.

An ancient, abandoned city rested in the shadows of the huge underground crater. Perrimen walked along the plated high rise, overlooking the thousands of structures below, each one unique in their own way. Though from this distance they appeared as little more than dwarven homes. He rounded the bend, spotting the ancient fortress of the Urdurnie. It'd been some millennia since anyone had laid eyes on the keepsake, abandoned so long ago when Ozmodius removed his smiths from the realm. The sanctum itself served as a weapon against those who would seek entry. The darkstone structure would hinder most, but he was special, unique you might say.

Perrimen heard the voices scream their displeasure, urging him onward. He knew the fortress had been opened, he could feel it. *Why does it call?*

Stop him!

Stop who?

Him!

Lost in the argument within his mind, Perrimen reached the gargantuan doors. Memories flashed through his mind, though not his own. He recalled the first gifts the Urdurnie gave to Ozmodius. He was present that day. The day the dragons where born. The darkstone twins, crafted by the dwarves and used to model all others. The image of the monstrous creations filled his mind, both exciting and terrifying. How something so massive could exist was beyond his understanding. Yet he knew it was true. Moreover, there two of them.

The memories faded, begging him to continue. Perrimen stepped into the ancient structure, following the breadcrumbs laid out for him.

Nezial stood in the antechamber, holding the attuned dagger in front of the mirror. The mystical flames hovered from the mounted scones, their eternal visage dancing in the nonexistent breeze. That was the trick to seeing the magic of the mirror. It was invisible to the naked eye. But the flickering light revealed slight fluctuations that he was able to identify.

Perrimen stood just inside the door, watching the unaware dreualfar. Why would such a unique creature waste so much energy on something he couldn't begin to understand? Truth was, he didn't understand it himself. But the mask had a way of guiding him to the correct path. It's strange. He had control over himself, yet the mask always seemed to lead the way. Was it the illusion of free will? Or something far more advanced? *I don't have time for philosophy!* Shaking the thoughts from his mind, Perrimen returned focus to the imbued creature before him.

Nezial sniffed at the air, attuning himself to his surroundings. "I smell power. Tell me, who might you be?" Stuffing the blade into his waistband, Nezial turned to face the masked figure.

Perrimen cocked his head to the side. The tendrils of his cap slithered about in search of something unseen. Instinct drove him, conflicting against his desire. Perrimen stared at the tiny, silver bell clipped to the hem of the dreualfar's tunic. He didn't know how he'd attached it, but he was certain he had. And more importantly, he knew what it meant.

Nezial studied the newcomer, unable to identify any features beyond humanoid. "What are you?" There was something odd about the figure. His demeanor shifted rapidly. Like he was multiple emotions all at once. But the truly interesting part was the magic radiating of him. It was ancient and immense, rivaling his own.

Perriman's head was still cocked. He knew the creature was trying to learn something about him. Though there wasn't much to learn. *What are you doing?* He tried giving the words voice, finding them impossible. Only now did he realized his will was not his own. He was a tool, carrying the will of his prison.

"I'm becoming annoyed by these constant interruptions. If you aren't going to do anything, leave. I've enough to deal with!" Nezial turned, presenting his back to the silent figure. Returning his attention to the mirror, he found the strands of magic he'd altered in an attempt to make it work.

Perrimen took a single step, appearing between Nezial and the mirror. He stared into the creature's deep, blue eyes, a rarity for his kind.

Caught off-guard by the masked man's speed, Nezial took a step back. "So it's death you seek. Very well, I shall indulge you and then return to my work." Knowing his magic wouldn't work properly, Nezial funneled it into himself, turning his body into a reservoir. Building up as much as he dared, he forced the energy to manifest, altering his natural abilities. He could feel the power wrap around him. He felt stronger, faster, more alert. But something wasn't right— it continued to build around him, growing to dangerous levels. He wasn't sure how much more he could take. He was full. And yet it kept building. Unable to stop, Nezial let the arcane energies explode from him. He wasn't right. Not since the dreuslayer lashed out at him.

Perrimen could smell the power. Not even the masters of his time possessed so much. Unable to move, unable the cast his own defenses, Perrimen stood helpless to the mask's desires. He closed his eyes, anticipating the pain that was sure to follow.

The blast wave filled the room, soaking into the stone. It erupted like a bomb in the antechamber, halted only by the darkstone.

Perrimen felt the energy wash over him. He was surrounded in the mystical waves, swimming among their number. It was then he noticed the thin, shimmering globe of his own making. It protected him from the misfired spells, rapidly being pulled into the structure. His head cocked a bit further, mocking the mage in his silence. He stared into the creature's soul, reading the magics inside him. He was different than most. Something dark and powerful graced him. But he was also broken. A piece of him was missing. Without he, he'd never have full control over his magics again.

Nezial's amusement turned to worry. The room was rapidly draining him and his limits were nearly reached. He wasn't sure how much longer he could remain. One thing was certain, it made dealing with the intrusions much harder than he preferred. "I suppose I'm just going to have to do this the hard way." Drawing his sabre, Nezial took an offensive stance, preparing to cut the trespasser down.

Perrimen watched the dreualfar raise his sword. He wanted to grab a weapon of his own, but the mask wouldn't allow it. Sighing his defeat, he gave in. The mask hadn't let him come to harm yet. Perhaps it was best to trust it. Relaxing, he gave full control to his master.

Nezial swung, using his full speed to cut the foe down. To his surprise, the strike missed entirely. Though he knew his aim. And it was dead on. There was no way he missed, yet the figure didn't appear to move. Baffled, he swung again to the same effect.

Perrimen watched the dreualfar attack. He moved so slow, like a sloth reaching for him. The slightest lean made the attacks easy to avoid. It was then, Perrimen noticed the magics around him. He was altering time and hadn't realized it.

Nezial stood perplexed. He couldn't touch the man. Not with steel, not with magic. He had but one final option. Sighing heavily, Nezial sheathed his sabre and drew the curved dagger. If his weapon couldn't do the trick, maybe Izaryle's could.

Seeing the wicked blade, Perrimen tensed from the shrieking voices in his head. They screamed in unison, driven by fear. *Protect the portal!* Regaining his composure, Perrimen glanced at the mirror, knowing it was the source of their concern. There was something ancient and dangerous about it. Something he was connected to, but unable to explain.

Nezial lunged forward, stabbing the imbued weapon at the trespasser.

There was so much power emanating from the blade, too much for one being to possess. Knowing he had to do something, Perrimen felt his body react on instinct. Taking a step forward, he intercepted the dreualfar and laid his hands on each side of his head.

Nezial didn't have time to respond. The figure moved so quickly.

A swirling vortex opened around them, and the small room disappeared, leaving the magical scones and ancient mirror behind.

Bits of dust lingered in the air, displayed only by flickering torch light. Shadows danced around the protruding edges of the rough, cavern walls, mimicking the actions of their witnesses. The two dreuslayers worked tirelessly, making their preparations.

Malakai grunted, heaving a large stone atop the others. He wiggled it, making sure it wedged itself into place. "You sure this is gonna work?" He glanced at his companion, who was dusting some dirt off his vest.

"It'll work. We just have to get out of here before all hell breaks loose." Ravion gave his vest one last pat, knocking the last bit free. His ears twitched, picking up the subtle echoes of the underground complex. Spinning around, he drew his longsword and took a defensive stance. "Hurry up, we've got company." Fears becoming a reality, Ravion leapt into the air and brought the ancient weapon down into the rapidly deteriorating darkness. A dark ichor ran the length of his blade, revealing the distorted face of the black-skinned alfar. Ravion pointed his toes toward the bedrock, letting his ankles absorb the shock of his landing. Feeling the stone beneath him, he spun on the ball of his foot and side-stepped, using the dead dreualfar as cover.

Malakai hurriedly tossed the final stones onto the pile, abandoning his perfectly settled stack. He reached for his dagger, drawing if from his belt. Pressing the sharpened edge against the piled stone, he scratched the dried paste off the side. A glowing sigil shined through the chipped cover, revealing the runed etching. As quickly and carefully as possible, he scratched another, watching the glowing runes disappear once they were fully revealed. Within minutes, the pile appeared as nothing more than mundane stone, piled with intent. The sounds of battle echoed off the walls, growing louder and closer. Stuffing his dagger away, he stole a glance to his companion.

Ravion ducked a narrow strike, deflecting another. Fighting like a master of precision, each strike was perfectly aimed and in preparation for his next.

"You need some help?" Malakai taunted more than asked.

"Only if you can find time in your busy schedule. I'd hate to put you out." Ravion panted through labored breaths. Placing his strike, he wrapped the tip of his sword up under the defenses of the attacking dreualfar. The sharpened steel punctured its flesh with ease. He placed his free hand on the pommel and thrust as hard as he could. The length of the blade disappeared in the creature's side and erupted out the other. As intended, it pierced another of the attacking beasts. Sword buried to the hilt, Ravion drew his dagger and deflected another scimitar.

Malakai pulled his rapier and charged into the fray. Hacking and parrying blow after blow, he cut into the dreualfar, clearing a path for his friend. A sharp pain erupted in his side. Wincing, he spun his wrist, severing the arm that had stabbed him. He reached down and pulled the crude weapon from his ribs. Inspecting the blade, he made sure there was no poison on the rusted iron. Glad it appeared dry, save for his blood, he discarded the weapon into the ranks of the swarming dreualfar. Anger in his eyes, Malakai bit his lower lip and pressed on. He squeezed the handle of his rapier and punched, the metal handguard connecting solid. The straight blade followed through, cutting into another. Malakai shouted over the cling of swords, twisting around to get the most damage from the attack. "If we're gonna' do this, now's the time."

Ravion twisted his embedded sword, tearing the wound further and releasing the suction on the iron. With a tug, he brought it out the side, ripping the impaled dreualfar in half. Spinning around, he snatched one of the fist sized stones off the shelved wall. "Sunstone!" He shouted, throwing the rock into the crowd.

The closest dreualfar scattered, shielding themselves from the renowned lethal blast.

Using the distraction, Ravion fell back, taking position beside Malakai. The dreualfar pressed forward, hesitant by the lack of explosion.

"Do we have an escape plan?" Malakai gripped his rapier tight, feeling his knuckles pop.

Ravion stole a glance at the pile of runed stones. "We've got two options, neither are good. Are they all set?"

"They are. But we're too close to the blast. There's no way we'll survive it."

"We're dead either way. We either take the city with us, or we die in vain." Ravion blocked another barrage, narrowly dodging an arrow. "And now they've got archers." An all too familiar thud sounded beside him. He glanced over, confirming his fears.

Malakai looked down at the thick shaft protruding from his chest. Another arrow plunged into him. He staggered back, weakened by the blow. Malakai glared at the swarm of dreualfar, letting his willpower fuel him. "Get out of here. It's too late for me. Run!" He demanded, pulling his last sunstone from his waistline. Launching it into the sea of monsters, Malakai threw his arm over his face to shield his eyes.

The eruption illuminated the darkened corridors, revealing every nook and cranny of the dusty chamber.

Ravion charged into the blinding light, feeling his flesh burn with its potency. The dreualfar on all sides charred, turning to ash. He could see the tunnel entrance ahead. If he was lucky, perhaps he could get Malakai through the ranks before they recovered. Slowing, Ravion spun around and found his friend. The distance was much greater than he'd realized. There was no way to get to him and come back before they'd be upon them again.

Malakai watched him turn. He was calculating. But it was too late. There was no time. Nodding his approval, Malakai pulling the ceramic vial from his pouch. Shouting over the mass of dreualfar, he saluted his successor. "Fight well, my brother. May your blade be ever sharp and the sun forever upon your back!" Without hesitation, he crushed the vial against his chest.

Ravion stared at the broken trigger. What had he done? The was no chance he could survive so close to the blast. The pile of stone began to glow, revealing the hidden runes marked upon them. Out of time, Ravion dove head first into the small hole, feeling weightless for several lingering moments. The roar of collapse echoed all around, shaking the cavern walls in his descent. He felt his feet hit, sinking into the pliable, yet hard substance. Liquid rushed into his mouth, submerging him completely.

The moonlight beamed through the trees, illuminating the band of dreualfar at the field's edge.

Lythus peeked through the shadows, watching them. He'd followed for nearly an hour, silently picking them off one by one. What stood before him was a manageable group, led by a single dreuki. Quietly sliding his sword from its scabbard, he leapt from the darkness and brought the thin blade across in an arch. It cut neatly into the creature's spine, killing it instantly.

The dreuki staggered and collapsed under its own weight. The thick, hair covered legs quivered and spasmed uncontrollably until the nerves finally died.

Refusing to leave it to chance, Lythus brought the blade around, cutting deep into the creature's throat, serenading his sword in the black ooze. The head rolled to the ground, coming to a stop a few feet away. A shocked expression remained on the twisted face. Lythus pushed his gloved fingers through the stringy, white hair and plucked the head from the ground. Raising it overhead, he displayed his victory to the squad of dreualfar, allowing them to look upon their dead captain. "You see this? You work for me now. You do what I say, when I say it, or your heads will be next. Are we clear?"

The dreualfar hissed their response, clearly not pleased by their position. But it was better than death.

"Good! Now that we have an understanding, you're going to do something for me. And mark my words, if you fail me, you'll spend the rest of miserably short lives looking over your shoulder, awaiting the day I slide a dagger into your ear." He tossed the severed head on the ground, letting it roll to the feet of his recruits. "The back way into Marbayne is unguarded. You're going to accompany me into the heart of the city.

Once there, I'll need you to distract the border wardens so I can take care of a few matters."

The sun beat down, making heat waves over the churned sand. The golden kernels were clumped together from gallons of blood that had been spilled over the years.

Krenin panted heavily, standing over the bodies of alfar. Their fragile forms were hacked in several places and leaking what was left of their fluids into the arena floor. Blood dripped from the dual axes in the half-orc's hands, the metal reforged from his great sword. His heart pounded, the beat nearly deafening to the roar of the crowd cheering his praise. A sense of pride washed over him. The acknowledgment of their presence, churning his gut.

The thick chains sprung to life, clinking out with each link that passed the massive sprockets to raise the portcullis

Turning to face the gate, Krenin casually walked toward it, throwing his axes into the sand. They struck blade first, sinking nearly half their heads into the moist floor. He ignored the crowd, defiantly marching down the ramp. They wanted more. They always wanted more. But he was not here by choice. He'd give them just enough to stay alive. Nothing more was required.

Passing the iron runs, Krenin ran his hand along the crude walls, feeling the change from iron to wood. He was in a long, dark tunnel. The thick beams were rough and nailed together, the excess ends protruding into the walkway. If he didn't know any better, he'd guess they were hacked into shape, rather than tooled. Rounding the corner, Krenin made way through the reinforced wooden door and into the slave pens.

The gladiators roared with his passing, shaking the bars of their cells and rattling empty tankard and bowls.

He smiled as he passed, trying to ignore their chants and cheers. His face tightened around his small tusks. There was a sense of honor to be had, slaying one's opponent in the arena. Such a welcoming was customary for the survivor of the games. It was a far better alternative than bleeding out in the sand. Though he didn't care for the attention.

Kicking the straw covered floor as he walked, Krenin noticed the gladiators grow silent. Something wasn't right. He caught a flash of movement out the corner of his eye. Reacting on instinct, he tried to duck, but it was too late. A large fist connected with the side of his head. Krenin jerked, hitting the iron bars lining one of the cells. Before he could recover his aggressor was upon him.

Krenin moved his head, avoiding the blows long enough to see his attacker. The human was larger than any he'd ever seen, dwarfing even Remle back home. He recognized the man as the friend to one of the alfar he'd just killed in the arena. Wrapping his legs around the man's waist, the half orc squeezed in an attempt to drain him of air.

The man twisted in an attempt the break the half orc's footing.

Krenin rolled with his movement and released him.

The large man staggered from the force and slammed face first into the iron bars. He impacted with a thud, staggering against the jarring blow. Glaring his vengeful anger at the prone half orc, he grabbed his broken nose and straightened it with a repulsive snap. Blood trickled down his face. Dropping his shoulder, he charged, hoping to finish the job before the guards arrived.

Rolling to his knees, Krenin searched for the next attack.

Boots echoed down the corridor in unison, the hurried footsteps timing the guard's arrival. The gladiators cheered louder than ever, witness to their own blood sport.

Krenin tightened his stomach in anticipation to the man's attack. Setting his feet, he prepared to intercept. The man smashed into his midsection, carrying him back. Krenin brought his elbows down on his back, forcing him to the ground.

The human gasped. His lungs unable to function from the unexpected blow. Panic set in, forcing him to catch his breath.

Wrapping his arms around the man's midsection, Krenin squeezed, hearing his ribs pop in protest. He wasn't sure if it was his own, it his opponent's. Bending at the knees, he lifted the large human and stood, the man's head dangling near the floor. Without hesitation he let go, watching the man crumple into a heap.

The man collapsed, resolved in his actions. Rolling over, he pushed his fist into the dirt and straw covered floor, trying to pick himself up.

Seeing the man's continued fight, Krenin knelt down beside him. Drawing back, his muscular arm flexed, displaying the dirt and sweat clinging to his green flesh. Squeezing a tight fist, Krenin released, punching the man across the jaw.

His head snapped and he arms gave out.

Fist locked and ready to strike again, Krenin stared into the swollen eye of the defeated man. "You are done. If need to finish, we fight in arena. Not here!" Lowering his fist, Krenin stood and backed away, hearing the guards bust into the room.

Spears aimed and shields forceful, the guards surrounded the half orc and his human counterpart, ready to attack any who gave them reason.

Krenin raised his hands. There was no sense in dying over something stupid. Their heavy grips secured him, yanking him out of the dusty chamber.

Krenin walked toward his cell, escorted by the orc guards. They pushed him through the open, barred door and slammed it shut behind him. Krenin heard it latch. Walking to his bed, he pulled the woolen blanket to the side, revealing a thin layer of straw matted atop the wooden cot. Sitting down, he placed his hands in his lap and recalled the battle in mind. There were mistakes, places he could have killed quicker. But he walked away. That was more than his opponents could say. If he remembered those mistakes, there was less chance to make them again next time.

The crowd above echoed through the rafters, signaling the start of another battle.

Closing his eyes, Krenin laid his head on the straw pile and pulled the green wool over himself. Within minutes he was fast asleep.

Gareth gritted his teeth, pushing the black ooze between them. It ran into his beard, matting the strands of red hair. Spitting a chunk of flesh onto the ground, he glared his hatred at the remaining dreualfar. Like a demon, he charged, digging his claws into whatever exposed flesh he could find.

The dreualfar screamed in pain, feeling his hide shred beneath the primal dreuslayer.

Gareth tore at him, finding the soft spots of his throat. Sinking his teeth, he shook violently, ripping away as much as he could. The chunk came free, leaving a large hole in the dying dreualfar's neck. He continued to shake the torn esophagus long after the creature quit moving.

Dreualfar cheered from the safety of their perch, watching the captured animal defeat the weaker recruits.

His sanity was slipping away. All he could feel was the sticky blood running down his skin. The hiss of their vile language echoed in his ears, whispering dark thoughts to him. What was worse, he was beginning to understand it. They taunted him. Reminding him of his child, his wife. How they tore her apart after they penetrated her body again and again. Gareth screamed, letting his hate radiate in the stone pit.

Several red strands of energy shot through the air, wrapping themselves around the cheerful creatures. They were helpless to the unseen power. Their bones crushed beneath the tightening grip. They tried to cry out in terror. But the vice like hold didn't leave any room for sound.

Gareth fell to his knees, his anger released. He felt empty inside, drained of determination. They could kill him now. At least he would be reunited with his family. "Didn't you bastards hear me? Kill me!" He paused, hearing nothing but silence. Summoning the strength to raise his head, Gareth couldn't see the wicked creatures. Picking himself up, he staggered toward the wall. Peeking over the ledge, he saw the crushed bodies of his captors. For the first time in weeks he felt hope. Did they find him? Was he rescued? "Ravion? Kane? Is anyone there?" The silence stung like a hot knife.

The whispers resumed in his head. *It's a trap. You're all alone. Nobody's coming to save you.* He knew how they got into your mind. How they made you see things that weren't there. They'd give hope just so they could snuff it out. *You're being broken. You're going to die.*

"Shut up!" Gareth charged the rock wall, jumping as high as he could. His hands pawed the jagged stone, searching for any place he could grab.

The sharp mineral cut into his flesh, but he pulled himself up. Once again, he was free. And this time, they weren't going to stop him.

Outside the Urdurnie fortress, two powerful beings appeared out of thin air. Frozen in the moment, they stared at each other, taking in what had just happened.

Nezial felt the freedom the cavern offered. The darkstone road was still pulling at him, but it was nothing compared to the sanctum. Out here he was the master. And this masked figure was going to learn that. Flexing his power, it radiated around him. Swirling and spinning, more for show than anything, a display of color splashed through the air. "You should have left me in there. I was crutched by the stone, unable to fully harness my power. Out here you don't stand a chance." The smile returned to his face.

Perrimen screamed, hoping to regain control over his body, but it wouldn't respond.

The mask tilted, seemingly curious to see what the dreualfar mage was going to do next.

Nezial channeled his power, launching a volley of arcane bolts at his unsuspecting prey. The multicolored bolts launched without fail, flying out in a barrage of missiles. They hit one after another, exploding against their target.

Perrimen closed his eyes, expecting his death to follow. He felt the power impact against him, but it didn't feel right. It was as if the energy dissipated as it touched him, like he'd dispelled it at the last second before impact. But that was impossible. Nobody was strong enough to dispel magic that quickly. It took time and focus, neither of which he had, even in the peak of his skill. But the facts said otherwise. He remained unaffected.

Nezial's smile faded to a frown. His magics should have torn the mysterious figure apart. Yet he remained unharmed. Straining his will, he fired another barrage, this time relying on destruction rather than evocation. Again, the man remained unharmed. It was as if he was immune. But nothing was immune to all magic. Not even the gods. Worry gripped him, forming a knot in his stomach. *Am I going to fail?*

Perrimen fought for control, hoping to finish the dreualfar mage. He needed to kill the creature before it got resourceful did the same to him. Try as he might, his body wouldn't reply. He felt his head tilt further, as if it was curious.

A sense of hopelessness washed over him. Unable to harm the figure in the slightest, Nezial did the only thing he had the power to do. He smiled. The masked man was too much for him. How anyone could best him was a mystery. He possessed the strongest magics this realm had to offer. Nobody should be able to rival him. And yet this man, this figure did so without lifting a finger in defense.

Perrimen recognized something in the dreualfar commander. A sweet stench. The smell of hopelessness and fear emitted from him. It was an acquired taste, one he hadn't realized he liked. Yet it brought an unexpected pleasure with it. Moving quicker than he realized was possible, Perrimen swiftly stopped in front of the dreualfar. He could feel his breath upon the mask. In one fluid motion, Perrimen ripped the kris dagger from the commander's hand and plunged it deep into the dreualfar's chin. It erupted out the top of his skull with a spray of blood and brain.

The mask pulled the wavy blade from the dead commander letting him fall to the ground in a puddle of tainted, black ichor.

The voices in his head screamed, erupting a deep pain in his core. They separated, filling him with worry and doubt, drowning him in their fear. Among the cries, he heard a question. *What have you done?*

"It wasn't me. He did it. Not me!" Perrimen argued with the voices, trying to clear himself of their accusations. He felt something extremely powerful flood him. Something much bigger than this one mage. Turning, he took a single step toward the fortress, disappearing in an orange glow. It wrapped around him and he appeared in the antechamber, staring into the ancient mirror. A black glow appeared in the center, growing wider. He watched helplessly, feeling the emotion of the voices weep inside his head.

The glow grew wider, reaching the reflective edges. The entire surface shimmered, releasing a wave of energy.

His feet left the ground, an overwhelming power exploded from the mirror, launching him into the far wall. Perrimen hit the ground with jarring force. He stared helplessly at the awakened vortex. "This isn't good!" Picking himself up, he glanced at the dagger, still in his hand. It was too powerful for just anyone to carry. And with this awakening, time was limited. He needed to find some way to share the load. Stuffing the blade under his duster, Perrimen disappeared from the chamber in a glow of orange.

The story will continue in Izaryle's Prison

Be sure to stay up to date with the newest Eldarlands books at
http://www.levisamuel.com

Please leave a review at your online retailer.

Author's Notes

Some stories come more naturally than others. One day you'll be thinking about how you're going to handle a particular section, striving to make it all come together in a fashion that's both believable and cohesive. The next, random pieces start falling from the woodwork and landing perfectly into place, leaving you, as the writer to ponder how the hell that fit so perfectly and why it took you so long to think of it. You run into these welcome plot hooks quite frequently when it's a story you enjoy.

This book took the latter. There were some major changes from my original vision, but I believe the end result was for the best. You see, it started when I was just reaching my teen years. I was in high school, sitting in my journalism class, at that point in time I never thought I would strive to be a writer of any sort. One of my friends, who just happened to be sitting next to me, was cleaning out his backpack when he pulled out this four-page sheet with all sorts numbers and text written in pencil. I studied it, lost in its function. I'd never seen a Dungeons and Dragons character sheet but I found it strangely wonderful, despite my ignorance to its purpose. My friend, noticing my interest, explained it to me, and while not directly related, he invited me to a gathering at one of the local parks. It started at 2 pm every Sunday and I desperately wanted to go.

When I arrived, I may as well have stepped into another world. People were dressed in the most fantastic garb and carried a wide array of duct taped covered weapons. Amidst all of these people, I felt at home. I continued to go and by the time the first monthly event arrived, I was a character living in this new world. At that first event I met some of my best friends, whom retain that status today. The day I was introduced to it, the LARP known as Eldaraenth truly changed my life. Over the years my friends and I formed a fighting company of mercenaries called The Order of the Trident. We specialized in combat against a race of black-skinned elves, which were inherently evil. I'd write their commonly used name, but, as was the case in using that name in this book, there's a lot of confusion surrounding the legality of its use. To be safe and prevent any form of law suit, I renamed them dreuaflar— It just doesn't have the same ring to it. Anyway, seasons came and went, members left and new ones arrived, but it was the family away from home that I cherished most. Well, that and dressing in armor and beating the crap out of each other with foam weapons.

The original draft of this novel was written at a low point in my life. My right leg had been shattered and I wasn't able to walk for several months. The fears and doubts that began to find their way into my mind were frightening on a level I never expected to experience. I'd already had another book published by that point, and my writing career was steadily growing, but it was in those months I was trapped that truly showed me the therapeutic power words can bring. I couldn't go for a walk outside, so instead I'd go for an adventure through my characters.

In the original draft, I took key events from the world of Eldaraenth and experienced them in manners suitable to the characters my friends and I portrayed. It went quite well for the first half. Then, like an idiot, I followed the storyline of the game and abandoned the potential story line waiting for me on other paths. A friend of mine read the manuscript, making sure there were no copyright concerns between the game and my story. And while that concern was minimal, he pointed out the mistake I'd made by sticking to the game world. I ended up scrapping the entire second half and went back to the drawing board. It took about a month to finish it a second time. And now, the story flowed in logical manner following the bread crumbs laid out in the first half.

I truly wish I could have published the second draft. It was by far the best thing I'd written at the time, and in my opinion, was a far superior story than the one before you. But due to a lack of foresight, and the stupidity accompanied with forgetting to back up and save multiple drafts, I had a computer malfunction and lost the entire manuscript. I was furious. I was heartbroken. And I was lost. I'd spent all that time and effort, just to have the entire thing gone in the blink of an eye. I tried rewriting it several times, but the words wouldn't flow. Outlining became a game of staring at a blank paper, struggling to recall the smallest detail. I spent hours staring at that blinking cursor, awaiting my command. And nothing happened. I'd write a line, and then erase two.

Unable to touch the story, I moved on. I took a few other contracts and published a couple books, but in my heart I desperately wanted to finish this story. One day I decided enough was enough. I opened the word processor and started plugging away. Before long, I had something resembling the start of a novel. I kept working at it, the complications of life and the need to pay bills slowing my progress. There were months of late nights and early morning, raising my daughter and working a day job in between, but I'd finally finished it.

At last, you've received a product, years in the making. I hope everyone enjoys reading it, as much as I enjoyed writing it. With your help, I'll continue to work toward bringing you better adventures in a timely manner. The next two books of this trilogy are complete and releasing shortly after this one. So please, if you enjoyed this book, or even if you didn't, but would like to give a few pointers, please take a moment to leave a review at your preferred online retailer. Reviews help us in every way.

Additionally, if you'd like a free book, as well as a sneak peek at some of my other endeavors, feel free to join my newsletter. http://eepurl.com/dxRUvL There, you'll have first access to every book, event, and detail that comes my way. Plus, each letter contains a piece of a new story that's never been published.

Thank you for your support. You guys are awesome!

Levi Samuel
September 2018